Praise for *New York Times* bestselling author Lori Foster

"[*No Holding Back* has] compassion, interesting family dynamics, troubled pasts, killer fight scenes, and of course, swoon-worthy romance. Highly recommended."
—*Harlequin Junkie*

"Emotionally spellbinding and wicked hot."
—Lora Leigh, *New York Times* bestselling author, on *No Limits*

"Hang on for this completely unexpected hard-hitting ride!"
—*Fresh Fiction* on *No Holding Back*

"No one writes alpha heroes and sexy, swoon-worthy romance like Lori Foster."
—Jill Shalvis, *New York Times* bestselling author

"Hot enough to start a fire!… A delicious and dangerous tale that proves why Foster is one of the best in the genre."
—*RT Book Reviews* on *Fast Burn*

"Count on Lori Foster for sexy, edgy romance."
—Jayne Ann Krentz, *New York Times* bestselling author

"Foster is a master at writing a simmering romance."
—*USA TODAY*'s *Happy Ever After* blog on *Fast Burn*

"Foster knows how to turn up the heat, delivering numerous steamy passages that crackle with chemistry and build essential connections between the characters."
—*Entertainment Weekly* on *Cooper's Charm*

"Teasing and humorous dialogue, sizzling sex scenes, tender moments, and overriding tension show Foster's skill as a balanced storyteller."
—*Publishers Weekly* on *Under Pressure* (starred review)

For more books by Lori Foster, visit lorifoster.com.

LORI FOSTER

THE DANGEROUS ONE

HQN

HQN

ISBN-13: 978-1-335-50637-5

The Dangerous One

Recycling programs
for this product may
not exist in your area.

For questions and comments about the quality of this book,
please contact us at CustomerService@Harlequin.com.

HQN
22 Adelaide St. West, 41st Floor
Toronto, Ontario M5H 4E3, Canada
www.Harlequin.com

Printed in Lithuania

MIX
Paper from
responsible sources
FSC® C021394

With every new book, I do a ton of research in hopes of getting it "right." It's incredibly helpful when I can email people with firsthand experience and get their perspectives. For that reason, I'd like to thank the following people:

Michelle Norwood, thank you for answering my numerous questions about basset beagle hounds. Your sweet dog, Betty, was great inspiration!

Noah Studebaker, I greatly appreciate the insight and background you shared in being a park ranger. Yup, I dramatized things quite a bit, but you gave me a great foundation to get started.

With other aspects of this book, I borrowed from headlines and news stories, and bugged a dozen different people on my Facebook fan page with "quick questions" that sometimes weren't so quick.

Thank you to everyone! You're all incredibly awesome.

Lori Foster

THE
DANGEROUS
ONE

CHAPTER ONE

YEARS, THAT'S HOW long it had been since the sight of a woman stopped him in his tracks, but… Wow. He'd feel bad about staring at her, except that this woman was noticed by everyone who happened to be out and about on this sunny, early-June Saturday, male and female alike. Triple Creek, Colorado, was small, but they were in the center of town, with a grocery, restaurant, barbershop and bank on one side, and a gas station, post office and car dealership on the other.

Plenty of people around to watch her with interest, so he wasn't alone in that.

It wasn't just about her looks either. Petite, trim and with a long ponytail swishing between her shoulder blades, she looked better than fine. That long tail of hair, a light brown highlighted with blonder streaks, seemed to point to cutoff shorts that hugged an incredible little ass and displayed slim thighs. Didn't matter that she also wore black lace-up boots over gray socks. Even they looked cute on her.

Yet it was about more.

She kept her narrow back straight, her legs braced apart and her hips slightly forward as she stood at the back of a gigantic stand-on commercial lawn mower. From business to business, she'd cleared the grassy areas, steering around landscaping and walkways effortlessly and in record time. Every so often, she paused to do trim work and use a blower to clean up.

Not staring at her had been almost impossible, she was such a mighty distraction. Hunter Osborn had tried, but no one else seemed to put up much effort.

Figured she'd be wrapping up at the car dealership... which put her very nearby.

To many, she might seem oblivious to the attention she drew. Not to Hunter.

Just as noticeable as her appearance—at least to him—was her charged awareness. She hid her eyes behind reflective sunglasses and gave the impression of focusing on her job, but he knew better. He *felt* her keen awareness of her surroundings, of every person in view and maybe even of things not visible.

"What a sight," the guy next to him murmured with a lot of innuendo.

That immediately drew Hunter's attention away from her. Disgusted with himself, he asked, "New landscaper?"

"First time here." Worth Linlow gave a sleazy smile. "Can't look away, though. Wish I'd known she was replacing Trent. I'd have cleared my calendar."

Like Worth would have a shot? Not likely. In his mid-sixties and with one of the more lucrative businesses around, Worth should have been more responsible, definitely more respectable. Instead, he was the opposite. He made inappropriate jokes constantly, lorded his position over others and tried to cheat everyone.

Currently he was trying to cheat Hunter.

"This isn't the price we agreed on." With Worth's '73 Corvette still on the trailer, Hunter folded his arms.

"Sure it is," Worth said, while lewdly gawking at the landscaper.

It took all Hunter's concentration not to look as well, especially when the sound of the mower drew closer. "You're short."

Worth spared him a quick, impatient glance. "That's the amount we discussed."

"No, it isn't." The buzzing sound of the mower died so that Hunter could almost hear the collective breath-holding of the twenty or so people still in the commercial area.

When Worth's faded blue eyes widened, Hunter couldn't resist glancing back.

As if she owned the town and even the mountains around it, the woman strode forward. Never mind that she couldn't be more than a few inches over five feet tall, she kept her chin elevated. Shoulders back. Her mouth deliberately void of a smile.

She stepped up to them, saying nothing as she pulled off thick utility gloves and tucked them partially in her back pocket.

Hunter breathed in the scents of sun-warmed peachy skin and subtle flowery shampoo.

When everyone stayed mum, she tipped her head toward Hunter. "Well?"

He saw himself reflected in the lenses of her sunglasses. "Well what?"

"You settled your business with him yet or are you still working on that, because I have one more job before I finish for the day and it's hot as Hades out here. I'd like to get to it but I don't want to be rude by jumping in line."

Amused, especially by Worth's surprise, and maybe a little entranced by her forthright manner, Hunter gestured. "Be my guest."

"Thanks. That's big of ya." She pushed the sunglasses to the top of her head, taking wisps of damp hair back, too, then pinned Worth to the spot with a direct stare of her light hazel eyes.

Worth's jaw loosened. Understandable. Hell, those eyes were pretty enough, but paired with that lethal directness? She might be petite, but she could level just about anyone with that gaze.

"So," she said. "Job's done."

"Yes," Worth breathed, his attention drifting to places it shouldn't travel. He even smoothed back his hair. For his age, Worth still had a very thick head of graying blond hair.

Hunter waited, curious about how she'd react to the rudeness.

When Worth said nothing else, she asked, "Ya got my money? Everyone else paid up front."

Jowls moving, Worth struggled and finally managed a smarmy smile. "Of course I do." He held out his hand. "I'm Worth Linlow, owner of the—"

"I know who you are." She pulled a folded paper from her front right pocket, shook it out and thrust it into his extended hand. "Your share of the contracted amount?"

Floundering, Worth glanced at the paper. "Right. Of course." Expression strained, he pulled out his wallet, freed some cash and offered it to her.

"You're short," she said without bothering to count it. "I need the full amount."

"Short?" Falling into his confused routine meant to cheat, Worth pretended to read the paper more closely. "Oh, there's some misunderstanding. I never agreed to—"

"Yeah," she said, "you did, though I was warned you wouldn't want to pay."

The smile slipped. "Who warned you?"

"Who didn't?" Cocking out a hip, her expression bored,

she heaved a sigh. "Ticktock, time's a wastin' and I have other places to be."

No longer quite so friendly, Worth asked, "Who did you say you are?"

"Didn't, but it's there on the contract that *you* signed, along with your agreed-upon amount."

Worth skimmed down the contract. "Jodi Bentley," he said in a suggestive purr. "I have to say, Jodi, you're a sight prettier than Trent."

Making a sound of disgust, Hunter weighed his need for detachment with the natural inclination to defend. Turned out he didn't need to do anything at all.

"Huh-uh," Jodi murmured, stepping closer, taking Worth by surprise and putting Hunter on alert. "I'm not prettier, definitely not nicer, because Trent put up with this sh…" She stopped herself, then corrected with, "*Baloney*, and I won't."

Trying not to curse? Amused, Hunter silently wished her luck. Dealing with Worth could test anyone's resolve.

Taking a step back, Worth scowled. "I have no idea what you—"

"Trent and everyone else in town—" she glanced at Hunter "—might let you bully them, but that's not in my DNA."

Now, wait a minute. She thought *he'd* put up with Worth? Not likely. "If you recall," Hunter pointed out, "I only allowed you to go first."

She smiled, and damn, that smile had a kick. "So you would've done some insisting of your own?"

"Notice his car is still on my trailer."

"Yeah? That's his?" Her gaze slanted back to Worth, and now she was so close, she nearly bumped into Worth's gut. "Guess you'll have to meet all obligations today, huh?"

"I'll have you know, I—"

Again she interrupted Worth, saying, "I'm not budging without my pay. Is this really how you want to spend your day?"

Hunter turned to Worth. "What's it to be?"

Blustering, Worth again tried to give her the money. "This is what I have. Now take it and go before things get ugly."

Unperturbed, she asked curiously, "What do you know about *ugly*?"

"I know little girls shouldn't go around issuing half-baked threats."

Damn it, Hunter did not want to get involved, but if Worth didn't let up, he'd—

"Little girls?" Her lips twitched, like she just might smile. "This little girl did her part, exactly as described. This little girl isn't going anywhere until she's paid. This *little girl* never gives in to bullies. Now, be a good *boy*—can't say the 'little' part, can I?—and pay up before we draw more attention from the masses. Won't bother me, but I have a feeling your reputation is already on the dirty, dingy side."

Furious, Worth glared at the onlookers, more of them than Hunter had realized. No one budged.

Hell, it was all pretty entertaining.

Jerking a few more bills from his wallet, Worth handed the money to her.

Now she counted it, gave a nod of satisfaction and shoved the money into a small pack strapped around her hips. With all signs of animus gone, she said, "Thanks. Enjoy the rest of your day." She turned to go, but hesitated, then glanced at Hunter again. "You gonna need any help?"

Amazing. Deadpan, he said, "I think I can handle it."

Her distrusting gaze went to Worth for three heart-stopping

seconds. Then she rolled one shoulder and dipped her chin in a barely there nod. "I bet you can." She replaced her sunglasses. "Later, gator."

Without her standing so close, Worth growled, "You just lost this job, girl!"

Hunter watched her freeze, saw her shoulders stiffen and then her neck. Predictably enough, she pivoted back around.

Funny, but despite the lack of expression, anger emanated off her in dangerous waves.

"Damn, Worth, you don't know when to leave well enough alone." Hunter found himself anticipating what she would do. The sleepy little town had never been this exciting.

Unfortunately, Worth had found his gumption and he stepped toward her. "You're rude and I don't want you back."

Unmoved by his statement, she ambled closer. "Here, you mean, because everyone else was pleased with my work. But no problem. I'll just cut around this area and leave your part to grow. I'll even have the contract adjusted to take you off it—since I've been hired for the whole season."

"I'll see you're fired."

As if in pity, she gently smiled. "Nah, you won't. I mean, you would if you could, I get that. The thing is, I know how to set up a contract, so you're pretty much screwed on the whole firing threat. But why don't you go ahead and try? Won't bother me."

Too dumb to quit, Worth growled, "I'll make you miserable. When I'm done, you won't *want* this job. You won't even want to be in Triple Creek!"

Up went the sunglasses again, and holy shit, unmistakable fury lit her eyes.

"Hey," Hunter said, concerned with the way she stared at Worth, as if sizing him up for demolition.

Jodi ignored him, but she did take a breath, then whispered calmly, "Do your worst. I don't care, and it won't run me off. If anything, it's going to make me dig in." Her smile was slow and mean. "But you might want to keep in mind that if you mess with me, I have the nasty habit of messing back."

Done with all the theatrics, Hunter pointed at Worth, who stood there blustering. "Don't disappear. I'll be back to get my pay in ten minutes." Then he strode to Jodi. "I'll walk you to your truck."

"Is that code for something?" Without any sign of that impressive anger, she fell into step with him. "Because, see, my legs work just fine and I know how to walk. I'm not a dog on a leash and I—"

"Yes," he said, thoughts churning. "It's code." Hunter didn't touch her. He didn't even look at her, and still he felt the energy all but bouncing off every small, dynamic inch of her.

She had presence big-time.

Who is she? Not a mere landscaper. Not by a long shot.

He had a nose for danger. Right now that danger was about five foot three inches, midtwenties and full of brass. Just what he didn't want or need in the backward town where he'd settled to get his fill of mundane, normal life.

Glancing at him, she said, "It's not a long walk, so if you have something to say, you might want to get to it."

"Who are you?" Not what he'd meant to say, but damn. He shook his head. "Not just your name—*is* that your name?" Somehow he doubted it.

Openly grinning now, she shared her amusement. "I

had a feeling, you know? That you'd be something different, too."

Ah, hell. That was an admission if he'd ever heard one. He *was* different. Too different. That was his secret, though, one he'd planned to bury here, where no one would ever find out.

JODI HAD TO ADMIT, it was sort of fun shocking the locals… and grabbing the attention of Mr. Quiet and Watchful. She'd uncovered the identities of most of the residents in the minuscule town—a town that had seemed perfect for her to experiment with nice and normal, everyday life for the nice and normal, everyday woman.

Somehow this dude had slipped under her radar. Weird, because he wasn't the kind of person she'd normally overlook.

When he went silent and suspicious, she blew out a breath. Seriously, was she that scary? Not that she'd mind… Scary was good in some situations. But now? *Everyday life for the everyday woman.* She kept repeating it to herself. If she did that often enough, she felt sure she could reprogram her automatic responses.

After all, she hadn't started out this way.

Casting him another look, she saw his set features, the grim mouth and blatant suspicion, and she almost laughed. "Okay, don't choke. I won't pry if you don't."

Oddly, that didn't ease him at all.

Trying again, she said, "So, yeah, my name is Jodi." She stuck out her hand, determined to be as normal as possible. "Nice to meet you."

He looked at her as if she might be setting a trap. Pretty funny, considering he was so much bigger than her. Like, topping six-feet big. With linebacker shoulders and seriously nice biceps.

Definitely not a local, but hey, now that she'd decided to live an uneventful life, it was sort of fun to meet other people trying to do the same.

Trying…because this man might think he was managing it, but she'd picked up on his nuances right away. Nothing alarming. Nothing…sinister. Just cagey.

She knew some cagey guys. Really good guys, so she didn't hold that against her new acquaintance.

Leaning a tiny bit closer, she said, "I won't bite." His dark blue eyes narrowed at her. "No? Maybe a high five, then?"

Finally loosening up in an effort to reclaim his manners, he clasped her hand. "I'm sorry." He gave a congenial smile to go with the warm clasp of his large hand engulfing hers. "You just surprised me since you clearly didn't want to touch Worth."

Wrinkling her nose, she confided, "He's oily, right? Not his skin, but his character. I don't like him, and no, I don't touch things I don't like."

Ending the handshake, and wearing another confounded expression, the big guy said, "Hunter Osborn, and yes, Worth is oily."

Pointing back and forth between their chests, Jodi said, "We both know it, proving we're both astute." They had that in common.

"Anyone who has more than a thirty-second conversation with Worth knows it, so don't think that you're graduating at the top of the class."

Jodi laughed. "You're quick. And correct." She glanced back at Worth, who watched them with ill intent. "He's such a creep."

"A dangerous creep, so maybe you shouldn't provoke him."

Huh. He wanted to…protect her? Funny, but in the time she'd been here doing her best to fit in, she'd met a lot of nice people. People without a clue. She liked them. They fit her agenda for the status quo. No close friends, she couldn't claim that yet, but casual acquaintances, people she'd waved to, maybe asked routine stuff. *How's it going? How's your day?* That sort of thing.

But with this man, well, he felt like a kindred spirit. How weird was that? She'd come here so she wouldn't be around people like her, so she could learn another way of life, but finding someone who'd really get it put her more at ease. Jodi knew that no one was ever really safe. She felt certain that Hunter did as well, and much as she'd wanted it otherwise, there was a measure of comfort in finding a like-minded soul.

When she just stood there, lost in introspection, Hunter made another grab for conventional conversation. "Nice mower."

Right. She had to do her part if she really wanted any-thing to change—and she did. She wanted that a lot. It was her big, shining goal. It'd not only make her happy but it'd please others, too. Win-win.

Smiling, Jodi turned back to her pride and joy, the key to making the future work. "Isn't it a beauty?" Once she'd shown an affinity for outdoor lawn work, the mower had been given to her as a gift, along with everything else she'd need to start up in a different place, as a different woman with a different outlook on life.

She was coming to grips with the generosity, but some-times it still leveled her. With happiness, gratitude and a zest to make the most of her opportunities.

"So this is what you do?" he asked. "Lawn work?"

"I'd accuse you of being nosy, but I guess that much is obvious, huh? Why else would I have the mower and all the lawn equipment in the truck?"

"So a safe assumption." He smiled with her.

Such a nice smile he had, too, with straight white teeth and notable lips... That thought stalled in her brain. Why the heck was she noticing his *lips*? "Yeah." She cleared her throat and glanced up at the bright blue sky. "I love the sunshine and fresh air." From now until the end of her days, she'd prefer it to being cooped up inside. "It's pretty much the perfect job for me."

Idly, as if it didn't matter, he asked, "Been at it long?"

So that was a little nosier, but hey, she rolled with it. "Not really."

He waited for her to expound on that, she stayed silent just to see what he'd do, and after a few awkward seconds, he gave her a crooked grin. "You handle the mower like a pro, so you must be a natural."

"Right? That's what I figured." Would he do a search? Try to figure out her background, what she'd done before lawn work, where she'd come from—and why she'd moved?

It's what she would have done in his position, what she'd planned to do as soon as she had time to research him. Yet she realized that wasn't the norm for everyone. Most people didn't suspect every person they met. Most, she knew, went about their daily lives oblivious to danger and how easily things could change.

It wasn't that she suspected Hunter of anything nefarious. Overall, he had a positive vibe. Still, it was good to be suspicious... *No.* That's why she'd moved here, right? To shake off those instincts?

Right. Might as well try to shake off her past, too. Not possible.

She decided she could be cautious without going overboard, as any sensible woman would.

Leaning against the truck, she asked, "How about you?"

"Sorry, you took so long thinking there, I've lost track of the conversation. How about me what?"

Oh, he was a funny one. She barely repressed her grin. "What is it you do?"

He hitched his chin back toward Worth. "Classic cars."

"You fix them up or something?"

"Or something."

Ha! He was playing her own game against her. "So, Hunter Osborn, do you live here in Triple Creek?" It was such a small town, she felt sure she would have seen or heard something about him already. A man like him didn't blend in easily.

"Actually, I live out a ways, forty minutes north."

No way. It took a second for her brain to absorb that. Tilting her head, she asked, "Where it's more remote?"

"Nothing but me, the foothills and one of the three creeks that gave the town its name." His dark blue eyes took her measure and his brows crowded together. "What's wrong? You look thunderstruck."

Because she was. "How much land do you have?"

"Now who's digging?"

Giving a theatrical wince, she said, "Sorry, I'm just surprised. There's only like two places out there, right? I was told each had something like twenty or thirty acres, with five acres between them."

"There's one house," he corrected. "Mine. The other is a dump that'll eventually fall down."

"Well, I hope not."

This time his brows lifted. "Why not?"

"Because I'll be living there."

SON OF A BITCH. Hunter was so pissed that by the time he returned to Worth he wasn't in the mood for diplomacy. "Are you paying me or not? If not, say so now so I can quit wasting my time. I have places to go." Like home, before Jodi Bentley started moving in!

"Looks like the girl put you in a shit mood."

"She's a woman, not a girl, and the mood is all on you." Liar...but then, the rest wasn't any of Worth's business. Not that he wouldn't know soon enough. Worth kept up on all the gossip, and always knew everyone in and around the town. "Now, pay up."

"This ain't right, damn it."

Hunter rarely threw around his size and strength, but at the moment, he used what would be most expedient. Stepping into Worth's space, he growled, "You have ten seconds to give me the entirety of my money, and like Jodi, I have a contract. So what's it to be?"

"That girl is a bad influence," Worth grumbled as he grudgingly dug out his wallet yet again. "Mark my words—I'll have her run out of town by the end of the day."

"Yeah, good luck with that." The *girl* had made mincemeat of Worth. Worse, she'd apparently settled in and planned to stay.

Who was she and what was she up to? And why the hell was she buying a shack that probably wasn't livable? At least, it didn't look livable. The one time he'd investigated the property, critters had scuttled under the collapsing front porch and along the roofline. He hadn't been inside the place, but from the outside... Hunter scowled.

The main body of the small house was stone, and

from what he remembered, that was largely intact, minus some crumbling mortar. A few windows were broken and boarded up. The eaves were rotted in places, one side with gutters swinging loose. The last winter storm had torn away pieces of aluminum siding from the addition, which Hunter thought had served as a sunroom.

Was there working plumbing? He didn't know.

The house had already been empty when he moved to Triple Creek eighteen months ago, and empty it had stayed. Off the more-traveled, blacktop road, a narrow dirt lane led to his property. The place she'd bought was beyond that, so he had no reason to drive by it, and oftentimes, when the spring and summer foliage was thick, he could barely see it.

By foot, he supposed it could be more directly accessible from the main road, but that'd mean cutting through brush and trees and rocky terrain.

He could ask Worth about the place, about whether or not it was habitable…but damn it, that felt disloyal, so instead, he snatched up his money and then went about finishing his business.

Worth followed as he unloaded the car. "What did she say to you?"

"If you had questions for her, you should have asked her instead of running her off." Edgy for reasons that didn't make any sense, Hunter added, "And if your car ever needs work again, you'll pay up front or find someone else to do it."

"You know there isn't anyone else around here! Why the hell do you want to crucify me for trying to get a bargain?"

"It's called reneging on a deal." At the moment, Hunter wouldn't mind saying a hell of a lot more—but he'd made a point of keeping his temper in check since moving here and he wouldn't let Worth prod him into blowing his cool.

He'd relocated to get a grip on the past, to put his life back in perspective, and he couldn't do that by overreacting to an idiotic confrontation.

Once the car was out of his trailer, he let Worth look it over again, then made sure to have him sign the invoice, stating he was satisfied with the job. With that done, he handed the keys to Worth and said, "Word of advice—forget whatever harebrained plan you have for annoying Ms. Bentley. From what I could tell, people around here like her, and those same people are your customers." Without giving him a chance to reply, Hunter stalked away and got into his truck. He had an urge to go straight home, but he made himself stop at the grocery to get a steak for his grill…and then, because he couldn't resist, he got one for Jodi, too. Not that he planned to ask her to join him. He wouldn't.

But just in case…

IT WAS WORSE than she remembered from her one time there. Hunter hadn't been around on that visit. She'd driven right past his place with no sight of him. If she had seen him, would he have factored into her decision to buy? Possibly. By appearance alone, she knew he wasn't an average guy. That might've spooked her then. After all, she wasn't looking for trouble—not anymore. These days, she hoped to take a different path.

Since she'd met him, though, she figured he'd be a reliable neighbor. Not that she planned to lean on him or anything. That wasn't what either of them wanted. No one looking for companionship—friendly or romantic—would move out to the edge of nowhere with only a rinky-dink town nearby. For a misfit like her, though? Seemed perfect. She had her solitude, and when the mood struck her, she could practice her social skills with friendly townsfolk.

Now, as the sun slowly sank behind the mountains, Jodi had misgivings. The plumbing was sound, the electricity, too; she'd ensured that before buying it. Unfortunately, many of the ceiling lights were missing bulbs. And seriously, she didn't do the dark, just like she didn't do confined spaces. Or basements. She definitely didn't do basements.

So far she'd found a dim light over the kitchen sink, one in a hallway and, thankfully, one in the small room she planned to use as her bedroom. Tomorrow, she had to buy some fixtures and bulbs. She'd take care of that before facing another evening. In the meantime, she also had a few battery-operated lanterns she could use.

Arms crossed, she turned a full circle, looking around. Mostly the interior needed a few simple repairs and perhaps some paint. The wooden floors were rough, but eventually, she'd have them refinished. Mentally, she added rugs to her list.

Some of the doors on the kitchen cabinets hung loose. No problem. She could fix those herself—but she decided new knobs would be great.

Draping cobwebs nestled in a few corners of the ceiling, and yeah, that creeped her out some, but she'd set off bug bombs right after buying the place. Once she got a ladder, she could get the webs cleaned out.

She'd already opened what windows she could to air it out. Luckily, new windows and a more secure front door would be installed tomorrow, along with some repairs to the eaves.

The bathroom was sanitized and in working order, with fresh towels stacked on the open shelf over the toilet, and a blind hung over the window. Her bedroom, too, had been cleaned top to bottom, and she had a cot set up with fresh bedding. Eventually, she'd get real furniture of her own. She'd make the house a home. She'd make herself normal.

You can do this.

Yes, she could, but first she needed to wear herself out. Cutting grass hadn't done it. Cleaning parts of the house hadn't done it. Setting up what she could only made her realize everything that still had to be done.

She needed a long jog to wrap up her day.

Heading into the bedroom, she thought about the time. She probably had a few hours before the mountain would shield the sunlight and shadows would cover the land. Night came a little earlier when you lived in the woods. She wasn't irresponsible enough to go tromping through unfamiliar terrain alone in the dark. Plus, there were animals. So far she'd seen deer and fox, but there were also snakes and the occasional black bear.

Shaking that off, she changed into loose shorts, an over-size T-shirt and running shoes. Her belly-band holster included utility hooks, so it not only held her Glock—mostly hidden beneath the shirt—but also made it easy to clip on a flashlight and her keys. Those *weren't* hidden, but who cared? She was out here alone anyway.

All her other weapons she stored in a locked closet in her bedroom. They'd stay there until she turned in for the night, and then she'd keep a few of them close at hand.

Some things were now ingrained—like the need to personally ensure her own safety, not only with bolted doors and windows but with as many weapons as it took to let her rest easier.

Stepping outside the house, she secured the entry door, stepped carefully off the deck that needed repairs and took another look around. With a deeply indrawn breath, she filled her lungs with the scents of pine and earth and clean fresh air. Trees grew everywhere, concealing a lot—but not her view of Hunter's house some distance away.

He'd cleared parts of his land so that his trees looked more like deliberate landscaping rather than overgrowth. Whereas her property was steeply sloping in places, with rocky outcroppings all around, his was gently rolling.

Behind the houses, the wide creek cut a swath across the land. Even now, standing in the front, she could detect the sound of rippling water. During heavy rains, it'd probably flood. Luckily, it was lower than the houses, framed by foothills that circled the mountain.

For only a moment, she resisted, then decided, why not? After a few brief stretches, she started loping in the direction of Hunter's property. She wouldn't intrude. Wouldn't get close enough to bother him, but in her bones, it felt safer than going the other way into heavier trees and rockier land.

PUTTING ASIDE THE BINOCULARS, Hunter muttered a low curse. *What are you up to, Jodi?* He hadn't exactly meant to snoop. Mostly he'd wanted to take a closer look at the house without her knowing. He had a feeling she wouldn't appreciate his worry on her behalf.

The binoculars were always accessible because he enjoyed catching sight of eagles, elk and even a mountain cat or two.

He'd been studying one boarded-up window when she'd suddenly stepped out wearing different clothes—loose clothes that showcased just how small and slender she was. The visual was enough, but then she'd looked around as if uncertain of her surroundings.

"Yes," he'd muttered low, as if she could hear him. "It's more isolated than you realized, isn't it?" Maybe that'd be incentive enough for her to change her mind.

Yet it hadn't changed his. Isolation was exactly what he'd wanted—what he still wanted.

Perhaps Jodi was the same.

It didn't surprise him when, instead of going back inside, she'd turned to stare at his place...and then started toward him.

Did she feel the same keen curiosity that plagued him? If so, that wouldn't do.

The whole point of the house and property he'd purchased was privacy. He didn't want to be around other people. He didn't want anyone else to suffer his foul moods as he dealt with unsettling nightmares.

He didn't want to deal with their optimism either. Their mundane complaints about shit that didn't matter. Their carefree chatter.

For eighteen months, he'd had what he wanted. Even his mail got delivered to the post office in town. No one came out this way—but now he had a quirky, somehow fierce and unpredictable woman literally jogging his way.

Hunter had no idea how to deal with her.

His body had a few suggestions... Eighteen months of seclusion meant he'd been a long time without the relief of sex. Too long, given the heat spreading through his bloodstream at the sight of Jodi in her too-big clothes drawing nearer. Odd, but until now, until *her*, he hadn't missed sex all that much. He'd been too lost in his own disturbing thoughts.

Now hot, grinding need interrupted his darkness.

Locking his jaw, Hunter wondered if he should just ignore her. For his own peace of mind, that seemed the way to go...until Turbo suddenly became aware of her. Rolling off the couch in awkward haste, the basset-beagle mix tipped his head, scenting or listening, Hunter couldn't tell, but the dog went nuts.

And the croaking began.

Running a hand over his face, Hunter accepted that he was probably the only man alive who would adopt a starving bag of bones with heartworms and a skin condition…who didn't know how to properly bark. As usual, that thought ended with a laugh.

"Why do you pretend to be vicious, bud? You know you're not, and that odd noise isn't going to convince anyone otherwise." He bent to stroke Turbo's head, reassuring the dog.

That only wound Turbo up more, until he issued mixed howls and croaks, each time propelling his big front paws off the floor but unable to get his heavy back end to coordinate.

Speaking over the hideous noise, Hunter said, "I don't think she's a threat, but how about I let you decide on your own?" Of course, Turbo didn't understand any of that. All the dog knew was that someone was out there. He knew, just as he seemed to know when fox were near the chickens. Hunter had never quite figured out if Turbo had superior hearing or if his sense of smell was just that good. Maybe a combo of both.

"C'mon." Turning toward the door got Turbo's attention real quick. No longer making a ruckus, he scrabbled along and shot out the second Hunter opened it.

And there she was on the dirt road that connected the properties, near where it turned into the long drive to his four-bay garage. She stood poised as if alert to danger, but she wasn't close enough for him to read her expression. He sensed her confusion as Turbo gracelessly lumbered toward her, pausing every so often for his weird rendition of a howl, accompanied by the front-legged hop, then taking off again, his ears flowing back and his heavy butt wiggling.

When Jodi started forward, he figured she was smiling.

It was there in her long, easy stride and her now-relaxed shoulders.

Before Turbo reached her, she knelt down and held out a hand.

Yeah, figured the dog would win her over. To entice her closer, Hunter sat on the bottom step of his deck and called out, "Hey, neighbor."

Ignoring him, Jodi lavished all her attention on Turbo, who promptly sprawled out in the grass. No animal could sprawl quite like Turbo. He was nine years old now and his furry skin spread around him like a blanket.

Didn't bother Jodi. She actually sat cross-legged in the prickly grass to pet more of him.

Well, damn. Guess he'd have to leave the deck after all.

He shouldn't.

He should call his dog and go back inside. Leave her sitting in the grass. Ignore her like she ignored him...

Of course, he didn't. He wasn't sure he could.

Annoyed with himself, Hunter strolled out to them. "Turbo will stay right there as long as you're petting him."

"Turbo," she repeated with a quirky little smile. "You have a great sense of humor."

Not really. Not for a long time had he indulged humor. Eighteen months... Hunter stared down at her, or more precisely, at the top of her head where her ponytail listed to the side. He noticed her ears weren't pierced. No rings on her fingers. Short nails. Loose-fitting clothes.

Decent running shoes, though, so at least she'd changed out of the lace-up boots. His attention continued traveling over her...and his eyes narrowed. "You're carrying a gun?"

Surprise brought her hazel gaze up to clash with his. With the setting sun reflected in her eyes, they looked like polished topaz.

She kept silent. Provoked, he said, "Guess I wasn't supposed to notice? If that's the case, you shouldn't attach a
flashlight and keys to the wrap holster. It's a dead giveaway.
No one straps on a holster just for a flashlight." Did she
think him unaware? Okay, sure, the average person might
not have realized—but he wasn't the average person. He
often saw everything in a single glance. It was a trait he'd
always had, one he'd underutilized during his time as a
park ranger, when that keen perception had led him straight
to… No. He brutally slammed the door on that memory.

With Jodi, he saw other things he'd rather not notice.
Like how smooth her open thighs looked in her current
cross-legged position. How her shoulders and neck tensed
just enough to convey awareness. How she breathed just
a little deeper.

Her gaze sharpened until she almost looked accusing.

He wasn't the one packing, so she had no reason for giving him the stink eye. "I hope you aren't planning to rob
me." Nothing. "Or shoot me?"

Still no reaction.

So. Damn. Cocky. Her stubborn hush was starting to
grate. "Yes? No?" His gaze moved over her face. "Still
deciding?"

She gave a small shrug.

"FYI, I'm not armed, but that doesn't mean I'm helpless."
Ruthless instincts were another of his natural attributes.

The corner of her mouth lifted…and she gave him a slow
perusal head to toes and back again.

Screw it. "Fine. Silence it is. C'mon, Turbo." He patted his thigh, but other than opening one eye, Turbo didn't
budge, the traitor. And why would he? Jodi continued to
gently rub his floppy ears. "Let's let our *neighbor* get on
her way."

After dramatically sighing, Jodi pointed out, "You sneered that." With one last pat to Turbo's rump, she gracefully rose to her feet and glanced at his house. "You took me by surprise, that's all."

By noticing her gun? "Was I supposed to be obtuse?"

"Most people are. I should have remembered that you're different."

Like she was different? He didn't like that comparison at all.

"So, yeah, I carry." She tucked a loose tendril of hair behind her ear. "I'm not familiar with the area, you know? I should have taken my run in the other direction—"

"Away from me?"

"—but I'd rather try that in the morning, when the sun isn't hugging the mountain." Shading her eyes with a hand, she frowned at the sky. "What time does it get dark out here, anyway?"

Avoiding his gaze? Interesting, especially with the way she'd used her stare to intimidate Worth earlier. Hunter crossed his arms. "You've got time yet. The sun hides, and it gets shadowy, but it's not actually dark until nine or so."

"What time is it?"

After giving her a long look, he said, "Dinnertime. Have you eaten?"

Something akin to consternation showed on her face before she masked it. "I'll eat later."

"Got the kitchen all stocked today, did you?"

For two seconds, her thoughts seemed to visibly scramble, and then, with a laugh, she shook her head. "Honestly? I'd forgotten all about food, so no, nothing in the kitchen." She gave another look at the sky. "Thanks for the reminder, though. I'll grab some stuff tomorrow."

And with that, she started to turn away.

CHAPTER TWO

JODI MANAGED TWO casual steps before Hunter asked, "You're serious?"

Right. Normal people didn't forget that they had to eat. She couldn't count herself completely normal yet, but she was making headway.

Turning back to face him—no hardship there, given how he looked—she smiled. "It was a busy day, right? And I just moved in. I was more concerned with finding lights that worked than stocking the shelves."

He tucked in his chin. "You don't have lights?"

"A few. I'll work on that tomorrow, too." She wrinkled her nose. "I still have some cobwebs up on the ceiling, so I think I'll get those cleared out before I bring in food."

Equally as casual as she'd been, Hunter stepped closer. "Your doors and windows lock?"

"Windows are mostly stuck, but the few that'll open also seem to lock." Should she tell him replacements would be installed tomorrow? Eh…maybe. "I'll have the door rigged." She gave him a look of warning. "Anyone tries getting in, they won't like the consequences."

Instead of being offended, or even wary, he nodded. "Good." And then, "Your refrigerator works?"

"Hard to believe, I know. Thing has to be two decades old. It's short with a rounded top. Three burners on the

stove work. There's a slightly newer microwave over it."
She pulled a face. "No dishwasher, though."

"I hadn't been in the house, but from the outside…"

"Looks rough, I'm aware." She stretched, gave a yawn
and popped her neck. "I worked on it earlier today. Had to
have a clean place to sleep, you know? After getting the
lawn work in town done, I came back and did more to the
house. That's when I realized I needed light bulbs. I mean,
there's enough light for tonight, but tomorrow, that's top
of the agenda."

"Along with buying food?"

She tapped her temple. "I have a mental to-do list."

Bypassing all that, he asked, "What did you have for
lunch?"

If she could read his expression, maybe the question
wouldn't bug her. She couldn't, though, so she couldn't
figure his motive for asking. "Why d'you want to know?"

"Friendly conversation?"

Not buying it, Jodi asked, "So you run around asking
random women what they've eaten?"

"Usually only those jogging with a gun and a flashlight."

Ha! He really was amusing. "I didn't jog far, did I? Hardly
counts." And yet much of her tension had eased. Weird.

Shaking his head, Hunter dismissed what she said.
"You're here, on my property, and you just moved in and
don't have food, so I was…"

When he stalled, she prompted, "You were what?"

"Concerned?" He watched her, and whatever he saw
caused him to suppress a grin. "No, forget I said that. I
take it back. No reason to get prickly."

Was she prickly? Definitely. Her independence was extremely important in ways he'd never understand. His frank

way of pointing it out took care of that, though. In fact, she almost laughed.

He tried again. "Let's say I was feeling *neighborly*."

The way he tried that on, almost tasting it before giving a nod, left her smiling. "Sure, let's say that. So neighbor to neighbor, I'll admit I don't remember what I had for lunch, but it's fine." She probably had an energy bar in her truck. "I'm not that hungry." A big old lie. Now that he'd made her think of food, she was suddenly ravenous.

"Or," he said, "I could invite you to join me." He held up his hands before she could even decide if she wanted to be surprised, offended or grateful. "I was about to throw a steak on the grill, but I can easily make it two."

"Is the second steak for your dinner tomorrow?"

"No, I got it just in case." His frown seemed directed more at himself than her, before he admitted, "After you told me you bought the house."

"So you figured I wouldn't have food?" She didn't understand him.

"I figured you'd be busy moving in—and I was right. I'll add baked potatoes, and I have fresh garden tomatoes. Sounds good, doesn't it? I can see that it does."

Before meeting Hunter, Jodi thought she was hard to read. He sure read her easily enough, though. That should alarm her—so why did she feel so lighthearted? "I don't know if that's a good idea."

"To eat? Everyone does it, I swear."

Such a comedian. She again looked at the sky while she considered things. As if to convince her, Turbo got to his feet and came to stand before her, staring up at her with his dark soulful eyes. His droopy face should have looked sad, but instead, he somehow looked hopeful. She couldn't resist rubbing his furry face. "He has enough skin for three dogs."

"Agreed."

"His ears are so velvety." When Hunter didn't reply, she peeked up and caught a weird expression on his face. "Well, they are."

"I'll agree to that, too." As if bothered by something, he rubbed the back of his neck. "So. What do you say to food?"

"Where?"

Took him a second to ask, "Where what? Will we eat?" He glanced around as if not sure—or maybe he wanted to figure out what she'd agree to. "Kitchen?" He discounted that immediately. "Or we could sit on the back deck since it's nice out. Our yards connect and obviously there is no fence."

Meaning she could get away if she wanted to.

Getting that close with him wasn't a smart move, though. Still, a steak off the grill sounded delicious. "I left the house dusty from cleaning, and after trotting up here, I'm probably sweaty, too." She hadn't run that far, but far enough. "I should probably shower."

He drew a slow breath, shook his head and said, "You're fine."

If only she understood men better, then maybe she'd know what was going on in his head. The men she had known... Well, they ranged from pure evil to avenging angels. A guy like Hunter Osborn... Where did he fit? Not evil. She'd gotten a sixth sense about that. But he also wasn't on a par with—

"Jodi?" Gently, he said, "It's just dinner, that's all. Food, maybe conversation if I can convince you to take part, but if not, that's okay, too. And Turbo for sure will want more affection, but that's it. That's as far as your commitment goes."

None of that sounded awful, so she gave in. "Okay, sure."

If he didn't mind her raggedy appearance, she wouldn't worry about it either.

"Great." He gestured toward the house. "Come on. I'll fire up the grill."

So, he might read her easily enough, but she didn't understand him at all. "Lead the way."

"With you armed? Not sure I want you at my back—no offense intended."

If she wanted to shoot him, he'd be shot, but she said only, "You're a funny guy."

"Not usually." As if it confused him, he shook his head and turned to the dog. "Let's go, bud. Time for dinner."

That got Turbo's interest and *he* led the way.

Jodi fell into step beside Hunter. His house was two-and-a-half times the size of hers, but then, hers was super small, or as she liked to think, the perfect size for one. Security lights were mounted all around his property. Cameras, too—especially on his massive garage. Made sense, she figured, because he worked on pricey cars.

She had only a ramshackle carport where she left her mower chained to a deeply buried stake. It wasn't the safest way to secure it, but no one could get it without making a racket, and she had plenty of ways to stop that from happening.

Unlike her stone house, his was made mostly of logs, with a pretty, dark blue metal roof. The tinted windows reflected the lighter shade of the sky, so she couldn't really see inside until he stepped onto the deck and opened the front door.

Latent misgivings crowded in. Pretty sure there were some things that would always stick with her. "You go ahead."

His probing gaze searched her face. Then he gave a

single nod of understanding and went inside, all the way through a comfy living room with high ceilings, past a dining area and into the kitchen. Turbo was right with him, making some crazy, croaking sound and bouncing off his front paws while Hunter went about refilling his dog dish.

Cautiously stepping in, Jodi tested the turn of the door knob, making certain it would open again, then closed the door. He had a sturdy dead bolt to secure it, and when she scoped out her surroundings, she saw that the windows had equally impressive locks as well as alarms.

The room opened into another with a dining table, and beyond that, the kitchen. She took note of a massive fireplace, a big-screen TV, a leather couch and chair, heavy wood furniture, and… *Why does he have binoculars on the table?*

From the kitchen, Hunter said, "Master bedroom and bath are to the right of the dining room. Spare bedroom, half bath and my office are to the left."

"Nice place." She noticed fishing equipment hanging on the wall in the dining room. Where did he fish? In the creek?

"It wasn't when I bought it, so thanks."

"Big garage."

"I work on cars, remember? That's part of how I support myself."

Part? She started to ask…and then changed her mind. If she asked questions, he'd do the same, and pretty soon they'd be sharing backgrounds or something equally appalling. "You do the remodel yourself?" *Damn it, that question wasn't much better.*

He paused with the food dish in his hands—until Turbo made that weird sound again.

"Your dog is broken."

That earned a smile. "My dog is awesome." He set down

the food and they both watched Turbo chow down until Hunter said, "You're the first person who's been in here, which means, yes, I did the work myself."

Wow, that seemed to be some grand confession, practically torn from him. Was it deliberate to get her to open up, too? Fat chance. Knowing she was the first only amplified her growing tension. Why the hell would he have *her* in, but no one else? Automatically, she searched for all avenues of escape.

When he casually leaned back against the counter, allowing a lot of space to remain between them, she forced herself to relax. A little.

After all, she felt the weight of the gun against her body.

"What about deliveries?" she asked, just to break the awkward silence—a silence she'd caused with her insecurity.

"No deliveries. I get my own supplies and bring them here. Pick up my mail in town. And…" Thoughtful, he rubbed a hand over his mouth. "I think you're cautious."

If by *cautious* he meant guarded against all threats, armed to the teeth and very mistrusting, then yeah, she was cautious.

He didn't wait for her to speak. "I am as well. After all, I moved out here to be alone." His brows pulled together. "Actually, I hadn't figured on ever having a neighbor."

"You said my house is a dump, so you assumed it'd sit empty?" The idea saddened Jodi, mostly because, on a gut level, she understood the need to shield herself from the world.

"Yet you're here, so…" He turned his head in what looked like frustrated resignation.

"I'm here and you wish I wasn't, so you invited me

to dinner?" Seemed like an odd gesture from a guy who wanted seclusion.

"I won't make a habit of it."

She laughed. She, Jodi Bentley, the girl who almost never laughed. Oh, she faked it sometimes, and on rare occasions, she laughed with one of her closest friends— because seriously, she did have friends now. *Everyday life for the everyday woman.* One step at a time.

"Tell you what," she said, already backing away. "I'll let you off the hook—"

"I'd rather you didn't."

Those softly spoken words, said with complete conviction, rooted her to the spot. "Yeah, well…"

"Dinner will be good. You look fine, even sweaty. And I won't interrogate you if you don't interrogate me. Deal?"

She couldn't think of a quick reason to refuse. Turned out she didn't have to, because without her uttering a single word, he pretended she'd agreed.

"Glad that's settled." On the move now, he said, "The grill is out here," and he went through a screen door to where a larger deck faced an awesome yard.

After another fast but thorough look around, she followed him out…and stalled when she saw a bunch of chickens in a fancy two-story coop and enclosed run. Even with the evidence right before her, she asked incredulously, "You raise chickens?"

"Of course not. Those are wild mountain chickens. For some reason, they hang out in the coop."

Ha! Going to the rail, she took in the impressive setup. "Wild mountain chickens, huh?"

"That's right. I've tried to run them off, and instead, they leave eggs in the nesting boxes. Go figure." He started the grill, then quickly went back inside. It was almost like he ran from himself; far as she could figure, she wasn't doing anything to set him off.

Well, except noticing his chickens.

Let him work it out, she decided, and went down two steps to the neatly cut yard. On one side was that really impressive coop filled with a dozen happily clucking birds, and on the other... Huh. A garden. Not just any garden, but one inside another enclosure with fenced walls and a wire-mesh roof—to protect his veggies from critters? Seemed likely. After all, just beyond the finished area were the same creek and woods and foothills that made up her own backyard.

Difference here? A big ax rested in a wide stump with split wood all around it. The sight of that sharp, heavy ax left her skin prickling. It was a tool, sure, but she also saw it as a weapon.

When she heard a sizzle, she jerked around and spotted Hunter up on the deck, placing steaks on the grill. Without looking at her, he said, "I never leave the ax outside. I'd planned on chopping wood, but then I got curious about you."

A thousand questions went through her mind. She thought of those binoculars, and she literally felt the presence of that ax behind her. She also heard the sound of the creek and the soft clucking of the chickens. She felt the warmth of the setting sun on her face and smelled the scent of grilling beef.

Still without looking at her, Hunter asked, "Would you like me to put it away?"

Why was she so damned tongue-tied around him? That shit had to end right now. "You planning to chop more wood?"

"Possibly."

She wouldn't mind seeing that... Wait. *What?* No, she didn't give a fig about seeing Hunter shirtless, maybe sweating, laboring while his muscles flexed... Definitely not.

Striding forward, she feigned a confidence she didn't quite feel. "Then why put it away? You just keep cooking so we can eat." And then she could escape to her miserable little home, where she'd likely be awake all night fighting invisible demons.

But hey, after doing that for so long, she was getting better at it. *Invisible Demon Fighter*—her own personal superpower.

Going up to the deck and leaning on the rail, she eyed him. "What do you mean, you got curious about me?" God knew, she was plenty curious about him.

With a shrug in his tone, he said, "You're small, and female—"

"So?" she asked with a lot of antagonism.

"—and as far as I could tell, the place wasn't habitable."

"You were wrong. It's fine."

"I'm glad." He stood in profile, his attention on the grill, his movements suspended...until he suddenly turned her way. "Not what you want to hear, I'm sure, but I was concerned."

A weird mix of insult and surprise narrowed her eyes. "Concerned about losing your privacy, or because you think I can't handle myself just because I'm a woman?"

His mouth twitched to the side and he went right back to staring at the grill. "If I say *both*, will that take the chip off your shoulder?"

"Definitely not."

Making it clear her affront didn't matter, he grinned. "So originally, it was the loss of privacy. I chose this place for a reason, and it wasn't to have a neighbor show up. But you have to admit, you're small. Granted, you have a big presence, but still."

"I do?" His continued teasing only honed her suspicion. "What do you mean by that?"

"Nothing insulting, I swear." He got rid of the grin, but she still saw the humor in his expressive blue eyes. "You carry yourself like a woman who can handle anything."

It pleased her that he'd noticed. "Most things."

"There, you see? No bragging, just confidence, but with the admission that you aren't invincible, which also makes you intelligent."

"You thought I was dumb?" she asked, just to be contrary.

"You moved out here, into a dump, so…"

"It is not a dump." Not entirely.

"If you insist the place is great, I'll take your word on it."

"Great?" She snorted. "Wouldn't go that far." Joining him by the grill, she asked, "Forget about my house. Tell me, what can I do to help?"

"Sit. Relax." He slanted her a look. "Tell me what you have planned for the place."

Jodi rolled her eyes, but she liked the way he bantered with her.

As she watched, he liberally seasoned the steaks. "You mentioned windows," he prompted. "Anything else?"

All in all, it seemed like a neutral enough topic to dig into. "Nothing fancy like your digs, that's for sure. Mostly I just want to repair what's broken, make sure it's clean—" and safe "—and make it comfortable."

Dark blue eyes met hers again. "Tell me, Jodi, what does it take for you to be comfortable?"

The way he asked that, she figured he already knew, but hey, she was going for the everyday life, right? Chitchat was part of it, so she sat on the bench facing him, folded her arms on the tabletop and answered as if she didn't have a care. "Not a lot. See? I'm easy to please." *That was the biggest lie of all.* "Like you, I'm big on peace and quiet. I enjoy honest work." She looked him over. "And as long as I have enough weapons to protect myself, I'm as cozy as I need to be."

SHIT. REMMY GARDNER stared at the signs of occupancy—a truck parked in front, lights in the windows—and he knew they had a big fucking problem. "Someone's moved in."

Beside him, Danny Giggs shifted with impatience. "So?" He touched the hilt of the deadly knife sheathed in his belt. "I'll gut the bastard. Problem solved."

There were times when Remmy felt like Giggs lacked a soul. "We won't do anything until I talk to the boss." Easing back into the trees, Remmy withdrew his phone. He was told that reception out here used to be iffy. Once the guy farther up the road moved in, things had improved. Fortunately, the neighbor's lights didn't reach this far, and it was—or had been—easy to slip in unnoticed.

They usually didn't come out here until night, but today was an exception. Danny was to retrieve something from inside while Remmy, as usual, kept watch. He didn't get into the weeds on details. He figured the less he knew about King and his business, the better off he was.

The boss answered on the second ring. "What's the problem?"

He knew Remmy wouldn't have called for any other reason. Getting straight to it, Remmy explained, "Someone moved into the shack."

Three seconds of tense silence preceded a surprised bark of "The hell you say," followed by a booming laugh.

King was nothing if not unpredictable. Then again, who would have thought someone would want to live in that dump? Giving the boss time to wind down, Remmy eyed Giggs. That lunatic looked ready to crawl out of his skin, likely with the need to hurt someone.

Finally, with one last chuckle, King said, "Check it out. Carefully."

"Understood."

"Just you, Remmy. Tell Giggs to wait in the car. Otherwise there's bound to be bloodshed, when I'd rather know what I'm dealing with first."

Screw me sideways. Remmy ran a hand over his face, but his tone hid all trace of frustration when he said, "Got it."

"If possible, get a photo of the interloper."

"And your package?" Whatever it might be.

"We'll leave it for now. Whoever moved in isn't likely to find it. It's safe, and I have a little time."

Time to torment someone, he meant. Remmy eyed Giggs with unease. The younger man wouldn't appreciate being sent away. His reactions could range from sulking to exploding, or anywhere in between.

One of these days, Remmy might have to end him.

Hopefully, it wouldn't be today.

ALTHOUGH HE KNEW she tried to hide it, Jodi looked both wary and belligerent. Nothing about her would be easy, and yet Hunter wanted to know her better. Why, he couldn't say. The woman was one contradiction after another. Friendly one moment, combative the next. Cocky and then unsure. Pushy but then so withdrawn that it made his chest ache.

There was a time when he'd enjoyed a good puzzle, especially the human kind. Discovering what made others tick had been a natural talent that he'd embraced. Not anymore.

Or… Not until Jodi.

And this time, what he felt wasn't familiar, because it seemed too personal.

The spring-hung screen door pushed open and Turbo came out, still licking his loose lips. His big beefy paws rushed over the decking as he headed for Jodi and more of her cuddles. Hunter understood that perfectly.

The look on her face when she'd stroked the dog's ears… Damn, it got to him. She'd looked incredibly sweet, as much as a messy, suspicious, pugnacious woman could. And she'd been open with the dog in a way she wasn't with him.

Who knew loving on his dog would wear him down so quickly? It was like seeing two wounded souls bonding right before his eyes.

I'll keep my own wounded soul locked away, thank you very much.

"He's just the sweetest, isn't he?" Without waiting for Hunter to answer, Jodi asked, "What's wrong with his barker?"

"No idea, really. He's just a little different." *Like me. Like you.*

"Where'd you get him?"

She couldn't know it, but that was the most personal question of all. Securing the gate on the deck, Hunter explained, "If Turbo hears or smells something, he'll take off—and he hears and smells everything. I don't trust the woods, so I don't want him to get away from me."

Surprising him, Jodi gave him an aggrieved frown.

"What?"

"You're explaining for me, aren't you? Because I've been weird."

"You haven't been weird," he denied, but yes, he'd explained for her in case she misunderstood his intentions.

Sure, she could still go over the rail if she chose, but he didn't want her to think he was trying to contain *her*.

The way she'd entered his home with so much caution— and yeah, he'd noticed when she'd checked the lock. The way she'd breathed a little deeper when looking at the ax, her hesitation to get involved even as a neighbor, it all troubled him. Maybe too much.

Acting like it was nothing, he said, "Just making more conversation."

"Bull." As if facing her own harsh truths, she looked into his eyes, and damn, she had a stare that could level a person. "You closed us in here, knew how I'd feel about it, so you explained."

True, and apparently in the process he'd made her more uneasy. "It's just a latch, and the railing isn't that high."

"Appreciate it." She didn't look away from him. After a long, tense stretch of silence, she muttered, "I'm working on some things."

The admission made his heart heavy. "I get it."

Her gaze sharpened, dissecting him, looking *into* him. "You do, huh?"

Oh, hell no. Never mind that he'd like for her to open up to him, he refused to be analyzed. "Let me grab the potatoes. I'll be right back." As he walked away, he felt that unnerving stare of hers, but he resisted looking back. Even while in the kitchen, he didn't let himself dwell on her compelling hazel eyes or how the bright sunshine looked on her delicate skin.

Or even the obvious affection she felt for Turbo.

No. Hell no. He would not let Jodi Bentley get under his skin.

Not any more than she already had.

When he returned to the deck, Jodi was different. More

closed off than she'd been before. He saw it. He felt it. Even as they idly conversed, she kept herself contained. More aloof.

The probing looks were gone.

Apparently, she'd given him that one opening, and since he hadn't taken it, she was done.

At least for now.

It didn't take long to get dinner on the table, but during that time, Jodi kept her comments superficial while continuing to stroke, pet and cuddle Turbo. Hunter pretended not to care. Hell, he shouldn't care. He had his own issues to work out, but seeing her so guarded bugged him.

"Gawd," she complained on a groan. "Knock it off already. You're starting to look like Turbo."

Taken by surprise, he went blank. "What?"

"You're all droopy and it's dumb. I liked it better when you were mocking me."

"I haven't mocked you," he denied.

"Ha. All that bit about my house?" Affecting a ridiculous deep voice, *she* mocked *him*, saying, "If you say it's great, I'll believe you."

"I was agreeing with you."

"Sure you were. We both know it's a dump, but I'm fixing it up."

Annoyed, Hunter set out utensils with precision, making sure he didn't snap them down onto the table. He added the salt and pepper shakers, and a dish of butter for the potatoes. "All this time, you've been sitting there stewing on one measly comment?"

"You won't let me help with prep. What else was I supposed to do?"

Was a quiet, friendly dinner so far out of her wheelhouse that she wasn't sure how to act?

"You want to help? Here." He handed her a sharp knife—how trusting was he, anyway?—and a fat, ripe tomato on a plate. "You can slice the tomato while I pour our iced tea." He'd have offered her something different to drink, but tea, coffee and water were all he had.

"Oh, yay. Look at me, such a big contributor."

Hunter couldn't help it—he laughed.

And that made her fight a grin. "There." She set the knife aside and presented the tomato slices with flair.

"Adeptly done. Thank you." He waited for her to loosen up, to say or do something else outrageous, but she settled back into silence.

It wasn't until he took his seat that she stated, "I like your dog."

"He likes you, too. Word of warning, though—don't feed him."

Since Turbo sat at attention, obviously hopeful, she asked, "Why not?"

Apparently, the topic of his dog would remain their middle ground. Hunter didn't have a problem with that. Focusing on the big goof had often helped him, so now he could help Jodi, too. "For one thing, he'll bug you through the rest of the meal. And for another, it upsets his stomach, which means he'll have me up all night for bathroom runs." He cut into his steak. "Let's eat."

Jodi surveyed the food. "Man, this all smells good."

Probably more so to someone who hadn't eaten all day.

While she dug in, Hunter surreptitiously watched her. She ate politely, but with obvious hunger. What if he hadn't offered? Would she have gone to bed without food? Seemed likely.

They were both silent as they ate, but this time, it felt

companionable instead of strained. Turbo gave up and sprawled out on the deck with a lusty groan.

When her plate was nearly empty, Jodi said, "It's really nice out here. Peaceful."

True. It was also quiet and remote. Perfect for sorting through problems. Was that what she intended?

"When I bought my place," she said, "I never thought about sitting outside to eat. Now I think I'll add a grill to my list."

"Does your house have a deck or anything in the back?"

She shook her head. "There's a little poured patio—and I do mean *little*. It's crumbling, so I'll probably break it up, but I could get a lounge chair or something."

He could easily envision her swinging a sledgehammer. Pretty sure there wasn't any type of work that Jodi would shy away from.

"Since it's only me, I don't need a whole table and all this seating." The look she gave him said she didn't quite understand why he had so much seating either.

Was money an issue for her? Was that why she'd bought such a run-down dump? "This all came as a set," Hunter explained. "The table, benches and two extra chairs. Plus, I like being at the table to eat, but then the other chairs are nice for just…" Sitting outside, thinking, *breathing*. "Relaxing."

She sipped her tea while considering that. "Won't be quite the same for me."

"How so?"

"I've got a lot of work to do. Not a lot of time for relaxing." Tipping up her face and closing her eyes, she said, "The sound of the creek is nice, and the breeze in the trees."

Hunter took in the smooth length of her pale throat. That stubborn chin and cute nose. The naturally dark lashes now resting on her cheeks. To him, she looked too young and, at the moment, far too innocent.

With a smile, she glanced at the coop. "I like hearing the chickens in the background, too. I've never heard that before."

Currently, the birds made quiet clucking sounds as they meandered around their space, pecking at the dirt and scratching. "I wish I could let them be free-range, but there are too many predators around."

In the smallest way possible, she stiffened—before stabbing her last bite of meat.

Her every reaction hyped up Hunter's awareness of her; he sensed Jodi knew a little too much about predators.

After a strained pause, she said, "You gave them a great setup. They've got a lot of room to roam around, fresh air and plenty of shelter."

Glad that she'd see it that way, Hunter ate his last bite and nodded. "I wanted them to feel free, even if they aren't."

She looked away, saying softly, "Yeah."

He had to fight the urge to reach out to her. "Jodi?"

"Man, you're a good cook." Shaking off her despondent mood, she shared a quick smile. "You said these tomatoes are from your garden? That makes you multitalented, right? Farmer, builder and great with cars."

In that moment, Hunter decided he was glad she'd moved in near him. Not because he wanted or needed company, but because he figured she did—and there were very few people who would understand her and her quirks.

He was the exception. Maybe fate had put her here for a reason.

"I prefer my own vegetables. For a while, I'd considered canning them for the winter, but that's a hell of a lot more complicated than you'd think."

Jodi grinned at that.

"Instead, when I go to the grocery, I pick up a few things here and there and store them in the basement."

Her gaze shot to his house with apprehensive realization. Over a basement?

Some might not see the deliberate, guarded stillness in her, but he did. He saw it, *felt* it. "Does your place have a basement?"

"Nope." Blowing out a slow breath helped her to appear relaxed again. "It's on a slab."

A deliberate choice on her part, he assumed, given her reaction. Awful suspicions cut through his mind, but he knew better than to ask. "Well, if you ever need something, just let me know. I'll probably have it stored away. In fact…" He pushed back from his empty plate. "Just a second." Turbo watched him go but didn't make a move to follow.

In the kitchen, Hunter located a notepad and pen and then rejoined her. "I'll give you my number." He scrawled it across the paper, folded it and handed it to her. "Any problems, just give me a call."

Jodi stared at the note without touching it. "Why would I have a problem?"

She wasn't that naive. She knew a woman alone, under any circumstances, faced a certain amount of risk. Actually, men did, too. Living out here, so far from town, without anyone else around, meant help wouldn't be easy or quick. "Leaky roof or truck won't start or a raccoon gets in your attic. No idea. I'm just saying, it can't hurt for us to exchange numbers, right?"

She frowned at the note.

Pretending he didn't see her reserve, he said easily, "Back when I first got Turbo, he was pretty sick. I found him starving in a field. He had a skin condition and he was afraid."

That shot her attention to his face. "Good thing you found him."

Hunter nodded. "Figured that, as I was trying to get him home, my truck stalled. Don't mind telling you, I could have used some backup then." Remembering made him miss his brother. Hell, it made him miss his whole family.

Jodi leaned a tiny bit closer. "What happened?"

"I spent fifteen minutes dicking with the ignition until it finally kicked over. Luckily, it kept running until I got to the vet's."

"Oh, wow. Poor Turbo—and poor you."

When she said his name, the dog rolled over and started wiggling on his back. Big paws in the air. His junk on display.

Laughing, Jodi quickly popped her last bite of potato into her mouth, then used both hands to scratch the dog's chest. "He's okay now?"

"Yeah, but it was a long road to recovery. He had heartworms, and I have to say, he looked like hell for a while there." After laying the note in front of her, Hunter folded his arms on the table. "And before you ask, his bark was already weird, and his skin is supposed to be that loose."

She smiled. "I think he's handsome."

"More handsome now than when I found him, that's for sure." It pleased Hunter to see that she'd cleaned her plate. Wishing he had dessert to offer, he took her dish and stacked it with his own. "My point is that things come up. So how about we exchange numbers?"

"Yeah, all right." Taking the pen, she wrote hers down in neat little numbers. "Have to say, it surprised me that my internet works and my cell reception is so good." She handed it to him, then tucked his note into her shoe.

"I enjoy roughing it. Chopping wood for my fireplace to help get me through the winter, growing my own vegetables and gathering eggs from my chickens, but if there was no way for my mother to reach me..." He shook his head and laughed.

Amused, Jodi put an elbow on the table and propped her chin on her hand. "What would she do?"

"She'd drive out here and build a house right next door. My brother, too."

"You have a brother?"

Appreciating her interest on a safe topic, he said, "Memphis."

"Younger or older?"

"Younger. I'm thirty-two, he's thirty, so not a big age difference." Talking about his brother always put a smile on Hunter's face. "You'd like Memphis."

"Why?"

"He's fearless, like you."

Her mouth quirked. "You think I'm fearless?"

Maybe more like dangerous—in many ways, which was exactly what she wanted the world to see. Overall, she pulled it off, but deep down, he knew something awful had happened to her and she was still dealing with it. "I think you're smart, Jodi. Determined, for sure, to take on that house as a project. And to live out here alone? You have to be somewhat fearless."

This time she outright laughed. "Somewhat, huh?"

"We're all susceptible to something." Maybe if she accepted that as truth—for him, for *everyone*—it'd be easier for her to accept for herself.

"Yeah, well..." After floundering a second or two, she downed the last of her tea. "You were talking about your mom?"

"She's always been protective of Memphis and me, and it doesn't matter that we're grown men now, twice her size. She has to be able to reach us or she'll turn the world upside down."

"So you made sure she could. Nice of you."

He wondered if she had anyone checking up on her, but he didn't ask. "When I bought the place, it already had internet and cable, but I stipulated that it had to be upgraded. I paid for it, but it was all handled before Turbo and I arrived. Even though we're isolated out here, we're still close enough to the town that cell reception isn't a problem—unless it storms, or snows too much."

"Or the wind blows?" she teased, proving she'd already done her research on that.

"Weather factors in, believe me. Doesn't take much to lose power." One thought led to another, and he asked, "You have lanterns or candles, just in case?"

"Lanterns." She thought for a second before venturing into another question. "You mentioned your mom and your brother. No other siblings? No dad?"

"No other siblings, but of course I have a dad. I wasn't hatched in a lab."

The joke fell flat, and it struck him that Jodi might not know her father. Did she have any family? Despite her current interrogation—which usually he'd hate, but now didn't mind—he hesitated to press her too much.

To test the waters, he asked, "How about you?"

"How about me what?"

"Family?"

"Ah, no." She shook her head to punctuate that. "No family." Then with a smirk, "Seriously, I might've been a mad concoction in a lab."

Another small piece of his frozen heart thawed. What could he say to that?

She saved him by adding, "Actually, I have like a... *stand-in* family, you know? Not blood related or anything, but they like to boss me around."

Given the fond way she said that and the twinkle in her eyes, she took their intrusion as caring, not control. "Family doesn't have to be blood related."

"That's exactly what they say." Her smile softened... but then, as if she realized what she'd admitted and how she'd opened the door to questions, she shed the emotion real fast. "Are you close to your dad?"

She needed space, Hunter knew, so he'd give it to her. "Dad's great but he doesn't hover like my mom. He's more the quiet type who trusts you'll do things right, and when you don't, when you screw up, he'll be there to help figure it out."

"Nice." With her curiosity obvious, she asked, "Have you screwed up much?"

Only his entire fucking life.

No, that wasn't accurate. He was getting it together... although it felt like he'd been spinning his wheels ever since he moved out here.

He'd just had more meaningful conversation with Jodi than he'd had with anyone in eighteen months—his family included.

Abruptly standing again, he said, "I'll take in the dishes."

"No, wait." Watching him cautiously, making him wonder if he'd somehow spooked her again, Jodi came around the table. "I'm sorry." She stared up at him, looking sorry, damn it, and then she took the dishes from his hand. "I shouldn't have pushed. That's my bad. You just... I guess I got a little too relaxed." And with that, she went into his house, leaving him empty-handed but overflowing with confusion. Too relaxed? Did she guard against even that?

Bemused, Hunter stood there, staring after her, until he heard the quiet clatter of dishes in the sink. Turbo leaned against his leg.

Glancing up at the darkening sky, Hunter frowned. Damn. Time had slipped away from him…because he'd had *fun*. Maybe it had been so long, he'd forgotten what that felt like. He wouldn't feel guilty about it, though.

He enjoyed her company. So what? He could point to some altruistic idea of helping her, but he didn't want to lie to himself. Much as he understood Jodi, he knew that she understood him as well. It was like a breath of fresh air.

Unlike his family, she didn't focus on him with the intent of helping him through a rough time. Likely from experience, Jodi knew that wasn't possible. Some things you had to tackle on your own, in your own way—except that maybe he and Jodi could tackle them together.

"Come on, Turbo." He held the door for the dog, then followed him in. Jodi stood at the sink, cleaning each plate. "I can do the dishes," he said, nudging her away and turning off the water.

"You cooked," she countered, and nudged her way right back in. One hundred pounds, maybe one-ten, of pure sass and gumption, pushing past his solid two-twenty like it was nothing.

Such a damn contradiction.

It made him grin. With a flourish, he opened the dishwasher. "Fine. Just load them in."

"Fancy," she quipped, reminding him that her kitchen was far more basic.

"Isn't it? And guess what? I even have indoor plumbing."

"Ha! Some amenities are super necessary, right? No way would I bathe in the creek."

She said it, then he pictured it… Jodi knee-deep in the moving water, naked, her loosened hair slicked back and trailing along her spine. That's as far as the imagery went.

Leaning against the counter, arms crossed, he looked her over, but in those clothes, it was difficult to get an accurate bead on her body. Thin, willowy but with strength. Few discernible curves…

And he shouldn't be trying to discern them anyway. If she knew the direction of his thoughts, she'd either shoot him or bolt—possibly both. "In the hottest part of summer, it's nice to get in the creek."

As she straightened from the dishwasher, her widened eyes locked on his in disbelief. "To bathe?" And then with a snort, "You kidding?"

"No. Well, I don't really take a bath in there. But some sections are wide enough and deep enough to cool off."

Skepticism leveled her brows. "In shorts or something, right?"

Was she doing her own visual? Just to test her, he shrugged.

Her jaw loosened, her brows went up—then she must have decided he was joking, because she laughed. "I'll believe it when I see it."

That made him stall for a second. "Did you want to watch me skinny-dip?"

She gave another, slightly forced *"Ha!"* and stepped around him. "I saw the fishing equipment."

"If you ever want to borrow a rod and reel, let me know. There are plenty of trout, walleye, bass and bluegill. Perch, too, but I don't catch them as often. Someday we could have a fish fry."

"Whoa." She stroked a hand over Turbo's head. "I'm not sure I could eat something I caught myself."

Earlier today, he would have avoided any type of involvement, yet now he said, "I'll show you. A fresh fish dinner is delicious."

"Maybe if I don't see it with its face." She shuddered. "Once it's looked at me...probably not."

So a woman with a backbone of iron, a smart mouth, a chip on her shoulder the size of a mountain, but she balked at hurting a fish. Her middle name should be Paradox.

"I need to get going." She tucked back wayward hanks of hair, not in any self-conscious way about her unkempt appearance, just to keep it out of her face. "It's been a long day and I'm looking forward to crashing."

He saw the lie. Like him, she probably had few restful nights. "How about Turbo and I walk you back?" The shadows were getting longer.

"Nope, I'm good, but thanks. Especially for dinner." Rocking back on her heels, she hesitated.

It struck him that at least she was more relaxed now than when she'd first arrived. "You're welcome." He did not want her walking home alone. "Something on your mind?"

"Yeah, actually. So, how's this work? Do I owe you a dinner in return?" Proving it was an unfamiliar offer, she rushed on. "I really will buy a grill, you know, but probably not right away. I wouldn't even mind getting two chairs if you think you'd want to...but hey, I understand if you don't. I just figured since we're neighbors and we're doing this whole neighborly thing—"

"We will." Hunter had the insane urge to kiss her. A quick, smiling peck—that of course he resisted. "Since I already have a grill and seating, why don't we meet here again? Next time, you can bring a dessert. There's a nice bakery in town where you can get a couple of cupcakes or something." Nothing too pricey, since he really wasn't sure about her finances.

"For real? Yeah, I mean, that sounds great." A genuine smile started to curl her plump lips…and suddenly, Turbo went nuts, bolting around as if goosed while also howling and croaking and slamming out the screen door to the back deck.

He and Jodi shared a quick, startled glance before they both raced after him.

Making a terrible racket, Turbo hopped and howled.

"What in the world?" Hunter grabbed for Turbo's leash just inside the back door and hooked it to his collar as an extra safeguard. "He never acts like this."

With her gun in her hand, Jodi quietly ordered, "Stay here," then hoisted herself over the railing and started jogging toward her house.

For three stunned seconds, Hunter watched her stealthily race through the shadowed trees along the creek line. She'd withdrawn her gun because she expected trouble.

And she'd told him not to follow!

Like hell! Going inside only long enough to grab his own Glock and stuff it in a pocket, Hunter held tight to Turbo's leash and opened the gate. Now that they were on the move, Turbo concentrated on sniffing instead of making a racket.

Hunter could no longer see Jodi and it worried him. Damn it, hadn't he told her there were wild animals around? The sky was now a deep purple, with a red haze the only sign of where the sun sank behind the mountains. Thankful that it was at least light enough for him to keep from tripping over rocks and fallen limbs, Hunter continued on until he could see the back of her house through the pines. Turbo looked back at him.

"Where are you, Jodi?" Hunter murmured.

She stepped out and said, "Right here," with laconic frustration. She held her gun loosely at her side while giving Turbo an affectionate pat, but her brows were down and her mouth tight. "I told you to stay put."

Tension gathered in Hunter's shoulders. How dare she give him an order? How idiotic for her to charge off alone! And then to snap at him? A thousand replies came to mind, none of them very neighborly.

In fact, he was pissed off enough to keep them all to himself, to actually ignore her in favor of speaking to his dog. "Go on, bud. We'll see what has you so riled."

Jodi caught his arm. "It's my business, so butt out."

Looking first at where her small hand attempted—and failed—to encircle his thick wrist, and then to her aggressively set expression, Hunter said, "Let go."

Her eyes flared, then immediately narrowed. She jerked away and literally took the lead, stepping around him and Turbo. They were within forty yards of the house when someone shouted, "Quit fucking around, will you? Let's go, already."

Jodi stiffened, then stabbed him with a glare. "Stay off my property." And *again*, she left him behind as she broke into a sprint.

Of all the asinine… Turbo went nuts once more. It dawned on Hunter that the dog had calmed once he found Jodi, but he didn't like seeing her leave. "Quiet," Hunter commanded. Turbo obeyed, but he continued to strain at the leash.

His dog was not an attack dog—but he was incredibly loyal, and apparently, Jodi had already won him over.

Holding the leash in his left hand, Hunter withdrew his Glock with his right. He saw Jodi edge around a tree, then dart to the rear of her house. She tried the back door, found it locked and inched around to the side.

Hating that she'd take such a risk, Hunter detoured to the other side. He had a feeling that the threat was in front anyway, so he'd get there before her. Other than light coming from inside the house, her yard was dark.

Unacceptable.

With his gaze constantly searching the area, he checked the front, where the door and window seemed secure, then the wild, rugged yard. No one would ever call it a lawn, not in its current state.

There were no cars around, only Jodi's truck, but Turbo stared toward the woods on the other side...that would lead to the main paved road.

Definitely intruders, but why? What did they want?

If it hadn't been for that deep voice, he might've blamed kids looking for a place to party—though, seriously, her house would never have been his first choice, even as a daring high school boy.

Turbo gave up his vigilance of the woods, telling Hunter the threat was gone. The dog now seemed more interested in joining Jodi. Wondering how that would go, Hunter went along. Jodi was sitting in the passenger side of her truck, staring at the open glove box.

She turned her head to glare at him. "The house is fine, but the bastards were looking for something."

Hmm. So her vitriol was now aimed at the intruders? Fine by him. They could clear up the whole issue of her giving him orders another time. "Is anything missing?"

"No, but my registration was out." She folded it, put it away and locked the glove box. Agitated, she left the truck, flashlight in hand, and began to search the yard.

"You need some exterior lights."

She shot him a killing glare. "No shit, Sherlock. Some alarms, too, and apparently a freaking garage." The second the words were out, she huffed. "Damn it, you made me curse."

That accusation brought out his own glare. "I *made* you?" Merely by being concerned?

"I'm trying to quit, but here you are, nosing in and..." She pressed the heels of her hands to her temples, and since she still held a gun, he flinched.

She was far more cavalier about weapons than he could ever be. Not that she aimed at herself, or him, or Turbo...

"Forget I said that." Dropping her hands, Jodi glared around the area with unspent rage. "I'm lousy company when I'm this pissed."

"And you're pissed now?"

"Oh," she laughed, making it sound like a threat. "Yes, I most definitely am."

To be sure, he asked, "At the intruder?"

"Two intruders, judging by the footprints." She pointed the flashlight to a clear path of disturbed weeds where her lawn should be. "This one circled the house, maybe looking for an easy way in." Next she aimed the flashlight toward the dirt road. "The other only came as far as that."

He followed the beam of light to see clearly defined boot prints—too large to be Jodi's—in the road. Amazing. "And you called me Sherlock?" In the short time he'd known her, which wasn't even a whole day, no matter that it felt longer, she'd made him feel too many things. Confusion was currently in the lead, especially with her bold assertion of two intruders. Protectiveness was close on the heels of that.

If Hunter had been searching, he'd have seen the same. But then, he was trained. And astute.

What is she...?

Besides trouble?

CHAPTER THREE

"So." AFTER GLANCING up at the darkened sky, then the darker road, Jodi strode over to him. Impatience seemed to emanate off her, as if she had a hundred things to do and none of them included him. "Will you get home okay?"

Of all the… "I'll stay until the cops get here."

"That'll be a long stay, since I'm not calling the cops."

No, of course she wasn't. What was he thinking? She never did the expected. "May I ask why?"

"No." She flicked the flashlight toward his house, then offered it to him. "You can take this with you."

Ignoring her outstretched hand, Hunter tried to decide her angle. Dodging cops often meant a criminal background. "Are you a felon?"

"Nope." Seeing that he wouldn't take the flashlight, she turned it off and tucked it away. They stood in the gloom of tall pines and long dark shadows.

"In some other kind of trouble, then?"

"Not currently."

That cryptic answer caused his curiosity to pounce. "Something from your past, then?"

The smile that curved her mouth wasn't friendly. It said loud and clear: butt out.

Damn it, he should…but he couldn't. "Someone is bothering you? An ex, maybe?"

With a harsh, strangled laugh, she headed for her front door.

Ah, so he'd hit a nerve with that guess. Had Jodi moved here to avoid someone? Maybe an abusive boyfriend? "Hold up."

When he started to follow her, she stopped and gave him a level look over her shoulder. "I wouldn't if I was you."

Now what? "Wouldn't…?"

"Keep pushing. You've got your own damn secrets, and any second now turnabout is going to be fair play."

Not likely. He had his past firmly stored away. "If you're saying—"

"I'm saying you should *go home*, Hunter. I have things to do."

Like what? "Don't you think—"

"I think it's my business, not yours. Besides, Turbo is tuckered out."

It suddenly dawned on him that while he'd moved, Turbo hadn't. The dog was sprawled in the grass, back legs stretched out behind him, his droopy jowls overlapping his front paws. The leash was stretched as far as it'd go. If he'd taken another step, he'd have been dragging the poor dog.

Hunter knew from experience that once Turbo quit, that was it. Diverted, he said to Turbo, "Sorry, bud. It was a hectic evening for you, wasn't it?" Hunter was about to pet the dog when he heard the distinctive sound of a key in a lock.

Turning quickly, he saw Jodi open her front door. He knew she would go inside, lock him out and that would be that. Incredible.

In rapid order, he weighed his options, and settled on total honesty. "I'm worried."

Sighing long and dramatically, her head dropped forward to show her annoyance—as if it wasn't already plain—and slowly she turned toward him. "Seriously, Hunter, I offered my flashlight."

That got his molars clenched, but he kept his tone moderated. "I'm worried about *you*, damn it. About this situation."

Disdain curled her lip. "About a woman alone?"

She did seem hung up on that. "Look at Turbo. He's worried, too."

This time she gave a dramatic eye roll. "Yeah, nice try."

Of course the dog was snoring. "How about this? How about I get a couple of my big outside lights for you? One for the front, one for the back." Lifting a hand, he forestalled her arguments. "Because it'll make me feel better. Tomorrow, or the next day, I assume you plan to install better lighting?" She wasn't a dummy. And despite all evidence, he didn't think she'd take unnecessary risks when given other options.

"You have lights just lying around, huh?"

"I have extra flood lamps, yes, and some long extension cords." One thought led to another. "Will your current electrical box support that?"

"No idea, but then, I wasn't planning to light up the mountain." She sent a doubtful glare at the bare-bulb porch light. "Not yet, anyway. But hey, if it really matters to you, you could loan me a few bulbs. Tomorrow, after the windows and eaves are done, I'll run into town and get what I need. I can repay you then."

"Perfect. Exactly how reasonable neighbors behave." He gestured between them. "You and me, I mean." In case she was just trying to get rid of him, he gave Turbo's leash a gentle tug and said, "Come on, boy. You can wait here with Jodi."

The dog lifted his head.

When Jodi started to protest, Hunter said, "Look at him. He's beat. No reason to make him walk to my place, back here, then home again, right?" As if he'd caught on, Turbo scrambled to his feet and, butt wagging, joined Jodi on the porch. Hunter handed her the leash. "I'll make it quick." In case she thought to refuse, he jogged off, going along the road this time instead of using the back of the properties. Once in his house, he took the time to put together a small bag of groceries. Jodi would probably harass him about it, but hopefully, she'd accept it anyway. He found the bulbs in his garage, but also grabbed a freestanding floodlight for her side yard with a heavy-duty extension cord.

He flipped on his own lights so he could gauge how close the beams came to her property, pocketed his keys and took off again, this time loaded down—and still with the Glock tucked in his back pocket.

When he got to Jodi's house, the front door was closed and she was nowhere in sight.

Uh-oh.

Praying that she hadn't taken off with his dog—seriously, he didn't know that much about her—he checked the side yard, saw her truck and bounded up to the porch with relief. He had his hand raised to knock when Jodi opened the door.

"Did you run the entire way?"

Pretty much, but what came out of his mouth was "Your house is *empty*."

Backlit by the light coming from the kitchen, she shrugged. "I just moved in, remember?"

"Why would you move in without furniture?" Literally, there wasn't…a thing. Not a chair, table or lamp.

"I have a cot to sleep in. I'll get some furniture soon."

A cot.

She planned to sleep on a freaking cot. *For how long?*

He looked through the small living room that opened into the kitchen and wanted to wince. It wasn't habitable after all. "When is soon, exactly?"

"In time frames, it's none-of-your-damn-business." She nodded at his packages. "What's all this?"

Hell, he'd brought her juice and food and snacks, but did she even have dishes? Anything at all? His curiosity didn't just double, it quadrupled. Turbo came around the corner, his nose to the floorboards, saving Hunter from more awkward gawking. "He smells something."

"Hopefully, all the cleaner I used."

While unloading everything to the porch, Hunter considered things. "I'll put in these bulbs."

"I can do it." But she looked in the bag with the food, and abruptly straightened. With all the enthusiasm she'd have given a two-headed snake, she pointed at the bag. "What is *that*?"

Screwing in a bulb gave Hunter an excuse not to meet her accusing gaze. "Hmm? Oh, just a few snacks for the morning. I'd never have eaten that whole pack of cookies anyway, so I put a few in a container for you."

"That's more than cookies."

"Juice, too. And some chips and a few bottles of water." He smiled as if he didn't see anything amiss in her tone or expression. "I'd have brought you a few scoops of coffee, but I didn't know if you have a coffee maker." Reaching past her, he felt inside the door, located a light switch and flipped it up.

The sixty-watt bulb was better than nothing, but she'd definitely need something better, and soon.

Jodi stood there, slack-jawed in disbelief as he plugged the extension cord into an outside outlet on the porch, then set up the freestanding floodlight so that it shone on her truck and mower. "Better," he proclaimed…though Jodi looked like a ticking time bomb ready to detonate.

Easing up on the pushiness, Hunter asked, "Okay if I put this other bulb out back?"

Two deep, calming breaths later, she nodded without looking like she might rip off his head. Took her just a little longer to loosen the obvious tension that made her shoulders rigid. She even popped her neck, dragged in another long breath and managed an insincere smile. "Thank you for the snacks."

Wow. That sounded almost civil. "You're welcome, neighbor." He was starting to feel like Mr. Rogers. "No problem at all."

Cynicism narrowed her eyes. "Do neighbors really do this?" She flapped a hand at everything he'd brought. "They go to this much trouble?"

"They help when they can." Going with the sudden inspiration, a way to make it easier on her to accept his help, he added, "That reminds me. I need to be in town tomorrow late morning. You'll be here with window installers?"

"Yes."

"Mind keeping an eye on my place? Now that we know intruders are around, I hate to leave it unattended. Know what I mean?"

To his surprise, instead of calling him on his BS, she nodded. "People think things only happen in the dark, but evil doesn't pay much attention to the time of day."

Thunderstruck by that observation, he stared at her as she scooped up the bag and headed in. "This way."

Inviting him into her house now? That momentarily sidetracked him from what she'd said. He could tell that she'd returned the gun to her belly holster. He should have grabbed his own holster, one that fit on the waistband of his jeans, but expediency had been his priority.

He didn't trust her enough to delay.

So odd. Both of them armed, both wary—and yet he followed her in. After all, Turbo seemed right at home.

She led him through that small, vacant main room, into the kitchen, where another door opened to the backyard. The kitchen... He looked around with interest. It was truly minuscule, without much storage space, but she'd obviously scrubbed it top to bottom. A few of the cabinet doors needed new hinges, but the white tile countertop, trimmed with black, looked chic—like a trendy vintage design instead of just...old. As she'd said, the refrigerator was ancient, but he heard it humming along.

With a peek to the left, he saw the bathroom and her bedroom. Indeed, she had only a folding cot, narrow but with a pad for a mattress, plus a pillow and quilt. She was small enough to fit on it, but no way would it be comfortable. At least those rooms had blinds covering the windows.

"I'd take you on a tour," she said, arms folded as she leaned against the open door, "but you've just seen it all."

"It has potential."

She snorted, which seemed to be her patented answer to many things.

"Here." He handed her the bulb to install herself so he could inspect the hinges on her cabinets. They were sturdy as only something old could be. The cabinets, too, were solid. Dated, yes, but a coat of fresh paint would help that. "These only need to be tightened."

"Yeah, I know. I was thinking of changing out the knobs."

"Not a bad idea, especially if you got something to match the hinges. What do you have planned for the floor?"

"Area rugs?" She grinned as she finished tightening the bulb. "There. Plenty of light now. Thanks."

He wouldn't say *plenty*, but it was better than it had been. "You have alarms?"

As she secured the back door again, she said, "That's on the agenda for tomorrow, too."

Exasperation overtook him. "Why didn't you just wait until tomorrow to move in?"

"Was everything perfect at your place before you got there?"

"I had furniture, a television, dishes," he shot back.

"I have dishes—some, anyway." She opened a cabinet to show off four dinner plates stacked next to salad plates, bowls, saucers and mugs. "Four-piece place setting, since that was the least they had. I got utensils, too, and a few pans, though I'm not much of a cook." Rummaging in the bag he'd brought, she put the cookies in an otherwise empty cabinet, the juice in the mostly empty fridge. "Are you a coffee drinker?"

"I usually have a cup or two in the morning."

"I have a friend who lives off her coffee. I don't think she'll be visiting anytime soon, but I should probably add a coffee maker and stuff to my list."

Hunter glanced around. "Where is this mile-long list you keep adding to?"

Tapping her forehead, she said, "I told you, I keep it up here."

He was about to question that when they both heard Turbo snoring again. "Where is he?" Hunter looked around but didn't see his dog.

Sauntering around him, Jodi followed the sound to the short hall that led to her bedroom. There, stretched out on her cot, with his head on her pillow, Turbo slept.

Not the least bit offended, Jodi laughed. "You big mooch."

Yeah, Hunter worried about the dog leaving fur on her bed, but more than that, he took note of the sparse room. Other than the cot, she had a square trunk with a laptop

and battery-operated lantern on it. There were two clos-
ets, one slightly open to show a meager amount of clothes,
and the other secured with a sturdy iron hasp and padlock.

What the hell does she have in that closet?

"Maybe you should get him home so he can rest in his
own bed instead of mine."

Hunter met her inscrutable gaze. She practically dared
him to ask her about it, but why bother when he knew she'd
never give him a straight answer? He got it together with
an effort. "I hope you won't mind the fur on your pillow."

Her lips twitched. "I've slept with worse things."

Not worse people? Testing the waters, he said, "Do tell."

"I don't think so. You've pried enough for one night." She
patted Turbo. "Come on, you slug. Time to hit the road."

The dog moaned and rolled to his back.

Jodi laughed again.

Hunter liked the sound of it. He liked her—didn't trust
her. Not at all. No way. But he liked her. "I'll stop by tomorrow to let you know when I'm heading out. Want me
to bring you a cup of coffee?"

"That's okay. The juice will be good, though, so thanks
for that." She eyed the dog. "Tomorrow, will you be leaving him alone at the house?"

"He usually goes with me."

"He wasn't with you when I first met you."

"Because Turbo hates Worth."

At that, the dog sat up and grumbled.

"See? Even the name irritates him."

"Now that I've met Worth, I understand why." Jodi patted her thigh. "Come on, dude. I have things to do." Still
grumbling, Turbo made a big production of getting out of
the bed and following her from the room.

With one last glance at that padlocked closet, Hunter trailed behind them. "You have my number, right?"

"Already programmed it into my phone." She stepped into the kitchen to retrieve the dog's leash, then hooked it to his collar.

Even knowing she wouldn't, he gave it a shot. "You'll call if you see or hear our intruders?"

"Probably not—and they're my intruders, not yours. Far as we know, they haven't bothered you." Taking Turbo to the front door, she opened it, stepped out to the porch and glanced around. "It's lit up like Christmas. I don't think I'll be bothered again tonight, but even if I am, I'm not helpless, okay? I take precautions and I can handle trouble."

"The way you handled Worth?"

"Worth is just a loudmouthed bully." Small and cute and with too much interest, she turned to stare up at him. The light added intriguing shadows to her features, making her bold stare even more mysterious. "Why do you put up with him?"

For so long now, Hunter had guarded his privacy with the people of Triple Creek. They asked questions and he dodged them effortlessly. For some reason, with Jodi, he had an urge to reveal just a little. Rolling a shoulder, he decided, why not?

"Worth Linlow is an annoying ass, but he's a bigwig in the town. He knows everyone and everything that's going on. He contributes just enough to town functions to keep people coming around. The local historical society needs something, they go to Worth. If he can't make it happen, no one can. Far as I can tell, no one really likes him, but they respect his influence."

"So you put up with him?"

Hunter stared toward his house, where lights shone

bright, especially around his garage. "I tell Worth what I want him to know. Enough to make him feel informed."

"Ah, I get it." Pleased with her deductions, she smiled at him. "You feed Worth a little bait, he spreads it around and everyone feels like they know you—but they don't."

Clever Jodi. Maybe this was why he'd felt an affinity to her right off. "Something like that."

"Smart. I like it. It's a solid plan." She nodded while thinking. "So, maybe I could do the same thing, right?"

"You," Hunter reminded her, "already alienated him. Pissed him off. Even threatened him, I believe."

"Eh, maybe a little." Her unrepentant grin made him grin, too. "It won't be easy, but I'll try to play nice whenever I run into him again. We'll see how it goes. My tolerance for creeps is on the low end."

When Turbo started to stretch out again, Jodi nudged him. "Seriously, you gotta get that boy to his bed or you'll end up carrying him."

It took all Hunter's concentration not to touch her. "I'll see you tomorrow."

"I'll be here, at least until the afternoon."

Hunter took one step closer. She didn't back up. "I enjoyed today."

With clear confusion, she said, "Yeah, me, too. Weird, huh?"

"A little weird." And maybe that's why he'd enjoyed it. "Rest easy tonight. And if you need anything—"

"Yeah, yeah." She waved dismissively. "The pathetic little helpless woman will call the big badass man if an owl hoots and makes her tremble."

Laughing as he stepped off the deck, Hunter said, "You're small but hardly helpless, and I have a feeling you're as badass as they come."

She beamed at him. "Thank you for noticing, Hunter."

Figured she'd take that for a compliment. "You're very welcome, Jodi. Good night." And that silly exchange kept him grinning all the way back to his house…and for a few hours after, as he attempted to research her.

He found nothing.

No social media. No mentions online.

As far as the internet was concerned, Jodi Bentley didn't exist.

When he turned in for the night, he sure as hell wasn't smiling anymore. In fact, he decided it was time to call in the big guns.

Tomorrow morning, he'd contact Memphis. His brother would know how to garner some info on Hunter's intriguing new neighbor.

STILL FUMING, Remmy waited with Danny in a dim, musty back room of the boss's house. "That was a dumbass move."

"Go fuck yourself."

He took great pleasure in saying, "Pretty sure you're the one who's fucked, bud. You know you were supposed to stay in the car. You know I was only supposed to look around. But you ran your mouth, and the woman was there. She heard you." Hell, the neighbor had heard, too, but Danny didn't realize that, and Remmy didn't want an innocent death on his hands. For now, he'd keep the issue of the neighbor to himself.

Danny, the idiot, wasn't innocent.

Keeping a wary eye on the door, Remmy listened to the sounds of men talking in another room. It was poker night, which meant all the local bullshitters were gathered together to waste money, brag about one thing or another, and likely get drunk.

It was never a good thing when the boss, Russ King, overimbibed. He was always ruthless, but more so when alcohol blunted whatever shreds of discretion he still possessed.

Beside him, Danny pretended not to care.

The door slamming open blew Danny's cavalier facade all to hell.

Both men straightened, but Russ merely closed the door behind him and then strode in with black eyes narrowed and lean jaw tight. With his straight, dark hair brushed back and the silver at his temples, he looked more like a stocky forty-year-old CEO than a thug. To shore up that impression, King wore a button-up shirt, the sleeves rolled to his elbows, and carried a glass of whiskey on the rocks in his hand.

Not a good sign.

"So," King said, his dark gaze stabbing Danny with accusation. "What the fuck did you think you were doing?"

The mild tone put Remmy on edge. Seriously, it might be past time to move on from this job. It seemed King got bolder and more unhinged by the day, while Danny continually pushed the limits. Eventually, one of them would kill the other. His money would be on King.

Petty crime was one thing. That, Remmy could handle. This shit? He didn't need it.

Trying for a bravado he clearly lacked, Danny said, "Remmy took too long. I didn't know if something had happened to him."

King laughed. "Idiot. I've already determined that Remmy is thorough, and he can take care of himself. You, though?" Clinking the ice in his glass, he strolled closer, making Danny's mouth tighten in dread.

The attack came fast.

Remmy barely had time to get out of the way before King nailed Danny in the temple with his thick whiskey glass. The drink sprayed, ice hit the floor and Danny slid off the chair to his knees, blank and disoriented from the blow.

Fuck, Remmy hated this unpredictable stuff, but he knew better than to get involved.

King's brutal kick caused Danny to cower.

Pity surfaced. Remmy hated bullies—but right now, King had a whole room full of them waiting for him to re-join them in cards. He didn't think King would go too far. Not with others around who might catch on.

Breathing harder, King curled his lip. "You'll learn to follow orders, Danny, if I have to beat them into you."

Holding a hand to his bleeding head, using the chair for support, Danny struggled to stand.

Disgusted, King turned away. "Get up, for God's sake. Stop sniveling."

With his back turned, King didn't see the killing glare Danny shot at him, and Remmy wasn't about to comment on it.

"Now." King faced them again, his expression once more contained. "So, a woman has moved in."

"Yes." Not by posture or tone did Remmy give away his apprehension. Never would he show either of these pricks a weakness. "Sorry I couldn't find out more, but she had the place locked up. Even the broken windows were secured."

"Don't sweat it. I have sources."

"Worth Linlow?" Remmy knew the car salesman was among the group of card players.

"He's a damned busybody and keeps track of everyone and everything. He was already bitching about her, saying she was rude and tried to cheat him."

Everyone knew that was bogus. Worth was the biggest swindler in Triple Creek.

"According to him, she's ballsy and mouthy, but he also said she's a looker." King waited for Remmy to verify it.

He did so with a shrug. "From what I caught, she's small, brownish or dark blond hair, on the skinny side."

"You said you didn't see her closely?"

"No. She was around back, maybe checking out the creek or something." *More like sneaking up to shoot me, but that's my business.* "It was getting dark, and I only saw her from a distance."

King wasn't deterred. "Did you know she's a landscaper? She cuts the grass and trims the weeds on the shitty little businesses in town."

Remmy thought of the woman, how her small form had silently, furtively moved closer, and the experienced way she'd held her weapon. She would defend what was hers, he didn't have a doubt. And damn it, he hated to see her needlessly hurt. "She had a big commercial-grade mower stored under her carport." Which had left her truck parked in the yard.

"So you said." King leaned against the wall, and they both ignored Danny. "From what he said, Worth pissed her off. Probably trying to cheat her."

Again, Remmy said nothing.

"Apparently, she did her best to intimidate him. He said she made a spectacle of herself and so he fired her." That idea had King grinning. "I admire a person who doesn't care about an audience."

Worth cared, because the arrogant dumbass thought he still had a good standing in the community. Too late for that, though. Remmy had been here long enough now to know exactly who and what Worth was.

King was the opposite. He thrived on his bad reputation, one that, from Remmy's limited acquaintance, made others fearful.

And Remmy... Well, he was just killing time and making a few bucks until he was ready to move on. If that meant cracking the heads of other thugs, so what? He wouldn't lose sleep over it.

But a woman? On that, he'd have to draw the line.

When the noise in the other room swelled, King glanced at the door. "Before the night is over, Worth will rethink his decision on Ms. Bentley. He'll hire her again, and he'll keep close tabs on her."

Because King would make sure he did.

Hoping to avoid a bigger problem, Remmy spoke before King decided to leave. "If she works in town, we could break in when she's not there. Danny could grab your package and we'd be gone before anyone knew."

"No." A nasty smile emphasized King's cruel bent. "She's got my attention now. I want to meet her. I want to play with her." He slanted a frown at Danny. "You," he said, "will do nothing until I tell you to. Do you understand?"

Dropping his hand from his head and trying to look cocky, Danny nodded. "Sure, boss." A trickle of blood seeped from his cheek, mixing with the liquor on his neck and in his shirt. "No problem."

"Good. I'm glad that's clear." He pinned Remmy with his black gaze. "I want you in town when she's there next. You're a good-looking guy, muscular. Flirt with her."

Well, hell.

"Make sure she notices you. I'm curious to how she'll respond."

To what end? Remmy didn't dare ask. Aware of the hatred emanating off Danny, and of King's vile intent, he rolled a shoulder. "Consider it done."

Now he just had to figure a way out of this…without leaving the woman at the sadistic mercy of Russ King.

THEY FELL INTO a comfortable routine. For now, Jodi was content.

Over the past week, she and Hunter had shared two more meals. She'd repaid all the foodstuff he'd given her and brought dessert to each of the additional meals. Now, with her own grill set up, she wondered if she should ask him over.

It was nearing the end of the day, but she hadn't seen him yet. Did he watch her through his binoculars? No way to know.

Hunter was cagey. Checking up on her while acting like he wasn't. He had this sneaky way of pretending he needed a favor, which he used as an opportunity to ask if anyone else had been around or if she'd had any trouble.

Not like she'd tell him if she did. But…it was kind of nice how he checked up on her without shoving it in her face. Sure, she knew he thought himself bigger and badder, and therefore superior. She snorted to herself.

Hunter didn't have a clue what she could do. What she *would* do if needed.

Circling back to the front of the house, she admired—for about the hundredth time—the new windows and eaves, the new, sturdy front door and the repaired porch. So she hadn't yet gotten much furniture inside. Who cared? Her cot was fine, considering she slept very little.

Food now filled her cabinets, though she'd be willing to bet her choices were very different from Hunter's. Frozen meals and snacks were more her speed.

Out of an abundance of caution, she walked to the road and again stared at the exact spot where her intruders had likely crossed from town, through the woods and onto her property. All along that stretch, she'd set booby traps that remained undisturbed. Nothing that would hurt the wildlife; she'd never want to do that. So far she'd enjoyed seeing elk, fox and a variety of birds. It left her feeling serene, when not that long ago, a sensation like serenity would have been nothing but a fairy tale for the likes of her.

Everyday life for the everyday woman.

Trespassers aside, her setting had become a big part of that.

So had Hunter Osborn. Having him for a neighbor wasn't a hardship in any way.

Other creeps lurking about? Yeah, that she planned to deal with—if they dared to show again.

She'd set out a few stacked twigs, arranged branches and such to see if they were disturbed. Little ribbons loosely tied here and there. Some soft piles of dirt.

So far all she'd seen were paw prints.

The security cameras she'd bought were closer to the house. Nothing as high-tech as her former employer had used, but they'd get the job done. It was one small house. And she was only…herself. Mostly insignificant.

Or at least, she used to be.

When her phone rang, she drew it from her back pocket while continuing to survey the property for security risks. A glance at the screen showed her a familiar name. Smiling, she put it on speaker. "Kennedy, hey."

Without preamble, her best friend said, "You're getting a delivery."

Incredulous, Jodi tucked in her chin. "Come again?"

"Sorry, hon. I tried to talk him out of it."

The *him* could only be one person. *"Parrish,"* she snarled.

"Afraid so. You already know he's keeping tabs."

Yeah, she had assumed he would. "We agreed!"

"Well, as to that, I'm not sure Parrish did." In a rush, Kennedy said, "It's out of love, hon. You know that."

"It's out of pushiness! It's him being a damned control freak!"

"Now, Jodi—"

"I'll call him." Holding the phone out in front of her, she began to pace. "I'll make it crystal clear that I'm doing this on my own, in my own way."

"No," Kennedy whispered in that heartfelt way of hers. "Please understand that you're *not* on your own anymore. You have us now."

Annoyance narrowed her eyes. "I assume Reyes is with you."

"Right here, doll," he said with his typical teasing humor. "The delivery will arrive in ten minutes—and don't you dare dodge out."

Frustration took out her knees and Jodi plopped down to sit on the top step of the porch. "What am I getting?"

"A couch and chair," Reyes said. "End table, television, few lamps."

"Jesus." Jodi had to laugh.

Kennedy jumped back in. "There are also some cool tech gadgets you can use so that we all know you're safe."

Resigned, Jodi closed her eyes and dropped her head forward to rest on her knees.

"There's something else." Kennedy hedged, but not for long. "Someone has been researching you. Madison said your trail is covered, so don't worry about it, but we thought you should know—"

"That'd be my neighbor."

"Hunter Osborn," Reyes confirmed. "Retired park ranger."

"Seriously?" Jodi straightened up again. "I tried to dig around, but couldn't find much."

"Like you, he's covered what he could—or he has someone to cover for him."

"But he wouldn't be a match for Madison's digital sleuthing skills." No one was. Jodi knew that. Reyes and Madison were siblings, and they, along with their brother, Cade, and their father, Parrish, excelled at what they did.

What they'd done for Jodi, what they'd given back to her, she could never repay. "Guess I should be thanking all of you."

Reyes said, "No, because we know you wanted to do it yourself. We understand your independence."

"Ha." She'd yet to see proof of that.

"But without us, you can't know everything you should." Reyes cleared his throat, and with a grin in his tone, said, "Like the fact that your neighbor is nearby and listening in."

Startled by that disclosure, Jodi literally shot off the porch, turned…and sure enough, there stood Hunter, all six feet plus of him, feet braced apart, muscled arms at his sides, his left hand holding the leash that kept Turbo, the wonder dog, silently beside him. *What. The. Hell.*

Jodi said the first thing that came to mind. "Why isn't your dog croaking?"

"It seems he's as fascinated as I am." Hunter's gaze searched hers. "Care to tell me what's going on?"

Kennedy sang, "I vote yes," while at the same time, Reyes growled, "Not yet."

Advice from them now only annoyed Jodi, especially with Hunter listening in. They could have told her sooner that he was hanging around. "Gotta go, guys."

"Wait!" Kennedy rushed to speak. "It wasn't just Parrish

who sent stuff. I picked out a few housewarming gifts, too. Pretty please, Jodi, accept it all. Enjoy it. That is, unless you don't like something, then feel free to exchange it. But…I also added a few personal things because I love you and I want you comfortable in your new home."

"At the moment, I'm the opposite of comfortable." Tension coiled in the twenty feet that separated her and Hunter, growing tighter by the moment. The muscles in her neck twitched. That familiar fight-or-flight response sparked to life.

But that was the old Jodi.

As if she'd read her mind, Kennedy whispered, "For me, you always fought."

True. Used to be, whenever she felt threatened, she ran away and only reappeared when she thought Kennedy, or sometimes other innocents, needed her.

Not anymore.

Hopefully, not ever again.

Patience personified, Hunter stood there while she worked it out. Finally, she drew a deep breath and released it slowly. "Thank you for the stuff, guys. I appreciate it."

"There you go," Reyes praised. "The delivery guys will set it up for you. Maybe let the neighbor hang around until they're done. It'll make Kennedy feel better to know you're not alone with them."

Jodi rolled her eyes. "Kennedy, huh?"

"Okay, so it'll make me feel better, too." He did another exaggerated throat-clearing. "Don't suppose you'd let me talk to him a minute?"

"Goodbye, Reyes."

"Love you, doll." For the cockiest of dudes with lethal skill, Reyes sure knew how to tug on the heartstrings.

Feeling like an idiot, especially with Hunter's unwavering gaze taking it all in, Jodi smiled. "Love you, too."

Kennedy went next. "I love you, Jodi. I don't ever want you to forget that."

No, she wouldn't. She couldn't. In so many ways, Kennedy was the sister of her heart. "Same."

In a rush, Reyes said, "Dad loves you also, so there." And then he disconnected the call—the goof.

Fighting a smile, Jodi stuck the phone back in her pocket. "Sorry."

"For?" Hunter asked, already coming closer now that she wasn't involved in a private call—a private call that he'd listened to.

"You said you've kept everyone off the property, but I'm here now and delivery guys will arrive soon, and sadly, I can't promise it won't happen again."

He bypassed everything she said. "Was that your family?"

"My sort-of family, actually."

"Ah. And someone in that family—I think I heard the name Madison—covered your background?"

No reason to deny it, since he'd heard it all. Not that she'd share details or anything. "Something like that."

He stopped right in front of her, his dark blue eyes studying her. "You're not a criminal."

That was a tricky question. Might depend on who he asked, but she wasn't about to explain it to him. "Been keeping you awake at night, huh? Did you think I was a serial killer or something?"

"Something," he agreed softly.

The sound of an approaching truck broke the disturbing spell and Jodi lifted a hand to shade her eyes.

Turbo hated the intrusion. Like Hunter, he wasn't used to

anyone else being out here. As if he thought she and Hunter might be unaware, the dog howled. Loudly.

"It's all right, bud." Hunter put a hand to the dog's head. "They're expected."

When Turbo saw that Hunter wasn't alarmed, he sat down to watch the truck, still with suspicion, but without howling alarm.

Damn it, she'd disturbed his life so much already. First meals, and then troublemakers, and now a big delivery. "I should have known they'd pull a stunt like this."

"A stunt like caring?" Hunter pressed. "Helping?" Before she could answer, he muttered, "You do seem to have a thing about accepting help."

Only because she'd taken too much of it in the last two years. "We'll be descended on in just a few minutes." Which meant she could quickly explain a few things, and he wouldn't have an opportunity to dig for more. "So how about I cut to the chase?"

"As you already know, I'm interested. Why else would I have been researching?"

"But you couldn't find anything."

"Actually... No, you go first. I'll get into my part of this whole thing later."

His part? Interesting. She couldn't wait. Until then, she might as well get it said. "So, I was this lost, miserable... *victim*." Saying the word, remembering how it had felt, made her chest tight and caused her pulse to quicken uncomfortably. Seeing Hunter's sympathetic expression, she shook her head. "No, I'm not going into detail on that." Not now. Probably not ever.

Her circumstances of victimhood were dead and buried and she planned to keep it that way.

"All right."

Damn, that soft voice sank into her, got under her skin, and that turned her brisk in response. "Point is, with the help of an elite task force, I was able to find a purpose. Like helping other women, you know?"

"Yes."

"I did that for a few years, and I enjoyed it." On a gut level, she'd been good at it. "The people on the task force trained me, helped me to understand what to say and do, the resources I could share, stuff like that." So many wonderful resources. Such an amazing family.

And they still wanted to save her.

"You made a difference."

God, she hoped so. Jodi lifted her chin. "The thing is, I finally decided I should take some of my own advice and help myself, too."

Hunter nodded. "That's what you're doing here?"

"Yup. Supposedly." She watched the truck pass Hunter's property—Turbo started to howl again—and she was glad her moment of confession was over. "I know what Reyes said, but you don't need to stay. I can handle it."

"I'd like to stay."

Of course he would. So far Hunter had gone above and beyond to be nice, and she'd been nothing but snippy. "Suit yourself." As the truck pulled to a stop, she walked out to greet the two men. Somehow, over the next few minutes, Jodi ended up holding Turbo's leash while Hunter helped them unload furniture—far more furniture than Kennedy had mentioned.

She'd had to remove her cot so they could fit in the full-size bed, nightstand and dresser. Her little kitchen now had a small café table and two chairs. The love seat and padded chair perfectly fit the dimensions of her living room, and the men even hung her television on the wall.

What the hell was she going to do with a television?

Beside her, Hunter said, "Nice TV. If you want, I can help you set up some streaming services."

She knew nothing about any of that. "Maybe. I've never been much of a TV person."

"No? A movie in the evening is a great way to unwind."

Doubtful that would work for her. Evenings meant escalating memories, too much introspection and plaguing regrets. She hadn't been a restful sleeper in a very, very long time. Sometimes it felt like a different life ago, when she'd been someone else.

Not the Jodi Bentley she was now.

Shaking that off, she walked out with the delivery guys. Misunderstanding, they promised her that they'd already been generously tipped—which wasn't something she knew to do, so good thing Parrish had covered it. No, she'd just wanted to ensure their complete departure, so she stood there watching as they drove away.

Hunter joined her. "Should you tell your friends that it's all done?"

"Why bother? I guarantee you, they already know." She looked around, didn't see the dog and asked, "Where's Turbo?"

With a half smile, he said, "The excitement of visitors wore him out. Sorry, but he's already in your bed."

The laugh surprised her. "Good. I'm glad it's getting some use."

Hunter lifted a brow.

Shock froze her to the spot. "I didn't mean... I wasn't saying..."

Now he grinned.

Jodi gave him a shove to his shoulder that barely budged him. "I only meant that I liked my cot just fine."

"I understand." Still wearing a grin, he gestured toward the house. "I'll get Turbo if you want to lock up. You can join us for dinner."

Already overwhelmed, she shook her head. "I've taken up enough of your evening."

"I enjoyed it. Besides, I came down here to invite you." As enticement, he said, "I made beef stew in the Crock-Pot, enough for both of us, and I picked up fresh bread from the bakery."

Damn. She'd forgotten to eat again, and now her stomach rumbled.

"You're hungry," Hunter reasoned. "I'm hungry. And there's plenty. What do you say?"

Good sense told her to refuse. He'd definitely use the time to grill her, to get her to expound on the info she'd shared.

He already knew too much about her.

She needed to stay guarded, but... *Everyday life for the everyday woman.* That wasn't her yet. Still...

"I promise not to interrogate you." He waited, then added, "When you want to tell me more, you can."

So beguiling. Damn it, she couldn't refuse. "All right, sure. Let's get the dog." And she could take one more look at her totally altered house...that was starting to look like a home.

CHAPTER FOUR

Jodi didn't trust him at all. Oh, Worth Linlow stood there with his slick smile pinned in place, and he sounded sincere enough, but she didn't buy it. "You want me to cut your area after all?"

"Yes."

Though Jodi could tell he tried to hide it, a bad mood hung around him like the lingering stench of skunk spray. "Why?"

"Everyone speaks highly of you. And to be honest, there really isn't anyone else."

Through narrowed eyes, she took his measure, but she couldn't guess his angle. "Pay me up front."

Visibly struggling to keep his smile from wavering, he said through his teeth, "Of course," and peeled off several bills.

As Jodi made a point of counting them, another voice said, "Hey, Worth, who's your friend?"

Jodi glanced up, saw a handsome guy several inches taller than Worth, fit instead of bloated and with blond hair shades lighter than her own. She folded the money, stuck it in her pocket, then held out her hand. "Jodi Bentley, landscaper."

"Remmy Gardner. You're new around here?"

"Moved in a week ago." Putting her sunglasses back in

place, she dismissed both men with a casual, "Enjoy your day," and started away.

A large hand closed on her upper arm. "Hold up."

So many reactions jumped to the forefront. Swing. Toss. Punch.

Maybe shoot?

Everyday life for the everyday woman.

Still, she couldn't help glaring at that large, work-rough hand until Remmy carefully opened his fingers and drew his hand away.

He did so with an exaggerated step back. "Sorry. Didn't mean to startle you."

Up went her sunglasses again. "I don't startle, but I'm not keen on getting grabbed either."

"My bad. Seriously. I just wanted a moment."

She glanced at Worth, who watched them with banked anticipation. So this was a setup? Fat chance. Transferring her gaze back to the younger man, Jodi gave him her most lethal stare.

Instead of retreating, he breathed a little deeper. Like… with interest?

Screw that. "A moment for *what*?"

"To get to know you?"

"Why?"

He smiled. "Why not?"

"Because I'm busy? Because I don't socialize much and I'm not interested in starting with you? Take your pick." Okay, so that was rude, but what did she care? "Look, I can see you and Worth have something cooked up, right? But I'm not playing, so I suggest you find a new game."

"Fascinating."

Damn it, he *sounded* fascinated! With a huff, Jodi stalked off. Behind her sunglasses, she scoped out the area.

Nothing seemed off, except that she felt Worth staring hateful daggers at her back and Remmy watching her with keen awareness. Not good. Not good at all.

During her first meeting with Hunter, she'd only been interested in the things they had in common. There'd been a nice vibe coming off him. Tones of protectiveness mixed with wary caution. Those were things she could relate to.

Now, with Remmy, sure, she sensed some relatable stuff there, too, but none of it was good. Her instincts put her on alert, and by God, she never ignored her instincts.

Once on her mower, she glanced at the new guy...and found him talking on his phone. She didn't much like that either.

So who had he called? Before she left the area, she'd try to find out. If that meant being a little less hostile to him, well, she could fake it, right?

She finished up all the other businesses before moving to Worth's lot. He'd long since gone into his showroom of cars, but Remmy stood outside in the heat, arms folded over a solid chest, making no bones about watching her intently.

Good. That'd make it easier for her to get some clues.

Pretending to ignore him, she went about her work, cutting the sparse amount of grass around the lot, trimming weeds along the edges of concrete and then shaping a few bushes. Finally, she cleaned up the mess. She was on foot behind the building, where inventory both new and used filled the lot, when Remmy joined her.

Alertness crept in, but she hid it. "You're still hanging around?"

"I wanted to apologize." This time he didn't get too close, wisely staying several yards from her. "I shouldn't have put my hand on you."

Hell, most women wouldn't mind. Most women would find him incredibly good-looking and be flattered.

As she already knew, she wasn't most women. "No problem. Just don't do it again and we'll get along fine."

Deliberately, she turned on the blower and removed grass clippings off the back lot. He couldn't keep talking over the noise, but she was able to keep an eye on him.

The second she turned it off, he came a few steps closer. "Jodi?"

Resisting the urge to roll her eyes, she faced him and waited with a display of impatience.

"I'm not sure what might have happened to you to make you so guarded."

"Nope. You wouldn't have any idea."

"If you want to tell me—"

"Not ever happening. Us playing nice doesn't include sharing secrets."

"So you do have secrets."

"Pretty sure you have a few of your own, sport." Taking advantage of the relative privacy here at the back of the building, she pushed up the sunglasses; it was a habit she had when getting serious. "Who'd you call? Someone who convinced Worth to hire me back? I know he didn't make that decision on his own."

He surprised her by saying, "Actually, yes."

So he'd admit it? Now what game was he playing? She repeated, "Who?"

After a long hesitation, where she could see him struggling with himself, he finally said, "My boss, Russ King."

"Never heard of him."

"You know everyone around here?" he challenged. "Doesn't seem likely since you said you only moved in a week ago."

Like she wouldn't find out important stuff first? "I know everyone who'd be a boss who might hire someone like you, yeah."

That long disclosure made his eyes widen. Deep brown eyes that contrasted nicely with his fair hair. Yup, plenty of women would be interested right now.

The fact that he left her cold was another stark reminder of her past.

Cautiously, he repeated, "Someone like me?" As if he didn't know exactly what she meant.

She stared into his pretty brown eyes and gave her meanest smile. "Yeah, you know, someone dirty enough to be hired, but smart enough to know I won't be easy."

Holding her gaze, he drifted closer. "You've got it all wrong."

"Do I? So why don't you tell me what it is you really want, and so you know, time is short and I have other things I need to do." Like talk to Hunter, ask him what he knew about Remmy and his boss, maybe do a little cybersearching, ferret out a few creeps.

Screw the *everyday life for the everyday woman*. There were times when it wouldn't work—like now.

He stopped six feet from her. "Worth has been running his mouth, claiming you're a troublemaker."

"So? I don't care what he says."

"Russ and Worth play cards together. It came up, and since Russ is looking for a landscaper but doesn't want anyone who'll be a problem—"

"Rules me out, doesn't it?"

"Not at all. Worth obviously doesn't understand that strong and astute is not the same as problematic."

Now, what was this about? Trying to sneak past her distrust using stupid compliments? By the second, Jodi's suspicion grew that Remmy was the man who'd been at her house. For what reason, she didn't know, but she wouldn't find out by telling him to fuck off. "You're smarter than Worth, I take it. You see the difference?"

"Absolutely. King only hires strong, loyal people."

"Those two traits don't necessarily go hand in hand."

"Definitely not, but in your case, I believe they do." His gaze dipped over her—and made her spine stiffen until he quickly focused on her face again. "See, Worth might think he's the money around here, but it's really King. He's just not as loud about it because he doesn't want people hitting him up for every little project. Don't misunderstand, though. He's generous. Anonymously. He doesn't do it for the clout the way Worth does."

"All goodness and light, huh?" She curled her lip enough to ensure he caught her sarcasm. "Sounds like a saint."

Remmy's laugh was low and rough, and some would consider it sexy. "Don't go overboard."

She didn't care about his lame, affected laugh. She didn't care about his congenial attitude. She definitely didn't give a flip that he'd glanced at her body with male awareness.

Hell no, she didn't care about that.

So why had it ratcheted up her anxiety?

Unwilling to show him a weakness, she stared into his eyes and asked, "What is it your boss does that makes him so well-to-do?" She'd be willing to bet it was something illegal—not that Remmy would admit it. Didn't matter. She had a nose for these things.

"He has a recreation business. Kayaking, river rafting, cabins and tent sites to rent, a few powerboats, just about everything to do with kicking back on or near the water."

"One location?" She'd check it out and get a feel for the place.

"Several, actually. None here in Triple Creek, though if you want a kayak, odds are the closest place to get it would be owned by King. He's never on-site at the businesses anymore. He has managers for that, but if you'd like to take a look around, I can give you a tour."

Was that a euphemism for "get you alone and murder you"? Possible. She'd give it a little more thought, but for now, with him waiting, she said, "Yeah, maybe."

"Really?" As if pleased by the prospect, Remmy smiled. "Say the word and I'll make it happen."

She didn't like his eagerness any more than she'd liked that intimate look. "It's not like I need a guide, right? I could just google it."

Something passed over his expression, regret or...worry? Hard to tell, but it definitely wasn't what she'd expected.

"Or," she said, pushing past his awkward hesitation, "you could just give me Mr. King's number and I'll call him, make arrangements to scope out the property he wants maintained." She lifted her shoulders. "Your mission will be accomplished, right?"

Hands on his hips, Remmy looked down at his feet, shifted his stance, groused something low that she couldn't quite hear, then lifted his head and locked her in his brown-eyed stare. "The thing is, Jodi, it'd be better if I was with you."

New, uneasy tingles sizzled along her nerve endings, making the troubled awareness spark hotter. "Uh-huh. Why's that?"

This time his grumbled *"Fuck"* reached her loud and clear.

She was about to insist on some answers when Worth came creeping around the corner, his cagey gaze scuttling back and forth between them.

Remmy was not pleased to see him.

Lifting his thick chin to prove he didn't care, Worth tried a smile that didn't look too convincing.

Now what was going on?

Shoving his hands into his dress-pants pockets, Worth nodded at her. "Good, you're still here."

"Did you think I'd left my truck and mower behind?" Both were at the curb on the street, more than noticeable in the quiet town.

"Ah…" He verbally tripped, then rallied. "Guess I wasn't paying attention."

Yet he knew to look for her back here? Crazy as it seemed, she took pity on him. "So, what's up?"

"I wondered if you would change the contract. Back to cutting my lot, I mean." His smile wouldn't fool anyone. "Now that we've worked out our differences."

Was that what they'd done? Jodi glanced at Remmy and caught him giving Worth a lethal glare that should have incinerated him. Man, she knew her stare was good, but his wasn't too shabby either.

"Sure, Mr. Linlow. No problem." At that point, Jodi knew her best bet was to get going.

"Call me Worth."

No, she wouldn't. "You keep paying and I'll keep maintaining." Hefting her blower and a heavy lawn bag packed full of trimmings, she walked away. Behind her, she heard a low argument that ended with Remmy jogging to catch up with her.

She kept going anyway. Luckily, her truck wasn't that far away, so she tossed in the bag of debris and dug out her mower keys to load it.

"We didn't finish our conversation."

"Pretty sure we did." Jodi eyed him askance while climbing onto her mower. Now that they were out front on the main street where anyone could see them, those twice-cursed nerves evaporated. Here, in the open, she was safer.

Isolated away from witnesses, like while at the back of the building, anything could have happened.

She knew that only too well.

It wasn't cowardly to be worried, she promised herself. As Reyes had told her many times, only an idiot wouldn't be. Not that Reyes would have worried. He and his family—sort of her family, too—were brave and brazen, confident in ways she could only pretend to be.

"Jodi." Remmy stepped too close. "Can I tell King that you're considering the work?"

Disliking the way he said her name—with familiarity and…something more, something smooth and warm, meant to soften her—she stuck the key in the ignition.

He sighed and eased back.

Yeah, he expected her to start the mower, and that had been her intent. Just to be contrary, she changed her mind. "I don't really know what the work is—unless you want to give me an address after all."

Appearing heartened by that reply, he relaxed. "Ten acres. Besides the detailed landscaping for the house and driveway, there are a bunch of trees surrounding the yard that you'd have to trim around."

"Sounds like a big job."

Nodding, he said, "Would probably take you two days, at least. Unless you have a crew?"

The sun baked down on her. Sweat left her skin sticky. Damn it, she hated mysteries. Plus, she could use the pay. What better way to convince people she was self-sufficient than building up her landscaping business? Ignoring his question, she said, "Tell you what," and hopped off the mower. Striding to her truck, she dug a pen and an old receipt from the console. "Give me the address and I'll drive by to get an idea of it."

He waffled way too long. "Just to take a look, right?"

That *was* concern she saw in his mellow brown eyes. Huh. "Can I even see it with all the trees?"

"From the driveway entrance you can. But don't linger there."

"Security cameras?"

One brow lifted. "Several."

"Got it." She waited until he wrote out the address. Then she tossed both the pen and the note back in her truck and turned away.

"I have your number off your truck."

Yeah, a business line that took messages where she could either call back or not. "So?"

"Would you like my number as well?"

Ha. Jodi gave him a level look to let him know he was nuts. "Later, gator. I have work to do."

"Jodi?"

With a big huff of impatience, she looked over her shoulder. Remmy was staring at Worth, who made no bones about watching them. *"What?"*

"Be careful, okay?"

She gave her best cocky grin. "Careful is my middle name."

LONG BEFORE SHE RETURNED, Hunter was watching for her. That was a new habit of his. An annoying one. He was not Jodi's protector.

He was a neighbor. And now a friend—or at least, he hoped so.

In some ways, yesterday had been a revelation. Jodi had friends-who-are-like-family who'd furnish her entire house for her. Wealthy, obviously. Given that they knew he'd been a park ranger, they also worried for her. Why else would they bother digging into his past?

The real kicker was how they'd so easily accessed her security cameras. There was no other way they could have known he was standing there.

Last night, he'd worried that they might have accessed his as well. He'd taken the time to change his passwords and codes, but in his gut, he figured it might not be enough. He'd bought good-quality devices—but he wasn't on a par with people who could determine that he'd covered his digital footprint. How would they know that?

Who were these people—and what did they do?

Okay, so Jodi said she helped women. He could believe that. Given her larger-than-life attitude, you could tie a cape around her and she'd pass for a superhero. Helping others was legit—so why was she holed up here in Triple Creek, living alone in a tiny house in the middle of nowhere?

Memphis had done some digging of his own, and his brother was better than good, but he hadn't found anything. The one time he'd spotted a lead, it miraculously disappeared. Memphis was impressed by that. Hunter was merely frustrated.

Allowing Turbo to lead him closer to the road where Jodi would pass, Hunter continued to muse on his million unanswered questions.

When her truck appeared, his heartbeat picked up pace.

When she stopped and rolled down the passenger window, something dark and heavy inside him lifted. Turbo was ecstatic to see her.

Hunter didn't want to name what he felt.

"Hey, guys," she called out, mostly to Turbo because that's who she looked at. "What a nice greeting."

Turbo wagged his backside with glee.

"You are so easy," Hunter told the dog. Leaning against her side door, he said through the window, "Done for the day?"

"Yeah, and I hope you're not cooking already, because I picked up groceries for our meal. That is, if you're free to visit so I can do a little payback."

Bowled over by the offer, noting the bags in the seat and on the floor, he met her gaze. "I'm free."

Her brows twitched together. "Good. Give me half an hour to unload the tractor and shower."

Nodding, Hunter started to retreat, and she spoke again. "Also, remind me to ask you about how you just said that."

Stymied, he pulled back. "What?"

"That *I'm free*. You said it different and I wanted to ask about it."

Having no idea what she meant, he said, "Okay."

"Thanks. Figured I could get some explanations from you. See you soon."

Watching her drive the rest of the way over the bumpy road, Hunter said absently to Turbo, "Confusing as hell, right?"

Turbo did more excited wiggling.

"So happy to visit her again, huh? Because I'm what? Chopped liver?"

The dog howled.

Laughing, Hunter led him across the yard. "Sorry, bud, but you have to wait the allotted thirty minutes, same as me." He should have offered to help her unload the tractor.

He should *not* imagine her all wet, lathering her petite, trim body in her very small shower.

Of course he did anyway.

And this time, he didn't even berate himself. Never in his

life had he met a more fascinating, enigmatic woman who kept so many secrets yet never seemed to hide her thoughts.

If you irritated her, she let you know.

Piss her off? You'd get the blast of that deadly stare.

Question her ability and she'd cut you down with her prickly ire.

She had a close relationship with powerful people, but she was as down-to-earth as a person could be.

After twenty minutes, he lost his patience and started a meandering stroll toward her place. If she spotted him, he'd claim Turbo wanted to roam. Given how the dog pulled at his leash, it wasn't a lie.

As they neared her property, Hunter glanced around, for once disliking how the surrounding trees insulated them from the rest of the town. If you cut through the woods, it wasn't quite a mile to the main road. But houses? People? Businesses?

Safety?

All too far away.

In a crisis, there was no guarantee anyone would be driving by to help, even if she made it that far. Through his binoculars, he'd watched her working in those woods and knew she'd set up little markers so she'd spot if anyone else trespassed. She'd even gone out after dark and attached a few hidden cameras in the trees.

What she'd do if she found anyone lurking around, he couldn't say.

Of course, he remembered that she was usually armed. Had she taken a weapon to town with her? On a hot Saturday afternoon?

Probably.

"Do you see something?"

Annoyed that she'd caught him unaware, Hunter turned

and found her on the front porch in an oversize T-shirt that she'd paired with pulled-on cotton shorts. Her smooth legs and bare feet kept him awestruck for a moment, before he caught himself. "I didn't hear you."

"I noticed."

Though she'd combed back her damp hair, the ends were already starting to dry. Her outdoor work left her with a light tan, and today her nose and the tops of her cheekbones were pink. She looked delicate, when he knew she wasn't.

Without any effort at all, definitely with no deliberate intention, she looked completely feminine. No makeup, no polished nails. No sexy clothes—though those shorts…

"What?"

He realized he'd been analyzing her, so he said, "You should wear sunscreen."

The corner of her mouth lifted. "Sure, Dad."

"Not how I'd have you see me."

As Turbo charged toward her, she grinned and sat on the bottom step, welcoming him with open arms and even a few kisses to the top of his head.

Squinting, she slanted her gaze up to see him. Here in the yard, beneath the setting sun, her eyes fascinated him. They were like a burst of shining amber rimmed with brown.

"Uh, Hunter?"

Fuck, he'd done it again. "Sorry. I'm distracted today."

While gently rubbing Turbo's ears, she nodded her understanding. "That business from yesterday, right? I figured you would be. I mean, in your shoes, I'd be going nuts wondering who knew what and how and all that."

Taking the initiative and hoping she didn't bolt, he sat on the step beside her. "I told you I wouldn't grill you, and I won't."

She'd stiffened at his nearness, but didn't move away.

He'd take that as a good sign. "So what's for dinner? And what can I do to help?"

Deliberately, she loosened her posture and continued rubbing Turbo. "You hadn't already planned anything?"

"I had hamburgers to grill, that's all, but they'll keep. We can have them tomorrow."

"So, um…" She watched the dog while petting him. "I'm eating with you tomorrow?"

"If you'd like." To give her a little space, he leaned back with his forearms on the porch and stretched out his legs so their knees didn't bump. "I enjoy our visits. Plus, my dog is mopey when he doesn't see you." Lower, in a teasing rumble, he complained, "Acts like I've been depriving him all this time with only my company."

As he'd intended, she grinned. "Yeah, I enjoy talking with you. So count me in for dinner tomorrow. Today, I figured on grilling pork chops. The grill is warming up now. I picked up potato salad to go with it."

"From the deli?"

She turned a little toward him. "Yeah, is it good?"

"Mustard or mayonnaise?"

Wincing, she confessed, "I got the mustard."

Damn, she was cute. Too fucking cute for a woman always armed—though he doubted she was packing right now. Assuming she'd slug him if she knew his thoughts, he smiled. "They're both terrific, but that's my favorite."

Suddenly, out of the blue, she blurted, "I met someone today."

Angry, anomalous emotion surged through his system. He held perfectly still and said, "Oh," in a way he hoped sounded unaffected.

"Yeah." She turned more, and now her knees were

against his thigh, but she didn't seem to notice. "You know anyone named Remmy Gardner?"

"Should I?"

"Eh, I figure if you'd met him, you'd remember. Big guy, good-looking, muscular, blond hair and brown eyes. Early thirties."

With every word out of her mouth, he clenched a little tighter. "Doesn't ring a bell."

"What about Russ King?"

That one he knew. "I've seen him with Worth a few times. An influential businessman." A prick. Birds of a feather and all that… "They've invited me to poker."

"Turned them down, didn't you? Like me, you'd recognize them as trouble."

Very slowly, Hunter sat forward again. "He gave you trouble?"

She eyed his new posture, not with alarm but curiosity. "I haven't met King, but Remmy works for him, and now that I've met him, I figure they're both up to something."

Hunter searched her face but didn't see any fear. They could have been talking about dinner still. "So this Remmy character did something?"

"It was just a feeling, you know?" Leaning a little closer, she confided, "I think maybe he was scoping me out."

A hundred different scenarios stampeded through his brain. It took a lot of concentration to stay nice and polite, and to ask with a civil tone, "Care to explain that?"

Licking her lips in thought—and tormenting him without realizing it—Jodi said, "He supposedly had a business proposition from this Russ King guy. I don't know, there were other vibes going on. Tension, I mean, between Remmy and Worth."

She ran down the exchange for Hunter, and he had to agree. Something wasn't adding up. "Worth rehired you?"

Waving that off, she went back to Remmy. "It was like he wanted me to take the job, but he was also worried about it." Visibly puzzling over that, she added, "And then he'd look at me in a certain way, like—"

Her long, confused pause had him prompting, "He found you attractive?"

She made a face. "I wouldn't say *that*." Showing her discomfort with the idea, she rolled a shoulder, flashed him a quick glance and said, "Like maybe he thought he could score."

"Because he found you attractive." When her mouth screwed to the side, he said, "Jodi, you do realize how pretty you are, right?"

"You think?"

The naked vulnerability he saw made him want to find this Remmy asshole and annihilate him. "Very pretty." Hunter got an awful suspicion. "You were flattered by his attention?"

Absently, she shook her head, not really in denial but more from confusion. "Sometimes *how* he'd say something was different, too. We were talking—mostly me insulting him, like I do—and he'd smile about it."

Yeah, Hunter assumed many men would be both amused by her biting manner, and equally challenged by it.

He certainly was. "How did he say it?"

Getting into her explanation, she scooted closer.

Was she even aware of doing it? He wasn't sure—but he didn't mind that she was drawn to him. He hoped it meant she felt safe with him…though he didn't yet know what she feared.

Only that she wouldn't run from it. Jodi was the type of person who'd prefer to face her demons head-on.

Like him.

With her so near, he picked up the light floral scent of her shampoo and lotion, and the earthier scent of her tanned skin, again being warmed by sunshine. He saw the striations in her fascinating eyes and he felt that ever-present vitality.

All of it, a turn-on.

"When I first pulled up and asked you if you were free for dinner? The way you said *I'm free.* It was different. It meant something, right?"

Good God. No way could she be that naive. Not at her age. Not with her bold attitude.

When he didn't reply, she surged on, her anxious gaze holding his captive. "It was lower and sort of darker and I think… That is, it meant you were thinking things besides dinner, right? Because that's exactly how Remmy would sound every so often."

"Low and dark?"

Exasperated, she straightened. "I'm not explaining this well, am I?"

"Actually, you are. Remmy was flirting with you, and why wouldn't he? You have mirrors. You know how you look."

Her brows shot up at that.

"Add your appearance to your balls-to-the-wall attitude, and I'm sure guys are hooked."

Her brows leveled out as her smile lifted. "Balls-to-the-wall?"

"Bold. Even pushy sometimes. A take-no-prisoners arrogance." He watched her fingers idly stroking the back of Turbo's neck. The dog was in heaven, his head on her leg, his body leaning into her. "So this Remmy person. Did you flirt back?"

The question earned a snort. "God, no. I don't flirt with anyone. If he *was* flirting, I didn't much like it. I hate to admit this, but it made me jumpy." Again, she rushed on. "Normally I wouldn't be. I can handle myself. But we were behind Worth's showroom and there wasn't anyone else around."

Disliking that image, Hunter raised a hand to stall her long enough for him to ask an important question. "Why the hell were you behind the showroom with him?"

"I was doing my job but he followed me! That was reason enough for me to put up my guard, right? But then he was all over the place, trying to schmooze me one minute, sort of warning me the next and trying to coerce me—"

What? Hunter fought back another surge of anger, this one more warranted. "Back up to the part where he warned you. You mean like a threat? And how did he coerce you?"

"*Tried* to coerce me," she stressed. "It was so weird, Hunter. I think he had an assignment or something, one that involved me, but he didn't much like doing it. He wanted me to agree to landscape for Russ King but didn't want me to check out the dude's house without him. When I insisted, he told me to just look at it from my truck, and not to linger. Isn't that strange? Why try to get me to take a job only to act like he was afraid of me doing it? And then the way he'd suddenly look at me, smile or lower his voice."

Fuck.

Fuck, fuck, fuck.

Hadn't he known she'd be trouble the second he met her? "Did it occur to you that these people might be the same who were snooping around here?"

"Of course it did. That's the thing, though, I need to know. Unlike *some people*, my curiosity gets to me."

Her look and tone made it clear that *he* was the *some people* she referenced.

"The only way I'll be able to sort it out is to go along."

"No." Hunter's flat denial had zero effect on her, not that he'd expected anything else.

"I'll be careful, though, maybe play off Remmy's confused feelings—if they're confused. If I actually read that right." She wrinkled her nose. "You may not have noticed, but I'm not much of a people person. I can judge ill intent, and he had plenty of that going on, but other stuff? It confuses me." Again she shook her head. "I don't think he was flirting or that he thought I was pretty or anything like that."

Exasperated, Hunter said, "That's exactly what he—"

"I think he wants to fuck me, though."

Blindsided by her language, it took Hunter a second, with her waiting for his reaction, to finally say, "I thought you wouldn't curse."

"That's what it is. No other word for it."

Of all the... "Sex?" he offered as an alternative. "Making love?"

She snorted. "I mean, I guess you could call it sex. Some would." Her mouth tightened and she stressed, "I would *not*. But the other? No, not with me. Ever."

There were so many things to dissect in what she said, but Hunter found himself focusing on one. "Why the hell *not* with you?"

Her mouth pinched and she looked away without further explanation.

He had a very bad feeling about all this. "Fine, forget

what you call it." For now, at least. "Are you attracted to Remmy?"

That brought her comical gaze zipping back to his. "*Attracted* to him? Ha! Get real." She shoved his shoulder. "Why in the world would you think that?"

Yeah, why exactly? "You described him favorably."

"Accurately, not favorably. So? He's a big, good-looking guy. Doesn't mean I want a piece of him, not the way you meant it."

"What other way is there?" Once the words left his mouth, he knew he shouldn't have asked.

Her expression darkened. "It's why I stay armed, right? If he causes me any serious trouble, if he means me any bodily harm, I'd—"

"Don't say it." Unwilling to hear her detail whatever brutality she envisioned, Hunter stood. Many things had changed in eighteen months, but he was still an honorable man and he'd never sanction an innocent facing threats on her own. Since he didn't know precisely how innocent Jodi might be, he figured a change in topic was warranted. "You mentioned food, and I'm getting hungry."

Groaning, she stood, also. "Keep your pants on. It won't take long to cook." Sashaying past him, she headed in but left the door open for him.

Turbo stared at him in accusation.

"Sorry, bud. I needed time to regroup. Let's go." He allowed the dog to enter first, removed his leash and hung it over the doorknob.

As if she'd done this many times—which he knew in his bones she hadn't—Jodi took the chops from the fridge, put them on a tray with salt, pepper and a fork, and started out back. With a wave of her hand, she said, "We'll have to eat at the little table in here. I don't have outdoor furniture yet." The screen door dropped shut behind her.

Left alone in her house? Wow, that was a shift. Unless… He glanced around to see if she had cameras anywhere, and sure enough, one was mounted near the ceiling. Interesting. If it recorded activity, later she'd be able to see everything he did. He stepped back in the main area and found another camera mounted by the front door that would encompass the entire small room.

The short hall was right there, leading to her bedroom, but no, better not do that much snooping.

Turbo, however, didn't hesitate. He disappeared into the room and no doubt planned to sleep on her bed. Back in the kitchen, Hunter saw the box in the corner filled with more tech equipment in it.

On top of the box was a framed photo that snagged his gaze. It showed a group of people, some of them really huge men—tall, broad shouldered, imposing even though they smiled—along with two stunning women nearly as tall as the men, and a smaller, grinning woman with honey-blond hair who was squeezing close to a painfully thin, stoop-shouldered and disgruntled girl at the center of the picture.

His heart didn't want to believe it, but he'd recognize that deadly stare anywhere.

"If you're staying in there," Jodi called, "go ahead and set the table."

Hunter rubbed the bridge of his nose. She'd come a long way from that sad scrap of humanity who'd so obviously been forced into a photo.

He'd like to ask her about it, but didn't dare. And yet… had she left it visible on purpose so that he would?

To give himself a moment, he said, "Turbo is napping in your room."

"No problem."

He had a feeling his dog got more use out of that bed than she did. "Should I pour drinks, too?"

"Sure. Chops will be done in ten minutes."

She sounded like a confident grill master. Trying to put things in perspective, Hunter opened a cabinet and got out plates. It was kind of nice that her home was small enough they could speak back and forth and be heard. That was probably true for any room in the house. She could be in the bedroom, him in the kitchen, and he'd hear her.

In his house, from one room to the next, Turbo could get into things and he wouldn't know until he walked in on it—like a pair of work boots missing leather laces, or the time the dog had gnawed on the leg of a table.

Luckily, those days were mostly in the past now.

Jodi ducked into the kitchen, pulled the potato salad from the fridge, found a serving spoon in the drawer and set both on the table. She got down a clean plate and started out again.

That's when she noticed the photo. In a nanosecond, she'd turned it over and shoved it deeper into the box, then shot him a killing glare.

Wearing his best impersonation of surprised innocence, Hunter asked, "What?"

She straightened in a snap. "You going to set the table or not?"

So bossy. *And so defensive.* "Working on it." He opened a drawer and found silverware.

She chewed her lower lip a moment, trying to see guilt that he struggled to keep hidden. Then she stormed away.

The woman rarely moved at a leisurely pace.

After arranging two place settings, Hunter leaned in the

doorway and watched her through the open screen. "That's a nice box of goodies you have here."

Another glare from her. Another show of innocence from him. Finally, she said, "Yeah, Reyes sent it and two other boxes. He's probably peeved that I haven't installed everything yet. I plan to get to the rest next week." She turned the chops. Casual as you please, she said, "You saw the cameras?"

"Yes. They're in every room?"

"Pretty much. Not the utility room or bathroom."

"Where's the monitor?"

"It just feeds to my phone or PC."

That wouldn't do her much good at night if someone came around again.

Knowing his thoughts, Jodi leveled a droll look over her shoulder. "I leave my PC on beside the bed. I see everything."

Not when she was sleeping, she didn't. Unless…she didn't sleep? That wouldn't surprise him. To test that theory, he pointed out, "Blue light is disruptive to a good night's rest."

Snorting, she turned back to the grill and lifted the chops to the plate.

So much of what she said and did hit his heart like a dart. "What does that mean, Jodi?"

"Nothing."

Her reply bothered him even more. Stepping out, he picked up the empty platter and held the door open for her.

"Such a gentleman." Being silly, she curtsied before going in with the plate of food.

He wanted to smile, but he had that image of her from the photo stuck in his head, and now his thoughts lingered on her not sleeping. "So, I take it you're not a fan of conking out for a solid eight hours?"

While putting the food on the table, she avoided his gaze. "Look, I get enough sleep, right? I mean, I'm not a zombie or anything." She took the platter from him, quickly washed it and the serving fork, and put them in the drainer. "Let's eat. I'm starving now, too."

He wished he'd brought some green beans or something, but he'd make do with what she had.

For a while, they ate in relative silence, finishing the food with nothing more than a hearty appetite from her and a few compliments from him.

She drained the last of her tea. Then, out of the blue, she asked, "What about you?"

"What?" He'd been so busy watching her throat move as she swallowed, how her slender fingers held the icy glass, that he had no idea what she meant.

"Do you sleep well?"

Usually, Hunter would have evaded a question like that. The instinct was there to cut and run. Politely if necessary.

Not this time.

Not after seeing that photo and knowing how much she'd changed, understanding how far she'd come. She was still thin, but she didn't look emaciated now. Instead, she glowed with health. She was still antagonistic, too, but rarely with him anymore. Overall, she was a beautiful, delicate woman with God-knew-what in her background and enough backbone and determination to change her circumstances by her own design, in her own way, on her own schedule.

Empty house to live in? No problem for Jodi. Isolated from help of any kind? She'd manage on her own. Wealthy and influential family to love and help her? She respected and cared for them, but resented their interference in her efforts.

She was an enigma. Contrary and foolishly brave.

But she was so much more than that—and he truly liked every facet she revealed.

Liked, respected…and damn it, desired.

With his lengthy silence, her smile went crooked. "Forget I asked."

Hoping she'd indulge a little give-and-take, Hunter shrugged and went for total honesty. "I'm a restless sleeper. I hear things I wouldn't have a few years ago." Noises in the night that now seemed ominous. A heaviness in the air that felt too much like danger. He awoke in battle mode, breathing hard and slow, his muscles tensed, his mindset deadly.

Jodi nodded, encouraging him.

More quietly, hating to talk about it but also wanting to reach her, he confessed, "When I do sleep, I sometimes have shitty dreams that make me wish I'd tossed and turned instead." Remembering things he'd rather forget, he set his fork on his empty plate, drank some tea, and concentrated on the here and now. The peacefulness of the mountains. His simple lifestyle. Turbo.

Jodi.

His gaze moved over her face, seeing all the complications, and all the beauty—inside and out.

She watched him with empathy and deep perception. Her golden eyes were intent on his, understanding what he said—and what he didn't.

Suddenly, she launched into motion, taking her empty plate to the sink, tossing the scraps in the garbage and washing with far too much energy.

More slowly, Hunter left his seat and carried his plate to her. She didn't acknowledge him, but that was okay.

Carefully, seeing she was on the ragged edge, he nosed in next to her, put his plate in the sink and took the clean one from her hands so he could dry it and put it in the drainer.

She breathed harder, scrubbing that plate as if she'd destroy it, right up until her hands stilled. Head down, she handed him the second plate and braced her hands on the counter. "I can't sleep at all."

His pulse thrummed. He held very still, unwilling to interrupt the moment.

"I mean, here and there for an hour or two," she explained, "but usually less. I wake up and can't help but listen, wondering what I heard, you know?"

"Yes. I know."

She shifted, leaning one hip on the counter, her face turned up to his. "I *have* to get up and check things, prowl around...*make sure*."

Make sure that she was safe. Make sure that no one had intruded. Damn, his heart hurt for her.

"I *am* tired," she admitted. "All the freaking time." As if accepting what couldn't be changed, she let out a big breath. "I don't know any other way to be, though. Sleeping pills are out. When I even sleep a few hours, I wake up and imagine everything that...could have happened."

To her, she meant. Things that could have happened *to her*.

The urge to tug her close, to surround her with his strength so she could finally let down her guard, crashed inside Hunter, but he tamped down those urges. Jodi would not want that, and more than anything, he needed her to know that he respected her reactions, and he understood them. Through pain and suffering, she'd earned her responses to life, and by God, he would never trample them.

Moving slowly in case she spooked, Hunter tucked a

long lock of tangled hair behind her ear. Her eyes widened, grew brighter, but not with fear, thank God. Taking a chance, he opened his palm against her warm, silky cheek and did more sharing. "I'm the same. You were right about that."

Smug, she gave a small smile. "Knew it."

"I was told many times by well-meaning people that talking about it would help."

"Don't believe it," she said. "Anytime I tried talking about it, it was awful."

He nodded. "I know." Her skin was so soft, he wanted to touch her in other ways, in other places—but this was definitely not the time to indulge his basic instincts, so he ignored them in favor of something even more intimate, something that filled him with dread, yet also teased his senses: *sharing with Jodi.* "I think talking things through might be different with a person who really gets it. Don't you?"

She surprised him by shaking her head and moving away. "No." Harsher, with sharp emotion, she snapped, "No one gets it." Her gaze clashed with his. "Not even you, Hunter. Whatever you did, or whatever you went through or saw, trust me—*not* the same."

Curling his fingers, he tried to retain the feel of her, her warmth and vitality on his palm, yet it had already faded. Her rejection hurt him on many levels, and made him feel like a fool for trying.

"I'm sorry to hear that, Jodi." Christ, he needed to leave. He needed that damned solitude now more than ever. "Thank you for dinner. It was great." He saw the table still cluttered even though the dishes were washed. Hell, his dog was asleep in her bed. Under other circumstances, it might have been funny. Here, with Jodi and the topic they'd just shared, he couldn't muster even a fake smile.

Jodi watched him warily, and with a tinge of regret.

Striding to her back door, he secured it, then gave a loud whistle for Turbo. "It's time for me to go."

"I didn't mean to run you off."

That small voice cut into him, but he couldn't deal with it now. She'd given enough, he'd taken enough, and staying would only cause him to make another misstep. Neither one of them wanted that. "It's dark and the air smells like rain. Lock the front door behind me." The second Turbo showed up, Hunter made his getaway.

That's what it was.

An escape from all the things Jodi Bentley made him feel.

Shit he didn't want to feel.

Shit she didn't want to share.

Not looking at her, he said, "See ya tomorrow," and with Turbo's leash held tight in his hand, he went out the front door, pulling it shut behind him.

Jodi hadn't said a word. She didn't have to.

Whatever she'd gone through was so bad it had no comparison? That was the worst of all…because he could imagine a lot. And all of it was pure hell.

CHAPTER FIVE

GRAY DAWN BARELY penetrated the still-stormy skies as Jodi repeatedly knocked. When he jerked open the front door looking a little wild with unkempt hair, dark eyes, whiskers on his face and no shirt, she knew she'd woken him.

Hello.

Since when did she notice male bodies with that kind of interest? Apparently, since Hunter Osborn. If she were honest with herself, and she tried to always be, she'd noticed more about him from the get-go.

With her cockiest attitude in place, Jodi lifted her chin and met his disbelieving gaze. "For a man who doesn't sleep, you sure look like you were out."

Howling and spinning, Turbo went nuts with glee. *At least the dog doesn't mind my idiotic crack-of-dawn visit.*

After the heavy rains last night, everything dripped—the trees, the grass, even the scattered boulders. Didn't matter. Like a woman on a mission, she had things to accomplish today, and the weather wouldn't change that.

Hunter just stood there, six feet plus of loaded confusion, staring at her with blurry eyes, so she pulled the door open wider and stepped in. "I'll make coffee, okay?"

He didn't move out of her way. "What the fuck, Jodi?" He said it without anger but with a lot of incredulity. "You realize it's not quite six?"

"Yeah, I know. I felt terrible after my stupid freak-out

last night." Still he didn't move. Damn. He wouldn't make this easy. "I want to apologize but I'm not good at it so I'm probably talking too fast and I figured coffee would give me something to do while you get it together."

Scowling, he stood his ground. "Maybe I don't want to get it together."

"Great. We can have grumpy coffee together." She smiled, hoping that would soften him. It didn't quite work, but he did sigh and close his eyes, so she sidled around him, Turbo hot on her heels as she headed for his kitchen. "I thought of something else with Remmy and King, too. Since you're the one who pushed all the let's-be-friendly-neighbors stuff, I figured you'd hear me out." Now that she was a safe distance away, she turned—and bumped into his naked chest. "Wow, way to sneak up on a person." He was like a big, warm wall, and for the first time in her life, she wondered what a man would feel like. She eyed his taut flesh, that light furring of chest hair, and considered touching him, but shook her head.

"I didn't sneak," he said, still sounding reasonable. "You're in my house. In my kitchen."

"Yeah, okay. Don't get territorial. Should I make the coffee or not?"

His nostrils flared. "Not."

Did that mean he'd throw her right back out? "Hunter—"

"I'm running to the john. Don't let Turbo out, but watch him so he doesn't take a leak in the corner. I'll be right back." He took two steps, paused and pointed at her. "Stay right there, Jodi. I mean it."

She lifted her hands. "I'll stand rooted to the spot."

"Good. Do that." He disappeared down the hall.

When Turbo bumped into her, she realized she'd been soaking in the visual of Hunter's wide shoulders, strong back and lean hips. His unfastened jeans had hung low and she'd seen a strip of black cotton boxers. "Sorry," she said to the dog, kneeling down to give him affection. "I'm not myself this morning."

Turbo tried to lead her to the back door. Despite her promise to Hunter, she looked around but didn't see the dog's leash. With the yard still dark, she didn't dare let him out without it. "Just hold on," she begged. "Hunter will be back soon."

At that precise moment, he emerged, still looking the same, hair untouched, jeans zipped but not snapped, no shirt, feet bare, but with a leash in his hands. "Now you may make coffee." He hooked the leash to Turbo's collar, saying, "Good boy," and making haste, man and dog went out the back door.

Jodi blinked several times. Okay, sure, she'd deliberately taken him by surprise. Her harebrained plan had been to brazen her way in, plow through her apology, then try to get things back on an even keel.

She *liked* having Hunter as a friendly neighbor. Dumb as she knew it to be, she'd gotten used to her relaxed meals with him.

A few times there, she'd even been so comfortable that touching him hadn't bothered her. In fact, it had been agreeable. Like when he'd stroked her face...

Remembering sent a warm curl of sensation through her stomach.

Coffee. If she didn't hustle, he'd return and she'd still be standing there like a dope.

In less than two minutes she'd located the coffee can and a filter, measured everything, and the scent of brewing coffee filled the air. Unable to wait, she headed out back and spotted Hunter standing near a line of trees, his back to her, while Turbo sniffed around. Drawn to him, she found herself quickly crossing the yard.

Hunter said nothing when she stepped up beside him, but she knew he was aware of her. He was aware of everything. All the time.

They had that in common.

She got the feeling he was especially aware of her, because Hunter was also intuitive. Whether she detailed things to him or not, he knew. From their first meeting a connection had sparked. An understanding gleaned from shared experience. A rapport that few could ever claim.

Maybe that was why, despite his desire to be left alone, he'd insisted on edging his way into her life.

Well, she'd opened the emotional door to him, damn it, and now she found she couldn't close it. Didn't matter if he wanted to slam it on his way out, far as she was concerned, they were stuck with each other and all their tormented idiosyncrasies.

Off in the distance, birds sang as they rejoiced in the rain. Somewhere in the woods, branches rustled. Heavy, dark clouds tumbled over each other with the promise of more rain to come.

Jodi stared at his strong profile. "I can hear your chickens." They softly clucked while wandering around their enclosure.

On a slow, deep breath, Hunter's shoulders expanded, then relaxed. "They can hear you, too. Wait—know what they're saying?"

Recognizing this particular tone of his, her lips twitched—with relief. "No."

"They're saying 'what the fuck, Jodi.' I hear it plain as day."

Her grin broke free. "I think they're asking about their food."

"No, they're definitely confused." His blue eyes looked darker in the gray dawn. "Usually when I come out here, it's closer to seven and I feed them right away."

Everything about Hunter fascinated her, from his fresh-out-of-bed, rumpled appearance, to how easily he let her off the hook, to his daily routine. "Before or after this ritual with Turbo?"

He rubbed his free hand over his face. "It doesn't usually take him this long, so the chickens get fed shortly after."

Turbo sprinkled again, chose yet another spot and locked eyes with her while doing his business.

"Clearly," Hunter stated, "you've thrown him off his game."

"Yeah, well." She nudged Hunter with her shoulder. "I'm a little off my game, too, so we're even."

"Have a need to use the yard, do you?"

This time she shoved him harder and got a snicker in return.

See, *this*. This was so nice. Joking around after a horrible evening where she'd mentally kicked herself multiple times. Being with someone who didn't have the deets to her entire, nasty, wretched past—so she knew it wasn't just pity he felt. With Hunter, she sensed that he liked her. He liked that they shared common ground, murky as the ground might be since neither of them had shared much. Well, he hadn't shared anything other than how he'd found Turbo. Oh, wait, and he'd told her about his family. And how he'd fixed up the house…

Well, hell.

He'd been opening up all along, and she'd stuck with being a snide, closed-off, unappreciative…bitch.

This time he nudged her, probably because he sensed her self-recriminations. "Listen to the creek."

"Yeah." Turning her face up to the turbulent sky, Jodi closed her eyes and let all the sounds of nature lull away her guilt. "The water is really rushing."

"Always after a storm," he said quietly. "The rain rolls off the mountains and into the creeks. It's probably over the banks today."

Such inane chatter, but she relished it because it meant Hunter wasn't holding a grudge. "So, last night—"

"Here." He handed her the leash, pulled a plastic bag from his pocket and went to clean up from the dog.

Eww. Letting Turbo lead her, she strolled nearer to the chicken coop and watched the fowl dig around in the wet grass and dirt.

Hunter went past her and into the house, but returned shortly wearing black rubber boots and carrying chicken feed and a bucket of fresh water. The second he unlocked the gate to the run, the chickens swarmed him. It was pretty hilarious to see him bending to pet a chicken, murmuring to another, then heading to food containers in an area kept dry from the storm.

Jodi decided it was a nice routine, communing with nature, enjoying the dog and the chickens, experiencing the fresh outdoors. "They like you."

"They know I have the food, but yes, chickens are more affectionate than most people realize."

And that's why he spent time with them. Probably the same reason he spent time with her.

Because he was a good guy who cared…and she, being a broken mess, had run him off last night. Trying to be fair, she warned, "If you cut me off again, I'm leaving."

He said nothing as he exited the coop and relocked the gate. Shifting both empty bucket handles into one hand, he took the leash from her. "Come on. We can talk in the kitchen."

"I have things to say, Hunter."

"I know." He walked off, but said, "So do I."

At the kitchen door, he and Turbo waited for her to enter before stepping in. Turbo tried to charge off, but Hunter said, "No, you don't," and, after removing his boots, he spent a few minutes cleaning the dog's wet paws and even drying his belly.

Realizing what was expected, Jodi pulled off her running shoes to place next to his boots, and then, barefoot, she went to the counter, washed her hands and poured two cups of coffee.

Hunter hung the leash over the knob, refilled Turbo's food and water dishes, then washed his hands, too, before dropping into a chair. "Thanks. This smells good."

"I feel like a slug now. You do so much first thing, and all I do is dress and feed my face."

"No coffee at home?"

"I grabbed juice and cereal. But this is good." She took another sip, and tried a heavy hint. "I think coffee with someone is way better than coffee alone."

"Agreed."

So far, so good. "So…last night."

This time he just waited, and damn it, now she wasn't sure what to say.

It wasn't like her to keep hedging, though—how was it he'd described her? Balls to wall? Well, it was time for her to find her balls. "First, I'm sorry." He looked receptive, so she continued. "I was really enjoying things last night—"

"Things?"

"Us talking. Dinner together. Just chilling."

He nodded.

"Then it all went wrong and that's on me. I know it." All she got was more patient listening from him. She cleared her throat, hated that she'd done something so clichéd, and forged on. "This is all new for me. Visiting and being friendly and everything."

"I heard you on the phone with friends-who-are-like-family, remember?"

"Yeah, but that's just it. For the longest time, it was just me. Then it was me and Kennedy, even though Kennedy wasn't always on board. Then she got hooked up with a stud and he sort of became a package deal. With his brother and sister, too, and their dad, and then their others..."

"Others?"

"The special people they hooked up with. You know, wives and husband and all that." Knowing it sounded like she was complaining, Jodi regrouped. Fingers tightening around the coffee cup, she carefully formulated her words. "That was a huge adjustment, getting used to them. But like I told you, they helped me get a job and find a purpose and all that. They're really good people, and I... I wasn't used to good people. Especially people who knew about my..." Words were so damn hard. She settled on, "Background."

Seconds ticked by. Though Hunter didn't change his deceptively relaxed posture in the chair, she felt his alertness ratcheting up, sensed the probing way he watched her.

It was so quiet, she could hear Turbo's breathing deepen into sleep.

Jodi drew an uneven breath that didn't really help. "I told you that I had a job helping women. That I'd been a victim. Well, like you said last night, it's easier to understand when it's something you've gone through."

"You and these women had gone through the same thing?"

The softly spoken, no-nonsense way he asked that helped her to spit it out. "No. They were trafficked."

Slowly sitting forward, Hunter put his coffee cup on the table. His gaze held hers, searching, wanting something she couldn't decipher. He seemed to be waiting, taut with suspicion.

"I wasn't."

His breath released with relief and he gave a careful nod. "I'm glad."

That made her laugh. "Don't start celebrating, okay?"

Without a word, he laid his hand, palm up, on the table before her—a silent invitation to share his strength.

God, she wanted to. Her palm tingled with the idea. "I've never held hands with anyone."

"Try it. You might like it—and if you don't, you're free to let go anytime."

His hand looked so large, easily twice the size of hers, with rough-tipped fingers, calluses and so much strength. With a feeling of inching toward the edge of a cliff, she loosened her hold on the mug and awkwardly placed her hand in his.

Hunter smiled, a beautiful smile that made her heart slam into her ribs as his fingers curled loosely around hers.

His thumb moved over her knuckles. "If you don't want to tell me, I understand and I won't pressure you. We're here, though, and there's no judgment."

If he knew the things she'd done, he would definitely judge.

Would he deem her a hero or a monster? She wasn't sure.

Oddly, holding on to him did help. She stared at their hands, instead of his too-perceptive eyes, when she said, "So, I was held prisoner for a while by this sick, twisted dick who liked to…" A vise seemed to clench around her throat, strangling off the confession.

Though he tensed all over, Hunter's thumb continued to stroke, gently, with encouragement.

She tried to meter her breathing but couldn't.

She tried to keep her eyes from getting glassy but already her vision blurred.

Her teeth clenched. Her heart thundered. Without realizing it, she ground out, "He liked hurting me, locking me in the basement without food, and I…" She gasped, unable to get air into her burning lungs. Oh, God, it was all closing in on her, memories slamming her, stomping her down.

She wasn't aware of what was happening, but suddenly, Hunter was standing and she was held carefully against him, and he was whispering, over and over again, "Jesus, Jodi, I'm so sorry. So fucking sorry. You're safe now. You're with me. You're safe."

Safe now.

With him.

Yes, yes she was.

It dawned on her that her hands were on his shoulders, her fingers digging into his muscles, though he didn't complain. Her cheek rested against his warm chest, and that light covering of chest hair felt really nice.

The scent of him… She'd never smelled anything like it, but it encouraged her to draw a slow, deep breath.

Darkness receded. Her calm gradually returned. Outside, a streak of lightning cut through the gray morning sky, followed by the low rumble of thunder. "I should go before it starts pouring again."

The comforting stroke of Hunter's hands paused on her back, then continued after a brief hug. "I have a better idea."

"If it has anything to do with me being plastered against

you, acting all wimpy, forget it. This is an oddity not likely to happen again." She wasn't sure how it had happened this time. She hated it, hated her own weakness…

Yet she didn't step away. Since she was already there, she didn't want to. Not now. Not anytime soon.

"I was going to suggest we spend the day together. Have breakfast. Shop for groceries and whatever you need for your house, or more security if you want. You mentioned Russ King and this Remmy prick. We could check out his property together."

Laughing just a little with a residue of nervousness from opening up, losing her shit, and being in a new and unusual, but comforting, position with a guy, she said, "Every time you mention Remmy, you call him a name."

"Accurate names. He bothered you." Hunter briefly tightened his hold in a careful embrace. "So I don't like him."

"And you'd prefer to be with me when I check out King's property—not because you pity me or think I can't handle it, but because you like my company?"

He pressed her back, stared down at her for one heartbeat, two, three, and then nodded. "All that, yes. And also because no one should venture into trouble alone."

Oh, how she loved that idea. It was what she'd wanted anyway, the reason she'd told Hunter about King and Remmy. "Safety in numbers?"

He shrugged his agreement to that. "Later we could watch a movie on demand."

Wow, he had the whole day planned out—with her. No one had ever done that before. "I have a few things I have to do to my house today." If she slacked off on it now, she'd get behind schedule and then her sort-of-family would try to take over.

"I could help with that."

Knowing she couldn't continue clinging to him, Jodi forced herself to step away. Odd, but she felt different now. Like she'd just experienced something new and exciting yet equally dangerous, and there was a little thrill of the unknown racing through her bloodstream.

Dare she spend more time with him when she was all twitchy like this? Looking up at him, she wondered how she could possibly convince herself to refuse. In recent years, she hadn't wanted much from life. Safety. Independence. The death of a few monsters…and the resources and ability to avenge a few innocents.

Now she wanted this, a day with Hunter, a simple thing that felt extravagant. A little foolish. Like disappointment waiting to happen.

"It'll be fun," he promised. "Try it and see."

Jeez, her whole world was changing. She wasn't sure how she felt about it. "You really wouldn't mind doing all that?"

"You should know by now that I wouldn't offer if I did." Again, he put a hand to her cheek. Using his thumb, he brushed away a stupid, infuriating tear, without saying anything about it or making it a big deal. "I get it, you know. I moved out here because I wanted to be left alone. I only wanted to see people on my own terms, when I damn well felt like it."

"Gee, thanks." Odd that after a panic attack, she could find a little humor. With Hunter. *How did he do that?*

"I'd still feel that way if you hadn't shown up."

Overcome with curiosity, she asked, "Now you feel different?"

Grinning at her, he lightly knuckled her chin and then dropped his hand. "You've changed things and I'm realizing I don't mind a little company. I won't invite Worth to have his poker night here or anything. I'd still rather keep the rest of the people in town off my property. You, though?"

"Do I even want to hear this?"

"You're good company."

Wow. Jodi had never received a compliment like that. Her, good company. It should have been laughable, and instead, it just made her smile. "You mean it?"

He did a rewind with his finger. "Have you been paying attention at all?"

Er...mostly she'd been staring at him, feeling vague, soft sensations, and trying to sort out her confusion. "Yes?"

Hunter shook his head. "I don't say things I don't mean."

"Oh, that part." Yeah, he had said that. And true, so far he'd been pretty up-front with her.

"If we shop, what will you do with Turbo?"

"He goes along. The places I visit don't mind."

"I assume you'll put on a shirt first?"

His slow grin caused a dipping sensation in her stomach, like she'd just driven too fast over a hill. So many new things she was feeling with Hunter, and maybe because it was with him, they didn't scare her quite as much as they should.

THEY HAD A big breakfast while the storm raged outside. It was nice, Hunter thought, being sealed inside with Jodi and Turbo. Intimate. Cozy.

For once, he felt more like himself—the person he'd lost. The person he'd deliberately buried while he dealt with his demons. The person his family loved, and the person appalled by the unspeakable things he'd done.

It was like they'd crossed some invisible bridge, each allowing the other in.

He had no illusions that Jodi still hid a lot. He certainly

did. But the walls were no longer so high, or quite so impenetrable.

With care, they could be surmounted. Not just yet, but maybe soon.

They'd just finished cleaning up when the power went out.

Hunter left her in his kitchen, with a lantern to brighten the stormy gloom, and took a speed shower, but skipped shaving. Feeling scruffy, dressed in his most comfortably worn jeans and a pullover navy blue shirt with his weatherproof boots, he drove them the short distance to her house.

Only because he'd insisted, Jodi wore his rain slicker as she raced to the front porch and unlocked her door. She held it open as he and Turbo barreled through the downpour. Once inside, he was careful to catch the dog at the entrance while Jodi got a towel to dry his paws.

Giving him a grin, she also closed her bedroom door. "I don't mind sharing my bed with a dry dog, but a wet dog is a whole different story."

"Very true. The smell of wet dog can be pretty nasty."

"Hush. You'll hurt Turbo's feelings." To make up for the perceived insult, she put a few more towels on the floor in a pile so Turbo could "nest." As he watched his dog kick them around, circle, then sprawl with a huff, it made Hunter think about things. Using Jodi's method of a mental list, he tacked on *dog bed for Jodi's house.*

They visited often enough now that it made sense.

Hands on her slim hips, she peered out the window at the slashing rain. "I vote we see if this lets up a little before we head back out." Over her shoulder, she glanced at Turbo. "No reason to get him soaked again, right?"

"I agree we don't need to be out in a downpour, but I think we should scope out that address for King while it's still raining a little, to lessen the chances of anyone hanging around outside."

"You think he'd bring in his guards just from the weather?"

"No, but there's less visibility in rain, right? Makes more sense than showing up there when it's bright and sunny."

Jodi chewed that over, then nodded. "Agree." She looked around. "So what do we do in the meantime?"

Such a loaded question. He could make plenty of suggestions. He wouldn't mind holding her again, feeling the slight curves of her body, the softness she'd likely deny. Tasting that mulish mouth of hers would be nice, too.

If she didn't bite.

With Jodi, he never knew quite what to expect.

He'd also enjoy talking with her more, learning details to go with the startlingly tragic background, but he understood the need to ease into things. She'd shared a lot, far more than he'd expected, and he wouldn't push for more.

Trust, he reminded himself. Mostly what he wanted with her was trust.

While they stood there staring at each other, likely sharing very disparate thoughts, the house suddenly hummed to life. Turbo raised his head, listened, decided it was okay and flopped back down to sleep.

"Wow. Power came back quicker than I expected."

"Don't count on it staying on—at least, not until the storm blows over." Going to the wall by the door, he flipped a switch and a dim overhead light came on. He eyed it. "You bought some indoor fixtures, too, right?"

"Yeah, but I've still been researching how to replace them."

"I can take care of that."

She gave him a long, assessing frown before relenting with a slight grin. "You're a handy guy to have around, Hunter."

"That's what I keep telling you."

An hour later, Hunter was up on a stepladder in her bedroom, replacing that light also, when his cell phone buzzed. It rang five times before he finished his task and could answer it.

Memphis greeted him with, "Dare I hope I interrupted something?"

"Installing a light."

"Damn, that's not nearly as hot as I hoped."

Instead of being annoyed by the comment, as he'd have been in the recent past, Hunter replied, "With the way your mind works, nothing ever is."

Silence, and then, "By God, brother, was that a joke? It was, wasn't it?" More solemn, Memphis said, "Welcome back."

Damn, had he really been such an ogre? Most likely. "Memphis, listen…"

"No apologies necessary. Just tell me if it's the mysterious Jodi Bentley who caused the change."

Hedging, because he couldn't talk freely here, Hunter said, "I'm at my neighbor's house right now, helping her with a few things. We're stuck inside—"

"Together?"

"—because it's been storming like crazy. We'll be heading out soon, though. Have a few errands to run."

Again, with a little more incredulity, Memphis asked, *"Together?"*

Making his annoyance plain, Hunter blew out a long breath. "Did you have something to share besides astonishment?"

"Yeah, I mean… Way to go, bro. That's all." More earnest now, Memphis said, "There are probably a few things you should know about this girl."

"Woman," he corrected. *Why the hell does everyone*

refer to her as a girl? Probably had something to do with her size, but the distinction was important to him. Lowering his voice in the hopes Jodi wouldn't hear, he explained, "She's midtwenties."

"Okay, yeah, whatever. She has deep connections."

"I figured that out on my own." Hunter stared at her locked closet as he came down off the ladder. *Where does she keep the key?*

"Whoever it is, he's been hacking into your security cameras."

"She, not he, and I knew about that, too."

Another long silence before Memphis remarked, "You're taking it awfully well."

"I changed my passwords, but I doubt that accomplished much."

"It didn't."

Hunter didn't question Memphis. Whatever tech skills Jodi's friends had, Memphis could likely counter. He was something of a phenom with his ability.

How to explain to his brother. Walking closer to the closet, Hunter lifted the heavy lock and realized it was as complicated as Jodi. Both biometric and keyed, meaning it would take her longer to open it, but also make it harder to hack. "Jodi has very few people in her life, but the ones who know her want to look out for her."

"You included?"

"Yes."

"Then I should probably tell you, she doesn't need much help. In fact, she's a dangerous woman to be around."

Yeah, Hunter had figured that as well. "Examples?"

"Shit was buried, so it took me longer than usual to find it, and now it sounds like my warnings might come too late. Not that I'm ungrateful to her for bringing you back around—"

"Memphis."

With a grin in his tone, his brother said, "I think our gal has used herself as bait to lure a few men into her trap. She's a vigilante—or at least she used to be a few years ago. And from what I could uncover, the men she targeted were due some tough justice. The thing is, you're not."

Knowing where this would go, Hunter said, "Don't—" but got no further before Memphis spoke over him.

"So help me, Hunter, I will show up there tomorrow and whoop your ass if you don't listen to me."

His brows lifted. So did the corners of his mouth. "Threatening me, Memphis?"

"Damn straight." With more urgency, Memphis said, "You're back, Hunter. I can feel it. Okay, maybe not all the way back, but it's happening, and you should know, when I meet this girl—woman, whatever—I'm going to kiss her."

Too much time had passed since he'd last tussled with his brother. He missed it.

He missed Memphis, too. And his parents. Hell, he was starting to miss a lot, so yeah, maybe he was coming back. "She'd probably kick your ass if you tried, and so we're clear, she won't go easy on you like I always have."

"Ha! I like her more and more. But that doesn't change the facts. She has a history of luring in guys and delivering her own brand of justice. If she doesn't know the whole story with you, she might think you're in their league. You know how shitty rumors go."

"I don't think Jodi puts much stock in rumors." At least, he hoped not.

"Those guys you destroyed… No reason to rehash it,

except to say you were never in the wrong for that. You survived, and I'm damn glad."

Yeah, Hunter was starting to be grateful, too. "Break it down for me, Memphis. What exactly has she done?"

His brother's next electric pause was out of sheer surprise. Hunter understood that. Always, before this very moment, he'd flatly refused to cut himself any slack. What had happened that day…it hadn't been him. Somewhere deep beneath his civilized veneer, a cornered, wild animal had emerged, lashing out, caught up in bloodlust, doing things Hunter would have denied possible.

Yet he'd done them, and yeah, little by little, he was glad that savage part of him existed, because otherwise, he wouldn't be here now. If he hadn't reacted that way…he probably would be buried in a shallow grave, and his family might still be searching for him. It would have broken his mother, destroyed his father, and Memphis—his too-smart, too-determined brother—would never have given up hope.

Finally, Memphis said quietly, "One guy had outstanding warrants for suspected kidnapping and possible murder. From what I could tell of redacted info, Jodi ran him off the road. If a cop hadn't shown up, she probably would have killed him."

"You don't know that." But did he think Jodi was capable of such a thing? Yes, he did.

"Later, the guy was convicted of rape against a different woman, and I'm willing to bet that's why Jodi targeted him."

Huh.

"She picked up another guy at a bar and he was never seen again. Cops talked to her, but she was a little beat-up and said the guy had manhandled her in a park, so she walked home. He's still missing."

His brother sounded admiring…and damn it, Hunter was a little impressed, too—not that he'd admit it.

"A really fascinating detail?" Memphis continued. "She's close with Kennedy Brooks."

"Kennedy Brooks," Hunter repeated. He remembered that framed photo in the box in her kitchen. "Should that name mean something?"

"She's a well-known author and speaker. You should look her up. Her topic? Human trafficking, how to be alert to your surroundings, what to look for but also escaping capture, and how to survive if you can't. She speaks mostly at colleges, but she visits high schools, too, and other venues."

Strained breath left Hunter in a rasped, *"Fuck."*

"Yeah, my thoughts exactly," Memphis said.

Hunter briefly closed his eyes. He'd known. Jodi hadn't shared everything, but she'd shared enough to make it clear. And still it hurt him to have it confirmed.

So how must it have been for her to live through it?

Remembering her stricken face, the harsh, uncontrolled way she'd trembled while trying to tell him, he knew the answer to that, too. She'd lived through her own private hell and it would forever be with her.

"Another interesting tidbit," Memphis continued. "Ms. Brooks has high-level security now, though she didn't always. You can find out a ton about her professional life but nada on anything personal. Much like Jodi, if something shows up online, it gets squelched real fast. Those names you gave me? Parrish, Madison, Reyes—"

"Wait." Hunter's senses came alert from one second to the next. He glanced at the empty doorway. There was no shadow, no sound, but he knew he was no longer alone. Silently he strode forward, stepped out—and found Jodi, all narrow-eyed and mean, standing in the hallway. Well, shit.

Letting his brother know they had company, he asked, "Been there long, Jodi?"

Her patented smirk didn't fool him—she was hurt as well as pissed.

Pointing past him, she indicated the small camera on the trunk beside her bed. "Just finished in the utility room. But you've got video and audio, so I didn't need to be here."

Damn it. He'd assumed she was still busy cleaning. Her utility room, which was a very small space between her kitchen and bathroom, was crammed full with the water heater, laundry sink and a stack washer/dryer. He'd pulled out the appliance for her and then left her to remove cobwebs, dust and grime from the walls and floor.

Unsure how to handle her now, he made a quick decision and pressed the speaker button. "Memphis, you're on speaker now."

Wasting no time, Memphis said, "Jodi Bentley, my God, it's a pleasure. How did you do it?"

Suspicious at his motives and taken by surprise at his upbeat tone, Jodi folded her arms and narrowed her eyes even more. "How did I do what?"

"Bring my brother out of his self-imposed exile. Whatever tricks you used, you have my full approval. Keep it up."

Flabbergasted, Jodi said, "I didn't do anything."

"Cute and modest. I can see the appeal."

Her scowl turned ferocious. "I'm not cute."

"Oh, you are," Memphis rumbled to her in that low voice Jodi considered flirting.

"Back off, Memphis," Hunter warned.

"She's beyond cute and you know it—though she's not my type, so I promise I'm not hitting on her."

"I'm *so* relieved," Jodi shot back, obviously flustered by his outrageous brother.

"Hunter, though? Clearly you've worked wonders with him."

Done with that whole inane subject, Jodi snapped, "You've been snooping around about me."

"Guilty. For what it's worth, I applaud you—"

"Memphis." Hunter would not have anyone, not even his brother, encouraging her in illegal activity.

"—just keep in mind, though, big brother is a different type of man. More proper, a real stickler for walking the straight and narrow. Mum's the word, okay?"

"Jackass," she snarled, more with exasperation than rage. "You were just spilling your guts to him!"

"Oh. Interesting how you knew that, since I assume Hunter didn't have me on speaker the whole time."

Instantly clamming up, Jodi flushed.

Yes, Hunter decided, it was interesting. "Jodi?"

Her chin notched up. "Yeah, so? You already know you're being watched. You know I have powerful people— how was it you put it, Hunter?—looking out for me?"

"So they're hacking my phone?"

She shrugged one shoulder.

"Un-fucking-believable."

Going all kinds of defensive, Jodi said, "It's barely raining now. You and Turbo can take off. Thanks for the help."

No, he wouldn't let her brush him off like that. It was another of her damned defense mechanisms, acting like she didn't care, but he knew better. "We have the day planned."

Her lips compressed and she looked at the phone in his hand, instead of at him. "Figured you wouldn't want to now."

"I want to."

Memphis, the ass, choked. "Hang on, I'm getting another call, so I have to put you on hold. Don't you dare hang up, Hunter, now that it's getting so interesting. I'll be right back."

Once his phone indicated he was on hold, Hunter used the moment of privacy to slowly approach Jodi until she was within reach. "Your friends don't trust me?"

"You, your brother—pretty much they don't trust anyone, with good reason."

"How about you?" Hunter badly wanted to touch her, so much so that his fingertips burned with the need, but he'd learned to read Jodi, and right now she was blaring hands-off signals bright enough to light up all of Triple Creek—not from anger, but because she felt vulnerable.

Glassy eyes glared into his, but she couldn't quite muster up her usual toxic stare. "I don't even trust myself most of the time."

Hunter eased a little nearer. "But you trust me. I feel it, honey. And I trust you."

Her lip curled. "Only so far."

"Only as far as you've let me in."

"Don't act like I'm the only one with walls."

"No, I won't." Propping his shoulder against the doorframe, Hunter tilted closer still. "And that's why we understand each other, right?"

Her chest expanded on a quick breath as she sought other defenses. "Your brother doesn't trust me."

Hunter could feel her giving in and it warmed him from the inside out. Gently, he explained, "My brother loves me an awful lot, and I've been…absent for over a year now. He's protective, when he doesn't need to be. Much like your family."

"And it's annoying, right?" Copying his relaxed posture, she rested her back on the wall beside him, her hands at her hips, her face turned toward him. "That's the problem with walls, you know. You don't just lock out others, you lock yourself in."

Yes, that's exactly what he had done. "Sometimes, whether the person realizes it or not, the isolation can be…"

"Terrible. Defeating." A small smile softened the tension in her set features. "So here I am, starting over."

With him. As a neighbor, a friend, and something more. "Did you break down some of your walls, Jodi?"

"Nah. Someone else dismantled them for me, because she cared. And fair warning—if your nosy brother goes poking around where he shouldn't, it could land him in trouble."

That wasn't a statement Hunter could let pass. "Is that a threat?"

Her mouth twitched, a precursor to her quick laugh. "Let's say a warning, okay? I mean, no one's going to take his head, but especially where Kennedy is concerned, he shouldn't go digging around."

"Why her especially?"

"She's not part of the business."

"Ahem," Memphis said as he rejoined the call. "That exact sentiment was just explained to me in grave detail."

Hunter straightened with the start of anger. "So someone *did* threaten you?" He held Jodi's gaze, saw her shrug with a told-you-so attitude. "Who?" Hunter whispered. "Give me a name."

"I know that voice, brother. It's not like that, so don't go blowing your mellow mood."

"Who?"

Memphis sighed. "Her people. I started to explain this

to you, but the names you gave me—Parrish, Madison, Reyes—they clicked."

Now even Jodi looked alarmed. "Hunter gave you names?"

"Yes, and out of concern for you, he asked me to find out what I could. Parrish McKenzie is well-known in Colorado, mostly for being a wealthy businessman, but also for his charity work."

Jodi flinched.

Because she'd benefited from that charity?

"The thing is," Memphis explained, "he and his kids have been on the cops' radar multiple times. They're often tied to the demise of..." Memphis hesitated. "Really miserable cretins who have escaped the penalties of the legal system."

Hunter appreciated the judicious editing he'd used. No reason to mention traffickers, or monsters evil enough to treat women like property. They both knew details would only trigger Jodi's memories of her own awful history. "They're always cleared, but still—where there's smoke, there's fire."

This time Jodi looked away. To keep him from reading too much in her eyes? Or because even glossing over the facts was difficult for her? "Who spoke to you just now?" Hunter asked his brother.

"First Madison, who I take it is the tech guru, then her brother Reyes. Cool your jets, Hunter, because neither of them were unreasonable. In fact, Madison said she respected my skill."

Damned if his brother didn't sound flattered.

"Then there was another man, and that one sounded like a general."

"That would be Parrish," Jodi all but groaned.

Her reaction sharpened Hunter's irritation even more.

If the guy had been kind to her, why did she look agonized now?

"So you know, I told them to back the hell out of your business as well." Memphis laughed. "It was a comical standoff—for, oh, about two seconds. Seriously, they have me outgunned when it comes to cyberwarfare, apparently. That's what they claimed."

"Believe it." Jodi glared first at Hunter, then at the phone as if she could sear Memphis through the connection.

"I'm a believer, but—and it's a big *but*—I did manage to wrangle a promise from them that they would refrain from hacking into Hunter's private life unless they felt you were in danger."

"They *always* think I'm in danger."

"Maybe," Hunter suggested, "it's your tendency to find trouble wherever you go?"

"Yeah, maybe."

That she didn't deny it made Memphis laugh. "They made it clear that they trusted Hunter for now—"

"Yay," she said, deadpan.

"—but if that changes, all bets are off, and it almost sounded like they could nuke Triple Creek from space or something."

Jodi laughed, and that, along with Memphis's irreverent tone, told Hunter that it wasn't *quite* that bad.

"They wanted reassurances," Memphis explained. "I gave them. I suppose they'll be keeping tabs, but otherwise, you kids can carry on."

Shaking his head, Hunter couldn't withhold a short laugh. It was all so over-the-top and absurd, but he had a feeling Jodi was worth it.

As Memphis had said, she had him living again, instead of just existing.

"Thanks for handling things, Memphis."

"What good is a techie younger brother if he can't deal with the most mysterious and philanthropic organization this side of the country has ever known?"

"They're good people," Jodi assured them. "And they really are generous, often to a fault."

"Jodi?" Memphis said.

"Yeah?"

"Whatever is in your past, whatever you've done, I've always found my brother to be a good sounding board. Just remember that, okay? If things get rough, or you need someone to talk with who isn't playing as a mythical god, Hunter's a little more real."

Her smile stretched into a grin. "Each and every one of them could be Zeus, so I get the analogy." Her golden gaze lifted to meet Hunter's. "Someone a little more real has to be easier."

"Awesome. Either of you need me, hit me up. Otherwise, I'll give you some time before I drop in to visit."

Drop in to… Hunter straightened. "Wait—*what?*"

"Gotta run, brother. Keep it real!" And with that, Memphis disconnected the call.

"Damn it." Hunter stuck the phone back in his pocket. "Where is my dog?"

"Sawing logs in the front room, why?"

"It's not raining, I'm done here, and I assume you've finished in the utility room, so how about we go scope out King, then do some shopping?"

Jodi's alert gaze probed his, looking for answers and more. "You're really not scared off?"

"What?"

She gestured at his phone. "You heard your brother. You know the people I'm associated with."

"Good people, from what I understand."

"God, yes, they're good. They're amazing. And powerful. Few people want them for an enemy."

"I'm not their enemy," he said quietly.

"Whatever's in *your* past—"

"Is none of their damn business." He wouldn't discuss that—at least, not now. Eventually... Hunter shook his head, but he knew the truth. Sooner or later, he'd have to tell Jodi—before someone else did.

In disbelief, she laughed. "You're not dense, Hunter. You know they're already digging out of some misguided idea of protecting me."

"Protecting you is not misguided." He had to wonder, were they also digging into King? Remmy? Worth? Did they know that Jodi racked up the wrong kind of attention on a daily basis?

She looked away with a short laugh. "Yeah, well, you might not think so, but then, you don't know enough about them. If they see you as a threat, they'll deal with it."

"I don't scare easy," he promised. Not when something, or someone, really mattered.

"Just so you know, I told them to back off, too."

"Will they?"

She snorted.

That got Hunter smiling. "The important thing is that they care about you." *And so do I.* "So what do you say we put your snoopy family and my snoopy brother on the back burner for now and go about our day?"

"I say..." She considered it, considered *him*, and finally gave in. "Sure, why not? Stow your tools while I wash my hands. I'll be ready in five."

Watching her walk away, Hunter realized that the more he learned, the more he understood and the more he was drawn to her. He'd never come about wanting a woman by first being shocked by her manner, then impressed by her fortitude, pitying her for her past, wanting to protect her, astounded at what she'd survived, and finally, craving her like he'd never craved another woman ever. He wanted everything, every part of Jodi, the good and the bad, the carefree and the troubled.

It wasn't the easiest path, but this time, easy didn't really factor in.

CHAPTER SIX

SMOOSHED AGAINST THE passenger door with Turbo slumped against her, Jodi took in the towering trees still dripping from the rain. "That must be it."

"Damn." Hunter slowly approached the drive leading to the ornate gated entry of Russ King's sprawling, private estate. The tires of his truck made a quiet hiss on the wet pavement. "I don't think I've ever seen a home that big."

"It's nice," Jodi agreed. The decorative iron gates connected to two stone pillars, each topped by security lights, shining amber against the gloomy day. "Parrish owns a bigger spread. It's like this massive structure that hugs the mountain with rooms that go on forever. I used to wonder why anyone wanted a home that big." She observed King's house, and the surrounding grounds, with a critical eye. "Parrish has his set up like a fortress."

"You sound impressed."

"With Parrish, yeah. King? No idea what his twisted motives might be, but I know it'd take me three days to do all that yard work, even without breaks."

Hunter said nothing as he coasted past a well-lit, occupied guard shack. Somehow he'd shifted from easygoing Hunter to on-alert Hunter...and seriously, they were both pretty darned exciting. It stumped Jodi, because she'd never found a guy exciting before. She tended to see men in pretty simplistic terms. Harmless or a threat. Good or bad. Kind or selfish. Disgusting or...well, after meeting Parrish, Reyes and the rest, she acknowledged that some men were exceptional.

She'd never met a guy who was good and somewhat tarnished, kind but disgruntled about it, never disgusting but, oh yeah, *very* exceptional, at least to her senses, so no matter what, she couldn't seem to put him from her mind.

Turbo, not caring that the bench seat was crowded and he was already giving her no room, flopped his head in her lap and wriggled closer to get more comfortable. "You big goof." Drawn away from her inspection of King's property, which, yeah, seemed to go on for a bit, she told Hunter, "Turn around when you can so we can drive by again."

"I don't like it."

"Right, I know. Your mood is stormier than the sky."

He ignored the taunt to mutter, "It feels off."

"Big-time, I know." On one side of the road was King's property, strongly fortified and protected, and on the other, nothing but aspen trees closest to the road, backed by pine, spruce and fir trees that created an impenetrable wall.

"If you know," Hunter groused, "then why are we driving past again?"

Jodi turned her head to take in his stern frown. "Maybe this is why I should have gone alone."

"You wanted me to come with you."

"Before you got all pushy and had your brother invading my privacy."

"Don't do that," he growled, his tone sharp-edged. His alert gaze stayed on the road and their isolated surroundings. "Your family did the same to me, so don't start looking for stupid excuses to shore up your reasons for being alone. Don't cut me out."

Was that what she'd been doing? True, they'd started this little adventure with him smiling, but as she'd moped, he'd turned sour and become mean-eyed. So maybe he was reacting to her, in which case, it wouldn't be fair to him to keep being snide. "Sorry."

That earned a double take before he found a spot where he could turn the truck and head back the way they'd come. "Want to tell me the problem?"

Hunter did that a lot, asked what she was thinking and feeling as if he really cared. He didn't bulldoze her. He was considerate. *Does he really care?*

Was that even possible?

"I can't figure out why you'd want me to hang around."

Easily, as if it wasn't a stupid question, especially right here, right now, he answered, "Multiple reasons, actually."

"Like?"

"I've been alone for eighteen months. You nosed your way in and now I like it."

Despite herself, she felt a smile tugging at her mouth. He did that often, too, lightened her darkness and drew her out of her own troubled thoughts. "Pretty sure you could find a woman more agreeable to—"

"No, I can't." Clearly offended by the suggestion, he frowned. "You think I've walked around wearing earmuffs? Blindfolded? I've met women. I've been polite. I've conversed." Constantly vigilant, his gaze searched everywhere as they moved along the shadowed road. "All I'd felt was the need to be left alone. Hell, I'd cut out my own family."

She knew that, and it broke her heart for his poor mama. She thought of Parrish, how he'd react if one of his kids did that to him.

Pretty sure Parrish would have put an end to it, but then, Parrish was an over-the-top personality unlike anyone she'd ever known.

Hunter quietly continued. "Then there was you, and… I don't know. Maybe it's like you said back when we first met. You were something different and I was something different than we pretended to be, but we both recognized it, so we clicked."

The words sank in, leaving Jodi awed. "I've never clicked for anyone before."

"We click."

"Even though I'm so weird?"

A short laugh escaped him. "You're not weird."

"No? What would you call it?"

"Unique. Compelling." His eyes narrowed. "Fucking extraordinary."

Wow. That rasped adjective just added major punch to the compliment. No one had ever called her extraordinary before. Around a glow of pleasure, Jodi tried to sound unaffected. "If you say so." She would have liked to continue the conversation, since it was all complimentary for her, but then they saw the two men standing in the road. "The guy on the right is Remmy." He stood there, arms folded, feet braced apart, obviously waiting. Next to him was a dude who tried his best to look menacing. His best was pretty good, she had to admit. "No idea about the other one."

Hunter slowed even more, an almost electric charge of tense anger vibrating off his big frame.

Whoa. Jodi wasn't quite sure what to make of the transformation. This was a side of Hunter she hadn't seen before. "Don't run them over, okay? I'll ask Remmy what's up."

"You'll stay in the truck."

An order? Was that where he thought they were relationship-wise? Fat chance. "Here's a clue, Hunter—extraordinary women don't take kindly to being bossed around." She heard his low curse. "Relax, okay? We're still in control." She lifted the Glock she'd just taken from her holster to show him she wasn't unprepared.

He countered that. "You think they aren't armed, too? Look closer."

"So?" The other guy, who seemed impatient for trouble, fingered the hilt of a big knife while glaring toward the truck. "I see it." He had a shaved head, pale blue eyes and a deliberately nasty attitude. "I've seen worse. Besides, he's way over there, and look, Remmy's giving him shit."

"Stop saying his name like the two of you are friends."

Jodi did a double take. Another order? And this one sounded like...disgruntled jealousy? Couldn't be, except she wasn't sure what other emotion to pin to it. "Definitely not friends, thank you very much." She needed to keep an eye on the two men, yet Hunter's presence kept drawing her attention. If she ever figured him out, it'd be a miracle.

Appalled at herself for being distracted, Jodi forced herself to focus. "Seems the two of them came to a quiet disagreement." The cue ball relented, taking a step back. He didn't look happy about it. As Remmy came forward, he didn't appear too comfortable with the dude at his back either. "Hold on to Turbo."

"Jodi," Hunter warned.

"If they try anything, then you can run them over." She opened the door, badly startling Turbo, who jerked awake with a croak and a howl. "Stay," she told the dog, who did his utmost to follow her despite the command. It was only the hold Hunter had on his collar that kept him in the truck. To ensure the dog stayed safe, Jodi closed the door behind her and stepped toward the front fender. "What's up?"

Warily, Remmy eyed the gun that she held casually in her hand, not pointed directly at him but still ready. He eyed Hunter with even more unease. Dumbass. Whether Remmy knew it or not, she was far more of a threat than Hunter.

Directing his attention back to her, Remmy nodded at her weapon. "Is this how you check out a job?"

Lifting a brow, Jodi nodded at his buddy. "Is this how you interview people?"

"At King's personal residence… Yeah. Sorry. Precautions and all that." Lower, he said, "I tried to warn you."

Yes, he had. "So who's the skinhead and why is he mean-mugging me?"

"He works for King." Softer, he added, "Steer clear of him."

"Not sure he'll let me do that, blocking the road the way he is."

"I'll get him out of the way. I just wanted to catch you on the trip back."

Meaning they'd been aware of them the whole time? "Got cameras all along the road?"

"A few." He smiled down at her. "I wasn't sure you'd come, Jodi."

"Curiosity got the better of me."

Again, he eyed Hunter. "Who's the chauffeur?"

"He's none of your business." But even as she said it, she heard the truck door open and close. Then Hunter was standing there, no closer than the front fender but imposing all the same, tall and dangerous and doing a fair share of his own mean-mugging, only he was better at it than baldy because he looked completely, icily in control. *Be still my heart.*

Turning back to Remmy with a grin, she said, "I don't think he likes your friend."

"No one likes Danny Giggs, me especially." After looking her over, Remmy almost laughed. "You seriously aren't at all uncomfortable with this situation, are you?"

"The situation being that I might shoot you and your wired cohort? No, that doesn't discomfort me at all."

Even more amused, Remmy stepped closer.

"Back. Off."

Remmy froze.

Eyes widening, Jodi slowly turned her head to see Hunter. Holy moly. Yeah, those two words, stated with dire warning, had come from him. She wasn't sure how she felt about that, but she said to Remmy, "I'd do as he says, if I was you." Because seriously, Hunter looked ready and able to cause massive destruction.

Right before her eyes, the two men had a silent battle of wills, and even from a few feet away, menace radiated off Hunter like the quiet thrum of a giant fan starting up: *whomp, whomp, WHOMP...*

Feeling it, seeing the risk, Remmy held up his hands and retreated two steps.

Okay, so maybe she wanted Madison to do a little digging into Hunter after all. Sure, she'd known from the start that Hunter wasn't average. Now she knew he'd been a park ranger.

Pretty sure he was a hell of a lot more.

WHILE JODI HAD done a cursory glance of King's property— from the road, where he could keep an eye on her—Remmy had gone over what would be expected from her as a landscaper. The other guy, who Remmy had called Danny Giggs, waited with a lack of patience that said he'd be trouble, if not now, then eventually.

To Remmy's credit, he'd kept his own body between Giggs and Jodi.

Hunter didn't give a shit. He didn't want either man anywhere near Jodi.

When they'd finished and Jodi was ready to go, Hunter had made up his mind how to handle the situation. He hated it, he detested being drawn between two loyalties, but no way in hell would he let Jodi come to this snake pit alone.

When Jodi seemed to be considering the job—likely so she could cause her own store of trouble—he'd jumped in with both feet and announced, "Since I'm working for you now, it won't take as long as you're thinking."

Remmy had stared at him, incredulous.

Giggs looked ready to attack.

And Jodi, always so damn cool under fire, had glanced from one man to the other, then fashioned a placid smile. "Let's see how the weather goes. I couldn't do much until it dries up. Too messy." She accepted a card from Remmy and started away, adding, "I'll be in touch."

On the long drive back, she'd said little, but every so often, she'd chuckle.

Finally, Hunter had snapped. "That was a hell of a predicament you put me in."

"Me?" she asked theatrically. "Like you didn't throw a kink in the works, announcing yourself as my employee?"

"I had Turbo in the truck," he'd continued. "What if we'd both been mowed down? What do you think would have happened to him?"

All humor had left her in an instant, replaced by a visible wave of guilt. "I didn't expect you to get out of the truck."

"So I should have sat there and watched you get slaughtered?" Wound up and ready to detonate, Hunter had squeezed the wheel and again checked his rearview mirror. "We were supposed to drive by the place, period."

Hugging Turbo, her cheek against his floppy ear, she whispered, "I didn't know they'd block the road."

"You didn't know if it was only the two of them either! You deliberately put yourself at risk, and that put Turbo at risk, too."

Solemn, she pressed a kiss to the top of the dog's head. "It's usually just me," she explained softly.

"Not anymore."

After exploding on her, an extended silence filled the cab. Both Turbo and Jodi watched him, and Hunter had no idea what to expect.

Until finally she'd said, "Fine. Take a chill pill, already. I'll do my best to remember that we're working together."

And with that, Hunter wondered if he'd literally signed on for yard work. If it helped keep her safe, he didn't think he'd mind.

Hours later, after shopping for lawn furniture outside Triple Creek, and later, groceries within the town, they went to her house and he helped her to set up the small patio table and two chairs.

The air remained thick with the promise of more rain, which made it a great time to explore the creek. Turbo agreed. Hunter couldn't tell who enjoyed it more, Jodi or his dog. At a shallower spot, both insisted on wading across, so he'd handed the leash to Jodi…and Turbo had immediately lunged for a fish. Standing on a slippery rock, Jodi lost her balance and, arms and legs flailing, landed on her backside with a big splash. The rain had deepened the water, but not enough for her to go under. Turbo took it as a game, and in seconds, they were both completely soaked.

Hunter reached in and hauled her upright—noticing that, despite her fall, she hadn't let go of the leash. He relieved her of it and asked, "Are you all right?"

To his relief, she laughed like a loon.

For over an hour, he and Turbo walked along the receding land while Jodi explored, going to the deeper sections to spot various fish, finding elk prints in the mud and even spotting a small bobcat. Turbo saw the animal and went alert, but when Hunter whispered, "Quiet," Turbo obeyed and merely watched.

"How do you do that?" Jodi asked, once the bobcat ran off.

"He knows certain commands, but he's only ever heard them from me."

"You taught him?"

"More like I stumbled onto them by accident. Every so

often, I'd notice that something I said clicked with him. So I started experimenting. I looked up popular commands with trained hunters. They don't all fit for him, and he follows a few that weren't listed, like *quiet*. Given how I found him, I don't know if he was actually a hunter or not, but I did check with local shelters and veterinarians, in case anyone was missing him."

"I'm glad you were able to keep him. Whoever had him couldn't have been as good as you."

Her faith in him felt like the best of compliments.

Wading knee-deep along the creek, her gaze on the water, she added, "I really am sorry about putting him in danger earlier. I'd die before I'd want Turbo hurt."

Mostly, Hunter thought darkly, because she didn't value her own life. "So we're clear," he replied, watching her intently, "I feel the same about you."

Thunder chose that inauspicious moment to rumble loudly, shaking the ground beneath his feet.

Squinting, Jodi looked up at the sky visible between the trees. "Guess it's going to storm again. It's gotten awfully dark."

"Let's put your new seat cushions inside, then go to my place for dinner."

Silently, she slogged out of the water, then lifted the hem of her shirt to wring it out, giving Hunter a view of her midriff between her low-slung jeans and the shirt she held.

It baffled him that a glimpse of a woman's belly would affect him so strongly. Then again, he'd been celibate eighteen months, and this wasn't any ordinary woman. She was Jodi Bentley, and as he'd told her, she was extraordinary.

"Guess it's a good thing I left my gun in the house, huh?"

As usual with Jodi, he knew what she said had deeper meaning, so he tried for a neutral reply. "Might've gotten soaked otherwise."

"The thing is…I forgot it." With chagrin, she stressed, "I *never* forget it. It'd be like forgetting to breathe. But I had so much fun shopping with you, then putting up my little patio set…"

"Then we walked to the creek—and you're with me. I hope you know I would protect you."

Typical of Jodi, his sincere declaration caused a laugh. She looked at his face, saw his annoyance and laughed again, but at least she covered her mouth as though trying to stifle it. "I'm sorry. It's just that I wouldn't want you to protect me. If something happened, I'd rather you take care of Turbo."

Turbo looked as indignant as Hunter felt. The skies shook with more thunder, as if equally affronted. "Come on." He started them on their way. "We don't want to get hit with lightning."

Still wearing a silly smile, she trailed along. "It has been a nice day, huh?"

Most of it, anyway. "Yes."

"You sure you wouldn't mind dinner, too?"

The skies rapidly darkened, and off in the distance, he saw a streak of lightning. "I'm sure, but we better hurry in case we lose power again."

Once they reached her back door, it occurred to Hunter that not only had she forgotten her weapon, she hadn't locked up, either.

They'd both lost track of what they were doing. Even though her house had always remained in view, it was tricky seeing it through the trees. Someone could have walked in and they wouldn't have noticed.

He'd have to be more careful, too, and with that thought in mind, he stepped into her kitchen with Turbo, even though the dog was dripping. When Turbo didn't sniff the air or otherwise seem suspicious, Hunter relaxed.

While he dried Turbo, Jodi surprised him by taking a quick shower before changing her clothes. That she'd do such a thing, trusting him in her house, told him a lot— all of it promising. He remained in the kitchen until Jodi emerged eight minutes later in cutoff jean shorts and another loose shirt, this time with her holster in place. Beneath the shirt, he could see the outline of her flashlight and keys.

He could also see the outline of her breasts and it made him a little nuts, remembering how pale her stomach was, how toned and slender. She would be a pleasure for the senses—but she was also emotionally wounded, and he would never do anything to make her uncomfortable, so he forced his attention to her face.

With her damp hair combed back from her forehead and her cheeks flushed, she shoved her feet into sneakers and smiled up at him. "Ready?"

If she knew his thoughts… But then, Jodi didn't see him that way, because she didn't see herself that way. She had no real idea of her own appeal, assuming others viewed her within the narrow scope of her own perception. In her mind, she was only an escaped victim, determined to prove something—to herself, more than anyone else.

"You have beautiful hair."

Instantly alert, she touched her hair and, at the same time, took a step back. "It's wet and currently stringy."

Pretending he hadn't noticed her retreat, Hunter said, "It's thick and has a little wave to it. You should wear it loose more often." Then he locked the back door and led Turbo to the front. "At least the drive is short this time, so Turbo won't smash you for long."

"I'll drive up so you won't have to bring me back later."

It was a challenge, but Hunter kept walking. "I'd rather you just ride with me."

"Why?"

She hadn't budged from the kitchen. At the front door, he glanced back, acting like it was nothing to see her so far away, drawn tight with wary uncertainty.

"It's our day together." He smiled and opened the door. "I'm enjoying it." One by one, emotions crossed her features— distrust, surprise...yearning—but she resisted each of them, doing her best to keep her feelings hidden.

He imagined she did that a lot, in part because she didn't want to feel too much.

After five seconds that felt like a lifetime, she gave a stiff nod and strode forward. "Sure, why not. But if you and Turbo get soaked bringing me back, remember that you only have yourself to blame."

She remained withdrawn on the short drive up, but after a quick and easy meal of canned tomato soup and grilled cheese, she finally started to relax. Another storm did blow through, but the power stayed on, and after an hour, the thunder and lightning passed, leaving only a steady downpour that in many ways seemed soothing.

With Jodi appearing relaxed and drowsy, Hunter tried to refuse her help with the cleanup. It was like trying to hold back a tsunami. She took personal affront at the idea that she wouldn't pitch in. Though it was only seven o'clock, the dark skies gave the illusion of night by the time they finished. Knowing Jodi could mention heading home, Hunter suggested a movie.

She thought about it, glancing twice at the window, now streaked with rain, before saying, "Why not? But make it something good."

Having an idea of what she might like, he offered her choices in sci-fi, horror and action. After giving it a lot of thought, she chose *John Wick*.

"One of my favorites, too."

She rolled a shoulder. "What's it about?"

"You've never seen it?"

"Told you, I've never been a TV person. I just picked it because the blurb said he's an ex–hit man and it was action-packed. Sounded good, you know? Better than some corny comedy or sugary romance nonsense."

For several reasons, her comments saddened him. "Will it bother you that there's violence? Mostly John Wick kicking ass and taking names, but—"

"For real?" she asked with enthusiasm. "Count me in."

Throughout the movie, Jodi's attention stayed glued to the screen.

Hunter spent most of his time watching her. It was endearing, to see her enjoying something so simple, something that most people took for granted. When it ended, he asked, "How about a horror movie, or will that bother you?"

"Pfft, no." She glanced toward the windows. "But it's getting late."

Knowing how she'd react to a goad, he said, "Okay, Grandma."

"Hey!" She playfully shoved his shoulder and, taking up the challenge, settled back against the couch and even crossed her bare feet on his table. "You choose something this time."

Because she'd taken such obvious enjoyment in the fight scenes, he put on the newest version of *The Invisible Man*. "This one's been done a few times, but the remake is great. Later, you can go through my personal library to see if anything else looks good to you. If you don't like it, just say so and we'll pick something else."

Forty-five minutes into the movie, Hunter wasn't at all surprised that she loved it. There were times she went utterly still, eyes opened wide, and other times that she jumped in surprise. Once she murmured, *"Oh, man,"* with feeling, making him smile.

When the action lagged for a bit, he took Turbo out for a bathroom break, then grabbed a few packaged cookies and two cups of milk. She accepted both with a hushed, "Thanks," and got right back to the movie.

Sitting all cozy on the couch with Jodi, sharing snacks and smiling at some of her over-the-top reactions, he knew this would be a memory he'd hold on to forever, even while he hoped to make it a regular occasion.

It was during the third movie, with the house dark and Turbo snoring, that Jodi started to yawn. "We might have to put this one on hold. Much as I've enjoyed it, I'm getting too sleepy just sitting here in the dark."

Hunter considered the situation, but why not? "If you doze off, I won't mind."

Appalled, she stared at him and asked, "Here?" as if he'd suggested she sleep on a hot stove.

"Why not? Maybe you'll actually get some rest. Look at Turbo. He knows he's safe." The dog sprawled on his back, paws in the air, junk on display again and his tongue lolling out.

"He looks like someone drugged him."

Staring hard at her, Hunter tried to see some signs of association. Had she ever been drugged? But no, she half smiled, as if amused, so clearly just a humorous observation. "He has no modesty, that's for sure."

Jodi heaved a sigh. "If I'm sleeping, what will you do?"

"Nothing pervy, I promise."

Her slim brows climbed high. "Describe *pervy*."

What would be her first concern? Since he couldn't know for certain, he tried to cover the bases. "I won't check you out—even if I'm tempted. I can't swear I won't look at you at all, but I'll keep it fleeting. I'll do my best to just watch the movie and not disturb you."

After all that, still looking slumberous but also a little more aware, Jodi asked, "Why would you check me out?"

Not the reaction he'd expected.

It was chancy, but he reached out to finger a lock of loose hair, now dry and a little tangled, testing its silky texture before tucking it behind her small ear. He let his fingertips graze her warm cheek. "I get that you're unaware of it, but as my brother said, you're extremely cute—and no, don't snort. You might disturb Turbo."

She subsided, her mouth now twisted to the side.

"You have beautiful features, Jodi."

She continued to watch him, her expression doubting.

"Small, proud nose. High, smooth cheekbones. I especially like your eyes." That caused her to blink and briefly look away, but not for long.

As if she couldn't help herself, her gaze came back to his. "Why my eyes?"

"They're like...sunshine."

Humor flickered over her lips. "Poetic."

Hunter ignored that. "Your big personality is also a draw." He shifted, trying to find the right words to explain. "On a lot of levels, you appeal to me, *but...*" He waited, and when she held silent, he continued, "I would never, under any circumstances, do anything to you that you didn't want me to do."

Her attention strayed from his eyes to his mouth. "What would you want to do?"

Such a loaded question, and there were a hundred ways he could answer. "Right now? I'd really like to kiss you."

Alarm shot her gaze back to his, where it locked on with wariness, defiance and...something more?

His heart beat a little harder, but he kept his tone gentle when he said, "Remember, I wouldn't. Not unless you made it clear that you wanted me to."

"I would never."

"Never is a really long time."

She considered that. "Men don't really want me."

Taking that as another opening to something important, Hunter asked, "Why wouldn't they?"

She turned to face the TV, and Hunter didn't know if that was a refusal to answer, or a way of buying time. She surprised him when she spoke softly.

"I've been seen as a nuisance by parents who weren't really cut out to parent. Then as property by a psycho guy who didn't see me as a real person. And I've been a charity case that...that my family wanted to help so I could survive. None of that is what you're talking about."

"No, it's not." Hunter badly wanted to touch her, but she had her arms crossed and strain kept her face stiff. "The first, I can't speak for that. If you tell me it's so, I believe you and I hate that you went through that. Parents should always take care of their children."

"Like your mom and dad do with you?"

"Yes." He brushed his knuckles along her upper arm, down to her elbow, back again. It pleased him when her muscles loosened and her posture relaxed. "The last, though, I think you're wrong about your family. I heard them on the phone with you, remember? That wasn't pity."

She turned her head to stare at him again. Almost desperately, she asked, "Then, what?"

It occurred to Hunter that despite everything that she'd learned and all the ways she'd been helped, she didn't yet comprehend her own value. Not fully. "I heard affection—especially in the way Reyes teased you. That wasn't the sound of a man who felt pity, but one who really cares. It's the same way Memphis and I harass each other or the way we tease our mom because she's the runt in the family."

"Reyes and his brother and sister give each other crap all the time. It's hilarious."

"Because it's done with love." Her skin fascinated him. So warm and smooth—soft packaging for such a prickly personality. "With Kennedy, I heard worry, because she loves you and wants guarantees that you'll remain in her life. My dad is the same. He'll drop some heavy stuff on us sometimes, all quiet-like and out of the blue, and it makes us stop and think."

She shared that sweet, quirky smile with him. "You're nuts. No way could you get all that from a short convo through my cell."

"You don't think so, huh? Well, tell me, smarty. What did you hear when Memphis was giving me shit? Did he sound bossy, or like he didn't care?"

"No. He obviously loves you and wants you back in his life, enough that he'd even thank me for doing something I hadn't done."

"See, there you go again." The movie droned on in the background, completely forgotten by both of them. Because she slumped into the couch cushions, he did the same, and their shoulders sank closer. "You don't know what I was like before you started provoking me."

"I never—"

"Just hush and listen." Maybe because he said it with a teasing smile, she clammed up instead of protesting.

"Everything about you puts me on high alert. You gave Worth hell that first day, and I wanted to cheer you at the same time I wanted you to go away."

With a short laugh, she said, "Gee, thanks."

"You set up house out here, where no one else has been in the eighteen months I've lived here, and I both wanted to be angry while at the same time I felt driven to find out more about you."

"You're the one who's insisted on us socializing." She said it without heat, and in fact, her tone was comically accusing.

"You make me laugh when I haven't laughed in a very long time."

"At me?"

"No." Since her arms were no longer defiantly crossed, he carefully lifted her hand and carried it to his mouth, where he brushed a kiss over her knuckles. "Never that, okay?" At her confused nod, he continued. "I laugh at your quick comebacks."

"That's more you than me. I noticed right off how funny you are."

"That's the thing, though. I hadn't been funny, not since…" Damn. In one respect, he wanted to tell her; he had a feeling it would help her to share more, too. Yet in another, he wanted this to be for her, not about him. "Can we come back to that?"

"Sure."

Never, ever did she pressure him. "That's another thing, Jodi. You have a big heart and a clear way of seeing things. You understand situations that others can't begin to imagine. You're astute, a little too brave, and as I've said before, you're dangerous."

After a few seconds where she just looked at their linked hands, she whispered, "I've had to be."

"I know, and it makes my heart feel trampled."

That got her protesting real fast. "Hey, I don't need you or anyone else to—"

"What? Understand? Care?" The kiss he pressed to her knuckles this time was firmer, lingering. Stark, painful emotion had him closing his eyes as he thought about how easily her small frame could be hurt.

"Hunter?" she asked unsteadily.

Making himself do it, he opened his eyes and looked into

hers, allowing her to see everything he felt, both tenderness and rage. "Do you think any rational, normal person with a fucking heartbeat could possibly *not* care?"

Pragmatic, and a little fascinated, she said, "They shouldn't, not about me."

"Most *especially* about you." He freed her hand and instead cupped her face, drawing her slowly closer. "You don't want to be kissed, but have you ever tried it?"

Instead of alarmed, she half smiled. "Not the way you mean."

"How, then?"

Gaze fixed on his mouth, she shifted closer still. "Reyes has hauled me up and kissed my ear, usually after giving me crap about something. Parrish puts little pecks to my forehead after telling me something I did the right way." Lower, she muttered, "He treats me like he would a grand-daughter or something."

More and more, Hunter was liking this crazy family that had claimed Jodi. "And Kennedy?"

"She knows I'm not big on being touched, but sometimes she'll squeeze me tight and kiss my cheek." Jodi licked her lips. "That's not what you mean, though, right?"

What about the man who'd kept her captive? "Never on the mouth?"

"God, no."

She said it as if repulsed, but she didn't move away. In fact, their shoulders now touched, and with him cupping her face, she was practically in his embrace. "So your family— that's the sum total of your kissing experience?"

"If you want to know about the bastard who locked me away, you should just ask."

"I'd rather you tell me when you want to."

"Fine." Her breathing hitched. Lashes lowering, she turned her cheek more fully into his palm. "The only blessing to him being so twisted and sick is that he didn't see me that way. It wasn't what he wanted. Mostly he just wanted to be cruel."

Very, very softly, Hunter asked, "Is he dead, Jodi?" In the deepest, darkest part of his soul, Hunter hoped someone from the elite family who cared for her had gone one step further and eliminated the bastard—for good.

If not, he'd see to it himself.

"Yeah, he's dead." Her lashes lifted, and her gaze bored into his. "He's dead because I killed him."

IT GOT SO SILENT, Jodi heard her own heartbeat pounding in her ears. It wasn't a normal rhythm, more like each beat clanged into the other until it sounded like a riot going on.

Hunter didn't blink, and he didn't look away. Finally, after drawing a bracing breath, he nodded. "I'm glad."

"Yeah, me, too." Jodi straightened. "It's late and dark, and I should get home."

"Don't go."

Losing her cool, she jerked free of him and asked, *"Why?"*

The explosive question didn't faze him. He didn't change position on the couch, didn't reciprocate her overflow of emotion. "Because I like having you here." Then, slowly, he sat up, too, but he didn't reach for her. "You look ready to punch me, or run, and that has me at a disadvantage since I don't want either to happen."

Punch him? If she tried it, she'd only hurt her hand. "Not planning either, so relax."

He did the opposite of relax. "If you leave, I'll walk you home."

"I can get myself home."

"You could, but it wouldn't change how I'd feel. Not after that stunt at King's house today. Those guys are unpredictable—almost as unpredictable as you are. I don't trust them, so I'd want to see that you were home safe, that you didn't run into a snake or an elk."

"Or Remmy?" she sneered, remembering how he'd disliked the guy for some reason.

He shrugged. "Or any other men King might have on his payroll. You know it's possible."

"If I'm not there," she protested, "they'll go through my stuff."

"If you're there, they might hurt you."

Offended, she said, "I would—"

"I know, I know." He held up a hand. "You'd rip out their hearts, crush their kneecaps, castrate them, et cetera."

She had to pinch her mouth together to keep from grinning. "Something like that, but maybe not that graphic."

"You could hold your own, and they'd probably regret it, but what if things didn't go your way? I'm sorry, Jodi. At this point, I wouldn't get any sleep at all from worrying about you. I'd end up standing at the window, trying to see through the dark and the rain. I might even end up on your porch."

She threw up her hands. "For what reason?"

"To make sure you're safe."

With a dramatic eye roll, she reminded him, "You said you wouldn't do anything I didn't want you to do."

"I didn't mean walking you home—and I think you know it."

After a moment, she grudgingly said, "Yeah, I do."

"Look at it this way—I'd have to wake the dog and he's already comfortable."

When they both turned to look at Turbo, they found him in the same position, but now with one eye open, watching them. Hunter smiled. His dog was goofy, but he wasn't dense.

"So." Hands on his thighs, he asked, "Will you stay?"

Even though she knew what he meant, she asked, "For how long?"

"Why not all night?"

As she considered it, she narrowed her eyes. "What would we do?"

"Finish the movie. Clean up. Anything you want."

That was the crazy part. At the moment, she wasn't sure what she wanted.

"Sleep." To push his advantage while she was listening, he added, "So far we've spent the day together. Why not finish it off together, too?"

God, he was so damn tempting. "Where would I sleep?" *With you?* The thought didn't alarm her like it should have.

"We can share."

Seriously? Jodi felt her eyes go huge. "I've, um, never really slept with anyone." *In any way.*

"I have no problem with the couch if you want to take my bed, though."

Swear to God, she could feel her heartbeat everywhere, in her chest, yes, but also in her clenched abdomen, in the fingertips that wanted to touch him as he'd touched her...

And in places she didn't want to notice.

Stop it. If you stay—what was she thinking?—*it won't be for that.* Allowing him to kiss her hand had been a huge concession. Nice. Stirring in ways she'd never considered before. Reyes's brotherly smooches were one thing, a kiss from Hunter would be altogether different. "I don't have my stuff here."

Taking that for what it was, her giving in, he relaxed. "What stuff do you need?"

"Toothbrush? Laptop, a few more guns..."

"I have an extra toothbrush. Your phone has Wi-Fi, so you can access whatever you need using it." Watching her intently, he asked, "What other weapons would you like? I have several."

"And ammo?"

"Yes."

Figured he would. Hunter wasn't a dummy. She looked around at his comfortable home, trying to think of more excuses but coming up short. "You know what? This would have nothing to do with the *everyday life for the everyday woman.*"

Hunter tried to decipher that, but couldn't. "Come again?"

"That's my motto." If she was staying—and pretty sure she was—she may as well make the most of it. "That's what I'm going for, you know? *Everyday life for the everyday woman.* So far I'm striking out, but I *am* trying."

Immediately, he held out a hand to her. "Trusting me would be another step in that direction."

She already trusted him, to a degree, and that was part of what alarmed her. For much of her life, trust hadn't come easy, with good reason. Then there was Hunter, and as he'd said, from the first *hello*, she'd known he was different. She'd felt it then.

She felt it now.

Part of it was his never-ending patience. He kept his hand out, his expression impassive. If she rejected him, he'd be okay with it. Not mad, not insulted. And if she accepted, he'd be okay with that, too. No assumptions made. No expectations.

With a touch of reluctance, she took his hand and allowed him to tug her down beside him. He even put his arm around her and hugged her into his side. "Now, what have we missed in the movie? Look, the shark just ate someone."

See? That was *so* Hunter. Chuckling, she snuggled a little closer and felt herself relaxing. "You do smell nice."

He went blank for a heartbeat, then said, "You smell pretty nice, too."

"Really?" She'd never noticed. "Maybe it's the shampoo?" She lifted a hank of hair to her nose and inhaled, but she didn't detect anything.

"Take my word for it."

For another twenty minutes, they sat like that, his arm around her, his body warm and firm against her. Every so often, his longer fingers, rough-tipped with calluses, would tease lightly along her arm.

She liked it. She especially liked feeling so snug and secure, like her bones were melting and worries didn't exist and she wasn't Jodi Bentley but someone else. Someone normal.

Someone special...to Hunter.

When she turned her head to peer up at him, he tipped his down and stared back. It took her breath away, how he looked at her. No one had ever looked at her like that. "You said my eyes are nice, but I really like yours. I'm not much for poetry, but if mine are sunshine, yours are midnight. Really dark blue, right before the stars come out. They're alert, but also... I don't know. Attentive?"

He cupped her face again, and God, she loved that. He had such big, capable hands, but they were so gentle with her. His fingers sank into her hair and he gave a small smile. "What am I going to do with you, Jodi?"

Was that supposed to be a serious question? Well, she suddenly had a serious answer, and for some reason, it made her all breathless. "I maybe wouldn't mind if you tried kissing me." The second the words left her mouth, her pulse started rushing, both in fear of humiliating failure, and with scorching expectation.

His gaze dropped to her mouth, and dang if her lips didn't tingle.

Warning him, she added, "As long as we both know it might not go well. If I can't take it, I don't want you to be all grumpy or morose about it."

"I would only kiss you if you wanted me to. 'Not minding' isn't good enough."

What felt like a lifetime stretched by in coiling anticipation. Jodi heard the movie, but it didn't distract her. The shark could have devoured an entire town and she wouldn't have noticed.

Her heart struck her ribs like a sledgehammer. "I am kind of curious. Does that count?"

"Yes." Hunter turned toward her. "It definitely counts."

CHAPTER SEVEN

BRACING HIMSELF FOR possible negative reactions, Hunter eased closer. Jodi had her face upturned, her tawny eyes shining and absorbed. No shying away for her, not with this.

He felt like his whole life hinged on the success of this one kiss. "If you say stop, I will. I swear."

"I know." She tilted closer. Waiting.

Damn. Hunter leaned down and barely brushed his lips over hers. Tentative, light. She didn't move, and she kept her eyes open, watching him, but he felt the rush of her breath, and a slight trembling.

Easing back to assess her, he saw that her lashes were heavy and her cheeks flushed.

"That wasn't horrible."

Slowly, he smiled. "You are so wonderful. Again?"

She nodded and, sounding a little rusty, said, "Might as well."

He was a complete and total goner and he knew it. Somehow this one, small, traumatized woman had bulldozed into his restricted world, demolished his walls and ripped his heart straight out of his chest. It left him overwhelmed, and grateful that he'd found her.

Or she'd found him.

Whatever miracle of mistakes had brought them together, he knew he didn't ever want to let her go.

With his thumb under her chin, he tilted her face slightly

and delivered another chaste kiss, lingering this time, tracing her bottom lip with careful pecks. Gently, he rubbed his mouth over hers, keeping the friction so light that she leaned in, increasing the pressure. Following her lead, he let his lips nibble at hers, and heard her sigh.

Breathing deeper, she sat back and said, "You're good at this."

"What an endorsement."

She grinned. "Hey, I'm surprised. I mean, it was really nice." She swallowed heavily. "Want to do it again?"

"Yes."

She touched her lips, and then she touched his, her fingertips trembling slightly. "You were holding back, though."

"I was." Stringing even two words together seemed far too difficult.

"So how about you kiss me how you want to, and if there's something I don't like, I'll speak up and tell you."

How many ways could one woman tempt him? Hunter put his forehead to hers. "The very last thing I want to do is push too fast."

"You won't."

So much faith. "You're sure you're okay with this?"

"I'm actually pretty excited about it."

Hunter went still, wondering if she meant what he hoped she meant. With Jodi, he could never tell.

Then she expounded, and he had to laugh at himself.

"I figured I'd get kissed and totally freak, you know? I *knew* I was going to hate it. Before now, or maybe before you, it was just…yuck. I wanted no part of it. But now it's like…well…" After floundering for words, and then giving up, she released another soft sigh. "I guess *never* rolled around pretty darned fast, right?"

"I'm glad." Wondering how he'd gotten so lucky to be "the one" she'd find acceptable, Hunter decided he would make every single step of her awakening pleasurable—even if it killed him. He'd go slowly no matter how difficult that might be, and for tonight, he'd limit himself to kissing, and superficial kissing at that. He wouldn't let her tempt him into losing sight of her past.

She lifted her brows, waiting.

"Let's try this." He sat back, sinking comfortably into the couch cushions, and easily levered her onto his lap.

If she noticed his erection, she made no comment, just braced her hands on his shoulders and stared at him expectantly.

Hunter slid a hand around her narrow waist and urged her forward. "Kiss me, Jodi."

Confusion brought her brows together. "I thought you were going to kiss me."

"I will."

Still frowning, she looked at his mouth. "You think I won't? Is this some kind of dare?"

Well, damn. Talk about missing the mark. "I thought that, this way, you could easily move away whenever you wanted."

"Dude, I'm armed. I don't need to be on your lap."

Not laughing was a strain, but he managed it. "How about you don't threaten to shoot me while I'm trying to figure out the best way to do this?"

Now she grumbled, saying, "I didn't mean I *would* shoot you." She slanted him a glare. "I assume you wouldn't give me reason. Otherwise, I'd already be gone."

"I'll do my best." He moved his hand down to her hip. "I like you on my lap. You don't like it?"

"I don't know. Maybe." She looked him over. "It's not bad."

"Okay, so kiss me, and I'll kiss you back, and we'll go from there."

As if they'd ironed out a business contract, she nodded. "Fair enough." For another three beats of his heart, she stared at his mouth, then gradually leaned in until her lips met his. Her hair fell forward, teasing his jaw, the side of his neck. Mimicking his moves from earlier, she kissed his bottom lip, nuzzling his mouth with her own.

As promised, he reciprocated, turning his head and nudging her lips to part. Using his tongue, he touched the corner of her mouth, lightly licked along her lips and teased just inside.

Jodi melted against him, her trim, soft little body naturally reclining in his arms. Though she weighed next to nothing, her natural vitality encompassed him.

While he ordered himself to strict control, the kiss grew hotter, and deeper. They were both breathing hard, tongues twining, and Jodi's hands were starting to roam over his chest when suddenly Turbo joined them on the couch.

Jodi sprang out of his arms so quickly, he lost his hold on her. She fell onto the coffee table, shoved away and landed on the floor. Eyes wide, her hand under her shirt to grab her gun, she breathed brokenly and stared at Turbo.

The dog stared back in confusion, his tail giving a single thump.

She muttered, "Jesus."

"Jodi," Hunter said softly, trying to gather his wits.

She glared at him. "Your dog scared the hell out of me!" Sitting there, her bare legs sprawled, her body shaking, she whispered, "Jesus," again, then ran both hands through her hair. A second later, she was on her knees in front of the couch, hugging Turbo. "I'm sorry, baby. I'm not mad at you."

Confused, Turbo looked to Hunter for help. He reached

over and rubbed the dog's ears. "She's okay, buddy. Just a little turned on and surprised by it."

Jodi laughed. "A lot turned on. I swear, I forgot where I was. I forgot all about Turbo. I forgot you even had a dog." After hugging Turbo again, she stroked his back, and finally stood. "Well, that was a stupid way for me to wrap it up, huh?"

"Nothing about you is ever stupid." Hunter had his own difficulty getting it together. "Probably just as well that we got interrupted, though, because you're not the only one who got a little lost there." He ran a hand over the back of his neck. "Not that I would ever push you—"

"Yeah, I know."

"—but everything felt so natural—"

"It did, didn't it?"

"—that I might have tried something I shouldn't, something I'd already told myself I wouldn't do."

"Like what?"

Figured that while he was desperately trying to regroup, she'd have already recovered and be hitting him with questions. "I'm going to plead the Fifth for now. Since you've decided to stay, what do you say we do whatever we need to do before bed, then try watching the movie again? I often fall asleep doing that, so maybe you will, too."

"I guess I should check on my house."

His gaze sharpened. "I don't want you to go."

"No, I mean through my phone. You're right that I can check the security cameras that way. You have an extra power cord, by the way? I'll set up my phone like I do at home, so it can alert me if any shenanigans happen, like if Remmy or any of King's other men come snooping around."

Hunter didn't think they would, not after they'd just

been out to King's house, but he appreciated her caution. "Sure thing."

A few minutes later, he'd just returned from the bathroom where he'd brushed his teeth and changed into flannel pants, when Jodi's phone dinged.

With no show of alarm, she lifted it, then shook her head. "Madison."

"Is everything okay?"

"Yeah." Jodi rapidly texted a message, waited, then grinned. "She asked why I wasn't at home, so I told her I was staying here with you."

Damn. Hunter wasn't sure how he felt about his every move being scrutinized. "How'd she take that?"

She showed him the screen, where Madison replied, You go girl!

"She's probably messaging Reyes right now, and—" Her phone dinged again. Rolling her eyes, Jodi read it, then laughed. "He said he's proud of me. I sent him back the finger emoji. I bet he's running to tell Kennedy right now." Another ding.

Hunter folded his arms and waited. When Jodi's face softened, he figured Kennedy had said something nice. Damn, he was glad Jodi had these over-the-top protective people in her life.

"You want to brush your teeth while I take Turbo out one more time?" The dog immediately perked up.

"I'd rather go with you while you do that, then get ready. Is that okay?"

Hunter was pretty sure anything she wanted to do would be okay with him. On impulse, he stepped forward and, moving slowly so he wouldn't startle her, bent to take her mouth in a soft kiss. He knew why she wanted to stick close, and he was glad of it. If she was in the bathroom while he was outside, that'd mean the door was unlocked, and Jodi didn't take chances. "I'd prefer that, too." Making her feel safe was now his top priority.

Soon enough she'd figure out that she couldn't have the *everyday life for the everyday woman*—because Jodi wasn't an everyday type of person. As he'd told her, she was extraordinary...and he loved that about her.

Now she only needed to love herself.

"WHAT DO YOU MEAN, she didn't take the job?"

It was nearing midnight, but according to King, it was the first moment he'd had to spare. God only knew what had occupied him all day. Probably something shady, Remmy thought, but the less he knew about Russ King, the more easily he could sleep at night.

"She didn't exactly turn it down. She's still considering it, I think." For once, Remmy saw King without Danny Giggs involved. According to King, Danny was on an errand tending *other matters*.

"You were supposed to convince her. Guess I overestimated your appeal."

Remmy shrugged. The bigger point was that in a hundred different ways, King had underestimated Jodi. "Eventually, she'll take the job." She was far too curious not to. Add to that, she seemed to feel challenged, and Remmy was pretty sure he wouldn't be able to redirect her, even if he gave her all the actual deets. In fact, knowing just how vile King really was might seal the deal for her. The little dynamo—and he did mean *little*—liked to bludgeon everyone with her attitude. She had great instincts, was far too damned daring, and overall, it was obvious that she considered herself invincible.

Except for that moment at the back of Worth's showroom. Alone with him, she'd realized the danger and had bristled because of it. He'd literally felt her agitation. Oddly enough, it not only made him want her more, it made him want to protect her, too.

Whatever experiences had carved Jodi Bentley into the dangerous personality she was now, they had to have been unpleasant.

"So what the fuck use are you?"

Remmy paid no attention to King's growl. He'd learned to read the man and knew when he was spouting off for show, and when he was actually pissed. Besides, if it came down to it, he would demolish King without breaking a sweat. The biggest advantage the man had over most was his standing of power. Since Remmy didn't give a shit about that, King could kiss his ass.

"For one thing," he said, "she's not quite as antagonistic with me as she is with Danny. She doesn't trust me, pretty sure she doesn't trust anyone, but at least she'll speak to me. When she looks at Danny, it's like she'd rather gut him than acknowledge him."

King smiled. "Yeah, Danny has that effect on a lot of people. Usually it's to my advantage, but apparently not with this pain-in-the-ass girl." He swirled his drink. "Wonder what her holdup is?"

"She's smart." That was the biggest holdup…and the fact that Remmy had already warned her, *if* his warning had even been necessary. He had a feeling not much got by Jodi. "There's another issue."

Sighing, King propped a hip against a table and downed the rest of his drink. "Let's hear it."

"The big guy—her neighbor—claims he's working for her now. If she does take the job, she'll have him with her." *She won't be one small woman alone.* That part relieved

Remmy. "He drove her when she came by earlier to check out your grounds."

King snorted. "The stupid girl stayed on the road. She couldn't even see the scope of the job. Did you tell her what I'd pay her?"

"She didn't really give me a chance, but I'd already explained that you'd be generous."

"Find her," King said. "Go to her fucking shack if you have to. Give her an astronomical sum that she can't turn down."

"And the big guy?" Remmy asked.

"Let me worry about him."

Not what Remmy wanted to hear. He had a feeling Jodi would go ballistic if anything happened to the guy. It was almost humorous seeing the two of them acting all protective of each other. Humorous—and annoying. Remmy wanted a little time with Jodi himself, and that couldn't happen with both Danny and the hulking neighbor hanging around.

He was a good judge of people. Danny he could handle. The neighbor? That one carried himself like he'd take on an army and enjoy it. He had ability, he sure as hell had strength, and the look in his eyes… Yeah, given a preference, Remmy would rather not tangle with him.

Getting back on track, he asked with mild interest, "Plan to have him killed?"

Bragging, because there were few things King enjoyed more, other than money and brutality, he said, "If it was necessary, of course I would." He smirked at Remmy. "You wouldn't balk at that, would you?"

Feigning nonchalance, Remmy lifted a shoulder. "I do what I'm paid to do," he lied, because yeah, he'd have a big fucking problem with it.

"Good. Not necessary, though. I have another idea."

Holding out his hands as if he had the answer to world hunger, he said, "Worth can order more work on his fucking baby."

"Worth has a baby?" Everything inside Remmy clenched.

Finding his reaction hilarious, King guffawed. When he finished laughing, he explained, "His stupid '73 Corvette. He treats that car better than he does any person alive. Hunter Osborn, the neighbor and current asshole in my way, works on vintage cars."

"What if Worth doesn't want anything else done to the 'vette?" Remmy tried to think fast. "I know you have a stranglehold on him—" and more power to him with that "—but if his car is that important to him, Worth might resist that idea."

"Good point." King gave a small smile. "I knew there was at least one reason I kept you around."

Ignoring the gibe, Remmy said, "I have a suggestion. Buy an old car that needs a lot of work and keep Hunter so busy, he won't have time to get in your way." *Or* my *way*.

Looking struck by the thought, King nodded. "I like it. I'll talk to Worth and see if he has a contact. Maybe I'll even create an offer for the car that Worth can't resist, just to keep me in the clear. In the meantime, visit the girl, pressure her in whatever way you see fit but get her to accept the job."

"I can do that more easily without Danny around." He didn't particularly want Danny's death on his conscience, and telling the boss what a fuckup Danny was could have that exact result, but either way, Remmy didn't want him around Jodi.

As if reading his thoughts, King smiled again. "For now, he sticks with you. Except for tomorrow." Straightening from the table, King poured another drink. "Tomorrow, you will visit her at home, and if the opportunity arrives to fuck her, take it."

Hoping he meant that literally and not figuratively, Remmy said, "Not a problem."

"Once that's done, convince her to take the job. After she's here, I'll handle the rest."

Remmy wouldn't mind getting Jodi into bed—but he had serious doubts that it would happen anytime soon. As to King handling anything… No. He couldn't let that happen.

For now, he wanted out of King's house, off his grounds and as far from the prick as he could possibly get.

"YOU'RE NOT SLEEPING," Hunter said without opening his eyes.

"Yeah, well, neither are you." For her part, Jodi didn't want to miss a thing. This had been the most wonderful, awesome day of her entire life. Not the most impactful— no, that had been the day she'd escaped. But for fun? For heart-thumping excitement? Couldn't beat making out with Hunter Osborn, and then curling up against his big, hot body on the couch while watching one movie after another. She didn't want any of it to end.

She rested against Hunter's left side, his arm around her, her cheek on his chest, her legs stretched out on the couch. Turbo had curled up close behind her, with his head practically lodged against her butt. Hunter, the only one upright, had his legs out on the coffee table, his head slumped into the corner of the couch. He'd put a light quilt over her, but all that covered him was a soft cotton T-shirt and even softer flannel pants. Who knew a man's body felt so good through cotton? She wouldn't mind feeling him without it in the way, but that'd probably lead to more than she could handle—at least for now.

"I can't sleep," Hunter grumbled. "I keep thinking about your family."

He referred to them as her family so confidently that she felt she should make it clear. "I told you they're not *really* my family." They were just wonderful people who'd felt the need to help her.

"As good as," he replied. "They love you and that's what really matters. So what'd Parrish do that irked you so much?"

Sneakily drawing a breath of his awesome scent, Jodi tipped her face up. "I actually respect Parrish a lot. He's bossy, but usually that's a good thing because he keeps order and sets things right and makes sure people are…"

"Safe?"

"Yeah, that. He's also generous. *Too* generous."

"And that bugs you?"

"Eh, sometimes. When the generosity is aimed at me, I guess. I don't want him to see me as someone who needs it, you know?" She wanted Parrish to give her the same respect that he gave his sons and daughter. She may as well have wished for a trip to the moon. Parrish—heck, all the McKenzies—knew deep down she was still—

"News flash, honey," Hunter said, interrupting her thoughts. "Everyone needs help now and then."

"Unfortunately, I needed it more than most."

"Through no fault of your own."

"Actually, that's not entirely true." Telling her innermost thoughts while snuggled against Hunter wasn't nearly as awful as when she had to look him in the eyes. And even then, it was tolerable, at least more so than with anyone else. "I'd gotten in the habit of helping women who needed it, Kennedy especially. She was my first real friend after…" No, she wouldn't go into her awful ordeal again, so instead, she said simply, *"After,"* and figured that was explanation enough.

Given the gentle squeeze Hunter gave her, it was.

"It made me feel useful to watch her back, but then some serious stuff went down."

Hunter stirred. "How serious?"

"People were trying to kill her, mostly because she knew me." Jodi shook her head. It was all too convoluted. "That guy I escaped? He had a deranged brother who seriously wanted to see me suffer for giving his lousy excuse of a sibling what he deserved."

Hunter silently watched her now, without censure but with keen interest and a quiet rage. Yup, the rage was an appropriate response, far as she was concerned.

"I didn't know Kennedy had gone to Reyes for help, and when I found out, I didn't trust him either."

Wearing a slight frown, Hunter said, "Trust is an issue for you. I get that."

"I'm glad, but Reyes sure didn't get it, and he definitely didn't trust me. Especially after I sort of tripped them up. None of them liked that."

"The McKenzies?" he asked.

"Yeah. They were plenty peeved—mostly because they thought I might get hurt." It still confused Jodi, how total strangers had looked at her and…cared. "It didn't make any sense," she whispered.

"It made perfect sense," he countered, tipping her face up for a too-brief, very soft kiss.

Relishing the warmth of Hunter's chest and how indescribably nice it felt to touch so much of him, she explained, "They put me in this crazy, posh hotel—a whole freaking suite of rooms, like the penthouse or something—and covered whatever I wanted. Food, different clothes…" She remembered, and wanted to wince because she'd felt so lost. "I swear, I could hear my voice echo, and I had this amazing view out the windows." A view she couldn't bear.

"You wouldn't like that for long."

Knowing that he understood her, Jodi felt warmed from the inside out. "I didn't like it at all. Not a single second of it. I didn't belong there. I didn't even come close to fitting in with all the swanky stuff."

"Few people would."

"I like your house a lot more. Heck, I like my house a lot more."

Hunter smiled, and she badly wanted to kiss him again. It had to be midnight, they'd spent the whole day together, and it wasn't enough.

Jodi wondered what would be enough, and when she couldn't find an answer, it put her on edge. Already she'd shared her deepest, darkest secrets with Hunter...and yet she knew very little about his past. She knew he'd suffered something that made time alone a necessity. He'd cut out his own family, even though she could tell he loved them. But the vital stuff? *His* deep, dark secrets? He'd kept those to himself.

That could only mean one thing: she was far more invested in their friendship than he was. Dumb. She knew better than to rely too much on others, but somehow Hunter had gotten past her guard, and now she was...vulnerable. *Screw that.*

"Go on," he prompted. "Then what happened?"

Tomorrow, she silently vowed, she would keep her distance, even though that decision made her start missing him right now. It was still the smart, safe thing to do. "Kennedy wanted me protected, and her guy, Reyes... He made some good points."

"How so?"

Grinning, Jodi admitted, "Basically, he shamed me for being so petty, and unlike Kennedy, who is sweet and gentle, he insisted that I had to knock off the stupid shit and *care*."

Appearing satisfied, Hunter stated, "About yourself."

"Yeah." And she was trying. She really was. "Then Parrish, that overbearing, bighearted, superior king of badasses..." The teasing comment trailed off. She had so much gratitude for Parrish, sometimes she couldn't find words to cover it. "He showed me a better way to help women, one that would also improve my own life in the bargain."

"Because," Hunter stressed, "your life matters."

He stated that firmly, with so much conviction. Unlike when others said it, she liked hearing it from him. That, too, was dangerous. "Yeah."

"Jodi..."

With her decision made, she no longer felt like chatting, so she forced a big yawn that turned into the real thing. "I'm wore out. I'll try to sleep if you do."

He considered her for a long moment, then reluctantly nodded. Shifting around until he had one leg on the couch, the other over the side, he pulled her higher against him and she ended up half sprawled over his upper body. *No problem.* In the current position, she was super comfy.

Turbo grumbled, but he repositioned, too, and Jodi ended up sandwiched between them. She heard Hunter's steady heartbeat under her ear and felt the strength of his chest beneath her palm. His arms were loosely draped around her, his hands at the small of her back. Some of Turbo's weight rested on her hip, but she didn't mind.

These two guys, man and dog, were fast becoming her favorite companions.

Tomorrow, she promised herself, she'd get her head together and readjust her priorities. For tonight, she just drifted to sleep.

HUNTER CHOPPED WOOD with a vengeance, but it didn't help.

Place the wood, swing the ax, move the neatly split pieces into the pile.

Think about Jodi… Repeat.

With the evening sun on his bare shoulders and back, he felt sweat drip, and he felt the turmoil in his brain.

Damn it, she confused him.

Sleeping with her had gone better than he'd expected. She'd awakened him with a kiss, her hair draping either side of his face, one of his hands inadvertently resting on her small but perfect ass.

Jodi hadn't seemed to mind. With her palms framing his face, she'd nuzzled into the kiss with a near desperation that had him drawing her a little closer, holding her tighter—and then she'd abandoned him for the bathroom. When she'd emerged, she was ready to go and no amount of fast talking on his part had dissuaded her.

Claiming the night had been *awesome*, that she'd slept better than she could ever remember, she'd stepped outside and called negligently, "Later, gator," and that was that.

Both he and Turbo had stood at the window, watching her stride up the road to her property. He'd grabbed the binoculars to ensure she got inside, that everything was still secure, and then…he'd gotten irked.

Two hours had passed before he'd heard her truck and stepped outside. She'd been polite, stopping to tell him she was heading into town for cleanup from the storm. Plenty of businesses needed fallen limbs and messy debris removed from their storefronts. She'd smiled and asked if he needed anything while she was in town.

Unsure what to say or do, for once unable to read her, Hunter had asked about dinner, but she'd declined, saying she'd likely just grab something in between jobs.

Hadn't been easy, but he'd resisted asking when she might be back. Her pleasant expression couldn't conceal a cooled attitude. What it meant, he couldn't guess.

He'd had his own yard cleanup to do, but luckily the chickens had hunkered down in their coop, none the worse from the storm. They were now happily attacking bugs and worms that had risen to the surface of the dirt within their enclosure.

With his lead connected to a grommet on the chicken coop, Turbo slept peacefully in the sun. He was used to Hunter chopping wood in the early evening.

Hunter kept going over it again and again. During the night he'd heard Jodi's breathing even into sleep and felt the heaviness of her limbs that proved she was truly out. He'd dozed off and on, waking to ensure she was still there, that she was settled.

That she was safe.

She'd awakened several times, too. Though she didn't move or make a sound, he'd felt it whenever she'd stirred. She'd go alert, listening, waiting for God knew what, and then she'd relax again, only to repeat the procedure every hour or so.

In so many ways, it had felt right keeping her that close.

At least to him. Apparently, not to her—but then, Jodi was different, from other women, from every other person he knew…even from himself. How she dealt with trauma was unique. His head told him that he had to let her figure it out.

His gut told him something altogether different.

Long after her work hours should have ended, she finally returned. He heard her truck again—the one consolation to having her live so close. He stepped to the side yard and saw her drive by. She didn't stop, and he didn't bother waving her down.

Now, with every beat of his heart, he fought the urge to go after her.

He was just bringing the ax down hard, his muscles flexed, when Turbo burst into a state of alarm by croaking and howling and jumping. Deliberately, Hunter sank the ax into the stump and reached for his discarded shirt, using it to swipe the sweat off his face. "Easy," he told Turbo, and wondered if Jodi had managed a change of heart all on her own.

Taking the dog into the house, he secured the back door and headed for the front, reaching it just as a heavy knock sounded.

No, that wouldn't be Jodi. Her knock, a sort of *rap-rap-rap*, had sounded entirely different from the heavy thump hitting his door. What the fuck? No one came to his house. No one dared. He looked out a window...and saw Worth Linlow.

Glad to have a target for his simmering discontent, Hunter jerked open the door and glared.

Worth automatically took a step back before he caught himself. Then he tried on a smile and came forward again. "Hunter." He made a point of looking around. "Damn nice spread you have here."

"Did you not see the No Trespassing signs? Several of them?"

"Well, sure." Uncertain now, Worth tucked his hands into his slacks. "Figured those were for strangers and solicitors."

"They're for everyone—and you know that."

"Sorry, I don't mean to show up unannounced."

Yet that's exactly what he'd done. Hunter knew there

had to be a reason, and whatever it was, he didn't like it. "What do you want?"

Trying to sound jovial, Worth said, "Fuck you, too, buddy. Guess you had a bad day with the storm?"

"My day was fine." His day had been totally fucked. "I've made it clear to you and everyone else that I don't accept people on my property."

"I know, but it's not like you're burying bodies out here, right?"

Hunter narrowed his eyes. "You have one minute."

"Right." Worth cleared his throat. "Can I come in?"

For an answer, Hunter held on to the door with one hand and propped his shoulder on the frame, making sure Turbo couldn't get around him. His dog loved everyone, with few exceptions—and Worth was one of them. Turbo was trying his damnedest to push past Hunter's legs. To do what, Hunter couldn't guess. Since he'd had him, Turbo had never bitten anyone.

"Fine, I'll get right to it. I bought another car." Looking proud of himself, Worth rocked back on his heels. "I've had my eye on a '65 Mustang Cobra for a while now. Surprisingly, the guy just sold it to me for way less than he had been asking. Interior is in great shape, but the body could use a little work. I figure after you do your thing, it'll be prime. What do you say?"

"I say you could have called me as you've done in the past. Why show up in person?"

"I was in the area."

"What area is that?"

"Look, I was driving by after paying for the car. Is it that big of a deal? Jesus, get a grip." Reverting to form, Worth growled, "It'll be delivered to me tomorrow, so tell me you'll come by and give me a price and I'll get out of here."

"I'll come by and give you a price."

"When?"

"I'll call you when I figure it out."

"Great, thanks." Throwing up his hands, Worth turned to go, his heavy stride making it clear that he was now pissed, too, not that Hunter cared. On any given day, he would have set Worth straight about showing up where he shouldn't be, where Hunter did not want him or anyone else, but today? He'd picked the worst possible time to prick Hunter's temper.

Reaching his SUV, the vehicle Worth drove for everyday use, he dropped into the driver's seat and slammed the door. Leaving far too much dust in his wake, he backed quickly out of the drive and then accelerated back toward town.

Glad that was over, Hunter turned and Turbo shot past him. It wasn't Worth's retreating vehicle that the dog headed for, though. No, Turbo was charging as fast as a chubby basset-beagle hound could go—straight for Jodi's place. It took Hunter only a glance to realize why.

A man stood just outside the woods, heading toward Jodi's front porch.

He recognized the build, and the blond hair... Remmy Gardner.

Shit had just gotten real.

Cursing, Hunter stepped back inside to grab his keys and Turbo's leash, then locked the door and took off in a sprint. As he ran, he dug his cell phone from his pocket and called Jodi.

She answered on the first ring. "I see him."

"Well, Turbo got loose. He's headed your way."

The phone disconnected, and a second later, Jodi stepped out of the house. She held a Glock in one hand, and even from several yards away, Hunter saw her practically vibrating with menace. Striding out to the yard, she said to Remmy, "Not another step," and then to Turbo, "Come here, buddy."

Turbo didn't listen. With his ears flopping and his butt bouncing, he headed straight for Remmy.

Damn it. Hunter called out, *"Stop,"* and wonder of wonders, Turbo actually obeyed. Sure, he was great at most commands, but that one hadn't always been successful.

Jodi reached the dog before he did, and she hooked a hand in his collar while glaring at Remmy. "What are you doing here?"

Deadpan, his gaze on Hunter, Remmy said, "Scaring dogs and neighbors, apparently."

Not in the mood for more bullshit, his temper rapidly fraying, Hunter went past Jodi until he stood mere inches from Remmy. "What," he snarled low, "are you fucking doing cutting through the woods?"

Remmy sized him up. "I came to visit Jodi, not that it's any of your business."

Wrong thing to say to a man on the ragged edge. Hunter took another step until only a breath separated them. "You figured skulking through the woods like a chickenshit was better than driving?"

"You," Remmy replied evenly, not backing down, "have fucking No Trespassing signs on the only road in here."

Jodi said, "I ignored those." Then to Hunter, "Leash?"

He felt a tug and realized he had Turbo's leash caught tight in his clenched fist. It took a lot of effort, but he got his fingers to loosen.

"There ya go," she said, as if praising Hunter for his control. "Turbo could use a few reassuring words. Poor boy wore himself out."

Damn it, he didn't want to act like a berserker. He stared

hard at Remmy until finally the bastard lifted his hands and retreated. "Farther," Hunter demanded.

With a rough laugh, Remmy took five more steps back. "Now may I live?"

"I'm still undecided." With the other man far enough away, Hunter gave quick attention to the dog.

Turbo continued to sit obediently, but he was badly huffing, his tongue hanging out and his sides bellowing. "Good boy." He patted Turbo's shoulder gently. "Take it easy, now."

Jodi gave Hunter a long look. "Why don't you take him inside and get him some water?"

"No, but you should feel free."

She rolled her eyes. "You'd let the poor dog suffer?"

"Would you?" If she thought for even a single second that he'd leave her alone with that bastard, she obviously didn't know him at all.

Remmy laughed. "We could all go in—"

Interrupting him, Hunter said, "He's begging to be flattened."

"And you're begging to do it. But," she stressed, "you will both behave or I'll start shooting people and then think how upset Turbo will be."

Ignoring all that, Remmy said low, "I have to talk with you."

"You saw me in town," Jodi said dismissively. "Could've talked to me then."

What. The. Fuck. So she and Remmy had visited while she was working? He frowned, which clearly surprised her, but instead of reacting with anger, she gave a small shake of her head.

Her idea of reassurance? It didn't work. He was still too pissed.

Remmy said, "With half the town watching and listening in? No, not a good idea." He glanced at Hunter, looked like he didn't really care if he listened, and said, "I need to talk to you in private."

Hunter took a step—and Jodi moved in front of him. With her back to Remmy! Did she trust the guy? If so, that'd be too bad, because Hunter didn't trust him at all.

Putting a hand on his bare chest and smiling up at him, Jodi whispered, "You seriously need to take a chill pill."

He seriously needed her.

Damn, just having her small, warm palm on his skin left him primed. Last night made him want more. More time with her, more touching her and tasting her.

More trust.

And instead, she'd taken off.

Remmy waited, one brow lifted, arms crossed.

Smug prick. She was right, though. Ripping off Remmy's head wouldn't give him any answers. "What are you doing here?" he asked more evenly, which earned him another sweet smile from Jodi and a quick pat on the shoulder.

"It occurs to me that you're not working for her." Remmy dropped his arms. "You weren't with her in town, and the place was a mess. An employee would have been along for the cleanup."

"We had our own messes here," Jodi said. "Divide and conquer, you know?"

"And," Remmy continued to her, "he doesn't act like an employee."

"Fuck off," Hunter said, his tone succinct.

With a truly exaggerated eye roll and a huff of frustration, Jodi faced him again. "My property. My rules. Let me handle it."

Hunter returned her look with an expression of *not happening.*

Watching them, Remmy ran a hand over his face. "So here's the thing." He glanced at Turbo, frowned and said, "Seriously, someone take care of that dog before he drops over. Go together if you want. I'll stand right here."

Hunter looked at Jodi, waiting.

Jodi muttered, "Fine," then added to Remmy, "Right there, understood? Not on my porch, not on the driveway and not looking in a window."

Remmy, the bastard, grinned and crossed his heart.

Together, with Hunter making certain that Jodi went first, they headed in, Turbo happily lumbering behind them.

The second they were inside and Jodi had secured the door, Hunter turned and kissed her. He needed it, whether she did or not.

To his surprise, she didn't fight him. In fact, after sticking her gun in the waistband of her shorts, she grabbed his face and returned the kiss wholeheartedly, even going onto her tiptoes and leaning into his chest…for five seconds.

Releasing him, she touched her fingertips to his mouth, his jaw, then down along his chest until her hand fell away. "Dog first." She lazily strode to the kitchen, no more worried about keeping Remmy waiting than he was. "Your asinine behavior second," she decided. "And Remmy third."

"How about Remmy not at all?" Hunter stalked after her. "I could send him off in a way that he won't be back."

Grinning, she set down a bowl of water. "I believe you, but now I need to know what private stuff he wants to say."

Yeah, much as he hated to admit it, Hunter was a little curious himself why Remmy would dare show up here. He'd met Jodi, so he had to know exactly how she'd react. If by *private*, he meant he wanted to come on to her, he was going about it all wrong. If it hadn't been for the dog, he imagined Jodi's reaction to Remmy would have surpassed Hunter's to Worth.

And come to think of it, were those two aligned? Seemed more than possible.

Turbo did take a few drinks, but clearly his biggest issue had been worry. Looking back and forth between the humans, apparently satisfied now that Hunter and Jodi were together, he licked the dripping water from his chops and ambled out of the room.

Hunter warned her, "He's going for your bed, you know."

Eyes widening, she grabbed the dish towel and raced after him. Hunter stepped into the hall to watch and saw her when she came out of the room, carrying the dish towel between finger and thumb. She pitched it into the utility room toward the washer. Feeling a special kind of peace, he smiled.

Jodi swiped her hands over the seat of her shorts. "Got the slobber off him before he soaked my pillow."

"Glad to hear it."

She stopped in front of him. "He's already sawing logs."

By sheer force of will, Hunter resisted touching her. A long day of working in the sun had left her cheeks, brow and the tip of her nose shiny pink. Her hair, caught up in a high, loose ponytail, was a little sweaty, telling him that she hadn't yet had time to shower. She smelled earthy, and his cock twitched at the scent while his heart drummed with the need to gather her close.

Sighing, she dropped against him, her forehead to his chest. "This is dumb, but I can't seem to help myself."

Closing his eyes in relief, Hunter wrapped his arms around her, silently vowing she'd always be safe with him. "Nothing between us is dumb."

"Says the man who hasn't bared his soul."

Immediately, Hunter clasped her shoulders and held her back, his gaze searching hers. *Of course* she wanted them on equal footing. How could he have been so blind? Jodi had shared so much with him, and he'd shut her down anytime the questions had veered his way. Grossly unfair, and it was past time he stopped doing that. "I'm sorry."

"Yeah, well, we can go into that soon, but right now I'm thinking if we go outside to talk to Remmy, Turbo is going to lose his ever-lovin' mind again, when he's only just gotten to sleep."

Very true. Turbo had shown that he was extremely protective of Jodi. "How about I go out and—"

"Thanks, but no." She lifted a brow. "I have a feeling you'd use any excuse to attack him."

"What if I only hit him once?"

Half smiling, Jodi lifted his hand, looked at his knuckles and said, "Once might be all it'd take. We need his mouth intact, remember?"

He could punch him in the gut, but Hunter kept that to himself.

"I assume you won't wrap up the caveman act and wait in here while I—"

Tossing her words back at her, he said, "Thank you, but no."

She grinned. "So I guess I have to let him in."

Hunter hated that idea most of all. "Fuck."

"Hey, I'm trying not to curse, so rein it in before you tempt me."

In so many ways, she softened his heart. "I can do that." Sometimes, though, *fuck* was the only noun, adjective or adverb that worked for him, and now was that time. "If he does anything he shouldn't, I'm mangling him."

"Get in line." Jodi opened the door with Hunter right

behind her. Remmy stood there, hands on his hips, his eyes narrowed at how long they'd made him wait. "You may as well come in."

He dropped his arms. "Finally." With long strides, he came across the yard, bounded up to the porch and stepped through the door. Immediately, he glanced around with interest. "Damn. It looks totally different."

"Meaning you've been in here?" Hunter asked, ready to dismember him for admitting as much.

"Several times, actually." He zeroed in on Jodi. "Could we sit?"

With a roll of her shoulder, she led him into the kitchen, indicated a chair, and once Remmy dropped into it, she leaned back against the counter. Grinning to himself, Hunter stood beside her, watching as Remmy realized he'd be the only one sitting.

He looked at Jodi, then at Hunter—and the dick dared to be amused. "I'm almost sorry that I can't do things King's way."

"What way is that?" Jodi asked.

"Get you in bed, soften you up and then deliver you to him."

Hunter's fist hit him so fast, Remmy didn't have time to duck. The chair crashed back and he sprawled over the floor, dazed.

"Hunter," Jodi complained, but she didn't look overly bothered by the violence.

"Son of a bitch." Slowly, Remmy got back to his feet, his shoulders bunched, his eyes hard. He rubbed his jaw, then widened his stance and faced Hunter. "Try that again," he dared.

Smiling, Hunter hit him again. This time he got the gut punch and dropped to his knees with a wheezing groan.

Jodi glared at him. "Got that out of your system?"

"No." He badly wanted to take the other man apart.

"You're disturbing the dog," she complained.

They all looked over to where Turbo stood, his gaze slumberous and not all that interested in seeing Remmy on the floor.

Hunter shrugged. "As long as neither of us are upset, he doesn't seem to care what I do. Remember, Turbo didn't like the prick either."

As Remmy got back to his feet once more, he muttered, "Christ, you're fast, and you hit like a fucking cannonball."

"It was a stupid thing to say," Jodi pointed out. Then to Hunter, she added, "Seriously, no more, though. I don't want to prolong this visit."

Bored with it all and seeing that Hunter was fine, Turbo headed back to bed.

While Jodi laughed, Remmy released a pained breath.

"If you have something to say," Hunter warned, "say it."

Remmy held up a hand. "Understand, I said that was *King's* way. Obviously, that won't work—as much because of my conscience as the fact that I actually like her."

Beyond provoked, Hunter started to move, but Jodi put a hand on his arm, so he relented. After all, he'd gotten to hit the dick twice.

"That's actually why I'm here," Remmy explained.

"To warn me?" Jodi asked with doubt.

He shrugged. "And to clue you in on just how danger-ous Russ King can be."

CHAPTER EIGHT

GLAD THAT HUNTER had gotten control of himself, Jodi reluctantly took the seat opposite Remmy. She removed the gun from the back of her shorts and, holding it, crossed her arms on the table. If she needed to, she could shoot Remmy before he moved an inch. "Let's hear it."

"So we're clear, I work for King, and I don't mind making his idiot associates pay up when they're due, or enforcing rules with his redneck buddies, but I draw the line at hurting women."

Very softly, Jodi said, "Try hurting me, and you'll be eating bullets."

He glanced at Hunter, who stayed silent. With his aggrieved attention back on Jodi, he frowned. "I just said I wouldn't."

"Because you have some hidden morality, or because you realized it might not be as easy as you first thought?"

His brows gathered together even more. With an insulting laugh, he sat back in his seat. "You've got brass, I'll give you that. I even admire it. But I hope like hell you don't go around challenging the likes of King or his ilk."

Hunter straightened again.

He'd impressed her. Jodi wasn't sure she'd ever seen anyone move with that kind of speed, or hit with that much accuracy and power. Oddly, she liked it, even though she could have handled Remmy on her own. "Don't tell me you're worried for me."

"Yes, damn it! Whatever skill you have with that gun, you're still just a woman, and a tiny one at that."

Hunter whistled. "You deserve whatever she does to you."

Ignoring him, even though she appreciated the sentiment, Jodi smiled. "Some men are so stupid. See, I'm *really* good with my gun, and I know when I need it. I see someone like you, and even before you open your mouth, I know you. I know how you operate. You think you're the first *man* to threaten me? You think I haven't survived worse than you?" When he glanced uneasily at Hunter again, she said, "Don't look to Hunter. He's protective, but he knows I won't hesitate to end you if it comes to that, so again, if you have a point to make, I suggest you get to it before I lose my patience."

This time when he turned to Hunter, it was with sympathy. "I don't envy you, dude."

Hunter shrugged. "Proves her point, that you're an idiot."

Remmy grinned. "Yeah, maybe." He rubbed his bruised jaw, then flexed it a few times. "I won't go into details, but I can tell you that King is sick. You're on his radar now. He wants you—for what exactly, I don't know, but I'm sure it won't be pleasant. His mind is twisted and he doesn't know what it means to let something go."

"Why me?" Jodi asked.

Another laugh. "Seriously? You don't know what a stir you've caused?"

"I haven't done anything." She was trying to have the everyday life for the everyday… *Screw it.* Who was she kidding? That life wasn't for her. Not yet, anyway.

Now *she* glanced at Hunter, because whatever her life might be, she couldn't help wanting him to be a part of it.

"I told you," Hunter said evenly. "You show up and people take notice." Remaining awesomely on alert, he narrowed his eyes, ready to rip Remmy apart with the least provocation. "Especially men."

"Yeah, you did, but I don't get it." She wasn't that pretty—or at least, she didn't think so. She was still a bit on the scrawny side…only not as much as she used to be. She didn't try. Didn't fuss with her hair or wear makeup or polish her nails. Her clothes were for comfort, and to conceal her weapons. Gaining that kind of attention from a guy, well, she'd never wanted it—except with Hunter.

Remmy, even being so gorgeous, left her cold.

In a mere flash of a second, she realized that with Hunter, it was the whole package, the strong bod, the handsome face and insightful eyes, and that *link*, that thing that told her he was an incredibly good man, yet somehow, in some way, he was also like her.

She wanted him.

No, she didn't like that idea much at all. Whatever had driven Hunter to seek a solitary life on the outskirts of an unknown town, her presence wouldn't help things. Yet she knew, he wanted her, too.

All the confusion she'd felt last night melded into acceptance, and that helped to give her clarity.

"So how did I end up on King's radar? Have anything to do with you and that malicious pal of yours snooping around my property?"

Holding up his hands, Remmy said, "He's not a pal, but yeah, that was me with Danny Giggs. At the time, we didn't know you'd moved in. Last we'd been out here, the house was empty."

Obviously, they had some interest in her property. But what? "Don't stop now," Jodi said. "I'm all ears."

"No," he corrected. "You're all attitude, and it's wasted on me."

Smiling, she tapped the muzzle of the Glock on the table.

Remmy folded his arms on the table and sat forward. "This house was empty for a long time." He glanced at Hunter. "He can tell you that."

"Long enough that I figured it should be condemned."

"Looked that way from the outside," Remmy confirmed. "Inside, though, it was still solid."

Hunter shifted. "So King's been using the house for something? And now that Jodi's here, he somehow feels slighted?"

"In his mind, she stole from him. Or at least, she disrupted his plans. Either is a cardinal sin to a man used to power and doling out punishment. What's odd is that she's in his way, yet he wanted to play with her—his words, not mine."

"In his way for what?" Jodi asked, not all that concerned about the warped mind of a madman. What she needed to know was his intent, and what he had planned for her.

Remmy shook his head. "Don't bother prodding me for details. I was only ordered to keep watch. Each time I was here, I stood in the doorway while Danny came inside. He hid…something, somewhere. The last time, we came to retrieve whatever it is, but then I realized you'd moved in. That changed things for me and I called it off."

"You expect me to believe that?" Jodi asked.

"Do or don't, it's the truth. I've been with King short-term, a month or so before you got here. He likes my ability, but he doesn't confide in me, not yet. He tests me constantly by saying shit he might do, or asking if I would do it for him. Telling me to screw you is another test."

Jodi said, "Ha."

Insulted, he said, "I get it, okay? Don't drive it into the ground. I came here to warn you, then I'm taking off."

"Taking off?" Jodi repeated.

"I'm done with King. He's unhinged, more so every day, and Giggs is even worse. I don't trust either of them, and neither should you. Not for a single second."

"If you can't tell us King's connection to the property, why bother coming here at all? You could have called."

"King might be keeping tabs on me. He told me to come here, so I did. Hopefully, that'll buy me enough time to get out of here alive." His expression softened and he leaned forward. "It's not safe for you to be here."

Not giving an inch, and nowhere near ready to trust Remmy, Jodi said, "Actually, it's not safe for anyone who tries to break in. I shoot to kill."

"You're a smart woman, Jodi. Stop being so unreasonable."

"I'm not sure I like how you use my name."

"I *know* I don't like it," Hunter growled.

Remmy glared at them both. "If I could tell you more, I would. I've given you what info I have. Eventually, you'll sort it out, and then you'll call in the cops. I want no part of that."

Jodi couldn't help but bark a laugh. "And you think I do?"

"You will." He shrugged his head toward Hunter. "He'll probably insist."

"He," Hunter said in an ominous overtone, "would like nothing more than to beat information out of you."

Holding Jodi's gaze, Remmy said, "I'm not surprised, but she's fair, and she's calling the shots."

Hunter took a step forward. "You think so?"

Uh-oh. Jodi thought she might have just lost control of

things. "Hunter? I'd appreciate it if you didn't murder him in my kitchen. Seriously, for numerous reasons, I don't want the cops here."

His jaw tightened. His broad shoulders flexed, big hands curling into devastating fists that, as they'd already seen, could deliver real punishment. Every inch of him appeared primed and ready to annihilate.

Where the heck was her easygoing neighbor?

Flown the coop, obviously.

Remmy held Hunter's gaze. "I've told you what I know. Beating me won't make a difference, but I can promise you, it won't be as easy as you're thinking."

Jodi said, "It was already easy, you idiot."

Hunter surprised her by calmly asking, "Does Worth have anything to do with this?"

Taken aback, Remmy's gaze ping-ponged between them. "How did you know that?"

"He came to see me right before Turbo noticed you."

"What a dumbass," Remmy said in disgust. "He'll be lucky if King doesn't kill him."

Damn it, Worth Linlow was a royal pain in the butt and a supercreep for sure, but he wasn't evil. He wasn't on a par with King. He was just your average, everyday jerk—so Jodi didn't want him murdered. Brought down a few pegs, sure. But dead? No.

With a long-suffering sigh, she asked, "What's the connection?"

"So you know, King isn't big on sharing the particulars, so Worth probably doesn't understand what he's gotten into." For a few minutes more, Remmy explained about the car, and how it was supposed to keep Hunter so busy, she'd have to show up on the job alone. "It was the only thing I could think of to hold back the collateral damage."

"Me?" Hunter asked.

"King likes the game. He wants to play with her, but you'd just be in his way."

Uncaring about King's preferences, Jodi asked, "So why does he want you to hook up with me?"

Remmy shot a cautious glance at Hunter before answering. "King could come after you, but he'd rather you come to him. The idea of me—someone who's working for him—screwing you, then convincing you with a lot of cash to take the job, was a big enticement for him. Once you're on his property..." Remmy trailed off. "I don't think he'll do anything right away. Like I said, he enjoys the game."

"But it's not worth taking the chance," Hunter said, more or less agreeing with Remmy.

"That's how I see it."

Jodi wasn't yet certain what she wanted to do, but she did realize that Remmy had helped her. "You didn't expect King to reach out to Worth so quickly or for Worth to immediately fall in line?"

"I didn't think Worth could even find a car that fast. I figured it'd give us at least a week. He must have jumped on the opportunity for King to buy him something."

"He told me he'd had his eye on a Mustang Cobra and suddenly got it for a low price." With complete loathing, Hunter said, "He's car crazy, so yeah, King probably knew that if he manufactured the deal, Worth wouldn't hesitate."

Jodi kept thinking of how Worth risked his own life by getting involved—and about the chance Remmy had taken by explaining this all to her. She really, *really* disliked that others might be hurt...because of a stupid plot against her.

"Think whatever you want about me," Remmy said, bringing the subject back around. "By tomorrow morning, I'll be out of Triple Creek, and I suggest you do the same."

"Leave my house?" Jodi asked, incredulous that he'd even suggest such a thing. Then with more feeling, *"Run?"*

Hunter went to stand behind her chair, one hand on her shoulder.

Funny that having any other guy at her back would make her antsy, but with Hunter, she relaxed, appreciating his show of support as she said to Remmy, "I'm not going anywhere."

"I was afraid you'd say that." Holding up his hands in surrender, Remmy slowly stood. "I've done what I could, so I'll be on my way."

"You're not skipping out tonight," Hunter stated.

"Yeah, I am."

"No," Hunter countered, "you're not. You're going to see King as usual, and you'll report that Jodi slept with you."

Together, Remmy and Jodi said, "What the hell?"

Hunter didn't budge. "You'll brag to King about how you rocked her world."

When Jodi started to surge from the seat, he held her in place. Now *that* pissed her off.

Remmy grinned. "Not a stretch—but is there a reason I'm boasting?"

Lightly rubbing her shoulders as if to soothe her, Hunter said, "You'll tell King that between the sex and the amount of money he's offering her for the job, she's decided to do it."

Stumped, Remmy asked, *"Why?"*

As Hunter's reasoning dawned on Jodi, she grinned with full acceptance. "Your car idea didn't work, since Worth isn't reliable, but this will buy us time to figure out what he's hiding in my house." And it would help her decide how to handle it. Now that she understood, she liked this plan. "If you bolt, King would probably decide to kill me and be done with it."

Both Remmy and Hunter went rigid with that statement.

"No," Remmy said, and it was clear the idea bothered him.

Not as much as it bothered Hunter, though, who said through his teeth, "I would never let that happen."

"I wouldn't either." She patted Hunter's hand on her shoulder to reassure him. "If King thinks I'll be coming to him, that he'll eventually have his way, he's more likely to be patient, right?"

Thoughtfully, Remmy nodded. "Maybe. But if you take too long, I'll end up going down with the ship." His shoulders tightened. "I don't want you hurt, Jodi, I swear it, but I don't particularly want to face King's wrath either."

"Did you kill anyone?" Hunter asked.

Remmy narrowed his eyes.

"Anyone innocent?" Jodi clarified.

For the longest time, Remmy remained stiff and silent, before giving a low curse. "Look, I'm not a random murderer, okay? Have I stood back and seen shit happen? Yes. To fuckers who deserved it. Have I taken part on occasion? Also yes. *To fuckers who deserved it.*"

Jodi noted that he seemed really hung up on the distinction. She got that, since the distinction mattered to her, too.

"Someone like you? A woman, or a kid? Hell no." He stared at Hunter. "Even someone like him? *No.* King's business is one thing. His sick sport is another."

"Somehow my house is part of his business," Jodi pointed out.

"But you're not."

"No, she's not," Hunter reasoned. "So if you want to help her, you have to stick around a little longer."

That only seemed to infuriate Remmy more. "By helping her, I could get myself killed."

"I understand the risk." Jodi scrutinized him, her gaze unflinching when he tried to stare her down. "I don't think you're completely lost, Remmy."

"Don't use that soft voice on me now, woman. You've made your preferences known."

Hunter started to move, and Jodi quickly tightened her hand over his. She understood Remmy, and because of that, she needed to give him the same opportunity that the McKenzies had given to her.

When Hunter subsided, she let out a breath. "Over the last few years, I've found that it's sometimes worth it to risk yourself for a different way of life. You're not cruel, and you're not completely without a moral compass."

As if to deny that, Remmy made a rude sound.

"You're a good-looking guy, and you seem smart enough."

"Such lavish praise," he mocked with a half laugh, while avoiding her gaze.

"I realized I had to take big chances, so that I could make big changes." She curled her fingers with Hunter's. "I'm glad I did. I hope you come to the same conclusion."

"Fuck," he muttered, turning away. "Fuck, fuck, *fuck*."

"Is that an agreement?" Jodi asked with a grin.

He glanced back at her with annoyance. "On one condition."

"You don't get conditions," Hunter said.

At almost the same time, Remmy said, "You can't stay here alone."

Immediately, Hunter retracted his statement. "I agree."

Jodi had to laugh at them both. It occurred to her that throughout her short adulthood, she'd encountered some of the most evil men alive…but she'd also met the very best the world had to offer. First the McKenzie men, then Hunter, and now she had to admit that Remmy wasn't too bad either. He still wasn't for her—only Hunter could take that dubious credit—but she appreciated him. It had taken guts, and yes, a deep sense of decency, for him to not only warn her but to want to protect her.

Standing, she handed Hunter the Glock, then went to Remmy and offered her hand.

Nonplussed, he gave her a long look, then a reluctant smile, and enfolded her hand in both of his. "You're one of a kind, Jodi Bentley. Don't change." After a brisk but gentle squeeze, he released her and headed for the front door. "I have your business number. Will you answer if I call?"

"Probably not." Opening a drawer, she dug out a notepad and pen, then wrote down her personal cell phone number. "Use this, but share it with anyone and I'll make you sorry."

A brief smile touched his mouth. "I'll call if I hear any definitive plans. Stay cautious."

"Don't go overboard on the bragging," she warned, but she was still amused. After closing and locking the door behind him, she went to check on Turbo to make sure he hadn't been disturbed. Stretched across her bed, the dog slept on.

Turning from the room, she almost ran into Hunter. And wow. He still looked really, *really* dangerous.

Now maybe more so than ever.

Funny thing, but that only made her want him more. Today. This minute, in fact. Given the way she lived her life, who knew how much time she'd have with him? Whether it was a day or a lifetime, she wanted every single second possible.

Stepping up against him, she put her hands on his chest. "I don't take orders."

"Neither do I."

Huh. He countered instead of objecting. Interesting. "Someone has to be in charge," she pointed out.

"Not in a partnership. Not where two people trust and respect each other. The answer is to work together, hold back nothing and be honest."

That was part of her problem—she'd dished out all the honesty. "I can handle that. Can you?"

"Yes." Hunter held her face as he lowered to take a long, deep, tongue-thrusting kiss that left her on her tiptoes, leaning in for more. "Come home with me and I'll tell you everything."

Of all the offers he could have made, all the arguments he might have offered or reasons he might have given, that was the one she couldn't refuse.

"Okay."

NEVER IN HIS life had Hunter wanted to do something as old-fashioned as stake a claim on a woman. But now, with Jodi, that's exactly what he wanted.

He tugged her up the hall so they wouldn't wake Turbo, then turned her to the wall and caged her in with his forearms braced at either side of her head.

Instead of seeming bothered by that, Jodi lifted one hand to his jaw, her gaze searching.

She was his.

Down to the marrow of his bones, he knew it. He'd probably known it within minutes of meeting her. It didn't make sense, it had happened too fast and he didn't care. "It'll be dark before too much longer. I'd rather we get settled into my place for the night."

She said, "All right."

Damn, he wasn't used to Jodi being so agreeable. "There are things we'll need to do here…"

"Tomorrow," she whispered, her fingers sliding along his scalp with a singular fascination, as if she'd never stroked a man's hair before.

Every masculine instinct he possessed urged him to rush her out of there now, before she changed her mind, but his heart also told him that he needed to prioritize her safety. "Your family, would they be able to do a deep dive on King?"

"I can put Madison on it. Within twenty-four hours, I imagine she can tell us all there is to know."

Relief coursed through him, leaving more room for the lust. Wanting her agreement, needing it, Hunter said, "Can you get together enough belongings for a few days at least?"

Her gaze softened. "I can grab some things for tonight. Tomorrow, we can sort out the rest."

He put his forehead to hers. "Jodi, do you understand what I'm asking you?" With her, he could never make assumptions. She saw the world differently than others might, just as she saw herself differently.

"I think so." Her busy little hands went down to his waist, then up his back as she explored him. "You want me safe—"

"I want you, period. Safe. Now and tomorrow. Next week. I want you with me. I want your complete trust. I want…everything."

In a carefully neutral voice, she asked, "Do I get everything in return?"

"Yes." He gathered her close, his arms around her, his body shielding her. It was an uneasy thought, but Hunter knew he'd die for her without hesitation. Hell, he'd almost died for a total stranger. For Jodi? He'd do whatever was needed to keep her from harm.

She *was* his...and he was hers, whether she realized it yet or not. "Anything and everything you want."

"That sounds perfect. I think I want sex first, though."

He choked on a laugh. "I'm with you a hundred percent, but you want to tell me why?"

She tucked her face against his chest, her nose nuzzling him, and he heard her draw in a slow breath. "I could live without knowing your past, but this body? That's asking too much. I'm suddenly way too curious to wait."

That suited him just fine, assuming she dealt okay with the intimacy. That was a concern, given everything she'd told him and what he'd witnessed of her reluctance to get too close. He'd like to think that things were different with him, but he wasn't willing to risk her feelings for it.

Despite how desperately he wanted her, he'd go as slowly as she needed him to. "If at any point you feel uneasy—"

"You already know me better than anyone." She didn't wait for him to answer, just stared up at him earnestly, her gaze unblinking, almost a challenge. "If I have something to say, I'll say it, and I want you to do the same. I mean, if there's something I should be doing that I'm not doing, or if I should be doing it differently."

Could she be more lovable? He didn't think so. He gave her a soft, gentle kiss and promised, "It'll be good between us." He'd make it so.

Running her hands over his shoulders, she said, "I believe you."

Thinking out loud on how they should progress, he murmured, "I need a shower." Despite her willingness to rush to bed, she probably needed dinner, and he had to get Turbo settled back home where he could really rest.

She plucked at the front of her sweaty shirt. "I need a shower more than you do."

He thought about offering to shower with her, but he wasn't at all certain of his control. And speaking of control... "Damn." It only just occurred to him. "I don't have a condom."

Blinking fast, she asked, "For real?"

"I haven't touched a woman since I moved here."

"Oh." She half smiled. "Guess you're all bottled up?"

Another choked laugh escaped him. "Definitely bottled up since meeting you." Once he'd realized how special she was, he should have picked up protection right away. Although, the small drugstore in town wasn't really the place to do it. Too many nosy people would have noticed, and they all considered him a recluse. Immediately, they would have speculated on Jodi.

"Well, you'll be glad to know I'm on the pill, but no, I haven't been busy in the sack either. Before you, the thought was just gross."

Her broken past and how it had molded her never failed to hurt his heart, especially when she was so cavalier about it. Hunter cupped her face and teased her cheeks with his thumbs. "Then why—"

"I don't like taking chances. I can protect myself. I trust my own ability." Her shoulder lifted. "But things sometimes happen that we can't control, and I figured if anyone ever got the best of me, I'd be covered against pregnancy."

He closed his eyes against that awful idea. She'd tried to protect herself in every way she could. But what good would the pill be if someone held her prisoner again...? *No.*

In a voice rough with emotion, he said, "Let's both ensure that never happens."

"Sounds good to me." She smiled up at him. "So, how about you get my laptop and cord and stuff together while I take a quick shower here, then I'll change into clean clothes and grab a few things for tomorrow morning. When I'm done, we can head to your house and I'll get hold of Madison while you clean up."

"I'd rather be with you when you call them."

"Okay," she said, not the least bothered by his request. "Still… I need that shower, so give me ten, okay?" Putting another firm kiss to his mouth, she pivoted away and went silently into her bedroom, emerging moments later with a change of clothes. She went into the bathroom and closed the door, and a few seconds later, he heard water running.

Rather than stand there visualizing her, Hunter got busy gathering up her laptop. Ignoring that locked closet as much as he could, he found a satchel she used for a purse and put it all on the small coffee table in her living room. Going from room to room, he checked that the doors and windows were locked. He ended up back in her bedroom, where the framed photo of her with the McKenzies sat on a nightstand.

Holding it, Hunter remembered how this room had looked when she'd first moved in. Stark, barely functional, definitely not comfortable. In such a short time, she'd settled here and, thanks to her family, everything was now nice and cozy.

Much like Jodi herself. Yes, she was definitely cozier now—but that intractable edge remained. Jodi could be softened, but she would never be the average person, shielded by ignorance of just how ugly life could get.

Slowly, he sat on the end of the bed, studying her image more closely. She looked so young, though she'd probably been in her early twenties. Her eyes, which were so beautiful to him, showed guarded uneasiness—as if she'd forced herself to go along with the picture but was far from being at ease with it. Thin to the point of looking sickly, except that even then, in the stillness of a photo, she possessed a sort of contained energy.

One false move, and Jodi would have detonated.

"Hey." She stepped into the bedroom while combing her hair, but stalled when she saw what he held.

Hunter started to apologize, then changed his mind. Reaching out a hand to her, he asked, "Will you give me names so I can identify everyone?"

After only a second's hesitation, she placed the comb on the dresser and allowed him to tug her down next to him on the mattress. Leaning into his side, she pointed to a tall, slender woman with long dark hair. "That's Madison, the tech genius. She's a beauty, right?"

"Yes." Madison looked like she could model, annihilate or host a fun party.

"Next to her is Cade, the oldest brother, and his wife, Sterling."

Sterling, he noted, was just as tall, equally beautiful, but with a sturdier build than Madison.

"That's Reyes." Briefly, she smiled. "He likes to give me a hard time, but then, he does that to everyone. He's the joker of the family, and a royal pain in the butt—but I like him a lot."

Hunter heard the affection in her tone. He looked at Reyes, and yeah, he wore an expression of merciless teasing, whereas his brother, Cade, looked like the definition of rigorous discipline.

Touching the photo, Jodi traced a line around the small woman with honey-blond hair. "This is Kennedy."

When she said nothing more, Hunter bent to see Jodi's face. "You okay?"

"Yeah, of course." Her hand dropped away. "Kennedy's the closest thing I have to a best friend, a sister, a… I don't know. Everything." She heaved a sigh. "She's really sweet, and one of the most caring people you'd ever meet."

Sensing all the emotion she tried to cover, Hunter gave her a one-armed hug. "I guess the older guy is Parrish?" Handsome and with a tall, athletic build, Parrish looked as if he could give orders to the pope, the king and the president, all three, and they'd obey.

She grinned. "Yeah, that's him—the big fraud. He always looks like that, but he's really nice—when he wants to be. And now that he's married again, he smiles more." When she stood, she noticed that they'd awakened Turbo. She stepped around the side of the bed to give the dog a pat. "Sorry, my man, but you needed to wake up anyway." Going back to the dresser, she opened drawers and pulled out a shirt and jeans, panties, bra and socks. At the unlocked closet, she found a big tote bag and packed her belongings.

Hunter was still boggled by the tiny beige underwear and bra he'd seen. Damn. Who knew she'd wear something so…sexy? Or maybe it wasn't sexy, it was just that he knew the little bits of nothing would go on Jodi, and that made them extremely hot.

Not noticing his preoccupation, she said, "Parrish had wanted Bernard to be in the photo, and he was going to take it. Bernard is this really cool guy who loves animals and cooking, and pretty much keeps them all in line. Parrish isn't used to anyone not obeying when he gives orders, but Bernard is different. He only obeys when he feels like it. It's extra funny because he likes to pretend to be a butler or something—you know, all stuffy and formal with his nose in the air. Then he just does as he pleases, and says whatever he wants to everyone. I like Bernard a lot. He keeps them all humble." She smiled at the photo a few seconds more. "This was taken before Madison and Crosby

220 THE DANGEROUS ONE

got married, or he'd be in the photo, too." Giving a wary look, she added, "Crosby used to be a cop."

He could imagine how that unsettled a bunch of vigilantes—Jodi included. "Doesn't bother me."

"Good. The family is a weird mix of people. They take some getting used to."

Weird, Hunter allowed, but he was certain they were also wonderful. After all, they cared about Jodi, and that told him everything he needed to know. "Will I ever meet them?"

"Eh, depends on how we go, I guess. If we're together very long, yeah, you can count on it because they'll insist. Otherwise, probably not."

Hunter stood, took her bag from her hands and dropped it on the bed, then turned her face up to his. "We'll be together."

"You think so, do you?"

"Yes." Tonight, he'd prove it to her. Testing her just a bit, he said roughly, "I'm going to love loving you."

Her eyes flared, then stayed that way, like the proverbial deer caught in the headlights. He saw the fight-or-flight response in those wide eyes, and knew she had no idea how to deal with him. A plus for him, since he rarely knew how to deal with her.

Hunter waited, her golden gaze searching as she appeared to go through several calculations before managing a slight nod and a tentative smile. Stepping around him, she went first to the side of the mattress where she withdrew a key from a hidden seam, then to her secured closet. "Let me grab a few more things, and we can be on our way."

His entire body—blood, pulse, breath—all stilled as he watched her deftly open the lock, not with just the key, and not with just one fingerprint. He didn't know a device like that existed, but after turning the key, she placed first her forefinger, then her thumb in different locations of the lock, and finally her pinkie...and he heard it click open.

Fascinated, he drew closer. She'd done it quickly, likely with lots of practice, and he wasn't sure most would even notice the complicated placement of her fingerprints. Little got by him, though, especially when it came to Jodi. He couldn't wait to see what warranted so much caution.

Standing right behind her, Hunter watched as she opened the sturdy wooden door...to a fucking arsenal.

Various rifles had been meticulously arranged along the walls of the closet, held in secure racks. An AR15, which would be good for her, given her slight size, was front and center. He grudgingly approved. To the left of it was a Mossberg pump shotgun. Seeing it as a great deterrent, Hunter smiled. Everyone recognized the sound of a shell being chambered, and once they did, they knew it wasn't going to end well for them if they proceeded.

Jodi reached inside and withdrew a Walther PPS M2 9 mm. "I like my Glock 45 since I've practiced with it more, but this one has a nice grip, it's lightweight and I prefer it when I'm working."

The gun wasn't much more than an inch thick, so easier to conceal. "You carry that when you're mowing?"

"Yup." She stroked it before putting it on the dresser. "The trigger is like butter." She glanced at him. "You have night-vision binocs?"

"I have sights on my weapons to see at night."

"Sweet." She grabbed the binoculars and added them, along with boxes of ammo, to her stack. "I should get those, too."

"Jodi, you won't need all that."

Her look now was full of humor. "Like the missing condom, I'd rather have them and not need them than need them and not have them." Using a multipocketed tactical bag the size of an overnight bag, she stored everything and added it to the pile on the bed.

It struck Hunter that Jodi didn't want to pack a lot of clothes, but she had no issue with taking an array of weapons. Embracing her quirks would be easier than fighting them, so he calmly asked, "All done?"

"Sure."

As she zipped up the bags, he turned back to the closet, noting the rest of the weapons—like batons, a stun gun and a Taser—and, there on the floor, propped in the corner, an oddly placed piece of broken wood, like a slat of some sort with jagged edges. "What's this?"

She glanced over her shoulder, then slowly straightened, color staining her cheeks and throat. Trying to sound dismissive, she said, "That's more a keepsake than anything else."

Sensing it had stark meaning for her, Hunter asked, "Will you tell me about it?"

"I guess I should." With a touch of antagonism, she met his gaze. "You might change your mind about wanting me."

"No," he assured her. At this point, there was no turning back for him. More softly, he insisted, "Trust me."

She firmed her lips, her brows drawing together. "Sometimes, when I try to talk about it, I…freak out."

He remembered how she'd lost control when telling him about the bastard who'd imprisoned her. So the wood had something to do with that?

Yes, he wanted to know it all, but more than that, he sensed Jodi needed to share it. Why else would she have let him see the contents of the closet? "Let's try this," he said, reaching out for her and drawing her against his body until they touched from knees up, thighs pressing, her breasts to his lower chest, and his arms around her protectively, her face nestled against his throat. "Take as much time as you need, okay?" To make certain she understood, he whispered, "I'm not going anywhere."

Releasing a strained sigh, Jodi relaxed, her hands settling on his lower back, her fingers tucked into the waistband of his jeans.

She seemed to have no idea how that not-so-innocent touch affected him.

Time ticked by, and Hunter knew she was gearing up, bracing herself for the awful memories. He hugged her more firmly, until he could feel the steady beating of her heart.

In a mere whisper, she said, "I knew if I didn't get out, he'd eventually let me die. There were times I was so hungry, and so cold. Always so damned cold." She shivered with the memory. "As miserable as it was…I wanted to live."

Thank God.

"I didn't have any weapons. There was nothing in the room with me except an old pallet, like the type used to stack feed to keep it off the ground."

"I'm familiar," Hunter murmured, picturing the pallet, or skid, a simple frame of wood with open sides for easy forklift access.

Jodi slipped into another silence that lasted half a minute. "The pallet was rough, and if I moved much, I'd get a splinter. Some of the nails were popping out at the corners. One slat of wood had started to curl from being in the damp basement. I realized how flimsy it was—and then I realized I might have a weapon after all."

It wasn't intentional, but his gaze returned to that jagged piece of wood. Her ingenuity impressed him, especially under such awful conditions. He turned away from the closet and pressed his mouth to her temple.

"It was easy to break up the pallet. I just bashed it against the floor. Every time I swung it, I thought he'd come stomping down the squeaky steps, but he didn't. Maybe he wasn't home, or maybe he was drunk. I don't know. I broke it up into several pieces, and sharpened the ends by scraping them on the concrete walls...and then I waited." Her voice broke on the last word.

Gathering her up into his arms, Hunter sat on the edge of the bed and held her. Turbo stirred, coming down to snuffle against them.

Absently, Jodi reached out and stroked the dog's ear. "All day, into the night. I thought he might not come back at all, that maybe I'd waited too long to come up with a plan." Her breath shuddered. "I felt weak from hunger, dehydrated, so cold and scared..."

That small voice was nearly his undoing. He rocked her, his face in her hair, his heart swelling so big that it seemed to choke him.

Jodi straightened. Her lashes were damp, her nose pink, but her tone was stronger when she said, "Until I heard him coming." Holding his gaze like a lifeline, she said, "Then I was just determined. I hated him and I wanted him dead. I wanted that more than I wanted to live. I heard his footsteps, then the rusty sound of the bar sliding off the door. He swung it open... I still remember his expression, all smug and gleeful, thinking he'd see me cowering there, ready to enjoy my misery." Her jaw tightened. "Instead, he saw me waiting. I screamed when I jumped at him, this loud sound of...rage, I guess. Before he knew what was happening, I was stabbing him, over and over, with the sharpest piece of wood."

"Good for you," Hunter said with feeling. God, she was amazing, and by some trick of fate, she was here with him. Whatever it took, he'd find a way to make it work between them. Forever.

"The wood broke off in his side, so I grabbed another piece. I had them all stacked and ready to go." Her gaze never faltered, but tears gathered again, clumping her lashes, ready to fall. "In the neck and the gut and across his face until he went down." Breathing harder, she said, "I locked *him* in the room. He was hysterical, saying he'd bleed to death, that I'd blinded him." Jodi paused to wipe her eyes, then sniff loudly, before she continued. "I yelled through the door that I'd call him an ambulance if he'd give me the combination to his safe." With a short, shaky laugh, she said, "He didn't want to die any more than I had, so he did it. I found everything I needed. A loaded gun, cash. The dick still had my purse, so I had my ID."

Soothingly, Hunter ran his hand up and down her spine.

"I was afraid he'd show up in the doorway any second, that somehow he knew a way out that he'd kept from me, so I did everything fast, grabbing some of his clothes, the keys to his car, and I...took off." Her chin hitched up. "I never called an ambulance. I didn't call anyone. I just put as many miles between me and that house as I could."

"I don't blame you." Hunter ran his fingers through her still-damp hair, then cupped his hands around her neck, making sure he had her clear attention. "I'm in *awe* of you, Jodi. When others would have given up, you persevered, and I think that makes you incredibly special." He pressed a kiss to her forehead. "Amazing." A kiss to her cheek. "Beautiful."

"Beautiful?" she repeated with a small, self-conscious, sniffling laugh.

"Mine." He covered her lips with his own, the kiss firm and, yeah, territorial. *"Mine."*

She wiped her eyes again, then hugged him. "So many times, I thought of going back, just to make sure he hadn't found a way out, but I never did."

"Good." In a thousand ways, Hunter hoped the bastard had suffered, that he'd died the miserable death he deserved. "You realize that because you were brave and smart and…"

"And what?"

"*You.* Because you were you, Jodi Bentley, a survivor against the odds, you probably saved other women from the same fate. If you'd given up, if you had…" Damn, he could barely get the word out. Saying it physically hurt, because he wanted her, needed her, with him. "If you had died, he would have found someone else to torment. You not only saved yourself, you saved others."

Her lips parted as she stared at him, and her eyes grew glassy again. "I never thought of that."

He loved that she didn't try to hide her tears from him. Jodi never hid. She was who she was, and people could either accept it or not. He loved that she'd come to trust him, at least enough to share her darkest, most difficult moments. He especially loved that she was with him now, and he wouldn't let Remmy, or King, or anyone else on the planet ever hurt her again.

"Every day, in some new way, you impress me."

Her smile went crooked. "You're into whiny chicks perching on your lap while telling horror stories, huh?"

"I'm into an energetic risk-taker who thinks to pet my dog while baring her soul—*to me*. Yeah, apparently, I'm really into that because I want more." He glanced out the window and said, "Before it gets any darker, why don't we get out of here and into my house? Let's drive up your truck and you can park it in my garage to keep it safe."

She laughed. "What about my mower?"

"We can take that up, too, if you want. There's only my truck and car in the garage right now."

"You have a car?"

Her comical surprise was cute. "I work on cars, so of course I have my own. It's a black '67 Chevy Impala, like Dean's car in *Supernatural*."

She gave him a blank stare.

"And…" he said with a laugh of his own, "that means nothing to you, because you don't watch TV."

Wrapping her arms around his neck, Jodi said, "I can't wait to see it." Then with more gravity, "But *after*, okay?"

"Definitely after." Amazed that he'd made it this long now that he knew Jodi was on board, Hunter waited while she relocked the closet, pocketed the key and got all her bags closed.

Then he spent the next fifteen minutes in frustration as he convinced Jodi to drive the truck with Turbo while he drove the mower. She treated that big piece of machinery as possessively as Worth treated his car. By the time they got to his house, the security lights had automatically come on, and the sun left only a red haze over the mountains. Because they parked in his garage, she ended up seeing his car right off, and while she admired it, she clearly wasn't all that interested. Reliability was her number one concern with transportation, not how a car looked.

Fine by him, since he wanted only to rush her inside. He forgot all about calling Madison McKenzie as he did a sweep of the house, ensuring everything was still locked.

With that done, he left her to get settled while he took a speed shower.

When he finished, he dressed only in flannel pants and, suffused with burning lust, stepped out of the bathroom and headed for the door, intent on finding Jodi in his living room.

He immediately stalled.

There she was in his bed, stretched out on her stomach, chin propped on one hand with her laptop open in front of her.

She wore only a T-shirt and panties.

The hem of the oversize cotton shirt bunched above her slim hips, showing off the perfect, plump curves of her stellar ass. Ankles crossed near the headboard, she presented an image hot enough to scorch his blood. Breathing deeper, Hunter visually tracked every inch of her body. She had beautiful legs, lightly tanned, and at the moment, even her feet looked sexy to him.

Glancing up with forced nonchalance, Jodi closed the laptop. "Turbo is conked out on the couch. I figured we'd let him sleep and keep the bedroom to ourselves."

Past the pounding of his pulse in his ears, Hunter heard the deliberately bold words. The hot way she looked him over felt like a physical stroke.

Above it all, though, he sensed her jittery uncertainty. Didn't stop him from getting hard, painfully so, but it did force him to collect his wits. This was very unfamiliar territory for her. As usual, Jodi hoped to bluster her way through it with a cocky attitude that would annihilate any insecurity she felt.

This time Hunter wouldn't let her. Whatever it took, he'd make this good for her, so good that he wouldn't have to convince her that they were meant to be, because she'd come to that conclusion all on her own.

Very quietly, he closed the bedroom door, then leaned against it and simply looked at her.

To REMMY'S SURPRISE, King himself was waiting on him, pacing the massive recreation room in the lower level of his home. Usually, once Remmy was escorted there by one of King's guards, he was left waiting. It was a power play for King, a way to subtly reinforce that he was boss and everyone else worked for him.

This particular area, down a curving flight of stairs, was where he usually hosted his poker matches. The dark, coffered ceiling—a description Remmy knew only because King had explained it—was high, with inset lights at every square except over the billiard table and a large round mahogany poker table, where heavy chandeliers ensured plenty of light. Leather couches and chairs were arranged in seating groups, and a sizable wet bar with eight stools took up most of the space on the far wall. Floor-to-ceiling windows gave a view of the private backyard, thickly wooded.

At the bar, seated nearby on the closest stool, Danny Giggs drank what looked like whiskey. Huh. So he was not only still alive, he was back in King's good graces? Remmy wondered what he'd done for King to make that happen.

"Did you fuck her?" King demanded, even before Remmy had secured the door behind him.

"Yeah." Smiling, he popped his neck, easing knotted muscles while trying to look pleased. "I did." He wasn't at all certain of Hunter's plan, but he'd do whatever was necessary to protect Jodi from a jackal like King.

It'd be better if Jodi took off, but even before she'd refused, he'd known it was a long shot. Jodi Bentley was not the type to tuck tail and run. She was the type to plant her feet and dare you to do your worst.

He couldn't help admiring her.

All along, though he'd tried to deny it, he'd known it would come to this. Him doing something reckless in an effort to keep safe a woman who looked at him with disdain— and rightfully so. It was so fucking stupid, but for reasons he refused to examine too closely, she did it for him. Made him feel both hot and tender, savage and protective. Damn, how he'd like to get her in a bed…

"Was she willing?" Danny asked.

Fury gathered, sending all Remmy's muscles to clench again. He stared at Danny, long enough to give the other man pause. Then, in a voice more deadly because of its softness, he said, "I'm not a rapist."

Giggs snorted a nervous laugh. "Had her begging for it, huh?"

Remmy badly wanted to hit something, and Danny's face would make a fine target.

King was not amused. He narrowed his eyes in a chilling warning. "Do you actually like the bitch?"

Staring right into the bastard's eyes, leaving no doubt as to how he felt, Remmy said, "I don't like anyone."

Oddly enough, that seemed to pacify King. "Good. Keep it that way." He thrust his empty glass toward Danny, who jumped up to get him a refill. Once Danny was behind the bar, King approached and asked quietly, "When will you see her again?"

He had zero idea. Pretending King's nearness didn't put him on edge, Remmy said, "Don't know. I told her I'd call."

From across the room, Danny laughed.

"Giggs is amused by everything tonight." King's dark

eyes reflected the chandelier lights. Under his breath, he muttered, "He's become a fucking nuisance."

"Say the word," Remmy replied softly. He'd rather dispose of Danny over Jodi any day, but if he got the chance, he could possibly just send the rat scurrying away.

When Danny handed him his drink, King smiled. "See, still so very useful."

"Want me to visit her?" Danny asked, while cupping a hand over his crotch. "Maybe let her make comparisons."

Remmy tried to show no reaction, but it wasn't easy when the thought of Danny getting anywhere near her made his blood boil. *Over my dead body.* Which, actually, might be how it happened.

He hoped like hell Hunter was as competent as he came off.

"You," King said to Danny, "would probably fuck her to death. I presume Remmy has a little more finesse?"

Since it was asked as a question, Remmy smiled again. "You already know she's a bold little thing." He fashioned a cocky grin. "She knows what she wants, and I gave it to her."

"Good." Idly, King clinked the ice in his drink while considering the situation. "Let her wait a few days. Don't be too accessible."

Perfect.

"Has she agreed to the job yet?"

Remmy shook his head. "She did, but the storm left everything a mess. She was scrambling all day, and has a lot more to do tomorrow. I think she's overwhelmed right now. Might be a few days before she can begin."

"That works," King said with satisfaction. "Soon her neighbor will be too busy with Worth's car to lend her a hand."

Obviously, King didn't yet know that Worth had jumped the gun on that. Remmy saw no reason to tell him. "That's how I figured it. You have a good plan. Just need time for the pieces to fall into place." He looked toward the windows at the immaculate lawn. "Besides, she's new at this shit. Your place is so perfect, I'm not sure you'd want her mucking it up now, while the ground is soggy from the rain. In a few days, it'll be dried out and she won't be able to do much damage."

After giving him a long, measuring stare, King nodded. "A valid point. I've had a three-man crew keeping this place pristine. No woman, for any reason, is worth damaging my image."

His image, Remmy thought, was a fucking shambles already, but whatever. "Something else occurred to me." It was a chancy move, the suggestion he'd give, but worth trying anyway. "Jodi lives in a dump. You could fit her entire house three times in this room alone. It's obvious that's all she could afford—so why not just buy her out?"

"Now, what fun would that be?"

Danny grew belligerent. "I have a suggestion, too."

"Oh?" Humoring him, King said, "I'm anxious to hear it."

"Let me grab her for you, you can have all the fun you want and then kill her. Tell everyone you bought her place and she moved away. Who would ever know?"

"Hmm." King considered it. "I could get her to sign it over before I finish her off."

Remmy asked low, "Is it really worth the risk, just to have a little fun?"

Turning to Danny, King clasped his shoulder and laughed. "I have to take my pleasures where I can, don't I, Giggs?"

"You've earned them—and then some."

Fresh alarm went through Remmy. The thought of killing Danny suddenly held more appeal.

"But not yet." Tossing back the rest of his drink, King started away. "You can both head out now. Remmy, if you hear from her, let me know. In the meantime, we'll let the girl miss you a little."

"But your package," Danny protested.

"I'll stall a little longer. It's fine. No one would dare cross me."

Glad to get away from them, Remmy headed for the door. Reluctantly, Giggs followed.

Right as they stepped through the doorway, King spoke again. "Although, it might not hurt to toy with her a bit."

Danny's pale blue eyes lit up, the psychotic prick.

Without making it clear who he addressed, King said, "I'll let you know what I decide."

The guard, who stood there waiting on them, gestured for them to precede him up the stairs.

Remmy wasn't sure what King was thinking, but he knew whatever it was, Danny was all for it. Now what?

CHAPTER NINE

JODI COULDN'T TAKE her eyes off Hunter. Man, he was put together fine, all long, thick bones layered in firm flesh and flexible muscle gained from physical activity. Real muscles, not the kind built from weight lifting and supplements.

The hair on his body enhanced everything, shadowing the groove between his firm pecs, dividing his flat abdomen and disappearing into a pair of loose, soft flannel pants that hung low on his lean hips.

Half sitting, Jodi put the laptop on a nightstand, then stretched out on her side again. With one hand, she smoothed out the navy blue sheets. She figured they had to be high quality or something, given their softness. His quilt was incredible, a geometric design of blues and greens that somehow blended beautifully. She'd folded it to the bottom of the bed. Obviously, he paid a lot more attention to the little details than she did. "I really like your bed."

"I like seeing you in my bed."

She grinned at his quick comeback, and the gravelly timbre of his voice. From the start, Hunter had amused her with his wit. "Maybe you'll like being in this big old bed with me?"

"Guaranteed." He turned the lock on the door and stepped toward her, walking to her side of the bed and sitting behind her, near her hip.

Confused, Jodi looked over her shoulder, but paused at

finding him transfixed by her butt again. Who knew her scrawny behind could fascinate a big, gorgeous guy like Hunter?

He lifted a hand, lightly touched her shoulder, as if savoring the texture of her skin, and then trailed his fingertips down her side to the dip of her waist, over her hip, the curve of one cheek and down her thigh to her knee. "I've never seen anyone as sexy as you."

His touch had sent her heart into a gallop, but at his comment, she laughed. "Yeah, right."

"Don't do that," he said simply. "I know what I know. You don't see it, but..." His fingers trailed back up her thigh, then over her behind until he opened one large palm to entirely encompass a cheek. "Perfect curves in a small package." His voice lowered. "I love your ass."

Yeah, she could kind of tell. "Want me to take off my underwear?"

Briefly, he closed his eyes before saying, "No. When I want them off, I'll do it."

He didn't want them off now? Well, that was insulting. "What if *I* want them off?"

Still with his hand lightly fondling her cheek, his gaze lifted to hers. "Do you?"

Not really. "I want to get on with things." The wait was doing her in, making her more nervous by the second.

As if he understood, he turned her to her back and got into the bed with her. "Sorry, seeing you like this... You're hotter than my imagination figured."

"Hunter," she chided, liking how it felt to be stretched out with him. "You don't need to say things like that."

"I'll say whatever I want." He cupped her face and finally, *finally* gave her a kiss that started out searching, but quickly turned scorching. The way he devoured her mouth had her curling toward him, getting as near as she could. He smelled faintly of soap and shampoo now, some subtle, masculine scent that she didn't mind, but she preferred him a little sweaty.

Probably not something she should say, though.

Honestly, she wasn't sure what she should say during sex. She'd always imagined that it'd be rushed, fast and rough, and if it came to it, if she got put in a bad situation, she'd withstand it and—

Hunter turned to his back, scattering her thoughts when he tugged her up and over him, so that she rested on his chest. One of his hands was at the back of her head, gently keeping her mouth right there so he could continue licking, exploring, making her nuts, while the other hand tracked a slow path back down her spine.

Seriously, the man did seem drawn to her butt. In the future, if she wanted his attention, she'd drop her shorts and see what happened.

After a few heated moments, his mouth moved to her throat, and—ho, boy—that felt incredibly good. Warm and damp, sending tendrils of sensation all through her body to land in key places—like her breasts, her belly, and lower... between her thighs. "I like that," she murmured, tipping her head so it'd be easier for him. She hadn't known a neck could be so sensitive.

"Keep telling me what you like." In another move, he returned her to her back and looked down at her with an expression both heated and tender.

"You don't have to be so careful with me. I won't break."

"I care about you, so I'll always be careful."

Since she was staring into his eyes, she didn't realize he was working up her shirt until his bare hand covered her breast. Whoa.

"Do you like this?"

With his thumb brushing over her nipple, yeah, she liked it. "It feels way different from when I do it."

An arrested expression froze on his face. His nostrils flared and heat colored his cheekbones. In a tone dark and husky, he suggested, "Tell me about that."

"Washing?" she asked. "Yeah, I do it daily."

Wry amusement flashed in his dark blue eyes and he dropped his head forward with a muffled laugh.

"What? Washing is funny?"

"I thought… Never mind." He kissed her again.

She knew he was trying to get her back on track, but no way would she let it go now. Turning her face away, she asked, "You thought what?"

For only a second, he hesitated. Then he smiled. "I thought you meant you touched yourself sexually. Super-hot image, by the way. Thinking it damn near put me over the edge."

Ha! Like she'd talk about *that* with him. Then again, the way he'd reacted, maybe she should. She put that on the list of Ways to Incite Hunter, along with flashing her butt. "So me in your bed, showing off my prettiest panties, didn't put you near the edge, but the idea of me indulging in a little personal play did? Maybe I should have—"

This time there was no escaping his kiss, voracious as it was, and the hand on her breast got extra busy, cuddling, stroking and toying with her nipple until she couldn't hold back a ragged moan. It seemed he'd caused an intense pulse point of pleasure that swelled even more each time he adjusted the kiss to make it deeper. His muscled leg parted hers, and he rocked oh-so-gently against her.

For the next fifteen minutes, Jodi forgot about talking.

She almost forgot about breathing, but then, who needed oxygen when Hunter Osborn was busy seducing her?

And how long was he going to take, anyway? Need escalated, and it was so awesome, she didn't want to chance letting it go, which meant he needed to get on with it.

"Great panties," he whispered, while sliding his hand inside. "Really pretty."

A smile almost crept up on her. The panties weren't all that pretty, but then, she didn't do fancy undies or anything. She'd chosen that pair because she liked the color, sort of a rosy peach, and—

"Let's lose your shirt, okay?"

This was all so new, yet equally awesome, more so than she'd expected, that she merely nodded. Wasn't like her to take a passive role, especially with her impatience, but he knew what he was doing, and she didn't, so she decided just to enjoy herself.

Hunter stood at the side of the bed, tugged her up to sit, and after another warm press of his mouth to hers, he stripped the shirt off over her head.

Okay, that was quick.

Before she had time to decide if she wanted to square her shoulders, or cover herself with her arms, or *what* she should do, he lifted her as if she weighed nothing and put her in the bed the right way, then slid in next to her and she was immediately back against him, getting kissed all over, and damn, Hunter knew how to kiss.

"Beautiful," he repeated again as he covered both breasts with his hands.

She was starting to believe him—at least, that he thought so. Maybe it wasn't just sex words. Maybe he really did like her look. Small, plain women could be his thing. And... she didn't want to think about her perceptions of being too scrawny and stuff. She'd rather enjoy the way his hands felt on her body, how they covered so much of her at once, sometimes stroking in broad sweeps, like over her back and along her thighs, other times concentrating on a single point, like when he explored the curve of her hip bones, or how his fingertips followed her spine down and along the cleft of her bottom. He'd given a low growl over that.

Her skin tingled as he placed hot, damp love bites to her throat, her shoulder and to her left nipple. When she'd felt the edge of his teeth, she'd braced herself, until he licked, circling with his tongue. That almost turned her liquid. Then he drew her in, softly sucking until her back arched and she let out another moan.

Without even realizing it, she had both hands clenched in his hair, keeping him right there—or so she thought, until he moved to her other nipple without her even realizing it. He drew on one, and toyed the other with his clever fingers, and the doubling of sensation was devastating to her senses. She couldn't hold still, couldn't be quiet.

Something started happening to her, some invisible coil growing tighter but in a really delicious way. Restless, she moved against him and whispered in surprise, "I'm really excited."

He didn't answer, and that was okay, because she liked his mouth right where it was. She kept trying to sort it all out, what he did and how it made her feel, but then he'd do something else, like tug at her nipple, or slide a hand between her legs, and coherent thought scattered.

She didn't realize he was taking off her panties until she had to lift her hips to help him. Then it registered and she was all *sure, let's do this. Naked will be great.*

If she got naked, surely he would, too.

Instead, he propped up on one elbow and looked at her

from breasts to knees and back again, his breathing harsh, his hair messy—her fault on the hair…and maybe on the ragged breathing, too—and his expression took on an intensity she'd never seen before.

"Christ, Jodi, what you do to me."

That sounded pretty awesome, and eventually, she'd like details, but right now, she only wanted more. "Don't stop."

Giving her a dark, carnal smile, he said, "Only if you tell me to," and came back to her mouth, his tongue twining with hers in a hot, eating kiss. He pressed his hand between her thighs, and she wanted that so much, she opened her legs more in invitation. Hunter made a low sound of approval.

His rough-tipped fingers were gentle as he explored her, first lightly petting, which wasn't near enough for her. It made her ache even more, until she started to feel frantic. When she lifted into his hand, he took the hint, parting her sex, touching her more deeply, finding places that were incredibly sensitive—and slippery wet.

With incredible care, he pressed one finger into her, slowly, inexorably, until she was gasping every breath and riding up against his hand. She needed *more*, but Hunter proved he had incredible patience and he seemed to want to use every speck of it.

The way he worked that one finger, slowly in, slowly out, had her near to crying. Just when she was ready to make demands, he pressed in a second finger, and though it hurt a little, it was also exactly what she needed. She freed her mouth from his and turned her face against his throat, somewhat desperate, and yeah, definitely unsure. She hadn't expected this, not for her.

"I'd have been happy," she gasped, "just being with you."

"I want everything." His fingers pressed deeper, twisting, finding some hidden place that sent tingles sparking through her.

She felt the wet rush of moisture, and reaching down, she grabbed his wrist and held him closer, ensuring he couldn't tease anymore.

Instead, he brought his thumb up and over her clit, lightly rotating that supersensitive spot on her body, and Jodi knew that was it. She was with Hunter, his fingers filling her, his body burning up beside her, and she heard herself cry out, surprised that she would, but unable to stop herself as an incredible orgasm rolled through her. That coiled spring of sensation snapped, allowing pure, hot pleasure to flood through her system. Eyes closed, head back, she embraced it all, safe with Hunter. Finally, by small degrees, her bowed body began to relax until she was limp and sated and feeling pretty damned impressed with herself.

Whew. If she'd known it'd be like that, she'd have propositioned Hunter on the very first day. Maybe she should tell him so. She got her eyes open in time to see him leave the bed, strip off the soft flannel pants in a rush, then he was over her again, one of his big hands drawing her left leg out so he could settle against her. His weight on her was a wonderful thing, and she loosely lifted her arms around his neck.

Hunter stared down at her, his expression hard and yet somehow so full of emotion it almost choked her up.

She said, "You are so easy on the eyes."

He didn't smile. Reaching between them, he opened her again. Her flesh was so sensitive now that she almost flinched. He was still gentle, moving far too slowly, but she felt his solid erection against her, saw the strain on his face and knew he needed her, in ways no one ever had before.

That rejuvenated her. She hugged him and said against

his throat, "If you're waiting for permission, then here it is. *Now*, please."

Without replying, he cupped a hand to her hip and pressed in.

Automatically, her legs bent and her heels levered against the mattress. She breathed harder, stunned at how it felt to be so close to a man, to feel possessed by him—and to actually like it. Damn, she wanted to possess him, too, and so far she hadn't done a thing. Soon, she promised herself, but for now, she wrapped one leg around him, then the other.

He breathed harder, shifting so that his cock fit more snugly inside her. Another shift, nudging forward, and he hit that deep inner spot again. Wow.

She adjusted with him, shifting when he did, until she had all of him to squeeze tight. Soon he was moving deeper and they seemed to find a rhythm together, one that, amazingly enough, sent her lethargy packing and sparked those incredible feelings once more. As she felt another release building, she gave thanks for his patience and his control. Every muscle on his body tensed. His labored breath was hot against her shoulder. Tautly muscled arms gathered her closer, held her tighter, and the second her orgasm started, he gave a long groan of relief and let himself go.

Smiling, Jodi held him, stroked his back, hugged him with her legs and… Damn it, she opened her heart to him. Completely.

It was an odd feeling. With her vision dazed and her heart thumping wildly, she acknowledged it. It was scary, and liberating, mostly because she hadn't known if she could ever fully trust another person.

She definitely hadn't known she could enjoy sex.

Then again, never in her wildest dreams had she counted on a guy like Hunter Osborn.

As HIS RIOTING pulse quieted, Hunter made no move to release Jodi. Though he felt numb in body and soul, he'd had the forethought to turn to his back, but he'd taken her with him. She was a small, warm weight resting on his heart, one slender thigh draping his, her fingers idly toying with his chest hair. When she spoke, he forced himself to focus.

"Big men used to unsettle me." She turned her face up to his. "I know my own ability, and against someone twice my size, I'm outgunned on muscle alone."

He was twice her size—but he would use that advantage to protect her, to shield her from ugliness, as much as she would allow him to. Letting his hand drift to her ass, he cuddled a bare cheek and waited.

Jodi squirmed against him. "When I met the McKenzies, I realized how overbearing big guys can be. They would never hurt me, but they always wanted to stand in my way."

"To keep you safe," Hunter rumbled, amazed that he could find his voice when every bone, muscle and bit of sinew in his body was currently lax.

"Yup," she said. "Even when it's not necessary." Spreading her fingers wide, she stroked over his chest, up to his collarbone and to the firm deltoid muscle around his shoulder. "With you, I'm finding big dudes are crazy-sexy, too. This body of yours…" She leaned down and took a soft love bite of his pec, then dampened it with her tongue. "Swear to God, Hunter, you smell so good and look so fine, I could just eat you up."

There went his drowsiness. Abruptly, he turned, pinning her under him again, loving the cushion of her warmth, the gentle softness that was such a contrast to her bold, larger-than-life persona.

Her breasts were modest in size but plump and round, her nipples a dark pink. He liked seeing her pale flesh held by his darker, rougher hands. She obviously had no idea, but her body was perfection, every curve in exact, enticing proportion. True, she didn't carry any spare weight. He could see her ribs, and her hip bones, but she didn't look too thin. Her flat stomach enticed him. Her smooth thighs and slender calves made her legs look longer. Everything about her was delicate—except her attitude.

He met her gaze and caught her wide, triumphant grin. Clearly, that comment about eating him up had gotten her the exact result she wanted.

"Tease." Once again, she'd proved that she had great instincts—even when it came to intimacy.

"Got your attention."

"Honey, you've had my attention from the second I noticed you on that big mower, wearing frayed shorts and work boots." He lightly nibbled on her bottom lip, and whispered, "Anytime you want me, you only need to say so."

"What if I always want you?"

Hunter lifted to his forearms to see her expression. Vulnerability and challenge vied for top honors. Not uncommon when it came to Jodi. Softly, he said, "You can always have me." He took her mouth in a kiss of ultimate possession that had her squirming, then asked, "And since that's a fact, do you want something to eat before I start devouring you?"

She pretended to give it some thought, then said with apology, "I am pretty hungry."

Though she wouldn't have said so on her own. She might not even have realized it. He'd have his work cut out for him, getting her on some sort of a routine. She'd had a long day, yet she didn't appear the least bit tired. Her energy level amazed him. "How do waffles sound?"

She'd been busy staring at his mouth, maybe doing her

own introspection about things, but now she widened her eyes. "Waffles for dinner?"

"You want something else?"

Brief amusement flashed in her eyes. "Look at us, planning dinner after sex. That seems so normal, doesn't it?"

If he had his way, it would become the norm very quickly. "We can be normal." He kissed her. "Or abnormal." Another, deeper kiss. "Or like you, extraordinary." He gave a soft tug to her bottom lip, then whispered huskily, "As long as we do it together."

Jodi hugged him tight, her face against his throat for a few seconds as she seemed to struggle with her emotions. When she dropped back to the pillow, she smiled at him, a soft, accepting smile. "Now that you've mentioned waffles, I think they sound perfect."

"Good. I'll plug in the waffle iron." He started to leave the bed, but she stopped him.

"I'm, um, sticky?" She scrunched her nose. "If I get up, the sticky is going to get all over your sheets."

Nothing with Jodi would ever be predictable. Grinning, Hunter said, "Let me do the honors. Stay put."

She frowned over that, gave it some thought and shrugged. "Yeah, sure. Knock yourself out."

He went into the bathroom and wet a soft washcloth with warm water. When he returned to the bed, Jodi was right where he'd left her, ankles crossed, one arm resting on her stomach, the other at her side. She turned her head toward him and waited.

Sitting by her hip, he gave her a long, heated look and said, "Open your legs."

"I like how you make that sound so sexy." Without hesitation, she bent one knee out.

God love her, her every reaction was distinctive. Never

would he be able to second-guess her. As he pressed the cloth to her, he again looked at her body. "Will you believe me when I tell you how fucking gorgeous you are?"

Her lips quirked. Sticking to her no-cursing rule, she repeated, "*Effing* gorgeous. Not just plain gorgeous?"

"No. With you, nothing is plain."

"I think you're effing gorgeous, too. Every inch of you. Not just your stellar bod—which really is spectacular—but your face, how you smile at me and how you make me smile, and the things you say and do, sort of serious but also funny."

He moved the cloth enough to distract her from the effusive compliments.

She went still, then bit her bottom lip.

"Jodi." Maybe feeding her could wait. He started to lean toward her, but caught himself in time. He'd made her a promise, and he needed to keep it. "Not to discourage you, but there were things we'd planned to discuss."

Turning serious in a heartbeat, Jodi scooted up in the bed, put her bare shoulders to the headboard and dropped a pillow over her lap. "I'm listening."

The eager way she'd jumped on that drove home just how unfair he'd been. Standing, Hunter took the cloth to the bathroom, rinsed it out again, then cleaned himself before draping it over the edge of the tub. In his head, his thoughts scrambled for the best way to begin, and how quickly he could end. When he turned back to the bedroom, Jodi was exactly as he'd left her.

In his bed, where he'd wanted her since the day he'd met her—whether he'd acknowledged it or not.

What if his honesty drove her away? No, the truth wouldn't do that. Out of the many people who'd be unable to deal with his confessions, Jodi wasn't one of them.

He came to stand at the side of the bed. "Most of the time, working as a park ranger was pretty routine."

Jodi stayed silent, listening with undivided interest.

He pulled the quilt free from the bottom of the bed and shook it out so that it settled over the mattress. Getting into bed beside her, he mimicked her position, but with the quilt pulled over his lap. "I'd taken on the wildlife-specialist duties, like monitoring wild game harvests, managing hunting units and food plots, wildlife surveys, making schedules, stuff like that."

Shifting slightly closer, Jodi put her shoulder to his, then drew up the quilt as well.

Once she'd gotten comfortable, he continued. "Occasionally, the job included responding to emergency situations. Some people thought nature was the perfect place to commit suicide. They'd go out alone in the woods and either put a bullet through their skull, or deliberately plummet off a cliff. One guy hung himself." Hunter stared at the foot of the bed. "Animals had eaten part of him before we found him."

"Gruesome," she murmured, and somehow she was closer still. Was she doing that for him, or for herself? In case she needed the nearness, he put his arm around her and drew her flush against his side. "We'd had three different women go missing over a month, all in totally different sections of the park. That wasn't uncommon, from lost campers to ditched dates to suicides." His chest expanded, as much with dread as need for oxygen. Forcing out the words, he said, "I had a hunch."

"Instincts," she confirmed softly. "Neither of us would ever ignore them."

"I was off duty one Saturday, but I couldn't get it out of my head that the disappearances of those women were somehow related. The areas had already been searched.

People had given up on the first two, assuming they were dead, consumed by nature." When her hand settled on his chest, small and warm, her fingertips gently coaxing, he realized that he'd gone rigid and consciously relaxed again. Jodi had been through enough, far too much, she didn't need his anxiety on top of her own. "I kept thinking through everything we'd been told about the women—they were different from each other, various ages, builds, types—and I scoured my brain for everything I'd ever learned about the mountains. Finally, I decided to check out an idea."

Jodi pressed her lips to his skin, then hugged him.

Such a compassionate woman, despite all she'd dealt with. That ability to not only understand, but truly care, was rare. *She* was rare.

And she was his.

"I'd already seen a lot of shit while working. I had a near miss from a poacher's bow and arrow in the middle of the night, busted up drug deals, kept watch on suspected pedophiles. Once I even fought a fire on my own, set by a small-time arsonist who recorded it from the woods." He flashed her a look. "I got him, by the way. My point is that you hear things, and learn things that stick with you. Clues, mannerisms. I'd been told more than a few times that I was a natural. Pieces come together for me when they don't for anyone else." Once again, he fell silent, but it'd be better to get it all said. "There was an area of the mountains that was nearly impassable. We forever heard rumors of things happening there. Noises in the night, cries that seemed to come from everywhere." He glanced down at her. "People claimed Bigfoot was around."

"Ghost stories," Jodi whispered.

"Or so we thought." But he'd had that damn feeling that he couldn't shake. "After fighting it throughout Saturday night, I took off at first light on Sunday morning, loaded down with gear, including a radio and my weapon."

"Smart."

God, he wished he'd taken more. "I knew where I wanted to go—but I didn't know what I would find." The seconds ticked by while he fought the images.

To her credit, Jodi didn't press him.

"It was damn near nightfall when I heard her screams." Sometimes, when he tried to sleep, he heard the tortured cries still.

They'd echo in his head, over and over...much like they had on the mountain.

Hunter lowered his voice, straining around the memory. "At first I couldn't tell if they were animal or human, or from what direction they came. I only knew that someone or something was hurt. My gut urged me to run to the person, but my caution is somehow ingrained." Furious at himself, he squeezed his eyes shut. "I radioed it in, giving my location, and then I started picking my way forward. It was shadowy enough, the woods rocky and rough, that I knew I could fall and break my damn leg, then I wouldn't be able to help anyone."

"You did the smart thing," Jodi reiterated.

"I should have given in to the urgency."

With no sign of condemnation, Jodi asked, "What happened?"

It wasn't easy, sharing something that he'd tried so hard to bury. Talking about it made it all fresh again, constricting his lungs, causing his muscles to tense. Sharing made it real, when he'd prefer to file it away as a nightmare.

Bad as it was, Jodi had a right to know, so he forced out the awful admission. "By the time I found her an hour later, he'd nearly tortured her to death." Regrets, as raw as ever, bombarded him. "He had her staked out naked on the ground, blood everywhere, and he was..." Bile rose in his throat, but he choked it back. "He'd cut her all over, long, shallow cuts, on her arms, legs and torso, a few on her face. I remember seeing her eyes, wide and wild, and in the firelight, her skin was so pale."

Surprising him, Jodi pushed back the quilt and crawled into his lap, nestling against his chest, her cheek on his shoulder, and her arm around his neck. "Go on."

Bemused, Hunter pulled the quilt over her and pressed a kiss to the top of her head. Her closeness was exactly what he'd needed, and somehow she'd known that. When suffering her own memories, she'd shied away from being touched, but for him...

The words emerged as a whisper. "He had the knife to her groin, in that tender spot between leg and pelvis, and he was making small cuts while smiling at her." *Miserable sick bastard.* Never again could anyone tell him that monsters didn't exist. He knew better, because he'd seen them.

Jodi breathed a little faster. "You had your gun."

"Yes, and I shot him, no questions asked. I should have ordered him to back up, should have restrained him."

"Screw that," she said with heated passion. "That's a shoot-first-and-ask-questions-later scenario."

Her attitude gave him a small smile, one of relief that she understood, but also admiration, because she was so fierce. "It was like I wasn't me anymore. I saw that poor woman, and without making a sound, I put one into his chest. He fell over her, the knife trapped between them. That had her screaming hysterically again, but she sounded weak, as if she had no reserves left." Hunter squeezed his eyes shut, but only for a moment. "God, I was afraid that I'd caused her death, that I'd been the one to force a fatal cut. I grabbed him off her and tossed him aside. The knife was in the ground be-tween her legs." Anger at himself forced him to draw a deep breath. "I didn't secure the area. Instead, I told her she was safe, that help was on the way, while I used the knife to cut her hands free. As soon as she could, she curled in on her-self, her body limp like a rag doll, but slippery with blood."

"Dear God."

His heart started pumping too hard, painfully slamming against his ribs. "The smells were awful. I don't know how long he had her staked out like that, but it was far too long. One fucking minute with that lunatic would have been too long, but he'd had her for more than two days. I could smell the infection on her, and urine, and all that blood." And now came the worst part.

"Did she live?" Jodi asked simply.

Such a difficult question. Hunter bypassed it for now. "Unfortunately, my shot hadn't killed the bastard, and I was still cutting her right foot free when he clubbed me in the back of the head. Stupid. So fucking *stupid* for me not to have secured him. I..." He shook his head, still fu-rious at himself. "I saw her and my only thought was get-ting her free."

"Pretty sure anyone would have felt that way."

"It was a rookie mistake because I let emotion cloud my judgment. I knew better. Remember, I was the guy who put things together, the one who saw what others didn't." What a joke. "When I left that morning, it was with a hunch that something awful was happening. And still it took me by surprise."

"You expected a kidnapper, Hunter, not a lunatic."

It was a sad truth that they both knew too much about the evil in the world. "The hit on the head dazed me, every-thing was swimming and combined with the smells... I almost passed out, but I saw him drawing back to hit her, the log aimed at her face and…"

"You couldn't let him do that."

No, he couldn't. "He wasn't alone, Jodi. Another man shouted from the woods. He yelled *Nevil*, like they were friends and he was worried."

"Damn."

She'd just broken her own rule about cursing. "I had the knife in my hand, and I knew with my head pounding that I couldn't take on two men, so I went on autopilot."

"Good." She hugged him again.

"I started stabbing him, over and over again, even after he fell back, I couldn't seem to stop myself. I stabbed him more than he'd stabbed her. In more places. Deeper cuts." Remembering the carnage he'd left behind, Hunter clenched. "I should have just cut his throat, but what I did was so much worse—"

"Survival isn't pretty."

No, it hadn't been. For either of them. "I'd just gotten my gun drawn again when the second man entered the clearing. He saw Nevil, or what was left of him, and he roared."

"You shot him, too?"

"I emptied my gun into him." Talk about overkill. "I didn't know if there'd be a third man, or a fourth, but the woman's cries were different. Less hysterical and weaker. I asked her if there was anyone else, but she just kept sobbing."

"What a hero you are, Hunter Osborn. No lie, your instincts are amazing. All day climbing in the mountains, then coming on to a scene like that. I mean, I wish you'd shot their balls off, too, but you did great. Even shocked at seeing that awful sight, and getting clubbed on the noggin, you did what a hero does. You protected the innocent." She kissed his chest, softly, a light brush of her lips, then his jaw, his chin, the bridge of his nose. "Autopilot is good. It means you function, no matter what. I think that's awesome."

"Jodi?" He didn't understand her.

"You were appealing from day one, but now? How could I ever let you go?"

That got his brain processing again. "You can't," he said firmly, crushing her close. "Not ever."

Her arms tightened, too, and she said softly, "Good."

They sat like that for a while. Luckily, Turbo slept on undisturbed, and Hunter gradually regained his control. Jodi remained Jodi, quirky and surprising and, as far as he was concerned, absolutely perfect. *For him.* "I knew it'd be a while before help arrived, probably not until the morning. Honest to God, Jodi, I didn't know if she'd make it that long."

"Did you have a concussion?"

Funny that, under the circumstances, she'd ask about him instead of the woman. "I did, yeah. There were times I saw double, and my head felt like he'd split it open. I worked by rote, just doing what had to be done, however I could do it."

"I understand."

"I got her covered and put up a shelter, first."

She lifted her head to see him. "From the supplies you had?"

"I had a survival backpack, so I had most of what we needed, including a two-person tent. Not fancy, but it'd be shelter if it rained. Small amount of rations, water, first aid kit, antibacterial wipes, heat packs, fire starter..." Seriously, Jodi didn't need to know the entire contents of his backpack. "A stream wasn't far away, and we could have used the water." Blood was *everywhere*, and all over him. "But she didn't want me to move. She was panicked by the idea that I wouldn't come back. Even when I threw up twice, she wanted to be able to see me." He let out a breath that was part laugh, part pain. "It was humiliating, showing so much weakness when I should have been stronger for her."

"Eh, you're mortal, dude, and a concussion is serious stuff. I think the fact that you stayed with her instead of seeking privacy, putting her needs over your own, *is* a show of strength."

Figured Jodi would see it that way. "I dragged the bodies a few yards away, tied them to a tree, and covered them with branches so she wouldn't have to see them."

Curious, Jodi asked, "Why'd you tie them? Did you think either of them might still be alive?"

"There was no doubt they were dead, believe me." Never would he forget the mangled, damaged bodies. "The smell of all the blood could have drawn in wild animals. I kept my gun and extra ammo close, just in case, but with a concussion, I didn't want to chance passing out, only to come to and find them gone. I thought…" His mouth tightened. "I *sensed* that they had something to do with the other missing women, too, and possibly even women we hadn't heard about. I knew investigators would need fingerprints, dental records… Hell, everything, probably."

"See, you were still sharp as a tack. I love it."

Love… He wanted that, and more, from her. "They had their own supplies. A bigger tent, backpacks with equipment. Other than the knife that I'd already touched, I used a stick to drag their guns closer in case I needed them. I didn't want to touch anything else and maybe dick up evidence. I concentrated on cleaning her up a little. Some of her wounds—he'd made them deliberately shallow so she wouldn't bleed to death, but there was definite infection and I knew she had to be in awful pain. Mostly she was in shock, though, as if she could barely feel herself anymore. I did what first aid I could, then got her covered and as comfortable as possible. She passed out shortly after that, gripping my hand."

Jodi turned to get his hand, carrying it to her face and kissing his palm. "You were her lifeline."

Yes, he had been. And he'd been so damned afraid that he'd let her down, that she'd be dead by the time help arrived. "If only I'd trusted my gut and done something on Saturday."

"You're not a mind reader."

"She was hurt so badly. Literally everywhere. Anytime she woke, I tried to get her to eat, but she couldn't stay alert long enough to get more than a few bites. I was afraid if I went to sleep, I might not come around when she needed me."

"Because of the concussion?"

"Yes. So I waited. Even when I spoke through the radio, she didn't stir. There were a few times I thought I'd lost her, but then she'd wail, remembering something, or she'd suddenly groan." He opened his hand against Jodi's cheek, cradling her precious face, thankful that she, too, had survived. "I had that man's blood all over me, but I didn't want to waste the rest of our water on me, and I didn't dare leave her alone to go to the stream."

"That had to be the worst night of your entire life."

When Jodi hugged him, he spoke against her hair. "When help arrived at dawn, they found the other women, both nearby, their bodies in different stages of decay."

Her slender arms tightened more.

"I was grilled endlessly." With a sardonic twist to his mouth, he said, "The men were brothers from an influential family. Their mother tried to claim I was the madman and that I'd just blamed them. After all, I'd mangled them pretty badly."

"Morons."

"For three days, the woman didn't talk. They kept her sedated while they treated her. She'd lost a lot of blood, but the infection is what almost did her in. For those three days, my name was dragged through the mud with endless accusations." His jaw worked. "Memphis, Mom and Dad had to put up with reporters calling and showing up on their lawns."

"I bet Memphis had a few choice words for them."

"Actually, it was Mom who lost her cool and told them they were imbeciles who had no business reporting the news when they couldn't get simple facts straight."

Jodi grinned. "Oh, I like her."

"On the fourth morning, the woman came around enough to clear up the confusion. I hated that she was put through that, and she was shaky on some of the details. But she made it clear, I saved her." He smoothed Jodi's hair. "Even though the brothers were eventually tied to other murders, some still whisper about it. They say I was involved or I brainwashed the woman. You know how that goes."

"They have no clue." Softly, slowly, she traced a fingertip around his mouth. "That's why you moved here?"

"In part. Plus, I needed to get out of my own head. When I was still there, I kept picturing her as I'd last seen her in the hospital. Haunted, as if a part of her had been stripped away. I guess it had. She'll always be afraid now." He hesitated. She'd be afraid in the same way Jodi was aware. Once you knew about the evil that existed, you could never discount it. "She thanked me, but said she should have just died, that it would have been easier."

"She was wrong, Hunter. I bet it's gotten a little easier for her every day."

For Jodi, that might be true, because Jodi was stronger

than most. Hell, she was stronger than any other person he knew. "I haven't seen her since she got out of the hospital."

Sitting up and straddling his lap, Jodi held his face between her hands and said, "Then she may be better already. She might be in love, married or have a kid. She might not. No one knows how long it takes for someone to recover, or at least recover enough to function. You and I both know stuff crawls into your brain and won't get out, no matter how you try to shove it away. But, Hunter, even if she's not yet happy to be alive, she's no longer being tortured. Her parents have her home, so they can sleep at night without wondering where she is, what she's going through or if they'll ever see her again." She put a firm, loud smooch to his mouth. "She's *not dead*, alone on a mountain with her last memory of pain and terror."

There was consolation in what she said. Was that what Jodi had feared? That she'd die alone? Had anyone missed her? It didn't seem likely, based on what she'd told him.

"You, Hunter Osborn, listened to your gut and saved her. You found the other missing women, so their families could have closure. Best of all, you removed two of the monsters. It's a terrible fact that more exist, but now there are a few less and I'm cheering."

"I lost my head."

"Bull! Against the odds, with a freaking concussion, you handled it. I'm cheering you. You need to cheer yourself and forget about idiotic reporters who only want a sensational story."

He'd like to forget, but… "I butchered the first man."

"Good." She smiled at him. "Remember, I did the same— only with a chunk of wood, not a clean blade."

"That was different." Hunter clasped her shoulders. "You didn't have a choice."

"Of course I did. I could have stabbed him once and then gotten out of there and locked him in. But we're both survivors, and we didn't take chances." She kissed him again, longer this time, with more feeling. She put her forehead to his. "Now that I'm with you, I'm glad I'm still here. I want you to be glad to be here, too."

"I am." He tumbled her to her back, as always, amazed by her. The brutality of what he'd done hadn't stunned her. Instead, she'd related to it, and taken solace in the fact that she wasn't alone. "Jodi, I—"

Whatever declarations he'd been about to make were forgotten when an alert sounded on her phone.

With a small jerk, Jodi went from warm and intimate to starkly aware. She twisted away from him and grabbed up the phone. "It's from Madison."

Hunter could see a message on the screen. You two have company. He'd forgotten all about calling Madison, but clearly she already knew they were together.

Shit. Rolling from the bed, he jerked on his flannel pants. A second later, Turbo started howling. Aware of Jodi yanking on her shirt and nothing else, he opened the nightstand and withdrew a Glock with a night sight on it.

She grabbed her own gun and her phone.

Bare assed.

She intended to handle whatever problem they faced *without pants*.

Without even *panties*.

Wishing he could tell her to stay back and let him handle it, Hunter cursed low and followed close behind as she unlocked the bedroom door and darted into the living area. Catching her arm, Hunter spoke over the racket Turbo made. "Wait."

Volatile, Jodi rounded on him—until she saw him checking the camera access on his own phone, then she crowded in next to him so she could see as well.

As the tall, broad-shouldered shape of a dark-haired man stepped out of a black Jeep in his driveway, Hunter relaxed. "Son of a bitch, I'm going to pound on him."

"Him who?" Jodi demanded.

"My brother." He looked her over. "Now, will you put on pants? He'll like you either way, but I'd just as soon Memphis not like quite so much of you right off."

JODI GLANCED UP over her bite of syrup-covered waffle. On one side of her plate, she had a cup of coffee, and on the other, her gun rested next to her phone. It was so quiet, she could hear everyone chewing. Were they always like this? Or had she caused all the tension?

She studied Memphis, specifically the way he put all his concentration on his food.

Hunter's brother was a looker. He had the same coloring as Hunter, and anyone could see they were brothers, but the angles of his face were harder edged. A meaner jaw, sharper cheekbones. His hair was slightly longer.

Were they pissed at each other?

Earlier, when Memphis had just arrived, she'd listened from the bedroom where she'd quickly pulled on panties and shorts. She'd heard Hunter demanding to know if their parents were okay.

Nice that he loved them so much, they were his first concern. Nice, too, that Memphis had immediately stated, "Everyone is fine. No, don't snarl at me. I had to see you." With what could easily be discerned as happiness, Memphis had added, "Damn, Hunter, I've missed you."

She imagined the silence after that meant some bear

hugs or something. It had been a different kind of silence, more peaceful, than what they had now.

Jodi had lingered just a bit—not long, because her curiosity was too keen for that—but she'd heard Memphis complimenting the house, heard Hunter's low voice replying.

She'd texted Madison that it was just Hunter's brother—to which Madison had replied: I know. :)

Sneaky. Guess that was Madison's way of keeping her on her toes. Jodi had decided to give her hell for that later. Right then, she'd wanted only to join the men. There'd been quick introductions, where Memphis had worked hard to keep his gaze just on her face. She hadn't bothered doing the same.

He'd shown up unexpectedly, and he was a stranger to her, so she refused to take chances. She'd checked him out, top to bottom. He didn't appear to be armed, not with the fitted T-shirt stretching from shoulder to shoulder. No bulges in his worn jeans, other than the usual near his crotch, and the outline of a wallet in one back pocket, a cell phone in the other.

Reassured, she'd followed Hunter into the kitchen while Memphis chose to play with Turbo, greeting the dog like a long-lost pal.

Hunter made the waffles and she tried to deal with her disappointment.

Her first night getting it on with Hunter, over before it had really begun.

He'd shared his past with her, and instead of being able to say all the things she wanted to say, they were sitting here now, eating waffles. Granted, delicious waffles. And she had been hungry, but still...

The silence was nearly suffocating.

After scooping in another buttery, syrupy bite, she went

back to studying Memphis. He was probably as tall as Hunter, but a little leaner. She supposed he could have a knife or gun strapped to his ankle, but he was Hunter's brother, so she should give him some leeway.

Hunter nudged her.

When she glanced at him, she caught his scowl. "What?"

"He doesn't like you staring at me," Memphis said, as if women staring was the norm in his world. "Great waffles, Hunter. Almost as good as Mom's."

"It's her recipe."

"She'll be tickled when I tell her."

Not the least put off by their inane chatter, Jodi clarified, "I was staring at you because you look a lot like Hunter. Do you two get that from your mama or your daddy?"

Slowly, dark blue eyes twinkling, Memphis smiled. "I love how you talk. It's like a mix of country bumpkin with a blunt edge."

Unsure if she'd just been insulted, Jodi sat back.

Hunter seemed appeased, but he warned his brother, "Say or do anything that bothers her, and you'll be back outside the door in a nanosecond."

"Do I bother you, sweetheart?"

Ah, she was starting to catch on. The two brothers loved each other, but they also had some sort of sibling bickering going on, not much different from how Cade and Reyes heckled each other. "First, not your sweetheart, so don't call me that again. Second, I don't know you, and other than the importance of you being Hunter's brother, you don't matter to me."

"Meaning if he ruthlessly tosses me out, you wouldn't mind?"

"Hey, it was my first sleepover, you know? I'd just as

soon you weren't here anyway." She shifted her gaze to Hunter. "I had plans."

Those same blue eyes were very different on Hunter. "Our plans haven't changed," he assured her. "Memphis will sleep at the other end of the house."

Grinning now, Memphis agreed. "I'll even convince Turbo to keep me company."

Huh. So Hunter didn't care if his brother knew his private business? Fine by her. "Appreciate it." Jodi went back to eating, aware of the two brothers smiling at each other. Yeah, she was an oddity and she knew it, but she wanted what she wanted. Hunter.

Getting up for more coffee, Memphis said, "Mom and Dad both have dark hair, but Mom's is curlier. We get our height and shoulders from Dad's side of the family. They're all tall, including our grandparents."

"You have grandparents?"

"Pretty sure everyone does."

Not her. She didn't have parents, aunts or uncles... Until the McKenzies, she'd had no one. "How is your mom built?"

Smile flickering, Memphis said, "She's bigger than you, but then, who isn't, right? Compared to us, she's short."

"I'm not short," Jodi denied, just to be contrary.

"I guess you're taller than Turbo." Memphis moved on. "Seriously, I am sorry to drop in unannounced."

Jodi wasn't sure if that was addressed to her or Hunter, until he continued.

"Once I talked to you, though, and knew you were coming around, I had to see you. It's been over a year."

Hunter accepted that. "I appreciate how patient you've been."

"It wasn't easy. Mom's going to kill me when she finds

out I visited without bringing her, but I figured one at a time—for now."

"I'll talk with her soon."

Memphis's gaze cut to Jodi and he carried over the pot to refill her cup as well. "You're not what I expected."

Jodi opened her mouth, but he didn't give her a chance to say a single word.

"You're better. So much better," he emphasized. "Hunter would never be content with the standard relationship, not after the life he's led."

Jodi was offended on behalf of all womankind. "Every woman is different."

"And yet some stand out."

"Memphis," Hunter warned.

"I'm just saying. She's different—in a good way."

Hunter's warm gaze moved over her. "On that, we agree."

Flustered by their praise, Jodi snorted. "What is it with the Osborn boys and outrageous compliments?"

"We both have eyes, we're intelligent and we can see beneath the surface." Memphis gave her a sincere smile that was markedly different, less teasing than what she'd seen from him so far. "I couldn't figure out what had happened, but now that I've met you…" His voice softened. "It all makes sense."

"Time out." Jodi pushed away her plate and scowled. "You don't know me."

"I know plenty." Memphis sat and he, too, pushed away his plate. Unlike her, he sat forward and folded his arms on the table. "One, you're hot." He said in an aside to Hunter, "It's cute that she doesn't know it."

"Yeah," Hunter agreed. "But I'm convincing her."

Damn it, she was going to stay in a state of embarrassment.

Why the heck was Hunter letting his brother carry on, anyway? He seemed...satisfied? Yeah, that was his expression. As if he liked that his brother had strong opinions on her. "Nothing about me is cute." Ready to disabuse him of that absurd notion, she narrowed her eyes. "Should I prove it?"

"Two," Memphis continued, not at all perturbed by her threat, "you speak your mind."

"Most people don't like that," she quickly pointed out.

"Intelligent people do. Three—" he nodded at the gun "—you have trust issues, and you're secure enough that you don't care if others know."

"Not trusting people makes me secure?" She shook her head. "That doesn't make sense."

"I have trust issues, too, but that's not what I meant. It's the fact that you don't cave to manners. Most people would, you know. They'd worry about offending someone, so even if they sensed something was wrong, they wouldn't do anything about it." He lifted his hands. "You don't care if they're offended."

Jodi muttered, "I always think something is wrong."

That amused him. "You have an answer for everything, don't you? It's not going to change my opinion. You're special, period. I see it, Hunter obviously sees it."

"I do," Hunter agreed.

"And," Memphis continued, "I promise to never give you reason to shoot me."

His good humor was starting to wear her down. It was hard to be grumpy with someone like Memphis around. "Okay, fine."

This time his grin looked downright wicked. She'd be willing to bet he gave women fits. And his poor mother. She'd had her hands full raising him, Jodi could tell. "If everyone's done eating, I'll clean up the mess while you two visit."

Somehow Memphis managed to look appalled. "I'll clean after I grab my bags from the Jeep. It's the least I can do after barging in. You two just...carry on."

Hunter pushed back his chair at the same time Jodi did. Knowing they shared the same thought, she smiled. It was nice to be in sync with someone. "You can't go out there alone."

Taken aback, Memphis glanced around as if assuming she spoke to someone else. "I'm thirty years old, not a kid afraid of the dark. Besides, Hunter's yard is lit up like a stadium."

"It's not that," Hunter said. "We've had too much trouble." Briefly he explained about Remmy's visit. "We don't yet know what's in her house, but I'm guessing it'll be evidence enough to destroy King."

"Well, that settles it. I'll bring in my stuff, then go to Jodi's house and start searching."

"No," Jodi said, appalled at the idea of him rummaging through her things.

"No," Hunter echoed, equally adamant. "If I didn't want Jodi there alone, I damn sure don't want my brother there alone either."

Memphis tucked in his chin with an incredulous expression. "You say that," he accused, "as if she'd be better equipped to defend herself than I would."

Frowning, Jodi asked, "You think I wouldn't?"

"Enough." Hunter stepped between them so that all Jodi could see was his broad back. "We'll all sleep tonight—"

"You're not planning on sleeping," Memphis pointed out.

"Hope not," Jodi whispered, and that stalled him for a few beats.

"Tomorrow, we can all three go to her house and search."

Stepping around him, Jodi asked, "Did I agree to that?"

Hunter put an arm around her and drew her to his side. "You're reasonable, so you would have."

True. Plus, she really didn't want to argue with Memphis. She got that his pride was bent a little, but then, he didn't yet know her well enough to see that she was *totally* better at defending herself than he'd be. And he didn't understand the level of threat posed by King and his goons. "Tell you what. You go guard your brother while I get started in here." To Memphis, she ordered, "No argument. Until we get this resolved, no one goes off on his or her own." To Hunter, she said, "Carry your weapon."

"I was planning to." He caught the back of her neck and drew her up for a firm kiss to her mouth, lingering just long enough that Memphis whistled.

That drew Turbo, who lumbered into the kitchen with a yawn.

Still holding her, Hunter said, "Keep in mind that I'm not an idiot, okay?"

Yeah, she really did need to quit insulting the brothers, even inadvertently. "Sorry."

"You're forgiven." As if to prove it, Hunter gave her another kiss, then took the leash from the back-door knob and headed off with the dog.

Jodi stood there watching while Hunter paused in the living room to pick up his Glock where he'd left it.

Next to her, Memphis murmured, "You've got it bad. I like it."

She turned and almost ran into his chest. Frying him with her deadliest stare—which had him backing up two steps—she said, "Don't sneak up on me."

"Yes, ma'am."

Jodi huffed a laugh. "And don't ever again call me *ma'am*."

"Yes, Jodi." He saluted smartly and sauntered out.

"Goof." Grinning, she stacked plates together near the sink, then put her own weapon near at hand. It didn't take her long to rinse the dishes and get them in the dishwasher. She cleaned the almost-empty coffeepot and put away the waffle iron, wiped off the table, counters, rinsed the cloth, rehung the dish towel… Out of things to do, she glanced around.

Hunter's kitchen wasn't that big, but the way it opened into the dining room, which was connected to the great room, made it feel larger. Curious, she stepped out of the kitchen and could see both men through the open front door. Memphis stood there beside his Jeep, holding a bag and talking quietly with Hunter, while Turbo investigated several spots.

Security lights kept the area bright. Other than a stirring breeze, all was quiet.

The fact that Turbo was at peace reassured her that none of King's men were lurking around.

While they were occupied, Jodi went to the smaller bedroom that Memphis would use. There was a full-size bed, made up with a quilt and two standard pillows, one nightstand, and a closet with folding doors, a few hangers inside. Overall, a utilitarian room, but it had everything he needed. Across from it was Hunter's office and a small bathroom. The bathroom had two hand towels hanging on a rod, a clear curtain for the shower, a bar of soap in a dish, but nothing else. Clearly, Hunter preferred the bigger bath connected to his bedroom.

She hadn't investigated these rooms before, so while she was here, she checked the locks on the bedroom windows and, as expected, found them to be as secure as the rest. The only way for anyone to get in would be to break the glass, and that'd set off an alarm.

The bathroom was windowless, so she moved on from

that and stepped into the office doorway. This room was small and simple, with a desk in front of the window that overlooked the backyard, the chicken coop, garden and all those trees. On the desktop was a calendar, lamp and a cup full of pens and pencils. A large swivel chair on rollers would make it easy to glide over to a bookcase filled with papers. On another wall was a tall, very cool gun-and-rifle cabinet.

Wow, they had more in common than she'd realized.

After admiring the cabinet and wondering what weapons he kept inside, she decided to get a few towels for Memphis. In Hunter's linen closet, she also found washrags and an extra shampoo, though Memphis might have brought his own. She set all that, with a bottle of water, on the bathroom sink.

Memphis would have what he needed, and she'd be at the other end of the house getting busy with Hunter. His brother would have no need to interrupt.

She considered going outside with the guys but decided they might enjoy a few minutes to talk, so instead, she headed back into the kitchen. She'd now seen every inch of the house and knew he had great security.

She no sooner had the thought than her gaze landed on the basement door. An innocuous door, the same as any other in his house, except that this door sent a cold chill running along her spine.

She liked his house, she really did, more and more every day.

The basement, not so much.

Half a minute later, both men came in. Memphis, trailed by Turbo, carried his bag to the guest room he'd use, and Hunter stepped into the kitchen. On his way to rehang the leash, he paused. "What's wrong?"

Jodi shook her head. "Nothing." To hide her rioting

thoughts, she turned away and busied herself at the sink, folding and refolding the dishcloth.

There was a moment of silence, then Hunter gently turned her. "You can tell me anything, remember?"

Yeah, she knew she could, but it still bothered her to admit to weaknesses. "It's nothing."

"Jodi." Bending his knees, he looked into her eyes. "Tell me."

Knowing he wouldn't let up, she rolled one shoulder. "I don't like your basement, that's all." She glanced past him at that door, knowing it opened to stairs that would lead down, down... She fought off a shudder. "It's dumb, but it gives me the creeps."

Drawing her in, Hunter folded his arms around her and rested his chin on top of her head. "It's our first time together. I shouldn't have left you alone for so long. I'm sorry."

Yeah, right. "I don't need a babysitter. I just need to get over..." She nodded at the door. Whatever that pesky *reaction* might be. Memories? Cowardice? She wasn't sure what to call it, but she hated how vulnerable it made her feel.

"Why?" Hunter asked. "I'm not over the shit I dealt with. You heard my brother. I was gone for almost two years. We each have a right to our demons, honey."

"We're fighting them, though." Of that, she was certain. Never would she give in to stupid fears.

"When and how we want. There's not a timetable." He pressed his lips to her temple. "I'll put a padlock on the door if you want. Would that help?"

Probably not, but she smiled. "Eventually, I'll have to make myself go down there."

Hunter frowned. "Not without me, okay? Promise me."

Now, that pricked her pride. "I can—"

He kissed her again, more demandingly this time.

Wow, she loved that.

He held her close, his mouth moving over hers, his tongue doing wicked things to her pulse.

By the time he let up, she wasn't sure she could get her eyes open.

"Not without me," he insisted softly.

Jodi figured she had to give in to him every now and then since he'd so often given in to her. Resting against him, she whispered, "Okay, fine."

"Thank you."

Silly Hunter. "What's it like down there?"

Another kiss, this one on her forehead. "It's like up here, really. Well-lit, neat shelves, a clean floor with a runner or two so my feet don't get cold in the winter." His hand curved around her jaw, his thumb touching her bottom lip. "I promise you, it'll be very different from where you were kept."

The way he described it, she probably could tolerate it. "We could go down there soon."

"Soon, but not tonight." Voice lower, Hunter added, "Tonight, we're going to clear up a few things."

"Yeah, like what?"

"Ground rules. For both of us."

To Jodi, that sounded like a promise. "Ground rules. I can handle that." She took his hand, ready to lead him back to bed…and her stupid phone rang.

Interrupted…*again*.

CHAPTER TEN

SITTING AT THE kitchen table with Hunter beside her, Jodi set the phone down and said to Madison, "I have you on speaker."

"No problem." In the background, the tapping of keys could be heard. "So, how are you kids doing?"

Chitchat? That's what Madison wanted? "You about stopped my heart with that damned text."

Laughing, Madison said, "Baloney. I bet you went all lethal and loved it."

"She did," Hunter confirmed. "But she ran out of the room without panties."

While Jodi stared at him, aghast, Madison hooted.

"Next time," Hunter said, "be more specific—for my sake, if not for hers."

"All right, all right." More tapping. "Will you forgive me for keeping an eye on your outside cameras?"

"Under the circumstances, I'm glad for the extra precaution." He reached for Jodi's hand, and after a few more glares, she gave in.

With that accomplished, Hunter went on to another priority—one *she* should have addressed as soon as they got to his house—but yeah, she'd been a little distracted with first-time lust.

"Jodi said you could research Russ King for us."

"I can research anyone. He's the local bigwig, right? I've

done some preliminary searching on everyone that popped. He and his goofy poker nights drew my interest."

It was Hunter's turn to be surprised. "You don't miss much."

"Jodi's one of us."

She said it so simply, Jodi's heart softened.

While Hunter explained the situation to Madison, Memphis stepped into the kitchen. He saw they were on the phone and started to leave, but Jodi waved him on in.

Clearly glad to be included, he dropped the reserve and, leaning against the counter, arms crossed, muttered, "I could have researched King."

Jodi shrugged. "Apparently, Hunter has decided to run the show."

"There's more to King than river rafting, cabins and tent sites," Madison said. "Though he has several locations, I don't think the businesses would generate the kind of money he seems to have. I'll do more digging and give a full report in the morning."

"Add another name to the list," Hunter said. "Remmy Gardner. He works for King. Tall, blond—according to Jodi, he's good-looking. He wants on Jodi's good side."

"Jodi has a good side?" Madison teased.

"I don't trust him," Hunter insisted.

"What do you want to know?"

Jodi decided to get a little payback for Hunter's comment on her panties. "Hunter needs to know if he's better looking than Remmy."

"Hang on." There were a few seconds with only the quiet clicks of Madison typing, and then she replied with firm conviction, "Hunter, by a mile, but yeah, Remmy's not hard on the eyes."

As if he couldn't take it anymore, Memphis crowded

closer, one hand on the back of Hunter's chair, the other on Jodi's. "Hey, Madison, it's Memphis."

"Hey, I was hoping we'd get to talk. How was your trip in?"

"Just fine."

Jodi lifted her brows. "You two are awfully chummy now."

"We're like this." Memphis crossed his first two fingers. "BFFs, don't you know?"

Madison said, "And it's awesome. I've never had a BFF techie friend."

"Same." Memphis got serious again. "Now that I'm here, I'd like to work with you to shore up the security. Encrypting passwords and all that."

"Since sleepy little Triple Creek isn't so sleepy anymore," Madison replied.

"Most small towns aren't." He glanced at Jodi, then gave a longer look at Hunter. "Small towns are a great place for people to hunker down or keep a low profile when necessary."

"Very true," Madison agreed. "So in the meantime, Jodi, don't trust Remmy too much."

She frowned.

"But, Hunter, seriously, Jodi is a great judge of character, so lighten up."

Hunter frowned, too.

Memphis snickered. "You have them both riled."

"Then my work is done. You two can go about your business. Memphis, let's do a virtual call so we can work through a few scenarios."

Memphis picked up *her* phone and carried it to the counter as he looked out the window.

When Hunter continued to appear disgruntled, Jodi put a hand on his thigh. "Leave them to it," she whispered. "They can catch us up later." She dropped her gaze to his mouth. "You and I could…discuss those ground rules you mentioned."

Realizing her intent, Hunter pushed back his chair. "Fine by me."

Memphis handed back her cell. "Madison said goodbye. I'm going to set up my laptop in the spare bedroom so she and I won't disturb you."

"She's married," Hunter reminded him.

"And she's scary as shit, so no problem." Memphis grinned. "I consider her a colleague, that's all. It's nice to talk to another cyberwhiz."

Jodi said, "I'm heading off to bed. Good night, Memphis."

He opened his arms. "One hug. Pretty please?"

She hesitated, but this was Hunter's brother, and he'd been pretty darned accepting so far. Frowning, she took a step toward him—and got hauled in for a gentle embrace. "There you go. It has been a true pleasure to meet you, Jodi. I can't wait to visit more tomorrow."

"Yeah, sure." Awkwardly, she patted his back, but she had to admit, it wasn't awful being hugged by another Osborn guy. He wasn't Hunter, he didn't make her heart trip up or shoot her pulse into the stratosphere, and the scent of him, while nice, didn't have her stomach doing somersaults. Yet it was still nice. "Tomorrow." She eased away.

Looking very pleased with himself, Memphis asked, "Does Turbo need anything in the room? A bed? Another trip outside? What if he wants out at night?"

Jodi picked up her gun and left the brothers to work out the logistics of Turbo's "sleepover" with Memphis. It wasn't that late yet, but the day was catching up to her.

In Hunter's bedroom, she put her stuff on the nightstand and then went into the bathroom to clean her teeth and wash up again.

It was a full fifteen minutes before Hunter slipped quietly into the room. Jodi stood at the window, noticing how the security lights had brightened when they took out Turbo.

"Memphis is right. The yard gets crazy-bright when the motion sensors kick on."

"I don't have blackout shades," Hunter explained. "When something moves out there, I like to know it. Usually it's an animal, or sometimes the wind moves the branches enough to cause the lights to brighten."

"Either way," she said, "I want to know, too."

He stepped up behind her. "Turbo is settled for the night, already snoring. Memphis is set up in his room. I offered him my office, but he didn't want to confuse Turbo by coming and going. I have a feeling he does a lot of computer work sprawled in his bed."

Smiling at that image, Jodi turned. "So now it's just us."

"You're ready for bed?"

"Yup."

He touched her face. "Give me a few minutes."

"Okay." She sighed. "But hurry."

As Hunter brushed his teeth, he noticed that Jodi had left a few things on the counter. Her toothbrush, her birth control pills, a wide-toothed comb. He thought about her uneasiness with the basement, but he wasn't sure how to fix the problem. Wasn't like he could fill his basement with dirt, and he was too settled in the house with his garden and chickens to easily uproot.

Somehow, they'd work it out, and until then, he'd just make her as comfortable as possible.

In an unusual way, it seemed that Memphis's presence

had made things easier, giving Jodi a target to focus on other than the massive step of staying with him. She'd faked umbrage a few times, but he knew her well enough to see the difference.

He thought again of how easily she handled most things. The awful reasons behind his move here. King's threat against her. Worth's harassment.

Her own past.

In so many ways, she rolled with the punches.

In every way, she was incomparable.

When he stepped out of the bathroom, he found her naked in the bed, the quilt pulled up to just beneath her breasts, her fingers laced together over her stomach, her hair fanned out on the pillow…and her eyes closed.

Had she fallen asleep? Regret mixed with tenderness because, yes, he wanted her again, but he knew she'd had a long, grueling day.

"About time." She turned her head and looked at him. "I was about to come after you."

Hunter grinned. "No need." He checked that the door was locked, then pulled the quilt to the bottom of the bed. Jodi turned to her side to face him, her head propped on one hand.

Getting into bed beside her, he did a visual map of her naked body, then coasted a hand from her shoulder to the dip in her waist, up and over her hip. So small, yet still so curvy. "My brother likes you."

"Yeah? I'm glad."

"Really?"

"Sure. He's your brother, and I can tell you two are close." She scooched nearer, tangling her fingers in his chest hair. "Plus, he's funny." Her golden gaze lifted to his. "I like him, too."

There was a lot Hunter wanted to talk about, but when she looked at him like that, innocently sultry, all her defenses down, he had to kiss her. Their earlier sex had taken the edge off, so now he could linger over her the way he wanted.

He kept the kiss light at first, playing over her mouth, licking the top lip, nibbling on the bottom, teasing just inside with his tongue.

When she tried to deepen the contact, he eased back and trailed damp, open-mouthed kisses along her jaw and throat.

Jodi liked that enough to tip her head for him, making her preferences known, giving him small sounds of pleasure when he happened on an extrasensitive spot, like beneath her ear, under her jaw, and especially where her neck met her shoulder.

Shifting her to her back, using one of his legs draped over hers to keep her still, he settled both hands on her breasts and felt her stiffened nipples against his palms.

"I want to touch you this time, too."

His body tightened at the thought and it took him a second to say, "Soon." Lowering his head, he drew her right nipple into the heat of his mouth while gently rolling the left.

Her back arched, encouraging him to suck harder. When he did, she tunneled her fingers into his hair and held his head closer. Loving that response, he switched to the other breast, holding it plumped up in his palm as he tugged at the nipple, first with suction, then carefully with his teeth.

Jodi's reaction was electric. Groaning, she lifted her pelvis against his thigh and started a sinuous rhythm against him. *So hot.* He loved her lack of inhibitions.

A few minutes later, knowing she was getting close, Hunter slid farther down the bed.

Immediately, Jodi protested, trying to bring him back up to her.

"Trust me." While kissing a path over her ribs and then her belly, he eased her thighs apart.

Jodi went perfectly still, and he could feel her building anticipation—because she *did* trust him. He licked her hip bone, took a love bite of her soft inner thigh, and with one hand cupped behind her knee, he opened her legs wide.

Fingers curling into fists at her sides, her breath coming faster, Jodi whimpered.

His Jodi, making that sweet, needy sound.

Damn, she smelled good. He pressed his face to her, inhaling her musk and getting so hard that he ached. He used his thumbs to open her so he could stroke in with his tongue. She was already wet, her flesh slick and hot. Hunter took his time eating her, dragging out her pleasure and his own until she clenched her fingers in his hair and tugged. If he hadn't needed her so much, he might have smiled at her impatience.

Instead, he eased two fingers into her, pressing them deep, then drew her small clit into his mouth and rasped with his tongue.

With a vibrating moan, Jodi lifted against him, her thighs stiffening, her breath laboring—and she came. Not a quick, easy come, but the kind that wrung a sob from her and kept her body suspended in harsh pleasure until, quivering, she sank back to the mattress.

Talking would have to wait. Hunter moved up her body and kissed her lax mouth. Her eyes didn't open. Sweat dampened her cheekbones and she still sucked air. He couldn't wait.

Reaching between their bodies, he positioned himself, then slid his cock deep in one firm thrust.

They groaned together.

Damn, he loved having her and only her, no condom between them.

Scooping a hand under her bottom, Hunter ground against her. He knew he wouldn't last, not with the taste of her still on his lips and the wet clasp of her body so snug. It took several hard, steady thrusts before she stirred, her excitement rekindling. Lazily, she twined one slender leg around him. Heavy eyes opened just enough for her to watch him with heated interest.

Hunter tilted her hips up more, dropped his forehead to her shoulder, locked his molars as he concentrated on not coming yet…and finally he felt her tightening again. The second her release started, he let himself go, and it was mind-blowing, even better than the first time.

Long minutes later, he realized he was still resting on her, and that she had one hand on his ass, lightly stroking while her lips played along his throat.

Wasn't easy, but he pushed up onto his forearms.

"Don't go," she whispered.

"I'm not, but I don't want to squash you."

"I like it. I…like you." Her eyes were big and filled with worry. "So much it's almost scary."

"No." He kissed her, a firm press of lips to lips. "Nothing between us is scary."

The corner of her mouth curved. "Is that an order?"

If only he had the power to give her orders. He'd start with insisting that she never again put herself at risk. For now, he turned to his side so that they faced each other. Smoothing her hair back, then brushing his fingertips over her swollen mouth, he gave a small confession. "I more than like you, Jodi Bentley. I want you to stay with me. I want us to be together. Not just tonight, not just this week or even this month."

Her gaze locked on his, almost like she was afraid to blink.

She looked so rattled, Hunter decided on a different tack. "Why did you dodge me all day?"

"I didn't—"

The press of his finger to her lips silenced her. "There should always be total honesty between us, okay? You dodged me, and I hated it." He traced over her lips, now soft and puffy from all their kissing. "I swear I'll always be honest with you."

Disgruntled, she said, "Fine." Fortifying herself with a deep breath, she muttered, "You spook me. You know I moved here to make it on my own, to prove to Parrish and the rest of the McKenzies that, while I appreciate their help, more than I can ever say, more than I can ever possibly repay, I *can* do this on my own. Their efforts weren't wasted. What they gave—trust and understanding and guidance—I've put it to good use."

It was clear Jodi had no understanding of how family worked. "They love you, and I'm pretty sure you love them. Like my brother showing up here, like my mom and dad worrying, family won't ever give up on you. Doesn't matter if you need them or not." Because she didn't look convinced, he added, "You know every one of them is capable, right?"

With a roll of her eyes, she said, "They're a bunch of Zeus imitators, remember? They're able to handle anything."

If that was her standard for herself, he had a lot of ground to cover. "Not true, honey. What if something happened to Kennedy?"

"No." Her eyes flinched as if the possibility actually hurt. "Don't even say that."

"I'm sure she's fine, but if the unthinkable happened, you don't think the others would show up in force to help her in any way possible? To help their brother? *You'd* be there, too. That's family. Through thick and thin, family is ready to do anything necessary. Nothing ever changes that." He framed her face in his hands. "They love you, Jodi Bentley. You're now a part of them and that means they'll be in your life, there for the good times and the bad, when it's fun and when it's inconvenient as hell."

As if pained, she closed her eyes.

"Hey, you know what'd make it easier for you?"

"Probably nothing."

Hunter smiled. She was such a hard case, but little by little, that massive chip on her shoulder got smaller. "Giving in." He couldn't resist another kiss, this one searching, wanting—*needing*—a response. "Giving in, accepting that they're a part of your life, acknowledging that they *are* family. Doesn't matter if you're blood related or not. You're one of them, and that means they're always going to be around."

With a groan, followed by a small laugh, she conceded, "You're probably right."

"I know I am. After all, that's my brother taking up space at the other side of the house."

Her mouth twitched again. "I think you sexed me up so awesomely, my brain isn't firing on all cylinders yet. It's unfair of you to expect me to think."

"Actually, this might be the best time for me to bring up those ground rules."

"Ugh." She dropped back and threw out her arms as if defeated. "All right, then, lay it on me."

"King is dangerous, we agree on that much." In case she

didn't agree, he moved right along…while also settling over her. "For that reason, we should keep each other informed. About everything."

Dubious, she arched an eyebrow. *"Everything?"*

"If we're apart for any reason—though we shouldn't be, not while there's trouble around—we need to check in."

The eyebrow came down and her chin tucked in. "I'm accountable to you now?"

"Same as I'm accountable to you." He smoothed back her hair. "Look at it this way. If you suddenly found me gone, wouldn't you worry?" Hoping she'd give the right answer, Hunter waited.

It took her a few seconds, then she slowly nodded. "Yeah, I probably would."

"Same for me. So…" While she was being agreeable, he figured he'd get it all said. "I don't want you making any moves with King—not even any decisions—on your own."

An electric stillness settled over her, then she hit him with that stare. "Come again?"

"I plan to do the same, once I've recouped." Hell, recuperation rapidly approached. With her naked under him, he already felt revitalized. "Until then, I want your agreement."

"Those are all the ground rules?" she asked with suspicion.

"All I can think of right now." He kissed her stubborn chin and smiled. "We care for each other. We respect each other. We team up and work together." Knowing he'd hit her with a lot all at once—sex, a brother, the invitation to live with him—Hunter said, *"Everyday life for the everyday woman.* This is how it's done, honey. It's called a relationship, and I promise, it won't be as hard as you're imagining. I'm even willing to bet that, once you get used to sharing the load, you'll find it easier."

In a barely there whisper, she confessed, "I don't know how to do relationships."

"Are you kidding me? You excel at it. Dinners together, quiet talks, caring for my dog and accepting my brother—"

"The sex is phenomenal."

Hunter grinned. "I agree."

Still in that quiet voice, she said, "I didn't know I wanted any of that until you. That's part of what's so scary about it." She placed her fingers against his mouth. "What if the novelty wears off? What if all of a sudden you realize I'm just too much trouble? What if your mom or dad doesn't like me, or...?" She inhaled a shaky breath. "What if my trouble gets you hurt? I couldn't live with that."

Hunter took her wrist and lowered her hand. "First, I'd had all that before and knew, with certainty, that I never wanted it again. Not until you." Anger started to edge in. "Caring about you is not a novelty, damn it. Do you think I'm so dense I don't know what I feel?"

"No."

What she said barely registered. "What if you decide *I'm* too much trouble?"

"I would never—"

Shoving up and away from her, Hunter sat at the side of the bed, trying to come to grips with her reserve. He'd basically bared his soul to her, and still he could feel her emotionally pulling away. It fucking infuriated him. Unreasonably so, because if she pulled away now, he didn't know what he'd do. "I care for you, damn it, and all you do is come up with excuses to keep me away."

Jodi's arms came around his neck, and hell, he felt her bare breasts against his back. "I'm not. I was just worried."

"You think I'm not worried, too? Especially for you. I *like* who you are, Jodi, but I damn well want you safe."

"I want you safe, too." Her lips brushed his ear, then the side of his throat.

Telling his dick to stay down, Hunter continued. "My mom and dad will love you, I guarantee it, but if they don't, so what? They won't be the ones living with you. We'd see them on holidays or other special occasions."

Jodi nipped his earlobe. "I'll make them like me."

He gave a rough laugh. "You're not listening to me. You won't have to make them. They'll react to you the same way Memphis did."

"Meaning if you care about me, they will, too?"

"Yes."

"And you care about me."

She sounded very soft and sweet, but with Jodi, he could never be sure. "I'm falling in love with you."

Three seconds of tense silence passed—before her arms clamped tight around his neck. Pressing her face to his shoulder, she took a gentle bite of his muscle and said, "Omigod, I'm falling with you, and I didn't even know what to call it."

Just that easily, his anger disappeared. "Chicken. You wanted me to go first." She laughed and tried to topple him to the mattress, but Hunter resisted, and instead, he pulled her around and into his lap to cradle her close. "So you're falling, huh?"

Her beautiful eyes glimmered with emotion, with love and laughter. "You make me feel things I can't identify. It throws me off balance, scares me a little and makes me want…more?" She held her breath.

Yes. More. Only with Jodi. "I like the sound of that."

All too serious, and a little anxious, she asked, "Are you sure?"

"Positive, because I feel the same."

To avoid eye contact, she became very interested in his chest. "You want me to change."

"You want me to change."

Her head shot up. "No, I don't."

"Jodi, I tracked a woman into the mountain because I thought she might need me. I stayed with her ten fucking hours—with a dead man's blood on me because she wanted to hold my hand. I carried Turbo out of a muddy field when he was little more than a bag of bones with a nasty skin condition, disgusting drool and a barker that didn't work right—then I babied him back to health. Until I moved here and isolated myself, helping others was part of who I am. Yet you want me to sit back and watch you face danger alone."

"I didn't say I wanted to do it alone."

"No, you just want to call all the shots." He lifted her chin. "That's not who I am. It's not who you are either. I'm offering you a compromise."

"Could I...?" She stroked her fingers through his chest hair. "What if I promise to do my best?"

"Your best will always be good enough for me."

"I might mess up sometimes. My temper snaps and I go into a mode..."

"I've noticed." To soften that, he kissed the tip of her nose. "You're not perfect, honey, but then, neither am I."

"You're so darn close, though."

Hunter couldn't help but grin at her forlorn tone. Even with all the trouble, his life was looking good, because Jodi was in it. He dropped back on the bed with her and started to turn, but she straight-armed him.

"No you don't. I have a ground rule of my own." She took his hands and pressed them to his sides, then sat beside him, her legs tucked under her, her gaze all over his body.

"I get to have a turn. No more overwhelming me until I've gotten to explore you a little."

Disbelieving, he asked, "That's your ground rule?"

"The first one."

"Oh, good," he said, deadpan. "There's more." Hunter stacked his hands behind his head and enjoyed how she looked at him. When her small hand suddenly wrapped around his erection, he forgot his amusement.

"Second one. Even if you get mad, you don't get to walk away."

"Agreed, as long as that rule applies to you, too." Her fingers lightly explored along his length before she gripped him a little more firmly.

"Last one. You have to tell me if you need or want something. I'm not a mind reader."

God love her, she really was amazing. For the next ten minutes, Hunter gave her detailed instructions, and she followed each one without hesitation, including enthusiastically using her mouth on him.

He didn't last long before he dragged her up and over his body with the final instruction to ride him. Neither of them could hold off for long, and after her release, she gently dropped to the bed beside him, saying, "You can do cleanup again. I'm beat."

By the time he took care of it and came to stand at the side of the bed, Jodi was sound asleep. For a while, he just looked at her, marveling that she'd come into his life when he'd thought he needed only time alone, and instead...he'd needed her.

Telling her he was falling in love was a giant lie. He was totally, irrevocably in love with her. For him, there was no pulling back.

As quietly as possible, he turned out the lamp and got

into bed beside her. When he reached for her, she helped, snuggling in close with a murmured, "'Bout time," and then fading to sleep again.

He didn't think Jodi slept soundly very often, but for the next hour, she didn't stir and he gradually drifted off to sleep, too. A few times through the night, he awoke. Once when she turned over in her sleep, yet even then, she wiggled her rump against him, ensuring they stayed physically close. Another time, she abruptly sat up and looked around. Hunter opened his eyes and listened, heard the house was quiet, saw the yard dim and said, "It's okay."

She turned to him, waited a second or two, and then collapsed half over his chest and went back to sleep.

Oddly enough, so did he.

Each time he stirred awake, what hit him was that he *could* go back to sleep—and so could Jodi. The connection between them was enough to remove the worst of the insomnia.

An hour before dawn, a light tap sounded at his door and he heard Memphis whisper, "Hunter?"

Shit. Knowing Memphis wouldn't intrude without a damn good reason, Hunter tried to slip silently from the bed. He didn't make it.

Bleary-eyed and confused, Jodi sat up. Her hair was everywhere, and she folded her arms around her naked breasts. "Memphis?"

"Yeah, it's just my brother. Go back to sleep."

She looked at the clock, rubbed her eyes and said, "I slept."

"I know." The room was dark, heavy with shadows, but he saw her leaving the bed.

"I'm awake," she said around a massive yawn. "See what your brother wants and I'll join you in a minute." On her way past him, she gave him a quick peck, then slipped into the bathroom. The door closed with a quiet click.

"Hunter?" Memphis repeated, a little more urgently. "Seriously, open up."

Glad that Jodi was in the bathroom, Hunter strode for the door. It had to be something important, but whatever it was, he wanted to spare Jodi for a few minutes more. He stepped naked into the hall and pulled the door shut behind him. "What's happened?"

With the kitchen light on, Hunter could see that Memphis wore unbuttoned jeans and nothing else.

His brother's gaze flashed over him. "Mountain life has been good to you. You're shredded."

Hunter's molars locked. "It's not even five, you woke Jodi from a rare sound sleep and I'm cold. You're about two seconds away from getting clocked."

Keeping his voice as low as Hunter's, Memphis muttered, "Right. I'm damned sorry to interrupt, believe me, but there's a fucking fire."

"Here?" Hunter started to push past him.

"No." Memphis leaned in, his gaze hard with rage. "Her place, Hunter." He put a staying hand on Hunter's shoulder when he again started to charge past him. "I already called it in. If Turbo hadn't started whining, I wouldn't have noticed, but he did, so I looked out the window..."

Turbo stood there behind Memphis, sniffing the air.

"Hunter, whoever set the fire probably assumed Jodi was in there."

Hunter drew a controlling breath. "Her truck wasn't there, so maybe not."

"Idiots set on destruction rarely notice details."

True, yet he had a feeling Remmy wasn't an idiot. So had

King acted without telling him? "They probably thought she would run out…"

"And they'd have had her, with time to get whatever is hidden in her house."

Just then, the sound of sirens reached them. Turbo started his unique rendition of outraged dog—bouncing, howling and croaking. Jesus. A hundred scenarios ran through Hunter's head, but first…clothes.

"Don't take a single step outside the house. I mean it."

"What about the dog? I think he has to go."

"Leash him for me, but stay inside. I just need a minute." A minute to dress. To arm himself. To alert Jodi.

To try to hold her back.

He wanted a lifetime, damn it. To get it, they'd have to eliminate the threats against her, once and for all.

JODI STOOD SEVERAL feet from the fire engine with Memphis at her side, each of them holding a hot cup of coffee. Every so often, his shoulder touched hers. Oddly enough, she appreciated the human contact. Hunter had wanted to do the same, but Turbo needed him more.

He was near her feet, squatting down to give the dog affection and comfort to help him deal with the chaos. Hunter's gaze continually swept over her, then lingered on her face, as if looking for signs of her losing it. Yeah, she wanted to. That wouldn't help the situation, though.

Her house, scorched.

A combination of rage, regret and smoke burned her eyes. All the beautiful things Parrish had sent her—would they be smoke damaged? Soon now, she'd be able to watch the playback feed from her security cameras. She'd see who had done this—and then she'd make them pay.

One firefighter walked over to her. "You're the home-owner?"

Playing it cool, Jodi sipped her coffee. "Yes. How much home is left?" To her, it didn't look that bad, but she wasn't a firefighter and she hadn't been allowed inside yet.

"The stone is intact. Most of the fire was contained to the outside back wall on the addition. Structurally, it's not bad, but you'll need a professional cleaner to remove the scent of smoke. Looks like some trees will be lost, too."

"I hate that," she whispered. Everything she'd done since moving here had been with the distinct attempt not to disturb nature. "The fire was set. Of course you realize that."

"Yes, ma'am." He eyed her, his gaze shrewd yet sympathetic. "We found accelerant near the back door."

"That confirms it, then."

"Generally speaking, if someone wants to burn a house down, the accelerant is in two locations, front and back. Your front door is intact, though, undisturbed."

If she'd been in the house, the back door would've been her first option. With that way blocked by fire, she'd have been forced to use the front door…where someone had no doubt been waiting for her.

She'd have made them sorry. So damned sorry.

"You know anything about arson?" the firefighter asked.

"Only that I wasn't here or it wouldn't have happened."

"You seem mighty calm about it."

Jodi took another sip before looking up and meeting the question in his eyes. "Nah. I'm nowhere near calm. Try *enraged* and you'll be a little closer to the mark."

Her tone and her look caused the guy to hesitate.

Immediately, Hunter was at her side. "She was with me." He nodded to his house. "My brother got in last night and we were all visiting until late."

The guy talking to them didn't look like a total dunce. Just because he couldn't read her mood... Well, few could when she chose to contain her fury. Hunter was one of those few.

"I'd already planned to stay the night, though," she admitted. "Before his brother got here, I mean. I have a big commercial mower I use for my business. Usually it's chained to a stake in the ground right outside my house." She lifted a hand and pointed. "I didn't want to risk leaving it here if I wasn't around to protect it. Hunter said I could park it in his garage, so I did. Same with my truck."

"You were expecting trouble?"

"I'm a woman alone, living off the beaten path with only a rinky-dink town around and not close enough to help if I need it." The orange sunrise looked hazy through the smoke-filled sky. Jodi realized her hand was trembling when Hunter took her cup and squeezed her fingers. "I'm not an idiot and I don't take chances."

The firefighter nodded. "Then good thing you moved them."

"She hasn't lived there long," Hunter calmly explained. "In the eighteen months I've been here, the house was empty. I didn't know it was livable until she moved in a few weeks ago."

Jodi noticed that Memphis stayed quiet while constantly searching the area. When he caught her stare, he smiled and took Turbo's leash from Hunter. "I'm going to walk this poor guy around, let him calm down a little."

True, Turbo wasn't at all sure how he felt about the ruckus. He puffed every breath and seemed agitated by the activity.

Hunter gave his brother a warning frown. "Don't go far."

"We won't," Memphis said.

Of course he headed toward the other side of the road, which was exactly how someone would have accessed her property—and was where she had a few trail cameras hidden.

To the firefighter, she asked, "Do you need anything else from me?"

"You'll be around?"

Jodi flinched, not at all sure how to answer. Even she with her daring didn't want to stay in the house under these circumstances.

The photo Kennedy had sent her—was it ruined? Were her clothes wearable? Never before had she realized just how territorial she felt about her things. Then again, until recently, she hadn't really had possessions—at least, nothing important.

Hunter put his arm around her and tucked her close to his side. "She'll be with me."

"That's probably best, then. We'll investigate, but we're a volunteer department without a lot of resources." He rubbed the back of his neck. "It's lucky you noticed the fire so quickly."

Hunter nodded. "If my brother hadn't stayed over, we might all still be sleeping. He was using the guest room at the end of the house closest to here. We were at the other side."

It struck Jodi. "I'd have come down here only to find I didn't have a house left."

The firefighter studied her again. "You'd have smelled the smoke the second you stepped outside."

Jodi locked her jaw. She knew what she had to do now. Looking up at Hunter, she said, "Let's go home. Er, that is…" His home was not hers, but hopefully, he knew what she meant. "To your house."

His gaze warmed and he gave her a gentle hug. He and

the firefighter shared a few more words, but Jodi tuned them out in favor of making plans.

They were almost to his house when Memphis jogged up to join them. Turbo happily ran along with him, glad to leave the commotion behind. Quietly, Memphis said, "I removed three memory cards. Were there more cameras I missed?"

"Nope. You got them. Thanks." If the firefighters called in an investigator, and they likely would, the area might be searched, and they'd find the cameras—but now they already had the cards.

Jodi went straight to the bedroom to get her laptop. If she had a choice, she'd check the feed without the brothers looking over her shoulder. She hated for Hunter to get further involved, yet without even asking, she knew he wouldn't tolerate that.

Hadn't they just discussed sharing this stuff? This was different, though. The danger had amplified, all because of her.

Hunter had followed her, so before she even left the bedroom, he took the laptop from her and slid an arm around her waist.

He kept doing that. Touching her, comforting her. "I'm fine, you know."

"I know." He walked with her through the hallway. "Somehow I think it's in my best interest to keep hold of you so you don't go charging off alone."

That sentiment was nice, and still a little alarming. She gave a wry smile. No one knew her as well as he did. That had to mean something, right?

He steered her to the kitchen, where Memphis had arranged three chairs close together and refilled the coffee mugs. Clearly, this was to be a group effort.

"I'm not a huge coffee drinker." That was Kennedy's

habit, not hers, and right now she didn't need the caffeine jitters. Taking the middle seat, Jodi asked, "Could I get a juice instead?"

"You've got it." Memphis removed her mug and filled a glass with haste, then sat to her left. Hunter was at her right.

It took only seconds to plug in the card and bring up the feed. As they watched the eerie black-and-white footage, Jodi repeated a silent mantra: *Don't let it be Remmy. Don't let my instincts be so far out of whack. Not Remmy. Not Remmy. Not Remmy.*

The image of a male came into view. Black knit hat. Dark clothing. Shorter than Remmy. Stockier. Jodi sat back in relief.

Until Hunter asked, "Why didn't Remmy warn you?"

Her heart crawled into her throat and she slowly turned to face him. "Hunter…I doubt Remmy knew."

He cursed low.

"What am I missing?" Memphis asked.

"Remmy would have told me," Jodi said. "I'm sure of it. This means they're keeping info from him."

Hunter rested a hand on her thigh, and said to Memphis, "Someone is probably on to him."

Jodi fought off the rush of panic. "That means he could be dead before we can get to him." Unless she came up with a plan, and fast.

CHAPTER ELEVEN

EVEN BEFORE HE opened the door to the insistent pounding, Remmy knew it was going to be bad. No one would have disturbed him except King, and King usually just called. When the boss wanted someone physically brought in, Remmy was the guy he sent.

But not this morning.

Surprisingly, Danny Giggs wasn't among the three men who informed him that King was waiting. They watched over him while he pulled on jeans, a T-shirt, socks and shoes. Even while he took a piss and quickly brushed his teeth.

Remmy didn't miss the guns on their hips, or their looks of satisfaction. While one guy took his cell phone and keys, the biggest of them ordered, "Hurry the fuck up. You're not going on a date."

That was pushing him a little too far. "Did King tell you to kill me?"

The guy grinned. "No, he specifically said he'd deal with you himself."

"Good." Remmy landed a heavy fist in his face, knocking him off balance and permanently damaging that smug smile by removing a tooth or two. Instantly, he was tackled. His shoulder hit the wall, his ass hit the floor, but the few bruises he got were well worth it.

Minutes later, angrily stuffed in the back seat of a mid-size car, with a goon on either side of him, the guy with the busted mouth driving, Remmy contemplated his chances of survival. They were slim to none, and unfortunately, slim was out of town. Hopefully, Hunter would be ready for any trouble sent their way. He detested the thought of Jodi being hurt because of his incompetence.

Hell, he didn't even want Hunter hurt.

Clearly, he'd gone soft. He should have moved on weeks ago. Yet if he had, would Jodi already be a missing person?

They drove away from the cabin, not toward town, and not toward King's property. The road turned to gravel, and then dirt. The farther they went, the more remote it became. Remmy glanced to the guy at his left, which prompted the dude to ask with wary belligerence, *"What?"*

"Nothing." The guy to his right leaned forward to say something—and Remmy threw an elbow at his nose. Judging by the spray of blood, he'd landed it perfectly. "Just that."

The car swerved as the driver's seat was jostled by the man on the left grabbing for Remmy. No time like the present, he decided, and drew up his legs to kick the driver's seat as hard as he could, folding the driver over the wheel.

The car veered off wildly while the driver tried to regain control. Not easy, since Remmy continued to kick his seat every chance he got. Blood went everywhere from the guy's broken nose. Fists flew, and he landed a few more elbows. During the melee, he managed to wrest a knife from the belt of the man on his right. Remmy even allowed a punch to the temple so he could shove the knife into his pocket. Before he could go for a gun, the car came to a quaking halt, inches from an enormous tree off the side of the road.

If he could get out of the car, he might have a chance to escape them in the woods— The barrel of a gun pressed into his neck.

"Fuck King, I'll end you now, you bastard."

Only because the threat sounded serious beyond the nasally whine of a smashed nose, Remmy relented. "Do," he reminded him, "and King will likely kill you, too."

The driver said, "We'll all swear you were trying to shoot us and killed yourself by accident."

Okay, so that was funny enough that Remmy laughed. "I'd like to see you sell that."

Rage smoldered in the driver's eyes. "Hold him."

Two sets of rough hands clamped down on his shoulders, pressing him into the seat. The driver leaned toward the back. Remmy expected a direct punch, and instead, the asshole brutally clubbed him in the temple with the butt of his gun.

Stars exploded in his vision before everything faded to black.

He came around as hard hands dragged him from the car and onto the rough ground. He landed on his face. Clearly, they hadn't had far to go, because he knew he couldn't have been out for long. Contrary to the BS pitched in movies, blackouts didn't last long. If someone stayed knocked out more than a minute or two, they were seriously hurt.

He wasn't.

Yes, he had a killer headache, and as two of them hauled him forward, it felt like they would wrench his arms from his shoulder sockets, but he wasn't dying. At least, not until King had his way.

A bullet would probably be easier than whatever he faced.

Knowing that, he subtly glanced around and realized they were at a rustic property not that far from the cabin where he'd been staying. A little wooden hunting shack sat on a cleared spot of earth, surrounded by thick woods. He detected the sound of a creek nearby.

Did King plan to bury him here?

"What's this?"

The second King's booming voice echoed around them, the bastards dropped him once more. He didn't have time to get his hands under him, so again, his face hit the dirt. If he managed to get out of this, he'd make them both pay for the abuse.

Spitting dust and gravel, Remmy sat up and glared around him. Oh, shit. Opposite him, looking maniacal, Danny Giggs grinned. Deliberately snubbing him, Remmy turned his gaze on King. "What the hell is this?"

Casually, King leaned against a tree, flanked by two other men. "It appears Danny is *dying* to tell you."

If Danny heard the implied threat, he didn't show it. Taking a step forward, the idiot said, "I went to her house. I knew you were lying. I could tell."

"Whose house?"

"Hers."

Danny had been to see Jodi? And he was still alive? "What did you do?" Slowly, driven by an internal rage that revitalized him, Remmy stood.

"I set her house on fire."

Without taking his gaze off Danny, Remmy flexed his arms. "Since you're not dead yet, I take it she wasn't there."

King laughed. "So much faith in your girlfriend?"

"Fucking her once does not make her my girlfriend, and against Danny? Yes, I have all kinds of faith that Jodi would have blown his fool head off."

Danny roared, ready to charge him.

Even with his brain pounding, Remmy relished the opportunity to destroy him.

King didn't give him the chance. "No" was all he said,

and Danny was forced to subside. "Now, finish explaining, Danny. I'm sure Remmy is anxious to hear it all."

"She wasn't there, you're right. I started the fire and waited for her to run outside. I'd have killed her for Mr. King, and his…" Hesitating, Danny glanced around at the others. "The stuff he doesn't want found would have been destroyed."

Such a shortsighted fool. "Did Mr. King say he wanted it destroyed?"

King answered. "No, I did not. Nor did I request that he go after her. As you knew—as you *both* knew—I'd planned to have some fun. I was looking forward to it, in fact. Now, however, with her house burned to the ground, we have no choice."

"The house is stone," Remmy pointed out. "It wouldn't burn to the ground."

King's eyebrows lifted. "Surely, everything inside would have."

"Might depend on how Danny handled the fire. With enough accelerant around the doors and windows, the fire might have spread inside. Of course, that'd make it tough for her to run out, too." He turned to Danny and asked, as if it didn't matter, "You stuck around to watch it burn?"

Belatedly realizing his error, Danny said, "I heard sirens, so I got out of there." When everyone stared at him, he got defensive. "She was up at the other guy's house, probably banging him! That means *you* never touched her. You lied to Mr. King. I think you're soft on her. I think you're protecting her."

Remmy laughed, and this time it was completely forced. "I said I fucked her, not that we have anything exclusive." He glanced at King. "Not yet, anyway. I'd planned to work on it, as you suggested." Actually, he'd ordered it, but whatever. He loosened his shoulders again. "That is, before you sent goons after me. Now I don't know what the fuck is going on."

King's small smile showed real amusement. "I see you didn't come along peacefully."

"Not when the assholes kept smirking. They said you wanted me alive, but didn't say shit about you caring if they lived or not."

At that, King actually chuckled. "You're the best I have, Remmy. I've been impressed, so I would never underestimate you."

"They're not as smart as you."

"No, they're not." As if it didn't matter, he walked up to the guy with the busted nose and said, "Gun."

The man handed it to him with alacrity, then braced himself.

To Remmy, King said, "It'll be a shame if you're lying to me."

Remmy stared into his black eyes and smiled. "Since you're not a fool, you'd already know if I was."

For several long moments, King studied him. Remmy was pretty sure he and King were the only ones breathing. Everyone else seemed to be holding their breath.

Then King turned and squeezed the trigger.

The bullet hit Danny in the forehead and he crumpled like a puppet freed of its strings.

Son of a bitch. All along, he'd known Danny would be a problem, but he couldn't hold back a twinge of sympathy. "You didn't have to do that. He's a hothead, and he wanted to please you." For that, King had murdered him.

"He's an idiot who jeopardized everything." To the other five men, King announced, "Relax, I'm not shooting anyone else today."

The collective relief was comical. Or maybe Remmy was just in a ridiculous mood. After all, he'd known his time was up. The smart move would have been to leave town.

Instead, he'd stuck around because a cute little ponytail asked him to.

Dumb. Far dumber than Danny Giggs.

"Clean up this mess," King said as he handed the man back his gun. "Then join us inside."

"Yes, sir." The dumbass seemed stumped as to how to accomplish that.

Running a hand over his face, Remmy brazened it out, pretending his future was secure. "Find something to wrap him in so his head doesn't leave bloodstains, and then put him in your trunk for now. We'll discuss how to dispose of the body later."

Again, King smiled. "You'll call her." He gestured for Remmy and the others to step into the shack. "You'll ask her to meet you here in two hours. If she doesn't sound like a woman who's been well laid, then I'll know you're lying. Do you understand?"

"I've got it." When he stepped into the small structure, the first thing he saw was Worth Linlow sitting on the floor against a back wall, badly beaten. With Worth's eyes closed and head slumped forward, blood dripping from his nose and mouth, Remmy couldn't tell if he was dead or alive.

King had flipped a sanity switch, obviously. He was in a literal killing mood. Not good—for anyone.

Somehow he'd have to end the bastard before he killed anyone else. All he had was a knife, but given half a chance, he'd make good use of it.

Remmy prayed that Jodi was as smart as he assumed her to be, so that no matter what he said, no matter how tough she thought herself to be, she would keep her sweet little ass far, far away from King.

Casual as you please, Remmy pulled out a chair and seated himself. "All I need is my phone, and for someone to tell me where the hell we are."

WHEN HER CELL RANG, Jodi jumped.

That was so unlike her, with her usual nerves of steel, that Hunter badly wanted to eviscerate someone for doing this to her. He also wanted to coddle her, to protect her, but he knew she'd hate that—as much as he would. So instead, he sat beside her and supported her the best he could. He *would* protect her, but he didn't feel the need to make announcements that would only insult her ability.

Overall, she was holding it together, putting on a good show, but he knew she was tightly strung, her emotions rioting. Resting a hand on her thigh, both to lend her his strength and to remind her that, no matter what, she wasn't alone, he suggested, "Put it on speaker."

Surprisingly, she agreed, but with a caveat. "Only if the two of you stay silent."

Memphis said, "No problem."

Hunter could tell she wasn't quite as pissed—or as hurt—as she would have been if Remmy had been involved. Like him, she wanted to be able to trust her own character judgment. Yet knowing the other man might die didn't sit right with him either.

Because she waited, he agreed to stay quiet, but with a caveat of his own. "As long as you don't try to keep anything from me. And remember, it's likely that Remmy's not alone at this point. He could have King breathing down his neck, so be careful what you say."

"Right." She inhaled, slowly exhaled, then hit the button and said, "Hello?"

"Hey, Jodi."

"Remmy!" She laced her fingers with Hunter's and blurted, "My house caught on fire. I was about to call you."

The silence stretched out, as if that quick disclosure surprised Remmy. "A fire?" he finally managed to ask.

At that point, he and Jodi shared a look. They could both tell Remmy knew about the fire, but that he hadn't expected her to bring it up. *Not alone*, Hunter mouthed, and she gave a slight nod of agreement.

"It had to be deliberate. I don't know what to do." Balancing between her role as Remmy's lover and the hedgehog she'd already presented to others, she said, "I'm freaking furious, and I have my suspicions, but I'm not sure what to do yet."

Her acting ability was astounding. Anyone who knew Jodi well would know she'd never admit to indecision. Memphis's acquaintance with her was short, but he sat back in astonishment, brows raised while a small smile played over his mouth.

Yeah, Hunter wanted to say. *She's incredible—and she's mine.*

"You, um, weren't in the house?" Remmy asked.

"No, I was visiting Hunter." Sounding disgusted, she growled, "I thought I heard something last night and it spooked me. Ever repeat that, though, and I'll make you sorry."

"I wouldn't," Remmy assured her with a short laugh, proving that he'd caught on, too. "You know you can trust me."

"Hunter let me crash on his couch." Jodi's blurted statement hung out there.

"I see." With more than a little sarcasm, Remmy said, "Sounds like a real accommodating neighbor."

At that, she took a turn laughing. "You're not jealous, are you? You know there's no reason." She glanced at Hunter. "I'm still amazed that I slept with you and liked it. Not my norm, you know?"

"I'm flattered." Remmy moved on quickly. "Listen, Jodi, instead of hanging out with some other guy, why not come stay with me? I'll give you a repeat. You'd like that, right?"

Jodi's expression turned shrewd, but her tone didn't change. "I have to figure out everything with my house. You could come over and help me."

"Not right now, but I don't want you there alone." He read off an address. "It's an isolated place." He added, voice low, "With a bed. C'mon, baby. We'll go back to your place later and I'll help you sort things out."

Jodi made an "Mmm" sound, as if deciding. "You were pretty good at helping me shake off tension."

Even knowing she said it all for King's benefit, hearing her discuss sex with another man sent a slow burn through Hunter's gut. Hitting Remmy twice wasn't enough. He wanted to pound him into the ground—but he wouldn't.

"The firemen are still at my house, and I don't think I can just leave. How about I'll call you as soon as they're done?"

There was another stretch of silence, and Jodi closed her eyes. Hunter could see her concern—an emotion she might deny, but felt it more keenly than many others did, because she understood exactly what could happen to Remmy.

She didn't want the other man hurt, but neither would she take chances.

"Just meet me here in two hours."

"Remmy," she complained, sounding pressured, but also

giving in. "All right, fine. I'll *try*. If I'm going to be late, I'll call. You better make it worth my while." She made kissing sounds into the phone. "Later, gator."

She disconnected with Remmy rushing to say something. Pushing back her chair, she stated, "They definitely have him."

"I know." Hunter, too, stood. He drew her back against his chest and crossed his arms around her middle. "You know you can't go to him."

"Not without a plan." She turned in his arms, went on tiptoe to kiss him and said, "I need to call Madison."

Her phone rang again before she could.

"Right on cue," Memphis said.

Yet when Jodi turned for her phone, she frowned. "That's not Madison."

"Then who?" Hunter asked, seeing the unfamiliar number. "That's not Remmy calling back." If it was King ready to pressure her, he'd go after the bastard himself.

"Eh, it's Parrish." Jodi lifted the phone and looked at him in apology. "Sorry, but this call I need to take on my own."

Hunter narrowed his eyes. "You're sure it's him?"

"Suspicious, much?" Probably to reassure him, she answered the call on speaker and said, "Hey."

The eloquent voice of a man said, "I know what you're thinking, because I know you, but you will hear me out, young lady. Is that understood?"

Hunter's mouth twitched, especially at the way Jodi rolled her eyes. Definitely Parrish, and he liked that the man himself had called to check on her.

Jodi said, "Yeah, so, before you start lecturing me, would you mind stating your name so my hunky guy isn't looking at me with doubt?"

A rough laugh sounded. "Hunky guy, huh?"

"Oh, dude, he really is." Jodi gave Hunter a very sweet smile. "Given everything that happened today, he's hovering big-time."

"The fire, I know. It's why I'm calling."

"Still waiting on a name."

"I take it I'm on speaker?"

"Yup. Until you reassure him."

"Hello, Hunter. I'm Parrish, and Jodi is like a daughter to me."

"Granddaughter," she corrected. "At least, that's what I already told him."

"Brat. I'm not as old as all that." In a less formal voice, he asked, "Did that satisfy him?"

"Judging by his grin, yeah."

Parrish laughed. "I need to talk to you."

"Give me a sec." She took the phone off speaker, went on tiptoe to kiss Hunter again and whispered, "Something to eat would be amazing." With an apologetic glance at Memphis, who sat there taking it all in, she darted into the living room.

Memphis waited until she was gone, then whispered, "Should we listen in?"

"No." Trust had to start somewhere. Hunter moved to the stove and got out a pan. The day had begun as a total clusterfuck, and he figured it was going to get worse very soon. Jodi was right—they all needed to eat. "If you hear her making a move for the door, let me know. I'm afraid she feels responsible, or indebted or something, to Remmy."

"She's loyal."

"And she wants to protect everyone." Him included. That burned his ass, but he'd known who she was before he fell in love with her. He couldn't see her changing anytime soon—and God love her, he didn't want her to. "I'm making scrambled eggs and bacon."

Memphis sat back and ran both hands over his face. "Whatever is in her house is key."

"And getting to it won't be easy with a fire inspector poking around." Hunter cracked eggs in a bowl, then glanced at Memphis. "She has a closet full of weapons, too. It's locked, but if anyone starts rummaging inside, it's going to be a problem."

"*She's* a problem," Memphis said with a smile. "A unique, fresh, beautiful, caring problem. I suggest you get used to it."

Hunter paused at the fridge. He could see through the dining room to the living room, where Jodi sat curled on the couch, the phone to her ear, Turbo tucked up close to her side. Lazily, she stroked the dog while talking. "I love her."

"Tell me something I don't know." Memphis stood and stretched. "She loves you, too. It's obvious, in case you didn't realize."

"I know. I'm just not sure she does." Jodi thought she was *falling* in love, and it scared her, he got that. He needed to be patient, but damn it, there was so much going on, every day a new issue. He wanted to hear her tell him, and soon.

Memphis grinned. "Want me to clue her in?"

"No." Hunter got out the bacon and laid it in the hot pan. "I'll make it all real clear to her soon, but first, we have to deal with the trouble."

"Got any ideas?"

Going on a rampage and killing King and his cohorts, that's what he wanted to do. "None that are viable." He nodded toward the doorway. "Pretty sure they're working it out, though."

"You think that's why Parrish called?"

"They seem to know everything, right?" Hunter still wasn't sure how he felt about that, except that now, with Jodi in trouble, he'd take all the backup he could get.

"It'll be nice having them in the family."

Hunter choked.

Clapping him on the back, Memphis said, "Seriously, it's going to be great. You'll get used to it."

"I guess." Not like he'd have a choice. And not that it really mattered. Hunter knew he could get used to anything—except losing her.

"I'LL GET YOU a new, better place," Parrish offered.

Jodi hadn't expected anything less from him, but still, it nettled her. "Thank you, no. I'll work it out."

"I can easily—"

"Just because you can," Jodi whispered, "doesn't always mean that you should."

Disgruntled, Parrish said, "Family helps family."

Jodi smiled. A sad smile, because here she was, back to square one, needing people again. Hunter, most of all. She needed him so much it left her trembling. "You've always done too much for me, and I've never done anything for you."

In a carefully neutral tone that immediately put her on alert, Parrish said, "If you believe that's true, would you repay me with a favor if you could?"

Jodi hesitated, sure that he was working an angle, but damn if she could figure it out. Finally, she said, "Yes." Truthfully, she'd do just about anything for Parrish, yet it would never be enough to balance all he'd done for her.

"Excellent." Back to sounding autocratic and fully in control, he said, "Then let me make the plans."

"What plans?" she asked with suspicion.

"The plans to take down Russ King. And no, don't act like you weren't—even now, while we're speaking—conjuring up ways to go after him. I know how that quick mind of yours works."

Sitting forward, Jodi shook her head. "No." How could she prove herself capable if Parrish stepped in before she could even get started?

"You already said you would."

"I did not! You manipulated that conversation and you know it."

"Yes, my children will tell you that I'm good at manipulation." His strident voice gentled. "As I said to Hunter, I think of you as one of mine now, so you may as well get used to it."

"But we both know I'm *not*."

"Shouting your denial at me won't make a difference to how I feel."

Emotions scrambling, Jodi tried to think of what to say. "You don't trust me to handle it."

"I trust you to do an amazing job within your set of abilities—the same as I do with Cade, Reyes and Madison. Yet you all know I have a hundred times the reach of influence. While the rest of you have cultivated different skills, I've cultivated contacts, power and the intuitive ability to plan." Again in that softer, more moderate tone, he added, "I want to plan this for you, the same as I would with the others."

A deep breath didn't ease the restriction in her throat. Emotions overwhelmed her. "Okay, fine." Hopefully that sounded grudging rather than grateful. "But I have a few stipulations that are important to me."

"Then they're important to me as well."

"You mean that?"

"I *do* trust you, so of course I want your input."

Jodi didn't realize there were tears in her eyes until Hunter sat beside her and pressed a tissue into her hand. When she glanced at the kitchen, she saw Memphis at the stove, cooking.

Good thing he couldn't see her. Showing vulnerability never failed to put her in a miserable mood.

Hunter's large hand opened on her back between her shoulder blades, coasting in small, soothing circles.

Amazing how much that contact helped.

And now that she looked at Hunter, as she took in the concern in his midnight eyes, she knew she had to accept that Parrish was correct. He was a better planner, with the clout to make things happen. If not for him, she might blunder into the mess—likely coming out the victor—but still, why risk herself and Hunter when Parrish was such a valuable resource?

Her risk was now *Hunter's* risk. She knew that with a certainty that shook her.

"Take your time," Parrish said gently. "But keep in mind, that young man loves you."

As if Hunter could hear, her face went hot and she scowled. "You don't know that."

"Of course I do, because I know you. If he wasn't committed and totally backing you, which he would only do if he was fully invested—because let's face it, honey, you aren't exactly easy—you wouldn't be there with him now."

Why did *everyone* have to see things before she did?

Again, Parrish read the situation. "Dear, dear Jodi. You're one of the most brilliantly astute, foolishly brave and sharply dangerous people I've ever had the fortune to meet, except when it comes to seeing yourself. One day I hope you realize exactly how precious you are."

Damn it. Those annoying tears flooded her eyes again, and this time Hunter pulled her against him, in the cradle of his arm while he pressed a kiss to her hair.

She had Turbo snuggled up to one side, Hunter on the other, and Parrish on the phone. Damn it, she felt too much.

Swallowing down the choking emotion, she said, "I love you, Parrish."

"Dear God," he whispered in alarm, and then with anger, *"Are you planning to die?"*

"What?" Jodi laughed and swiped her eyes. "No." But it was easier saying it to Parrish. She needed to ease her way into declarations.

Another pause. "So you really want to live?"

The unspoken *finally* hung in the air. "I really, really do."

"Excellent," Parrish said with relief. "I love you, too, have for a while. Now put the phone on speaker."

"Why?"

"Because I want to talk to both you and Hunter."

"You better not harass him."

"I'll harass anyone I choose, and no one will tell me different. As it happens, I only want to ensure a meeting of the minds on the plans."

"You're sure?" she asked skeptically. She, more than many, knew exactly how dictatorial the McKenzies could be.

"I will never lie to you, Jodi. You have my word."

Yeah, she knew that. "Sorry. Hang on." She covered the phone and turned her face up to Hunter. Before she could explain, he took her mouth in a firm, warm kiss that both incited and comforted. Against his lips, she murmured, "Parrish wants to talk to you."

Curving his hand around her cheek, he used his thumb to brush away a remaining tear. "Fine by me, as long as you know I'm not giving you up. Not to King, not to Remmy, and not even to Parrish McKenzie."

How did he always know exactly what to say? "You have a gift."

"In bed? Yeah, with you."

Laughing, she leaned into him more. She enjoyed him *so* much…that maybe it was more than falling in love. Maybe she'd done something really reckless, like already fall. *Hard.*

Forever.

In love with Hunter Osborn. Okay, so maybe it wasn't quite as scary as she'd figured. "At this point, you'd probably have to remove me bodily, and I might shoot you if you tried."

"Good." With a satisfied grin, Hunter took the phone from her and pressed the speaker button. "Hunter Osborn here."

Getting right to it, Parrish said, "Jodi has agreed to let me make plans, as long as I take into account a few suggestions she has."

"Of course she did. She's shrewd enough to always take the right path."

"Jodi?" Parrish said.

"Hmm?"

"He's a keeper."

She straightened away from Hunter, or at least she tried to, but he held on. "Behave, Parrish."

With a light laugh, Parrish said, "Both of you will stay away from King until I've finalized things."

"How long?" Jodi asked.

"Within a few hours or less." His tone became stern. "I don't want either of you alone."

Rolling her eyes, Jodi grumbled, "Now you're pacifying

me?" He probably knew she didn't want to be alone, so this was his way of helping to salvage her pride.

"I'm not one to pacify, you should know that. It's safer for both of you if you're together. You will each stay armed at all times. Even within your homes or vehicles."

Shrugging, Hunter said, "With you so far."

"The car you were supposed to work on for Worth, have you considered that it would be bugged?"

They looked at each other. It bothered Jodi that she hadn't thought of it. "No, but you're right, it's possible. Could be done even without Worth knowing." As an aside, she said, "He's not the sharpest tool."

Into the quiet, Memphis said, "If you don't mind me interjecting, I can sweep the car for listening devices, no problem."

"Ah, Memphis Osborn," Parrish said. "The somewhat-techie younger brother."

Instead of being insulted, Memphis grinned and squeezed in next to Turbo, leaning in and speaking into the phone. "Compared to most, there's no *somewhat* about it, but I'll concede I'm not in Madison's league."

"Few are," Parrish agreed. "I appreciate your realistic estimation of your skills. Far more useful than bloated boasting."

"Parrish," Jodi complained. "Don't insult Hunter's brother either."

Memphis grinned at her. "I'm not insulted, but thank you."

Parrish gave a rude clearing of his throat. "As you'll find out soon enough, I've already gotten started on arranging things."

"*Before* my agreement?" Jodi asked.

"Your agreement was a foregone conclusion."

Her mouth dropped open, then snapped shut. "It was not!"

As if to explain to Hunter and Memphis, Parrish said, "She's always more disagreeable when she's worried. You've been given fair warning."

They both smiled at her this time. Jodi threw up her hands.

"The firefighters are packing up to go. There will be no investigation."

There went her jaw again. She knew the leverage he had, and still it astounded her. "Just like that?"

"Of course. I also know where they have your friend. For now, he's unharmed."

Shoulders dropping in relief, Jodi said, "Thank you."

"How do you know?" Hunter asked, and Memphis looked equally curious.

"Once Jodi mentioned everything to Madison last night, she arranged some surveillance. It was easiest to pick up from King's residence, but also at one of his businesses, and at an office for the rental units where Remmy Gardner was staying. He was escorted out a while ago and taken to a more remote location. No security cameras there, but luckily, she was able to access Remmy's cell. Even now, she's connected to them. The problem is that the battery on his phone might run out faster, so we have to move quickly."

"So, let's hear the plan," Jodi said. She was much better at acting than she was at waiting.

"First, there's something else you need to know. For some reason that I don't yet understand, they grabbed the car salesman as well."

Omigod. "Worth? Worth Linlow?" Was he in on it? Or, as Remmy had suggested, did Worth sign his own death warrant by aligning with the wrong person? *Fool.*

"He was taken forcefully, and at present, I have no idea of his condition, so we don't want to delay too long."

"Just long enough," Hunter said, "to ensure Jodi is safe."

"That you're *all* safe," Parrish stressed. "And to that end, reinforcements are on the way."

Hunter and Memphis shared another look, but Jodi knew exactly what that meant. The big guns were headed in. Guess she was in for a family reunion.

"Until then," Parrish continued, "there's something important that I want you to do."

Sitting forward, Jodi nodded. "Go."

REMMY WAS STARTING to sweat. Figuratively and literally. There was no air in the shack, and with only two small windows open, every breath filled him with the scent of Worth's blood. Though King knocked back two mixed drinks, made from a cooler that had been carried in, no one else was offered anything.

Rude prick. He really ought to make a move while the others were equally uncomfortable. Maybe they'd help him to take out King, rather than jump to his defense.

No one said a word, and it finally pushed Remmy too far. "He's stinking up the place."

King's black gaze, now a little glazed from alcohol, shifted to Worth. "Stop playing possum, you miserable, ungrateful shit."

Worth groaned, but otherwise didn't move. Almost as if he was afraid to, he refused to open his eyes.

"Want me to drag him outside?" Remmy asked.

"So you can run off?" King smirked. "No." He nodded to another man. "Take him behind the shack and secure him somehow."

Blank faced, the man repeated, "Secure him… But how? We don't have any rope or anything."

When King looked ready to explode, Remmy said, "Here." He stripped off his T-shirt, then, using his teeth to start a tear, neatly ripped it into long strips. "Use this." Deftly, he twisted the cotton material until it created a short rope. "Tie one around his hands, then use the length of the others to secure his hands to a tree or something."

The guy nodded, grabbing the material and stuffing it into his pocket, then going to Worth in a rush. As soon as he moved him, Worth issued more groans, but he managed to get his feet under him and more or less stumbled out.

Remmy shook his head.

Disgruntled, King murmured, "Always so innovative. Never at a loss. If only all my men were as talented as you are."

"They need training, that's all."

"You can't teach common sense."

Fair point. You also couldn't expect excellence from two-bit thugs, but whatever. "Care to tell me your plan?"

King smiled. "I'm making it up as I go along."

"Bullshit. You're not a spur-of-the-moment type of villain." Two of the men who'd gotten him here stared at him, appalled.

The man who'd hauled out Worth came hurrying back in. "A truck's coming."

Satisfaction put an unholy light in King's eyes, making him look like the fucking devil. "Finish securing Worth, then hide in the trees."

That left King and two of the morons he'd already tangled with in the room with Remmy. Even if he could eliminate them—and there was a good chance he could—there were two more outside, already stationed somewhere, and the third man who'd have to finish tying Worth first.

"I see the wheels turning," King said. "I'd almost like

you to try it, then I could order them to mow you down and damn the consequences."

Remmy shook his head. "You want to go on being the boss, and that might jeopardize things. Danny is one thing. But Danny, Worth, me, Jodi… How many bodies are you going to pile up in one day and still expect to get away with it?"

Swirling the ice in his drink, King considered him, then gave a shrug. "Actually, Worth will live, but going forward, he'll be more careful about crossing me. Danny was a liability and you know it. You…?" He swallowed the last of the drink and set the glass on the table. "You, I'm still hoping to keep. Consider this your final test. Fail it, and you'll have the same fate as Danny. Help me eliminate the girl…?" He shrugged. "And we can continue to work together."

A horn blared.

Remmy didn't take his eyes off King. He wouldn't make the first move.

Amused, King gestured for the man with the broken, swollen nose to step out. "See if she's alone."

In only ten seconds, he reported in a nasally whine, "She has a man with her."

"Looks like you've been passed over, Remmy."

"He's a neighbor," Remmy said, striding forward. "And he works for her." What the fuck were they thinking?

"You understand I have two other men stationed in the trees."

"Yeah, whatever." Stomping halfway down the path, Remmy stalled and stared at Jodi. She stood in front of her truck, arms crossed as if she didn't have a care. Beside her, looking like a fucking sentinel, Hunter watched him, his gaze a laser beam of rage.

"Why the fuck are you here?"

Behind him, the dude with the broken nose laughed. "Giggs was right. You're whipped, man."

Jodi stepped away from the truck, her expression serene, maybe a little belligerent. "Is that your handiwork?" she asked, gesturing at the guy's mangled face.

Remmy flexed his hands. He'd tried…and it didn't matter. He was aware of King striding out with gleeful anticipation, and there Jodi stood, far more innocent than he'd ever expected.

She glanced around. "Let's see…" She pointed a finger at the different men, declaring, "Thug, thug…ah. That must be King."

"It's a setup," Remmy muttered, his brain scrambling and coming up blank. There was nothing he could do to help her now. Most likely, they'd all three die.

"Remmy," she said softly, "you actually believe I'd walk into a trap?"

"You have, damn it."

She gave him a mocking smile, full of fondness. "Doofus. *I* set the traps, not the other way around."

His aching heart slowed with comprehension, then shot into a frantic race. A trap. One she'd arranged? But how? He started to look around, but thought better of it. King had almost reached them and it'd be dumb for him to give anything away. "You better know what you're doing."

"She does," Hunter assured him. Then he stared at the other men, and hilariously enough, they faltered.

Yeah, he got that. Hunter made a damned imposing figure. "You're along for the ride?"

"I'm with her," Hunter stated. "Always."

Huh. Apparently, they were going the domestic route. Well, good for them—and no, that was *not* jealousy he felt. Hell, if he survived today, he would be officially unemployed and in massive legal trouble. He had bigger things to worry about than romance.

Softly, just to her, Remmy said, "I'm happy for you."

She grinned, and it was such an evil, anticipatory Jodi-like grin, he actually grew hopeful. Maybe, with her cunning and a bit of luck, he'd get out of this alive, too. If he did, by God, he'd change his ways. He'd get legit…somehow.

And then, *then* he could rethink his whole life, maybe do something right, and possibly even consider…settling down.

As JODI WALKED toward King, Hunter kept pace at her side. Without making it obvious, he took in everything—the trees, the shack, Remmy, King and his men. He knew her family was out there, and he trusted them. Overall.

But with Jodi's life? He wasn't yet willing to go that far.

Jodi was. She trusted them with herself, and with him. To Hunter, that counted for a lot.

"That's far enough," Remmy said, his gaze piercing. Lower, he muttered, "Whatever your plan is, don't push it."

"So, Danny was correct all along." King stepped up behind him. "You do have feelings for her, don't you?"

Amazingly enough, Remmy flushed.

Not in this lifetime, Hunter thought. He watched Remmy's gaze lock on Jodi as he tried to convey some silent meaning.

"Don't do it," Hunter warned. If the other man attempted to play hero now, he was liable to screw up everything.

King smirked at Remmy. "Planning to sacrifice yourself for her?"

"Aw," Jodi mocked. "That's sweet."

Hunter appreciated her bravado, but at the same time, he saw Remmy slip two fingers into his pocket, and he knew without a doubt that he had a weapon. "Not necessary," Hunter stated again.

King, who was oblivious to the moves Remmy made, announced, "My men have you surrounded. Make a single move and they'll kill that one first." He nodded at Hunter. "And then this backstabber." He leered at Jodi. "You, I think I'll save for later."

"Eww, no." Jodi pretended to gag.

King's expression hardened. "I'll make you pay for that."

"I don't think so. You see, we went through my house and found some interesting stuff."

That, at least, gave King pause.

"In the attic space—above a special closet—we found six hardware buckets."

"Bitch," King snarled, his whole body shaking with menace.

"Even though I scrubbed that house top to bottom, I didn't run into it at first because that's the closet I use to store my weapons. It was locked up nice and tight, so even if you or your buffoons had managed to break into my house without me killing you, you wouldn't have gotten into that closet, not unless you removed the hinges." Her lip curled. "Wanna know what was in the buckets?"

While King fumed, Remmy said, "I sure as hell do."

"I know you're enjoying yourself," Hunter remarked. He could see it in her eyes and in the line of her posture. He hated to spoil her fun, but Parrish had been clear on his instructions and the timeline. "How about we wrap it up here?"

Jodi nodded. "We found buckets full of cash, over two hundred thousand dollars."

Staring disbelievingly at King, Remmy whistled. "You hid *cash* in her house?"

"Also, four TEC-9 semiautomatic pistols. We were careful not to touch those, so fingerprints can be recovered.

Best of all, three wallets—containing IDs for missing men."
Jodi smiled. "Now, why do I assume those missing men
are dead, and that their deaths will somehow be traced
back to you?"

"You won't be able to prove any of it—especially once
you're dead."

"Ah, well, you're going to be disappointed on that. Men
are already going through your house. By the way, they
found another six hundred thousand in your safe, along
with heroin and fentanyl." Her lips curled. "And one more
wallet. Surprise, surprise. Another dead man."

King lunged for her.

Several things happened at once. In a blur of motion,
Remmy withdrew the knife and stabbed King hard in the
groin, causing him to scream out in pain. Hunter fired his
gun, hitting King in the shoulder and narrowly missing
Remmy, who swiftly turned with King's body held in front
of him, as if for cover.

Okay, so Remmy was fast, Hunter would give him that.
A knife in the privates was also a hell of a way to halt an
attack. He almost winced.

None of that made him good enough for Jodi.

"Relax," Jodi told him. "If anyone else dares to take aim,
they'll be shot."

Clearly not trusting her, Remmy maneuvered so that he
and King both protected Jodi. Over his shoulder, he snapped
at Hunter, "Get her out of here!"

Another shot. Then one more. Remmy looked around
wildly as King began to slump, his legs giving out from
his injuries.

"He's stealing your thunder," Hunter said to Jodi, and
got a grin from her in return. He realized she was enjoying
herself. God help him, that only made him love her more.

"It's okay, Remmy." Jodi started to pat his shoulder.

No way. Snagging a hand in the waistband of her jeans, Hunter drew her back. "I don't think so." She could be as cocky as she wanted, but she would not start touching other men right now.

Giving in on that point, she grinned again, then said to Remmy, "Those shots you heard? That means two of King's men are now disabled. He's already bleeding to death, so I think you can let him go."

Remmy cursed low.

"We have it covered," Hunter assured him. "Seriously, he's dead weight. Drop him."

"What the hell," Remmy breathed, seeing the last two men discard their weapons and lock their hands behind their necks. "Who did you bring along? Federal marshals?"

"You only need to know that she's protected."

King sought lost reserves and started to struggle, so Remmy spun him around and punched him in the chin. He staggered, then fell back unconscious.

"That wasn't necessary." Hunter stepped forward, flipped the man over and secured nylon cuffs on his wrists.

"It made me feel better." Remmy stared at King with hatred. "He killed Danny Giggs, and Worth is beat all to hell and back, tied up behind the shack. He's going to need an ambulance, I think."

Only seconds later, sirens sounded, and Remmy turned to stare at Jodi in awe. "Are you responsible for those, too?"

"She's responsible," Hunter said, "for you getting a second chance. Don't blow it or I'll personally make you pay."

"Hey," Jodi protested. "That was my line."

Remmy looked at them both like they were nuts.

Prodding him forward—away from Jodi—Hunter handed him more restraints. "You can help me secure them." After

Jodi had convinced Parrish that Remmy was a decent guy who'd gotten in over his head, they'd worked out the plans. Jodi got to have her input, and part of that was offering Remmy an opportunity to do the right thing.

Hunter trusted Remmy only because Jodi did, but he still wouldn't leave the two of them alone.

Quietly, Remmy asked, "Is it really over?"

"It is. And for now, unless you do something else stupid, you're in the clear, so I suggest you get it together, and fast."

"In the…" He rushed to catch up to Hunter. "How is that possible?"

"Jodi's doing." Hunter shot him a look. "And I agreed. You've been helpful. Don't make me regret it."

"But how?"

"She has connections. Now, leave it at that."

Appearing dazed, Remmy bound a man's wrists. "Who's in the trees?"

"Her family." Hunter moved to the other man. "And you do not want to be on their bad side."

"I suppose they like you?"

"Maybe, but it doesn't matter." Hunter stood again and looked to where Jodi walked with state troopers, men that Parrish specifically knew and trusted. She was explaining the situation to them while gesturing to paramedics, all in all, taking charge and looking incredibly beautiful. "She's mine. I love her. More importantly, she loves me." He pinned Remmy with a hard stare. "You don't have a chance."

Remmy laughed. "I never did, I know. But I meant what I said. I'm glad she's happy."

"Me, too." Hunter started back to her. "I plan to keep her that way."

CHAPTER TWELVE

One week later...

"I CAN'T BELIEVE they want to set Remmy up as an operative." Fresh from a shower, dressed in a loose T-shirt, pull-on shorts and nothing else, Jodi flopped onto the couch next to Hunter. "You know it's because they think I'll get into more trouble and they want someone to keep an eye on me."

Hunter said, "I'll be keeping both eyes on you." And his hands. His mouth. Every available body part...

"Not the same," Memphis said from the floor where he brushed Turbo. Supposedly, being left behind to watch over the dog the day they'd confronted King had unsettled not only Memphis but Turbo, too. Memphis had found the only way to occupy his thoughts and soothe Turbo was to groom him.

Using his own hairbrush, because he hadn't known where Hunter kept the dog's.

Turbo had enjoyed it so much, it had now become a nightly ritual.

He added to Jodi, "And you know you'll find more trouble, hon. Or it'll find you. Somehow, some way, we all know it's going to happen."

Jodi whipped a throw pillow at his head, but Memphis caught it and tossed it back, laughing.

Hunter pulled her into his side and kissed her forehead. "They love you."

"I know that," she grumbled.

"Aren't you happy for Remmy? He'll be better trained, so maybe next time I take a swing at him, he'll have the good sense to duck."

"There won't be a next time."

Hunter made no promise on that, especially since the guy would be hanging around. "He'll have a legit job—"

"Sort of legit," she corrected.

"—and he'll be helping people when they need it."

Groaning, Jodi dropped back dramatically across his lap and stared up at him. "You always see the best and I'm always bitching."

That had to be a joke. He'd never seen anyone who complained less. "If you want to hear bitching, you should have heard me burning Memphis's ears."

"It's true," Memphis said. "Hunter was not too happy that his competition would be sticking around."

"Competition?" Jodi turned her head to see Memphis. "Who?"

Hunter met Memphis's gaze and they both laughed.

"You see?" Memphis said to him. "I told you there was nothing to worry about."

"I wasn't worried." Hunter hauled Jodi up so that she sat on his lap instead of draped over it. With one hand on her thigh, the other at the back of her neck, he kissed her. "He's definitely hung up on you. I almost feel sorry for him."

Jodi snorted. "I'm not buying that. Remmy's not hung up on any woman, especially not me. Besides, everyone knows I love you."

She said it so casually, it took Hunter a moment to process the words, and once he did, he drew her in, taking her mouth in a voracious kiss that he meant to keep short, but couldn't. He wanted to carry her off to his bedroom and hear her say it a hundred times more—while he made love to her.

Then he remembered his brother was sitting only a few feet away.

He lifted his head enough to look into her eyes, those beautiful eyes that had caught him from his first glimpse.

"Wow." Jodi licked her lips. "What brought that on?"

Memphis snorted.

With her gaze going suspicious, she looked from his burning expression to Memphis's sappy smile and then to Turbo, who watched them alertly, his tail giving three hard thumps on the floor.

"What?" she asked, frowning at all of them. "It's not like it was a secret."

"No, it wasn't." Hunter had known she loved him, because he knew her. He understood her and what motivated her, just as she understood him. With another, gentler kiss, he whispered, "I still wanted to hear it."

She blinked at him. "I've told you before."

"No, you haven't."

She turned to Memphis. "Haven't I...?"

"The last week has been chaotic, hon, what with cops coming and going, your family dodging everyone, Worth recovering, and King's men getting picked up left and right. Still, I'm pretty sure I would have noticed if you'd finally put my brother at ease."

"Shut up, Memphis," he said, because he *was* at ease. Jodi was staying with him. Every night, she slept wrapped around him, and every morning, she smiled when she opened her eyes. She hadn't yet made it to the basement, but she no longer looked at the door with dread. He figured they had plenty of time to tackle life and all the issues. For now, he just wanted to love her. In a hundred different ways, she'd shown him how much she loved him, too.

But she hadn't said the words—until now.

Her gaze softened, then dropped to his mouth. "I love you, Hunter Osborn. From now on, I'll be sure to say it every single day."

"How about twice a day?" He nuzzled her ear. "Maybe every hour?"

She drew a shuddering breath and wrapped her arms around his neck. With her lips touching his ear, she whispered, "How about I show you instead?"

Standing with her in his arms, Hunter turned for the bedroom.

"Wait," Memphis said, causing him to halt. "Two things. I almost forgot, but Parrish called earlier while you were chopping wood and she was feeding the chickens. The IDs in those wallets led to a drug trafficker, a coyote, and get this, one of King's competitors."

"Interesting." Not that Hunter really cared at the moment. What interested him more was how chummy his brother had gotten with the entire McKenzie family.

"Parrish said he doesn't want Jodi in her house." When she started to protest, Memphis continued. "He'd prefer to demolish it, just in case anyone else comes sniffing around with ideas of revenge."

"What?" Jodi wiggled to get free.

Hunter tightened his hold. "No one is demolishing her house," he stated to Jodi and Memphis both. Again, he started away.

"Second thing," Memphis said quickly.

With a groan, Hunter turned back to him.

"I bought some property."

The way Memphis announced it, Hunter knew there was more. "And?"

"Near here?" Jodi asked at the same time. "I'd love for you to stick around." With a grin, she added, "You've grown on me."

"I'll only be thirty minutes away," he assured her.

Hunter asked, "What kind of property?"

"Basically, it's an RV park, currently vacant." Memphis launched through a fast explanation. "It has electric and plumbing at the designated lots, but needs a lot of cleanup work and repairs. I'll make it a location for low-rent vacationers— similar to what King had, only more affordable... I'll be on the up-and-up."

Hunter studied his brother closely, and knew he was plotting something. "We'll talk about this more later."

"There's a livable cabin already on the property." Memphis held out his arms. "So you'll be pleased to know I'll be moving out soon."

When Jodi started to protest, Hunter hugged her. Something was afoot, and they'd discuss it together before confronting Memphis. "You're welcome to stay as long as you like, you know that. We've enjoyed having you here."

"As a dog sitter, I know." He grinned at them. "I'll still be around to help out however you need, and you know Mom and Dad will be visiting soon. This way, they can divide their attention between us instead of overwhelming you."

For that, Hunter smiled. He anticipated seeing them again. Phone and video conversations weren't the same. He was ready to hug his mom, and talk quietly with his dad...because he was living again instead of just going through the motions. "Thanks, Memphis."

"Now you may carry her off. Turbo has decided to sleep with me, so you two are free for the rest of the night."

Hunter hesitated. "I really am glad you'll be nearby."

"Me, too," Jodi said. And then, as Hunter carried her down the hall, she called back with an impish smile, "Love you, Memphis."

They heard a thump, followed seconds later with a shouted, "Back atcha, hon!"

Grinning, Hunter stepped into the bedroom and closed the door. "I think my brother fainted."

Happier than he'd ever seen her, Jodi kissed his face all over, with small excited pecks. "I do love him, you know. And Turbo." With a frown, she said, "Don't laugh, but now that I've said it, I like saying it." She settled her mouth over his, teasing, taking and giving. "Especially to you."

"Say it."

Without hesitation, she whispered, "I love you, Hunter. I love you so much."

Hunter put her in the bed, coming down over her and settling between her slender thighs. "I love you, too."

Her hands opened on his shoulders. "I love this super-hot body of yours." She inhaled. "I love the way you smell, too, and what it does to me."

"What does it do?"

"It turns me on," she breathed. "Like a drunk needing a drink. Sometimes I just think of you and I want you." Being serious, she added, "I'm glad you're always agreeable."

Hunter started to grin, but thought better of it. "My pleasure."

"I love that we can be unusual together, and that you don't think I'm weird."

"Never."

"It's so dumb that I used to want the *everyday life for the everyday woman*. Now I have you and it's so much better."

That amused him. "Because you're extraordinary." He worked her T-shirt up and over her head, then tossed it aside so he could cup both her breasts. "There are some perks to everyday life, though—as long as that everyday life is with me. You see, we'll always be together like this."

"Awesome."

Now he grinned. She had a clever way of summing it up. Life with Jodi *was* awesome. "There are also dates." Briefly, he kissed her. "I want to take you on dates, Jodi."

"You mean something other than feeding chickens and watching movies from your couch?"

"Yes, other than that. Dating can be fun."

"I trust you, so count me in."

"I want to give you a ring."

Bemused, she blinked. It took her two tries before she managed to say, "I'm not big on jewelry."

"Then it can be a simple band." Staring into her eyes, he specified, "An engagement ring—after we've spent some time dating."

Her eyes widened.

Hunter worried that he was rushing her, but he needed their relationship to be official. "It's what the everyday couple would do."

"We're not that, though."

"We're extraordinary," he agreed, and then stressed, "together."

Jodi licked her lips. "How would things change?"

"They won't, except that we'll be more committed to each other."

"I'm already committed to you." Her frown eased. "I can't imagine my life without you in it."

For that, Hunter hugged her close and kissed her without restraint. "You'll never have to, because I'm not going anywhere."

After a second, she asked, "Will you wear a ring, too?"

Once we're married. Trying to be judicious, he asked, "Is that what you want?"

"I think I'd like to be engaged to you." With a little wicked smile, she said, "Imagine how Parrish and Reyes will react."

So far, so good. "After dating, and an engagement, after you've met my folks and you're comfortable—"

"I'm so comfortable with you, Hunter." She tangled her fingers in his hair. "I love you, remember?"

"Then we'll get married." In case that spooked her, he whispered, "When you're ready."

"Married." Her smile trembled, but not out of fear. No, she looked intrigued...and a little in awe. "I used to think my superpower was fighting invisible demons. Now I know that it's catching the hottest, most amazing, wonderful man in the world."

Humbled, Hunter promised, "We'll fight those demons together."

"Then we should probably get hitched." She tried to sound serious, and ended up grinning. "It'll be almost like the *everyday life for the everyday woman.*"

"But with you, it's going to be even better." He framed her face in his hands. "It's going to be extraordinary."

* * * * *

Do you love romance books?

Join the Read Love Repeat Facebook group dedicated to book recommendations, author exclusives, SWOONING and all things romance!

A community made for romance readers by romance readers.

Facebook.com/groups/readloverepeat

Get 4 FREE REWARDS!

We'll send you 2 FREE Books plus 2 FREE Mystery Gifts.

FREE
Value Over
$20

Both the **Romance** and **Suspense** collections feature compelling novels written by many of today's bestselling authors.